MOTHERLAND

A TOM GRANT NOVEL

SAMANTHA ADAIR

Editing and Publishing Assistance provided by:

Michelle Morrow www.chellreads.com

CONTENT WARNING:
This book contains mature themes that might make some readers uncomfortable. Foul language, criminal activity, and drug/alcohol use may be included in this book. Please proceed with caution.

For Rae and Michelle.
Commit and bin the bollocks!

CONTENTS

1. Tom 7
2. Tom 17
3. Isabella 26
4. Tom 35
5. Tom 41
6. Isabella 51
7. Tom 63
8. Isabella 72
9. Tom 79
10. Isabella 90
11. Tom 106
12. Isabella 118
13. Tom 126
14. Isabella 133
15. Tom 140
16. Isabella 146
17. Isabella 153
18. Tom 162
19. Isabella 168
20. Tom 176
21. Isabella 182
22. Tom 193
23. Isabella 204
24. Tom 213
25. Isabella 223
26. Tom 233
27. Isabella 242
28. Isabella 255
29. Tom 264
30. Isabella 275
31. Tom 287

32. Isabella 294

33. Tom 306

34. Isabella 317

35. Tom 323

36. Isabella 331

37. Tom 340

38. Isabella 351

39. Tom 360

40. Isabella 369

41. Tom 380

42. Tom 399

43. Isabella 409

44. Tom 419

EPILOGUE 425

1

TOM

"You should have shot him straight through the chest and not dithered around aiming for his head. You aren't good enough." Tom squints at the protein bars on the shelf, looking for the ones that taste best. *They're all like cardboard.* "So, one shot would have killed him— straight through the heart. Instead you ended up using six rounds. At least he's dead... but still."

He turns around after yanking a box off the shelf. An old lady peers at him. Her eyes wide and her mouth agape.

Oh, shit. "I've gotta go. I've just terrified a senior citizen."

"Yeah, okay. Thanks. I guess." James ends the call.

"Are you alright?" Tom asks the old woman. He steps towards her and goes to touch her elbow.

The old woman shuffles backwards and holds up a finger. "Don't touch me, you... you... psychopath." Her trembly voice bounces around the boxes of cereal and snack bars on the surrounding shelves.

Tom cringes and steps towards her. "That's a bit harsh. It usually takes people weeks to figure that out."

She lifts her cane and pokes him in the thigh.

"What the…" He rubs his leg and watches as she retreats backwards, glaring at him. "I have an elderly neighbour you know," he grumbles.

"I'm reporting you to the manager," the old woman sniffs and hobbles away.

Excellent. Just what I need. The overweight manager of Tesco onto me.

Tom walks into the next aisle and is confronted with loaves of bread. *I just want normal white bread.* He paws through the grainy, wholewheat, pumpkin seed— *pumpkin seed?*

A hushed giggle to his left catches his attention. A young couple, all of about nineteen, laugh together over which bread to get. He rolls his eyes. The boy squeezes the girl on the bum, and she squeals and slaps his arm. *Get a room.*

His phone rings again and he pulls it out and checks the screen. "Martha."

"Where are you?"

"Tesco. I'm trying to buy food. But it's irritating. I scared an old lady half to death, and she poked me with her stick."

"Did you say she… poked you with her stick?"

"Yes. And it smarts." He rubs his thigh again while reading the bread labels.

"You've bought food before, Tom. Surely it's not that hard."

"Well, I'm always in and out of hotel rooms and in other countries, aren't I?"

"That's fair."

"And I don't think Tesco does room service."

"I would think not." Martha pauses. "You've never heard of online shopping? How do you think I organised deliveries to your flat when you weren't being sociable?"

"Is that what we're calling it now? Not being sociable?" Tom grins and pulls a loaf of bread off the shelf. "I was drunk Martha. Pickled. Couldn't walk a straight line. Luckily, I didn't kill anyone." He turns and the old lady with the stick is glaring at him again, shaking her head. "Ah."

"What?"

"Nevermind. What's up?" Tom watches the old lady disappear towards the cat food, but not before throwing another glare over her shoulder. Tom grins, shaking his head.

"How are the meetings going?"

Tom rolls his eyes to the ceiling and huffs. "Fine. I don't go every week though. And you can't make me."

"That doesn't sound immature at all."

"Did you call for a reason?"

"Have you heard from Isabella?"

Tom's blood freezes. *Why are you asking me that?* "Not for a few weeks. Why? What's happened?"

"I've been made aware she's left Belgium and wanted to check with you."

She's left... Tom's adrenaline spikes and it's suddenly hot in the cool supermarket. "Where is she?" *Why didn't she tell me? Fuck.*

"Nevermind. It's fine. I'll see if we can get a track."

"A track?" Tom yelps, and the young couple who were giggling over bread scurry away from him.

"Well, Admiral Moore will still be wanting her no doubt. So, it's best we find her first." Martha pauses and Tom's pulse thunders through his ears. "We've spoken about this Tom."

"Yes. She was supposed to tell me when she left. After her father was well enough."

"Okay well, keep trying her phone, yes?" The line goes dead.

Tom dials Isabella's number and slaps the phone to his ear. The phone rings. *It's on.* His heart doubles its speed as he waits.

"Hello?"

"Iz!"

"Hey. I was just about to call you."

Tom frowns. *Why is she so calm?* "Where are you? Are you okay?"

"Of course, I'm okay. Why wouldn't I be?"

"Well… You're… where are you?" His heart hasn't let up and he pushes his hand to his chest to curb its insistence.

"How about we play a game?"

"A game? Iz. I'm really not… just tell me where you are?" He glares at the bread in front of him, hating it for no reason.

"Let's see if you can guess where I am."

"Iz? What are you on about?"

"I'll give you a hint…"

"Iz…" Tom rakes a hand through his hair and blows a hard breath out of his mouth.

"Relax. Or you'll squash your bread."

"Squash my…?"

Tom spins around and looks to the end of the aisle. He squints, leaning forward. His heart slams against his ribs and he balls his shirt in a fist over his heart. He pushes the phone harder into his ear.

"Iz..."

Isabella smiles and gestures to his groceries. "Bread and protein bars. All the major food groups, then?" She puts her phone in her pocket.

Tom drops the box of bars and bread and stalks to Isabella. He cradles his hands on either side of her jaw and pulls her face to his.

Her skin and soft mouth against his own send warmth through his chest. She kisses him back, running both hands up his neck and into his hair. They stumble into the bread, sending loaves crashing to the floor.

Isabella pulls her face away and laughs. "This isn't quite how I imagined it."

"Well, you ambushed me in the supermarket." He kisses her again, stepping on a loaf of bread.

She giggles into his mouth and puts both hands on his chest. "Stop."

"Can't." He rests his face against hers and breathes her in. "I missed you."

Isabella's hands are still against his chest and she digs her fingers in and nips his lip. "I missed you, too."

Tom grabs her hands and holds them against him. They stand in the middle of the bakery aisle with their foreheads together.

"There. Him." Tom hears the trembly voice of his supermarket nemesis behind him and he turns, holding Isabella against him. The manager is with the old woman. "He threatened to kill me."

"Wait what?" Tom drops Iz's hands and walks towards the old woman. "I did not."

"And I poked him with my cane!" She lifts her cane as though it's evidence and jerks her head towards Tom. "And now he's ruined your bread." She tuts and rolls her eyes.

The overweight manager in his crushed Tesco shirt sighs and rubs his forehead.

"I'll pay for the bread I ruined," Tom says.

The manager looks past him and counts the loaves on the floor, squished. "That's nine loaves."

Tom squints at the offending bread and steals a glance at Isabella who is stifling a laugh. "Yes," Tom grins and turns back to the manager. "All nine loaves." *It was worth it.*

"Right then." The manager goes to leave and the old woman swats him with her stick. "What now?"

"Have you forgotten something?" The woman curls her lip and taps her slipper adorned foot.

The manager takes a deep breath and holds both palms out towards Tom. "Please don't kill anyone in my store."

Isabella snorts and Tom squashes a grin as the old lady breathes fire at him. "I'll try and... contain myself."

The manager nods and walks off, the old woman trailing after him.

Isabella slides her arms around Tom's waist and leans against his back. "Are you scaring old ladies?" Her voice vibrates against him and he turns to face her.

He slides his hands up her neck and holds her face. "Only the evil ones."

"She probably has fifty cats at home."

Tom chuckles and swipes his thumbs across her cheeks. "Are you busy?"

"When?"

"Right now?"

Isabella smiles and wraps her arms around the back of his neck. "I can spare a few minutes."

"I require more than a few minutes."

"Okay."

Tom thrusts open the door to his flat and pulls Isabella in behind him. He kisses her while kicking the door shut. She draws her fingers down the front of his shirt before dipping her hands under it and sliding it up over his head. He throws it away as she squirms out of her own top and pushes herself backwards against the wall. They both hustle to kick their shoes across the room.

Tom slaps both hands against the wall over her head and pushes his mouth to hers. Isabella unbuckles his belt and rips the buttons of his trousers apart, they fall to his ankles, and he kicks them away. Isabella runs her hands inside the waistband of his pants and squeezes his hips. She digs her fingers into his skin, rubbing her thumbs back and forth. Tingles erupt under her touch and Tom drops his face into her shoulder. *Jesus.*

He holds his breath a moment and trails his mouth along her jaw and down her neck.

"Tom," she rasps. Tom rests his lips against hers and kisses her while his fingers trace the lace over her breast. He stops his hand over her heartbeat and rests it there.

Isabella whimpers into his mouth. She pulls her hands from his waist and slides her jeans off her hips, letting them drop to the floor. Her hot breath brushes against his skin and a tremble rips through his core and down his legs. He runs his fingers along the inside waistband of her knickers and she gasps.

They both still a moment, staring at each other, breath colliding.

Isabella grabs his hand and pulls him to the bedroom. She snaps her bra off with one hand and throws it on the floor. Tom pulls her against him, his hand nestled in the small of her back. He feels the warmth of her chest against him and her mouth nipping at his neck and all self-control is lost.

He walks her backwards and lays her on the bed. She arches her back, her arms reaching above her head. Goosebumps pop up under his fingertips as they glide down her arms, over the curve of her breasts, across her stomach and down to her lace knickers.

"Please," she whispers, her ragged breaths coming out in short bursts.

He traces the outline of her knickers from her waist and around each leg, slowing around the heat between her thighs.

"Oh my…" Isabella draws in a breath as he slips his fingers inside the lace.

His mouth is on hers again as he brushes his fingers back and forth.

Isabella lifts her hips and scratches her nails down his back, reaching his waist. She rips his pants down and he chuckles against her mouth.

"Forget the fancy stuff, Tom," she squeezes her eyes shut and tilts her head back. "I need you, now."

He can't resist her soft neck and slides his mouth down across her throat. He pulls her knickers off and hovers above her a moment and waits.

Isabella opens one eye and quirks a brow. "Stop being a tease."

"You love it."

"I do." She wraps her legs around his waist and tilts her hips up to meet him.

Tom pushes and feels her warmth wrap around him. Isabella

gulps in a breath and throws her head back. She rolls until she is on top of him and moves her hips in slow, hard circles.

"Jesus Iz," Tom closes his eyes and bites his bottom lip.

Seconds later, Isabella kisses him hard and he slides a hand through her hair to the back of her head, holding her face against his own.

"Oh God," she squeals against his mouth. She pulls herself up and tosses her hair down her back. She gasps in air before letting it out and collapsing against him, her nails clawing his shoulders.

Tom rolls her down next to him and drifts his mouth along her neck. Her pulse thumps against his lips. She drags her hands up his body as he grips the pillow and moans against her skin. She squeezes her legs tighter around his waist and pushes against him. His body tenses and he exhales in a rush against her neck. He lets go of the pillow and drifts his hands down her shoulders and chest, stopping at her waist, in the crease between her leg and hip.

He drops next to her and pulls her against him, kissing her deeply.

"I love you," he whispers.

She smiles against his mouth. "I love you, too."

2

TOM

Tom traces his fingers over Isabella's collarbone and the dip in her throat. She smiles and brushes the hair back from his forehead.

"I hadn't planned on getting this sweaty today." She pulls Tom's face to hers.

"Well," he mumbles against her mouth. "I like you this sweaty." He trickles his hand down her chest to her stomach and rests on her hip.

Tom's phone rings from the floor outside the bedroom door. He pulls Isabella onto his chest and ignores the phone.

"It can go to voicemail," he whispers. It stops ringing and Tom smiles against Isabella's kiss.

"You don't have voicemail." She wraps her legs either side of his hips.

"Exactly."

Isabella drifts her lips across his chest and down his stomach. He sucks in a breath and rakes his fingers through her hair.

The phone rings again.

Really?

Isabella crawls up from under the duvet and grins. "I'll go get it."

"No." He pulls her against him. "Let them wait."

"What if it's important?"

"More important than this?" The phone falls silent again. "See? Not important."

Isabella giggles and plants her hands on the bed above his shoulders and leans down to his face. "Ready for more sweat?"

Tom grins and rolls her onto the bed. "Are you?"

The phone starts again and Tom groans. *Fuck.* He springs out of bed and stalks to the hall. Yanking the phone out of his trouser pocket he checks the screen and rolls his eyes.

"Martha." He trudges into the room and falls into the bed. Isabella nestles against him.

"Are you at home?"

"Who's asking?"

Isabella traces circles on his chest with her finger and goose-bumps pop up.

"I'm on my way."

"Ah, wait. Why?"

Isabella's fingers snake down his chest to his stomach and dance across his abs. Tom squashes a grin and slaps his hand over hers.

"I found Isabella."

Tom's eyes widen. "Really? Where?"

"Well, I mean she's here. In London. Apparently."

Isabella snatches her hand out from under his and continues its journey down his body, resting on the inside of his thigh. She brushes her fingers up and down and kisses his neck.

"Ummm..." Tom inhales a sharp breath. "That's very interesting."

Martha huffs. "She's there with you, isn't she?"

Tom glances at Isabella who continues kissing his neck, moving to his throat and down his chest.

"Yep." Tom holds his breath.

"Right. I'll be there in half an hour. Please have clothes on." She hangs up.

Tom throws his phone on the floor and cups Isabella's chin in his hand, tilting her face to his. He nips her top lip. "Martha will be here in half an hour. She has requested we have clothes on." He smirks. "Presumptuous."

"Half an hour?" Isabella purses her lips and raises one eyebrow. "That gives us at least twenty-five minutes." She drops onto the mattress next to him.

He nibbles her neck. "Twenty-eight." He kisses her shoulder. "And a half."

Twenty-nine minutes later, Tom is pulling the fly up on his trousers as the intercom buzzes. He looks to the ceiling and lets out a breath. "A whole minute early."

Isabella giggles from where she's still lying in his bed. "Give me five." She stretches her arms above her head and Tom climbs over her on all fours.

"Take your time." He pecks her lips and jumps off the bed. "It's only Martha."

He presses the button on the intercom to let Martha in, wanders to the front door and pulls it open.

Leaning against the worktop in the kitchen, he folds his arms and waits.

Martha appears in the doorway. "Tom." She looks him up and down. "You forgot your shirt." She walks in, places her handbag on the coffee table and sits on the sofa.

Isabella appears and throws Tom a shirt. Her hair is a tangled mess down her back and mascara smudges under her eyes tell the whole story.

"Martha." Isabella leaps across the room and envelopes the tiny woman in a bear hug. Tom grins to himself as Martha struggles with the overload of affection.

"Yes, hello Isabella." Martha pats her awkwardly on the back.

"Oh, Martha." Isabella sighs and sits next to her on the sofa. "You've hugged me before. Stop getting all weird."

Tom snorts as Martha's lips press into a thin line. He sits in the armchair. "To what do we owe the pleasure?"

"A few things." Martha shoots a sideways glance at Isabella. "You've been in London since yesterday, my dear?"

"Yes, late last night, anyway. I stayed at the Best Western." She smirks. "Fancy."

"Yes, I know. I collected your luggage." Martha nods towards the hall and Tom goes out to retrieve it. He pulls the suitcase and hikers backpack into the flat and drops them beside the sofa.

Isabella stares at the bags a moment and blinks. "How did you know I was…"

"I spoke with you father's minder." Martha appears to hold her breath a moment while Isabella bites her lip. "I'm sorry, Isabella."

Tom sits upright in his armchair as his stomach contorts. *Sorry?* "Sorry?" He looks at Isabella, her eyes brim with tears. He scrambles out of his chair and sits on the coffee table, in front of her. "Iz?"

"Umm…" She swipes a hand across her eyes and shakes her head. "Papa died."

Tom drops to his knees, wraps Isabella in his arms and she buries her face in his chest. Her body trembles as she cries into his shirt.

Tom slides his eyes to Martha over the top of Isabella's head. Martha stares impassively back at him.

Tom drops his face next to Isabella's. "Iz?"

Isabella sniffles and raises her head. "I was going to tell you." She wiggles her nose and wipes her forearm along her top lip. "But when I saw you… I was so happy, and I didn't want to…

cry..." She hiccups. "I didn't want to think about it for a little while."

Tom pushes her hair off her face and looks in her eyes. "I'm sorry, Iz." He pulls her against him again. "I'm so sorry."

Martha goes into the kitchen and gets Isabella a glass of water. She sets it down on the coffee table and perches herself on the armchair. Tom takes the spot next to Isabella and holds her against his chest.

"When I was a child, I used to hate the smell of those awful cigars." Isabella sits up and takes a sip of the water. "I found him coughing into a handkerchief a few weeks after I arrived. He tried to hide it from me but I saw the bright red spots." She shakes her head and looks at her lap. Tom slides his hand under her shirt and strokes the small of her back.

"Did he see a doctor?" Tom asks.

Isabella lets a chuckle escape. "God no. Not my Papa. Everything can be cured with a few shots of vodka and a bowl of kasha." She takes another sip of water. "Anyway, by the time I convinced him to have a doctor come to the house, it was far too late."

Tom kisses her temple.

"It's okay. I was with him. And it was peaceful. Like it should be." She looks between Tom and Martha and smiles. "Thanks to you two."

Tom's arm tightens around her shoulder and she nestles under his chin.

"I need your help." She sits up, keeping one hand against Tom's chest. "I made a promise to my father. I intend to keep it."

Prickles awaken on the back of Tom's neck and he shifts so his body faces her.

Isabella takes a breath. "I'm taking him home to be at rest with my mother."

Ringing hits Tom's ears and he tilts his head. "Are you mad?"

Isabella pushes her hand harder against Tom's chest. "I promised him."

"Iz… you can't. If you're found in Russia, you're dead." He leans in front of her face. "Dead."

"They won't find me." She smiles. "Besides, I'm going to Belarus."

Tom rolls his eyes to the ceiling. "Six of one…" Tom scrubs a hand through his hair and studies her face. "It's not safe, Iz."

"He's right."

Tom turns to Martha, remembering she is also there. He nods at her before nodding at Isabella. "We don't agree on a lot. But we agree on this. You aren't going. You can't."

Isabella bites her lip and hardens her eyes. "Are you going to stop me?"

"If I have to."

Isabella scoffs and stands up. She stalks to her luggage and heaves the backpack off the floor. "I'm going to shower. Hope that's allowed?" She raises her eyebrows before spinning and stalking down the hall.

Tom hears the bathroom door slam and drops his head into his hands.

"Tom, she can't go."

"I know."

"If they get wind—"

"I *know*, Martha." He stands and balls his hands into fists by his side. "What exactly would you like me to do? Chain her up?"

Martha picks up her handbag and slides it over her forearm like the Queen. "That's extreme. But what you do in your own time is none of my affair." She gives Tom a wry smile.

Tom lets out a heavy breath and laces his fingers behind his head.

"Keep me posted." Martha walks out the door, closing it behind her.

"Shit," Tom mumbles and wanders to the bathroom door. He can hear the water running and knocks loudly. "Iz?"

"It's open."

He walks into the bathroom and is engulfed in steam. *What is it about women and hot showers?*

The shower curtain moves and Isabella peeks her head out. She eyes Tom and says nothing.

"You'll scald yourself." Tom folds his arms across his chest.

"I'm sorry."

"Don't be."

"Are you going to stand there brooding or get in?"

Tom lets a smile creep along his lips. "That depends. Are you going to attack me with the soap dish?"

Isabella smiles, pulling the shower curtain open and holds out her hand.

Tom pulls his clothes off and steps into the hot water. He pushes Isabella's wet hair away from her face and drops his forehead to hers.

With her hands clasped behind his neck, she tilts her mouth to his.

"I need to go. Please understand."

She kisses him and he rests his hands either side of her face, relishing her wet skin against him.

Tom looks into her eyes and sees determination wrapped up in grief.

"I'm coming with you."

3

ISABELLA

Half a jar of peanut butter, crackers and a packet of almonds. Really?

Isabella shuts the pantry and finds Tom leaning against the worktop with his arms folded. He grins as she shakes her head.

"How do you survive?" Isabella holds her palms up. "Your fridge has butter, a few beans and a half bottle of milk. And let's not talk about your pantry."

"Have you forgotten I was at the grocery store yesterday when you ambushed me?"

"And left empty handed."

"Who's fault was that?"

Isabella purses her lips. "I'll accept half the blame."

"I'll take you out for breakfast. C'mon." Tom holds his hand out and smiles when Isabella takes it.

"How do you survive on half a jar of peanut butter, Tom?"

"I order in. Or eat out." He locks the door. "I can't cook."

Tom leads Isabella down the hallway and she sees a small cat sitting at the top of the stairs. "Oh look." She bends forward and holds out her hand, rubbing her forefinger and thumb together. "Hello kitty…" The cat wanders to her and rubs its little face against her hand. She scoops it up and strokes her cheek against the top of its head.

Tom sighs and Isabella raises both eyebrows. "It's Pebbles." Tom walks to the door opposite his and knocks. An old lady opens the door a crack and Isabella smiles, holding the cat against her chest.

"Ahh." The old lady shuts her door and a chain jangles. Opening the door again she smiles at Tom. "Lovely to see you, Tom."

"And you Lorna, missing someone?" Tom jerks his head towards Isabella.

"Ahh, the pesky little diva." The woman shuffles into the hall and holds her hands out to Isabella. "Thank you, lovey. She's always getting out."

Isabella glances at Tom as she hands the cat over and he rolls his eyes and mouths, *always.*

Isabella pats the cat that now sits in Lorna's hands. "Well, I love cats. I'll give her a cuddle anytime, Lorna." Isabella winks as Tom walks over and puts both hands on her shoulders.

Lorna looks between Tom and Isabella. "Anytime? Do you… reside here now lovey?"

"Oh ah..." Isabella chews on her bottom lip. "For now."

"Well, that's lovely. Can I offer you some tea?"

"You should go inside Lorna. Don't want you getting a chill." Tom steers Isabella to the stairs. "Don't engage her too much; she won't shut up," he whispers in her ear.

Isabella giggles. "She's adorable."

Tom snorts as he opens the foyer door and steps outside. Isabella goes to follow when he whips his arm back and pushes her against the inside wall, her head narrowly missing the letter-boxes jutting out.

"What are you—"

"Shhh! Get upstairs. Tell Lorna you want that tea after all."

"What?"

"Get inside Lorna's flat and stay there."

"Tom you're not making—"

Tom whirls his head around and fire blazes in his clear green eyes. "Go!"

The urgency in his voice is enough to make Isabella scramble up the stairs. She sprints down the hall, skidding to a stop at Lorna's door. She hammers with her fist, hoping the old lady isn't trying to get out of a chair.

Isabella's heart pounds against the thump in her throat. She hops from one foot to the other and finally the door clicks open a fraction. She sees Lorna's sparkly blue eye peer at her. Isabella musters a smile and the door shuts, followed by the jangle of a chain.

"Lovey!"

"Hello again." Isabella fights to keep the tremble out of her voice. "I don't suppose tea is still on offer?" She smiles, hoping it conveys kindness and not a manic need to hide.

"Of course, lovey." Lorna steps back and ushers Isabella inside. "Please sit down."

Isabella eyes the dusty rose-coloured sofa and matching fluffy cushions. *Oh my.* She crosses the room and sits but keeps glancing back at the front door. Pebbles jumps into her lap and turns in a circle before curling into a ball.

"Ah, you've made a lifelong friend." Lorna gazes at her cat.

"Seems that way." Isabella nods and tries to stop her knees bouncing.

"I'll put the kettle on." Lorna shuffles to the kitchen.

Loud voices echo in the hall. Isabella slides the cat onto the sofa next to her and creeps to the door. She peers through the peephole.

"I must say you appear rather flustered." Tom's voice is loud and he appears in view of the peephole.

"Flustered? Flustered Grant? I'm not flustered. I'm elated. I know she's here and I'm taking her to face the music."

Isabella's heart flutters and she slaps her hand to her stomach.

"Open the door, Grant."

Two men come into view wearing Navy uniforms. The older one barking at Tom is covered in decorations. *Admiral Moore. Has to be.*

Tom pats himself down across his front pockets and then his backside. "Keys…" he sneaks a glance at Lorna's door and narrows his eyes.

Isabella leans back from the door a moment but realises there's no way he can see her. *He knows me too well.*

"Grant!"

Tom huffs and shoves his hand into his front pocket. "Calm yourself. I'm looking for my keys."

"I'll kick this door in."

Tom crosses his arms over his chest and glares at the highly decorated Naval Officer. "First of all. No, you won't."

"Why not?"

"Because you don't have a warrant. I'm letting you in out of courtesy to show you you're wrong."

"I'm not wrong. She's in London. Where else would she go?"

Tom shrugs. "A Best Western?"

Isabella snorts softly.

"She's with you, Grant. I know she is."

"Second. If you damage my flat in any way, I'll snot you."

Isabella bites her tongue to squash the giggle. *You haven't changed.*

"Open the fucking door, Grant."

"Lovey?"

Isabella jumps and turns around to see Lorna with a tray of tea and biscuits. "Oh, um… thank you. One moment?" she whispers.

Lorna gives her a quizzical eyebrow raise but sets the tray down and lowers herself into an armchair.

Isabella spins back to the peephole.

"... it only makes sense you would hide her."

Tom scoffs and slides his key into the lock. "You'll be disappointed. Oh and... don't touch a single thing. Or I'll knock both your heads together." He glares at the MP shadowing every move of Admiral Moore.

Tom throws one more warning look at Lorna's door before following the men into his flat.

Isabella walks over to the sofa and smiles at Lorna, who fills a dainty little cup from her teapot.

"One lump or two, lovey?"

"One please."

Lorna picks the cup up with its saucer and holds it out. Isabella takes a sip of the scalding tea and stops herself grimacing. "Mmm, thank you."

Lorna nods and picks up her own cup. "Lovey, I must say you are a lucky thing. Nabbing a handsome man like that. You'll have to give an old girl a few pointers." She cackles as she picks up a jammie dodger. "I can't tell a lie. Sometimes I let Pebbles wander the hall just so Tom will bring her back for me." She winks.

Isabella grins into her teacup. "You saucy minx."

"I'm seventy-seven, but I'm not dead." She takes a sip. "Yet."

Isabella picks up a biscuit. The unease in her stomach comes in waves as she wonders what's going on across the hall. She mentally accounts for her suitcases that she shoved inside Tom's wardrobe. Her father's ashes are inside the larger case on wheels.

If the Admiral touches him... She tightens her fingers around the handle of the teacup.

"Lovey?"

Isabella's eyes flick to Lorna, who sits with her eyebrows raised, obviously waiting for an answer.

"Oh, I'm sorry. What did you say?"

"I asked where you and Tom met each other?"

He protected me from crazy Russian mafia and we knifed a few people... "Tinder."

Lorna frowns. "I'm not familiar. Is that a fancy bar?"

"No, it's... yes. A fancy bar." Isabella takes another sip as the cat climbs into her lap. She strokes its soft head and smiles.

"I must say it's nice to see him with someone. He's been alone in that flat since he moved in."

"Yes, well. Sometimes it takes a while to find... someone."

"And his upbringing was so tragic. Poor dear."

Isabella swallows her tea. "Hmm?"

"Oh, with his mother dying so young. And then the violent foster home. I'm glad Martha finally took him in."

As though shoved hard in the back, Isabella leans forward. "What did you say?"

"His foster mother. Martha."

"His..." Isabella bites her lip and puts her cup down. "Martha?"

"Yes. Well of course, she organised the flat for him while he was in hospital after the motorcycle accident. Poor dear punctured his lung. Nearly died." She tuts and stirs her tea. "I came across her ordering a man around, bringing boxes in and such. I thought *she* was the one moving in. So I mentioned the stairs can be a hard slog to get up and down for a woman of our... vintage." She laughs and picks up another jammie dodger. "She seemed taken aback that I called her old."

"I bet." *Foster mother?*

"Anyway, we got talking and she said the flat was for a relative. Didn't seem to want to say much more after that. She's a guarded woman that one."

"Of course." Isabella bites into her jammie dodger even though her stomach is tied in knots and she isn't hungry. "So, who told you she was Tom's foster mother... guardian... person?"

"He did." Lorna shrugs. "O'course he probably has no recollection. He was rather... drunk when he told me. I was looking for Pebbles in the hall one night when he trudged in, completely legless." She shakes her head and tuts quietly.

"What did he say?" *Surely you're mistaken.*

"Well, I helped him unlock his door and he stumbled inside. I made sure he was okay and as I was leaving, he said I was as nice as his foster mum. I asked if that was the woman who organised the flat for him and he nodded. Then, promptly fell asleep. Bless him." She smiles into her tea and takes another sip.

Isabella realises she's biting on her lip so hard she'll end up with an ulcer. She sucks her lip a moment and puts her cup down.

"But..." Lorna leans forward in her chair and a twinkle lights up her eyes. "If you want something a bit juicy… Mr Chatton in flat fourteen… he has three mistresses. And they all come on alternating weeks! It's like a revolving door. I see them out the front." She juts her chin towards the window. "Poor Mrs Chatton has no clue…"

4

TOM

Tom leans against the door of his bedroom as Moore gets on his knees and looks under the bed. Tom rolls his eyes.

Moore stands up. "Where is she Grant?"

"Clearly, I have no idea."

"Clearly, you're a lying bastard."

"Now, now. You're in my flat. Maybe ease off the insults."

Moore scoffs and pushes past Tom out of the room. Tom goes to follow him down the hall when he stops and spins around to face Tom.

"What now?" Tom raises his eyebrows. "She's not hiding under the bed or in the kitchen pantry. What more do you want?"

Moore stands toe to toe with Tom and glares into his eyes. Tom glares back without blinking.

"Wait a minute…" Moore stomps back into the bedroom,

shoving Tom aside. Tom's pulse responds and he clenches his fists to stop himself landing a punch on Moore's jaw. Moore makes a beeline for the wardrobe.

Fuck.

He throws open the door and his eyes rest on Isabella's two bags. He pulls out the hiking backpack and case on rollers. "Going somewhere, Grant?"

Tom swallows and shrugs. "Who doesn't love a hike?"

"You don't strike me as a hiker." He throws both cases on the bed.

"What the actual fuck do you think you're doing?" Tom steps into the room.

"Investigating." Moore grabs the zip of the case with wheels and tugs it open.

Tom jumps across but it's too late. Moore picks up a pearly white box. He shakes it and it makes Tom's pulse spike. *Show some respect.*

"Stop!" Tom shoots his arm out and grabs Moore by the collar. "Put it down." His voice is low and dangerous. "Now."

Moore looks down at Tom's hand and grins. "It's heavy. Drugs? Diamonds? What game are you and the killer playing, Grant?"

"It's neither. And *I'm* not playing any games. Put the box down or I'll shoot you in the head."

Moore and Tom eye each other. Moore's fingers toy with the lid of the box.

Sweat trickles down the centre of Tom's back. *Don't you fucking dare.*

"Shoot me in the head, Grant? Really?"

"Try me." He twists the hand around Moore's collar and it tightens. Moore makes a squeaking noise. "Call for your MP. I dare you. I'm fairly sure he's poking around the lounge room. Finding nothing. Call him."

Moore drops the box on the bed. Tom's heart jerks. He let's go of Moore and scoops the box up.

Moore clutches at his throat while Tom inspects the box. *Intact.*

He looks up at the dishevelled Admiral. "Get the fuck out."

Moore straightens his tie and marches out of the room.

Tom cradles the box against his body and follows.

"We're done here." Moore snaps at the MP, who stands at attention beside the front door. Moore flicks his head towards the hallway and the MP moves out.

"So pleased you could visit. Maybe next time give me a warning and I'll bake scones."

Moore glares at Tom and sniffs. "Next time Grant, you'll be locked up with the killer and I'll swallow the damn key."

"You seem to be forgetting the graphic photographs I have of you with the prostitutes and the cocaine…some of them depict the cocaine *on* the prostitutes. Classy." Tom smiles as Moore's nostrils flare. "You ever come back here again or touch a hair on Isabella's head. Wherever she may be. I'll expose you." Tom reaches across and dusts his ribbon bar. "Are we clear?"

Moore's nostrils flare and realisation dawns across his face. "Get your hands off me."

Tom winks. "Again, thanks for dropping by. It's been super."

Moore marches down the hall and disappears down the stairs. Tom leans against the doorframe and blows a breath out. He looks down at the box, still cradled to his chest. "Sorry about that."

He walks into his flat and puts the box on the kitchen worktop. A glance out of his kitchen window confirms Moore has left. *Good riddance.* He walks across the hall and taps on the door.

"Tom." Lorna opens the door wide. "Come in. We were just starting on our second cup."

"I couldn't possibly. Thanks." He looks at Isabella on the gaudy pink sofa with the cat in her lap.

She gives Tom a lopsided smile and pats the spot next to her. "One cup won't hurt. Besides, Lorna is a wealth of information." She widens her eyes and tracks him as he walks across the room and sits beside her.

"Is she now?"

"Oh yes, Mr Chatton for example... he has three mistresses. Did you know?" Isabella sips her tea.

"No. I... who's Mr Chatton?" Tom scrunches his face up and swipes a jammie dodger.

"Flat fourteen Tom, dear." Lorna crosses her ankles and pours him tea.

"Oh. Right." Tom frowns at the milky tea. "You know, on second thoughts I—"

"He'll have one lump." Isabella grins. "Oh, there was also that other useful piece of information…" Isabella rolls her eyes to the ceiling and squints for a moment. "Oh yeah." She clicks her fingers and points at Tom. "Martha's your foster mum."

Tom tilts his head and blinks a couple of times. "Ah…" He puts the tea down. "Well, yes that's very interesting…" He looks at Lorna who raises her brows in anticipation. "How did you… I mean I don't…"

"*You* told me dear. A little while back. You came home drunk. I doubt you'd remember."

Tom cringes and laces his hands together in a knot on his knees. "No. I don't." *Well, shit.*

"Actually, maybe that's enough tea for now." Isabella puts her cup down and stands up, placing the cat on the floor.

Tom leaps up and tries to walk casually to the door, suppressing the urge to sprint out of it. "Thanks Lorna. I do love a jammie dodger." He holds an arm out and Isabella walks to him, grinning.

She slips under his arm and nestles against him. "We have so much to discuss!"

Tom lets a breath out and walks across the hall and into his flat. Once inside Isabella ducks out of his arm and turns to him. She smiles, folding her arms over her chest. "Forgot to mention it did you?"

"No. I… hadn't got around to it yet." He shoves his hands in his pockets and watches Isabella.

She's smiling. She's not angry.

"Do you not trust me?" She tilts her head.

Fuck.

"Of course, I do. It's…" He rakes a hand through his hair and exhales, looking to the ceiling. "It's weird."

"No, it isn't."

Tom quirks a brow. "Honestly?"

"Yes. And I must say it explains *a lot*." Her eyes fall to the box on the worktop and her hand flies to her mouth. "Papa." She slides the box against her and wraps her hands around it. "Why is he out here?"

"Moore found him."

Isabella's head snaps up. "Oh God."

"It's okay, Iz." Tom walks to her and slides his hands either side of her neck. "I reminded him of a few things. He won't be back."

"I'm not afraid of him," she whispers. "But he touched my father." She drops her face against Tom's chest and he wraps both arms around her. "I need to lay him to rest, Tom."

"Let's go see Martha. Our plans will go over a treat."

Isabella chuckles against his chest. "Will she ground you?"

Tom grins, his mouth against the top of her head. "You're a hoot."

5

TOM

Tom sucks a breath in through his teeth and pushes open the door to the warehouse.

"What's the matter?" Isabella hooks a finger in the back of his waistband and follows him inside.

"I hate being here when there's people about."

"Why?"

"Because—"

"Tom!" Penny waddles towards him, her smile is irritating as opposed to welcoming. *Exhibit A.*

"Penny." Tom swallows a groan. He pulls Isabella out from behind him, and Penny stops short.

"Oh. Hello." Penny's face changes to blank and she looks between Tom and Isabella.

"Penny, this is Isabella. Iz. Penny." He pulls Isabella further onto the floor before Penny can start talking. *She never shuts up.*

"Ah, nice to meet..." Isabella scurries along beside Tom. "That was a bit rude, Tom."

Tom shrugs. "She's used to me."

"Oh! Coffee," Isabella nods at the kitchenette. "I need to wash away the milky tea. You want one?" She walks backwards and holds her palms up in question.

"Sure, yeah. Ta." Tom scans the room, thankful there's only a handful of other people in the building. His eyes rest on Martha's office door. It's closed but she's in there. *She's always in there.*

The unmistakable chesty cough of Malcolm hits Tom's eardrums. Malcolm wheezes and giggles at his phone. Tom peers over his shoulder and sees a tabby cat and a Labrador fighting over a toy mouse. "You know, you could at least watch something worthwhile."

Malcolm jumps and fumbles his phone. "Tom."

Tom shakes his head and grins. "A cat and a dog fighting over a mouse? Really? No swimwear models or Victoria's Secret runways?"

Malcolm chuckles and wipes the sweat away from his fat face with a handkerchief. "Gotta keep it work friendly."

Tom hides a grimace as images of Malcom watching something not work friendly invade his mind. *Not safe for work indeed.*

"Hey, tell me Malcolm. Who owns the shiny new Porsche outside?"

Malcolm gives Tom a proud grin. "That would be me."

Are you fucking kidding me?

"You?"

"Yep. Picked her up yesterday." Malcolm's grins and his crooked teeth remind Tom of piano keys.

"You must be doing quite well for yourself."

Malcolm's grin falters and he shrugs. "Just saved up for a while."

And you still live with your Mum.

"And here I was thinking you spent all your money on prostitutes and KFC."

Malcolm coughs and gulps from his stained coffee mug.

Tom stares at him a moment before cracking a smile and slapping him on the back. "Calm down. I know you don't spend your money on KFC." Tom walks away suppressing a chuckle.

"Tom! Chap."

Tom rolls his eyes and stops walking. He turns and James is standing behind him. "Did you just call me chap?"

"Ah, I did. But… let's pretend I didn't." James winces.

"Hmm." Tom tilts his head and squints at James.

"What?"

"Did you…" Tom peers around the back of James' head. "You did. You cut that stupid man bun off."

James strokes the back of his head. "Oh. Yeah. Martha said that if I didn't get a decent haircut, she would tie me to a chair and cut it for me."

"She would have."

"Did she cut your hair for you? You know when you were—"

"Shut up James."

James cringes and clears his throat. "Anyway, Tom. Who's the bird?"

"Pardon?" *You did not just call Isabella a bird.*

"The hot bird making coffee?"

Yes. Yes, you did. Tom keeps his face neutral and looks at the kitchenette. Isabella is leaning over the small worktop fiddling with a spare coffee filter. Her shirt has ridden up slightly and her tattoo is visible on the skin peeking out. "No idea. Have you spoken to her?"

"I'm going in." James saunters across the floor.

Tom bites his lip and waits for the show.

James parks himself directly in front of Isabella and starts talking. Isabella's eyebrows raise and she gives him her friendly smile that Tom knows she reserves for the elderly and imbeciles. She shifts her eyes to Tom as James prattles.

Tom grins and gives her a head shake. *Make him sweat, Iz.*

Isabella smirks and steps towards James, pinning him between the worktop and her left hip. She tilts her head and nods as he keeps rambling.

Tom can practically see the sweat forming across his top lip. Isabella leans in and whispers something in his ear. She slides her hand over a letter opener someone left next to the toaster. She picks it up and rotates it in her hand.

She says something else and James glances down at the letter opener and back to her face. Isabella's eyes widen and she runs her tongue along her top lip.

James slides out from where Isabella has wedged him and

pulls his collar away from his neck. He scurries back towards Tom, looking over his shoulder at Isabella who winks at him and tilts her head.

"Not funny Tom."

"What?"

"You could have told me it was Isabella."

"Could have. But… where's the fun in that?"

Isabella appears next to Tom and hands him a mug. She turns to James. "Sorry. Didn't mean to scare you."

"I thought you were gonna stab me with the letter opener."

"I was." Isabella stares directly at James who chuckles and looks between Tom and Isabella who don't crack.

Isabella takes a long sip of her coffee as James stumbles backwards. He jerks a thumb over his shoulder. "Right, I should go… and…" He spins and jogs through the desks and out the back door.

Isabella leans against Tom and they both laugh. "He's a git." Tom sips his coffee.

"Be nice." Isabella winks. "Poor guy almost wet himself."

"What did you say to him?"

"I explained how easy it would be to stab him through the heart and not leave more than a tiny mark." Isabella shrugs. "I was just making conversation."

"Tom." He spins around and Martha is standing in the doorway to her office. "Both of you. In here."

"Oh fun…" Tom puts his hand on Isabella's shoulder and steers her into the office. "Just, let me do the convincing."

Isabella snorts. "Because that always goes so well."

Tom grabs one of the two chairs in front of Martha's desk, spins it around and straddles it. He reaches across and snatches a piece of the blueberry muffin sitting on the desk.

Martha thwacks Tom across the back of the head as she walks past. "That's my breakfast, Tom."

Tom coughs.

Isabella giggles. "Cute."

Tom's cheeks burn and he shoots Isabella a glare.

"Adorable." She winks.

Martha sits in her chair and folds her hands on the desk. She stares at Tom and Isabella and doesn't say anything.

Tom squints and chews on the muffin. "Martha?"

"I'm waiting to see which one of you is going to try and convince me that going to Belarus is a great idea."

Tom clears his throat and tries to swallow down the dry crumbs of muffin still stuck halfway. "Well, it's *not* a great idea."

Martha purses her lips. "Agreed."

"I'm going." Isabella folds her arms across her chest and watches Martha.

"*We're* going." Tom narrows his eyes at Isabella a moment before looking back to Martha, who sits back in her chair and taps her fingers on the desk. "She's not going alone."

Martha nods once and stands up. She paces behind her desk. "I figured as much."

Tom smirks to himself. *Of course, you did.*

"You did?" Isabella put her mug on the desk.

"Have you met Martha?" Tom grins at Isabella. "She'll already have the jet booked."

"You'll leave tomorrow evening." Martha stops pacing. "But as you can imagine, it's difficult to get clearance to even fly over Belarus, let alone land a plane. Not to mention you need to be completely undetected, my dear." She stops and rests her eyes on Isabella for a moment. "So, you'll fly to Poland where a car will be ready for you. You need to cross the border on the ground."

"Okay." Isabella nods.

"You get in and get out. Do you understand?"

"I understand."

Martha looks at Tom. "Tom?"

"In and out. Got it." He looks at Isabella. She's pale. He reaches across and grabs her hand, giving it a squeeze. She holds tight but keeps staring at a spot on the desk in front of her. "What about passports?" He directs the question to Martha but keeps his eyes on Isabella.

"Malcolm is working on them as we speak." Martha sits again and watches Isabella, who's eyes still haven't lifted from the desk.

"No, he's watching cat videos on YouTube."

Martha huffs and stomps around her desk. "Wait here." She disappears out the door.

Tom pulls Isabella's arm and she looks at him. "Hey. You okay?" Her blue eyes meet his and the uncertainty clouding them softens Tom's chest. He gets off his chair and squats in front of her. "Talk to me."

"I'm okay. I'm just..." Isabella shrugs and looks away. "I'm apprehensive."

"About?"

She shakes it out and brings her hands to Tom's face. "I haven't been home since I escaped. I haven't seen my childhood home since we were raided. I'm... frightened."

"Then, we don't go."

"I promised him. Tom." She runs her hands off his face and down his neck. "He asked *nothing* of me when I was there. Nothing."

Tom swallows and grabs both her hands that now rest on his shoulders against his neck. Her emotion is tangible. The slight tremble in her hands and the way her eyes are soft and fragile hits him in the heart.

"What can make this less frightening? What do you need, Iz?"

"You."

"Me?"

"You won't let anything happen to me."

"No, I won't."

"Then, you take away my fear." She rests her face against his and kisses his mouth. "*You* are what I need."

Tom pulls her against him and their heartbeats rest against each other. "Okay," he whispers into her hair. "Okay..."

The office door opens and Tom reluctantly pulls himself back onto his chair.

Martha marches in and slaps two manila envelopes on her desk. "Passports, Drivers license and birth certificates." She eyes

Tom and then looks at Isabella who is wiping tears off her face. "Do you need a moment, Isabella?"

Isabella sniffles and shakes her head. "No."

"Right then." Martha sits down and gestures to Tom. "Nathan Parker, meet Emily Maguire.".

"Emily Maguire. I like it." Isabella smiles and sifts through the paperwork in her envelope.

"There's some backstory in there too." Martha leans back in her chair, crossing her arms over her chest. She looks between the pair of them. "Am I going to regret this?"

A chuckle escapes Tom's mouth before he can reign it in. "Of course, you will."

Martha keeps her lips pressed in a thin line, leans on her desk and folds her hands. "In and out. I'm not kidding. I'll come and haul both your sorry backsides out of there if I have to. Do you understand?"

"Thank you, Martha." Isabella's voice is soft and delicate, and Tom has to check it is coming from Isabella's mouth. She brings her eyes to meet his and Tom falls in love with her all over again. *Damn it Iz.*

A knock at the office door shatters the fragile moment.

"Yes?" Martha stands up.

Malcolm peers around the door. "Ah, yeah. I thought you might like some burner phones. You know … well, if you need."

"Okay Malcolm, bring them in and stop dithering."

Tom grins at Isabella who giggles softly.

Malcolm hustles to the desk, his shirt is half untucked and doesn't appear to have made acquaintance with an iron. Ever.

"Here you go. All set." He drops the phones on the desk and appears to bow before hot footing it out of the office.

Tom stares at the door a moment and frowns. "Where the fuck do you find these people, Martha?"

"He's a tech genius. And a complete slob."

"And now the proud owner of a black Porsche." Tom shakes his head.

Martha plonks into her chair and takes her glasses off. She rubs her eyes. "Yes well, he *does* live with his Mum."

ISABELLA

I sabella unhooks the helmet from the pillion seat and slides it over her head. She swings her leg over and nestles herself against Tom's back, squeezing his hips with her thighs. *Right, that feels quite nice.*

"What do you do when it rains?" She leans herself forward and rests her chin on his shoulder.

"Stay home."

"What about catching the bus?"

Tom twists around, keeping one hand on the handlebars and lifts the corner of his mouth. "Me? On a bus?"

Isabella laughs. "Point taken." She sits up, leaning against the backrest. "Where are we going, anyway?"

"You'll see." He starts the bike and the rumble travels through the footplates where her feet rest and all through her body.

"As if you weren't sexy enough."

He tilts his head to her. "What?"

"The Harley. Of course, you ride a Harley."

"And here I was thinking you meant the leather."

"Well, the jacket's sexy too." She runs her hand under the jacket and across his chest. "But I prefer what's under it."

Tom slaps the visor down on his helmet. "Okay, we need to leave. Or… we won't."

Isabella laughs and pulls her hand away. "Fine. Party pooper."

The bike rolls forward and Isabella rests her hips against Tom's waist. The view of London is different on a motorcycle. She turns her head back and forth as though watching a tennis match while they weave through the congested streets. Instead of being locked away from the bustle of the streets in a car, on the bike she is amongst it.

They stop at a set of lights and Tom plants his feet on the ground. He slides his hands back and along Isabella's thighs, and leans against her. "You'll feel better once we are out of the city. Trust me."

"I do." She slides her hands over his as they rest on her knees. He squeezes her hand as the light turns green.

"Hold on."

They pull forward and get ahead of the cars. Around twenty minutes later they are on the A4. The freedom of being on the back of the bike is exhilarating and Isabella finds herself holding her arms out either side of her and catching the wind in her palms.

After an hour and a half Tom slows the bike as they roll into a country village. Isabella looks around at the small quaint stores and the green fields beyond them.

"Where are we?"

"Avebury." Tom taps Isabella's knee. She climbs off the bike and puts her helmet on her seat. Tom flicks the kickstand down and pulls his own helmet off, scrubbing his fingers through his hair.

"And what's in Avebury?"

Tom stretches his arms over his head before grabbing Isabella's hand and pulling her along. "You'll see."

"Stop saying that." Isabella laughs. They stop in front of a stone church. "Church of St James." Isabella reads. "Well, I didn't see this coming."

Tom turns to her and grins. "Not up for a church service?"

"Ah… I mean if you…" Isabella stares at him. *Seriously?*

Tom laughs and grabs her hand again. "Relax. We aren't going inside."

"Oh, thank God." Isabella presses her hand to her chest and Tom laughs again.

"But to be fair. Maybe where I am taking you is weirder than going inside."

They walk to an old graveyard behind the church and Tom weaves through the headstones to a lone one at the back. He drops Isabella's hand and crouches down next to it. He dusts the top of it and wipes dirt from the lettering on the stone.

"Hey, Mum."

Isabella's breath catches and she presses her hand against her throat. "Your Mum." She crouches next to him and rests her hand on his back. She leans forward to read the headstone. "Heather Grant. 1947 - 1994. Beloved Mother. May your soul wander, spreading peace and love forevermore." Isabella swallows the ache in her throat. "Forty-seven. She was so young."

Tom plonks onto his backside next to her headstone. "She was." He holds his hand to Isabella, and she takes it, sitting next to him. "You would have loved her, Iz."

The cemetery is deserted, and birds sing in the nearby trees. The sun warms her back and fluffy white clouds gently morph and change above them. "It's so peaceful."

Tom lays back on the grass and pulls Isabella against him. "That's why we're here. You're frightened."

Isabella opens her mouth to argue but realises it's pointless. "Yes."

"Well, when I was frightened, Mum always made me feel better."

Tom nudges his mouth to hers and kisses her. Flutters erupt in Isabella's stomach and chest. She savours every tiny second of his kiss and the warmth it gives her.

"Everything makes sense here." He squeezes her.

The ominous feeling that plagued her since it was confirmed they would leave the following evening evaporated here. With him.

"Tell me about her?" Isabella sits up and wraps her arms around her knees.

"She was the kindest human being I've ever known." Tom

shields his eyes from the sun and smiles. "Even though she made me eat kale and lentils."

Isabella laughs. "Sounds delicious."

"It wasn't." Tom sits up and wraps an arm around Isabella. "I can't tell you how good it felt to eat a juicy steak for the first time."

Isabella leans her ear against his chest and hears his heartbeat.

"It must have been painful to lose her," Isabella whispers, remembering her father's last breath. Pain pierces her heart and she pushes a hand against her chest.

"It was the worst thing I've ever gone through. Well, until Claire…" Tom stares at a faraway place that Isabella can't see. She bites her lip and Tom shakes his shoulders. "Sorry."

"Don't apologise. You loved her."

Tom's eyes find hers and she stares into the green abyss. "It's different with you, Iz." He rests his hand against her cheek. "I thought I wouldn't be able to love anyone again. But the thought of being without you…"

"I'm not going anywhere." She pulls his hand from her cheek to her mouth and kisses it. "Ever again." *Never.*

Tom falls back on the grass and pulls down Isabella with him. She nestles under his chin, against his heart and closes her eyes.

ISABELLA WALKED OUT OF THE BATHROOM TOWEL DRYING HER HAIR. *Martha huffed and shoved her phone into her handbag.*

"He's still not answering."

Isabella's heart sped up and she sat next to Martha on the bed. "He must be going out of his mind. I need to go to him." Tears pricked at the corners of her eyes. She swallowed and gulped in a breath. She stood up but Martha pulled her back down.

"You need to remain hidden for now. What if Kat sees you? You're supposed to be dead."

"I know, but—"

"But nothing. If she or one of those kids spots you. It's all for nothing."

The tears toppled from Isabella's eyes and rolled down her cheeks. "What if he drinks himself into oblivion?"

"I have no doubt that's exactly what he's done." Martha paused and Isabella tried to overcome the dagger that stabbed her through the heart as her fears were confirmed. "I'll keep trying him." Martha pulled her phone out again and slapped it against her ear. "And if he doesn't pick up, I'll go over there."

Isabella stood and walked to the window, staring out of it. She held her hand over the throbbing bruise on her chest and bit her lip. She looked across town in the direction of The Ritz. So close yet, so far. Too far. "I'm sorry. Don't hate me." She dropped her face and sobbed, wrapping her arms around her middle.

"It's almost three pm. I'll go over there."

Isabella's heart jumped. "I'm coming with you."

"Isabella—"

"No!" She stalked across the room and glared at Martha. "I love him, Martha. This isn't fair. To him." She sweeps her arm

out, gesturing around the tiny room. "I'm in some crappy motel pretending to be dead and he's drowning himself in whisky."

"We had to go to the closest motel Isabella. Less chance of you being seen."

"I don't care about the motel, Martha! I care about Tom." She crossed her arms over her chest and glared at Martha. "I'm coming with you."

Martha sighed and threw her hands up in defeat. "Fine. But let me speak to him first. I have no idea what state he will be in. Give me half an hour." She picked up her handbag and strode out the door.

Isabella stared at the back of the motel room door while tears rolled down her face.

TOM LEADS ISABELLA ALONG AND SHE SMILES AT THE LITTLE houses and shops they pass. Ten minutes later, Tom stops in front of a white cottage with a thatched roof. It has four windows facing the front and a wooden front door. Isabella looks at Tom as he gazes at the house.

"What is this place?"

"It's my house."

"Your what?"

"My house." He looks at Isabella and grins.

"When you say… your house…"

"I own it."

Isabella is well aware her mouth is hanging open. "It has a thatched roof."

Tom laughs and pulls her along to the front gate. "Yes. And the maintenance is a nightmare."

"Wait… I… I'm confused."

Tom opens the gate and walks up the path. "Are you coming?" *He's serious.*

Isabella joins him at the front door, staring up at the thatching that hangs over them.

Tom slides a key into the lock and swings the door open. He holds an arm out and Isabella walks inside the house.

She sees a lounge with a fireplace and a squishy sofa to her left. On the right is the kitchen. It's country style with an authentic wood fire stove and timber worktops.

"I rent it out on Airbnb these days." Tom looks around and taps the exposed beams on the low ceiling. Isabella turns and stares at Tom, waiting. Tom drops his eyes to hers and chuckles. "You look like you've seen a ghost."

"I'm pretty sure I have, Tom."

Tom pulls a chair out from the round dining table in the middle of the room for Isabella. They both sit.

"This was my mum's house. And before that it was her father's house, and before him his father… you get the idea. Anyway. I lived here with Mum until she passed. It was held in trust for me until I was eighteen. And now I rent it out for holiday stays." He shrugs.

"You lived here as a kid?"

Tom nods.

Isabella stands and goes to the kitchen window that faces out the back of the house. She peers into the distance and sees some large grey stones. "What's out there?" She leans forward and squints.

"The stone circle."

"The what?"

Tom stands next to her. "The stone circle. Avebury is famous for it."

"What is it?"

"A bunch of prehistoric stones that people come to worship and perform rituals around. Mum used to go out there and meditate." Tom rolls his eyes. "Hippy shit."

Isabella turns and leans against the worktop, folding her arms. "I can't imagine you hanging out with hippies."

"Well, until I was eleven, that's exactly what I did. Mum even dressed me in tie-dyed clothing."

Isabella purses her lips to squash a grin. "Stop it."

"It's true."

She steps into Tom and stands on tiptoes, kissing his lips. "I bet you would have been an adorable little hippie child."

"I did a lot of eye-rolling and playing in the dirt while they all chanted and played with crystals." He grabs her hand and pulls her into him. "Wanna stay here tonight?"

"Absolutely."

TOM THROWS A LOG ONTO THE FIRE AND STOKES IT WITH A STEEL poker. Isabella plonks onto the rug next to him, her hands wrapped around a mug of hot chocolate.

"Thank you for bringing me here."

Tom rocks onto his backside and smiles at her. "You feel better?"

Isabella nods and puts the mug on the table by the sofa. "Yes."

Tom pulls something out of his pocket. "I got you something."

Isabella raises her eyebrows. "When?"

"When you were busy in that tiny store buying things to cook for dinner."

"What is it?"

He shuffles behind her and brings his arms over her shoulders. He drops a pendant on a silver chain in front of her face before fastening it around her neck.

Isabella looks down at the pink stone and rubs her thumb and forefinger over the polished surface. "It's beautiful."

Tom traces the chain against her neck. "It's a rose quartz."

"What's a rose quartz?"

"A pink rock."

Isabella narrows her eyes at him, smiling.

"It's the stone of the heart."

Isabella's nose tingles and she closes her eyes before the tears come. "You got this for me?"

"I don't believe in all that magic crystal stuff. But Mum did."

He rests his lips against her neck and kisses her skin. "She never lied to me. And she told me it means love."

"It's never coming off." Isabella presses it to her chest, flattening her hand over it.

Tom's mouth trails up her neck and along her jaw. Her skin tingles and she closes her eyes.

"What about your clothes… can they come off?"

Isabella grins. "You're so smooth." She dips her face down to his and catches his lips with her own. She slides her hands up and under his shirt, resting them on his chest.

"So, that's a yes?" He undoes each button of her top and slides it off her shoulders.

"You don't need permission," she whispers against his mouth.

Tom kisses her again and pulls the straps of her bra down from her shoulders.

"You believe me, don't you?" Isabella whispers.

"About what?" He pulls his shirt off and throws it on the sofa.

"When I say I'm not going anywhere."

Tom rolls down to the floor and pulls her against his chest. "Of course, I believe you."

A sudden urge hits Isabella deep in her gut and she grasps Tom's face in her hands. "No. Tom. I promise I'll never make you feel that you've lost me again." She swallows back the sob that sits in her throat.

"Iz. I know." He pushes his face against hers, his hot breath surrounds her, and she breathes him in.

"I'm sorry I did that to you." *I've felt guilty ever since.*

"Stop." Tom strokes her hair off her face. "Stop…"

Her pulse thumps against her neck and she bites her lip. *What the hell is wrong with me?* "I'm scared that—"

"Stop…" He nuzzles her neck and trails his fingers down her back. She tangles her legs with his and kisses him urgently.

They roll until Isabella lays beneath him, her legs wrap around his hips. Tom pulls her arms above her head, lacing his fingers through hers.

He gazes at her and Isabella sees the reflection of the fire in the green of his eyes.

"You know I'll keep you safe right?" He drops his elbows either side of her head and traces her face with his fingers.

"I trust no one more than you." She runs her hands down his body and drifts her fingers up and down his back. "No one."

Isabella gazes at Tom and he smiles, crinkles appearing in the corners of his eyes.

She pushes her hand against his chest, over his heartbeat.

"I'm not frightened, Tom. Not with you."

7

TOM

Rays of sunlight stream in through the windows of the lounge. Tom wraps his arms tighter around Isabella and kisses the back of her neck.

"Morning." Isabella rolls over to face him. She tugs the duvet Tom pulled off one of the beds closer around her shoulders. The fire is out, with only a few embers feebly glowing.

Tom pushes her hair off her face, resting his nose against hers. "Sleep okay?"

"I did. To be honest I've never slept so well. Despite the fact I'm on a rug on the floor." She peeks under the duvet, and pops her head up again, grinning. "Naked."

Tom strokes his hand down Isabella's body, over the curve of her hip, resting it on her thigh. "Well, you didn't bring pyjamas."

Isabella leans up on her elbow and peers at Tom. "Who's fault is that?"

"Mine." Tom cradles her chin and pulls it to his face. "I take full responsibility."

"We need to leave, don't we?" Isabella mumbles against his mouth before kissing him.

Tom sits up. "We do." He runs a hand through his hair.

"Will you bring me back here again?"

He smiles. "Yes."

TOM DROPS ISABELLA'S HIKING BACKPACK BY THE FRONT DOOR OF the flat. Unease rises and falls in his gut as though the tide can't make up its mind. *Get a grip.*

Isabella peers at the backpack, shaking her head. "How did you manage to squeeze stuff for both of us in that one bag?" She holds the box with her father's ashes in her arms.

"I'm seasoned at travelling light." Isabella bites her lip and Tom rests both hands on her shoulders. "You okay?"

Isabella nods and blinks, sending a tear down her cheek. "I'm fine."

Tom wipes the tear away with his thumb and pulls her into his chest. "Say the word and we don't go."

"I have to."

"I know." Tom rests his hand on the top of the white box. "Let's take him home." He hauls the backpack off the floor and holds his arm out to the hall.

Isabella walks out of the flat and sees Pebbles in the middle of the floor. "Oh, you sneaky old lady."

"The cat's an old lady?"

Isabella laughs. "No. Lorna told me she does it on purpose, so you'll visit her."

"That crafty old fox." Tom grins.

"You knew. Didn't you?" Isabella scoops the cat up and taps on Lorna's door.

"Yeah. But if it gives her a thrill, what's the harm?" Tom shrugs. "I had avoided tea and biscuits though, until you made me go in."

The door opens and Lorna pushes both hands to her chest. "Ah, you sneaky little feline." She takes the cat and winks at Isabella. Tom looks at the floor and squashes a grin. *You sly hussy.* Tom walks to Lorna and gives her a peck on the cheek. "Look after yourself Lorna. We'll be back in a few days."

Lorna's mouth forms a perfect O and she touches her cheek. Colour fills her face and she stumbles against the door frame.

He drops the backpack. *Shit.* "Are you alright?" Tom grabs her elbow, and she nods slowly.

Isabella giggles.

"You're going on a trip?" Lorna manages to find her voice, though her hand is still stuck against her cheek.

"Just a short one. So, look after Pebbles." Tom smiles and picks up the backpack again. "We won't be here to rescue her from the hallway."

Isabella gives Lorna a kiss on the other cheek and they walk to the stairs. "You softie. Giving her a kiss."

"I won't be doing that again. She got all wobbly."

Isabella scoffs. "She'll get over it. We all do."

Tom grins and tosses the backpack into the boot of the car waiting for them. He gets into the back seat next to Isabella. "You don't get wobbly?"

She slides an arm through the crook of his elbow and rests her head on his shoulder. "I've built up a resistance."

"Really?"

"No."

"Aren't you cute." James' voice from the driver's seat cuts into Tom's interrogation.

Fucking James. "Shut up James."

James chuckles and pulls away from the block of flats.

"Why did Martha send *you*?" Tom leans forward.

"What do you mean?" James scratches the back of his neck, keeping his eyes on the road.

"You irritate me."

"You're welcome."

Isabella snorts. "By the way, James. Sorry about the other day. It really *was* nice to meet you."

"Don't mention it. I figured Tom put you up to it." He flicks his eyes to Tom's in the rear-view mirror.

"Actually, Isabella is more than capable of terrifying people without my help." Tom sits back in the seat and rests his hand on Isabella's leg. "Though you are quite easy to scare."

"I'm getting better. I killed that loon the other day."

Tom rolls his eyes. "Yeah, after six shots. Poor bloke was riddled with holes by the time you were finished with him."

"Well, he kept moving."

"They don't sit still and wait for you to kill them, James. They run and fight back." Tom stops and realises Isabella isn't participating in the ribbing of James. "Iz?"

She turns from where she was gazing out the window. "Yeah?"

"You're doing it again."

"Doing what?"

"Freaking out." He points to her mouth. "You're chewing on your lip, and your hands are bunched into fists." He reaches over and untucks her fingers from where she has balled them into her palms on top of her father's box. He holds both her hands with one of his and squeezes. "You're missing out. Making fun of James is a very relaxing pastime."

Isabella smiles but her eyes remain dull. Tom pulls her under his arm and she slumps against him.

"Where are you guys going anyway?" James changes lanes. "Martha said to take you to the airfield. She doesn't say much does she?"

"Does she need to?"

"Well... no. I... guess not."

"Maybe you irritate *her* too?" Tom raises his eyebrows and smirks at James as he eyes him in the rear-view mirror.

"Need I remind you how I saved you and her that time?"

"One time. Get back to me when you've come to the rescue a

few more times."

"Do you reckon I will?"

Tom snorts. "Doubtful."

James fixes his eyes back on the road and stops talking. *Small mercies.*

They drive in silence for an hour or so and Tom realises Isabella has fallen asleep against his chest. He strokes her hair and drops his lips top her head. "It'll be okay," he whispers into her hair.

"So, have you seen Malcolm's new Porsche?"

The unease that sloshed around in Tom's gut earlier is back. "Yeah. Seems a waste."

"Huh?"

"Well, what is Malcolm planning to pick up in it? Take away? A new video game? His Mum's gout medication?"

"Oh." James laughs. "Yeah right. I don't know." He shrugs and flicks the blinker, turning onto the road leading to the airstrip. "He reckons he came into some cash."

Tom narrows his eyes at James' reflection in the mirror. "He what?"

"Yeah, I asked him how he afforded it and he said some old Aunt died."

"What?"

"An inheritance. His Aunt in Ireland died, or something." James nods forward at the airstrip. "How close do you want me to get to the plane?"

"Stop here." Tom turns to Isabella and shakes her gently.

"Hey." He runs his fingers over her face and her eyes open. She blinks a couple of times and sits up.

"Sorry." She rubs her eyes.

"Don't apologise. It's not like you slept a lot last night."

Isabella giggles. "Not my fault."

Tom smirks and gets out of the car. "Wake up a bit. I'll sort our stuff."

James is at the boot pulling the backpack out.

"It's okay James. You aren't a chauffeur." Tom grabs the backpack.

"Sorry."

"And stop apologising. Listen to me. You need to not give a shit about what people think of you. Start being an arrogant arse-hole as opposed to an indecisive, annoying git. Yes?"

James swallows and gives Tom a lopsided grin. "Like you?"

Damn right. "Yes, James. Like me."

"Right." James nods and kicks a toe into the ground.

"Hey listen. I have a job for you."

James peers up at Tom and jerks the corner of his lip up. "A job? I thought Martha gave out the jobs?"

"Just… shut up and listen to me."

James leans in and puts a hand on Tom's shoulder. Tom peers at the hand and back to James. "What have I told you about touching me, James?"

"Fuck. Sorry." He pulls his hand away.

"And what did I say about apologising all the time?"

"Sorry."

Tom raises an eyebrow.

"I mean…"

"Stop talking."

James slams his mouth shut and stares at Tom. He flaps his hand around as though encouraging Tom to continue.

Tom glares at James a moment and rubs his eyes. *Jesus Christ.*

"Okay listen. Malcolm."

"I'm James."

"What?"

"You called me—"

"Stop talking before I rip your voice box out and shove it up your nose."

James presses his lips together.

"I need you to watch Malcolm."

"Watch him do what? Giggle at cat videos?"

Tom rolls his eyes. "Fuck, you're frustrating. No James. Something isn't right. I don't know what it is, but… keep an eye on him. Yes?"

"What makes you think…" James shrugs and holds his palms up.

"He told you his Aunt died."

"And?"

"He told me he saved up."

"Maybe he did both?"

"No, James. He did not do both. He's lying about the car."

James' eyes widen and he inhales a breath before whistling it out. "How do you do that?"

"It's not that hard. He told two different people two different things." Tom reaches across and tweaks James' ear. "You need to listen to people. They tell you a whole lot if you bother to use your ears."

Isabella slips her hand around Tom's waist and leans against him. "Are we ready?"

Tom kisses the top of her head. "We're ready."

He lugs the backpack over his shoulder and grabs Isabella's hand. "I'll be in touch. Yes?" He raises an eyebrow at James.

"Yes. I'm on it." He nods once. "Am I allowed to call you? I mean if I…"

"Yes, James. I'm expecting it. Oh and… maybe keep this between you and I?"

"What are you two on about?" Isabella looks between Tom and James.

"Nothing. I'll explain later." Tom squeezes her hand.

"Right. Yep. Have a great trip. Wherever you're going." James scurries to the driver's seat and jumps in.

"He looks like he opened the best Christmas present ever." Isabella waves as James pulls away.

"I gave him an ego boost. He's useless but he tries. I'll give him that."

"An ego boost?"

"He's spying on a fat slob that lives with his Mum. He can't possibly fuck it up."

"But he will?"

"No doubt."

8

ISABELLA

Isabella falls into a seat next to the window of the plane. Before she can attempt to buckle her seatbelt, Tom's hands are across her lap, clicking it in for her.

"I still remember last time." He keeps his hand against her stomach, and she leans her head against his. "I'm right here next to you. Okay?"

Isabella nods and claws her fingers into his hand. Her chest is tight, and she gasps air through her mouth.

"Iz. Look at me."

Isabella gazes into Tom's green eyes and tries to bring her breathing back to normal.

"It's not the flying this time is it?"

Isabella shakes her head and drops forward over her knees. She massages her scalp through her hair and concentrates on not passing out. *What the hell am I doing?*

She sits up and grabs Tom's shirt with both hands. "What am I doing, Tom?"

He slides his hands over hers and holds them. "Currently, wrinkling my shirt."

"I'm flying into hell, Tom. What if they find…" She gulps in a breath and moans.

"Iz. Look at me." He turns her face to him and runs his thumb across her lips. "I told you I'd keep you safe. And I will." He pulls her against his chest and wraps an arm around her. "And we aren't flying into hell. In fact, I've heard lovely things about Poland."

Tom's voice rumbles through his chest and she lets out a small giggle despite the impending doom looming over her. "What's in Poland?"

"Potatoes."

"Potatoes?"

"Yep." Tom grins at her.

The engines on the plane amp up and Isabella swallows the acid pooling at the back of her tongue. She clutches her knees, digging her nails in.

Tom reaches across, unhooks both her hands and holds them in his. She leans into him and grits her teeth. Her chest burns as her breaths come out in short sharp bursts.

"Tom, I… can't…"

The plane shoots down the runway and heaves into the air. Weightlessness hits Isabella's gut and dizziness envelopes her.

"Breathe, Iz. I've got you." His deep voice rolls into her ears.

She counts her breaths as she inhales and exhales. *One, two, three…*

Her heart throws itself against her ribs, looking for a way out. The tightness in her chest keeps it caged in. She counts. *Eight, nine, ten.*

She swallows and exhales a breath tinged with a moan. "Are we in the air?"

"We're in the air." Tom lifts her face and looks into her eyes.

"If they find me, they'll kill me."

"Yes. They will."

"The day I left, Kotsya told me that if I tried anything stupid or didn't report back to the plane, they would never stop hunting me. And they didn't."

"And now they're dead."

Isabella gazes at Tom.

"You killed the head of the snake, Iz. Remember? Or, more so you sliced his femoral artery and he bled out on the floor of a strip club."

Isabella snorts softly.

"It was a fancy demise." Tom shrugs.

"There's always someone who will replace the head of the snake. We're talking about organsied crime, Tom. And I'll be on their most wanted list."

"Only if they know you're there. And how could they possibly?"

Isabella shrugs. "They got to Jack."

"Well, I'm kind of glad they did."

"Why?"

"Because I would never have found you." He presses his lips against her temple and the warmth of his kiss spreads down her body, calming her.

She grasps the pink pendant around her neck and squeezes it. "Okay, I'm glad Jack sold me out too."

"But this time. No one knows we'll be there. We're in and out. Just like Martha said."

Isabella nods.

"And we're together."

Isabella nods again as tears pool in her eyes. She looks at the seat across from them where she placed her father's ashes. "We're almost there, Papa."

"If he'd known what you were risking taking him home, would he have asked you?"

"No."

"Why didn't you tell him?"

"He was dying, Tom. And he had no idea what became of me while we were apart. He thought I'd been trafficked to some rich man on a yacht."

"He did?"

"Yes. That's what he'd been told. I didn't bother to correct him. Imagine if he knew what I did?" The ache in her throat comes back and she fights to swallow it away but it's no use. She coughs and sobs against Tom's shirt. "All those people they made me kill." Isabella wipes her nose with a tissue from her bag. "The thought of it would have killed him faster than the cancer did."

"So, it was more palatable for him to believe you were sold into sexual slavery?"

"I wouldn't have been taking people's souls. Desecrating their dead bodies." Tom's muscles tense under his shirt and Isabella sits up, looking at him.

Tom drops his forehead against hers. "What?"

"You never did tell me."

"Tell you what?"

"What was it about the carving that got to you so much?"

Tom stares at her a moment before resting his head against the headrest, peering at the ceiling.

"Sorry, I didn't mean to…"

Tom shakes his head. "No. It's fine." He takes a breath. "My mother always told me that the worst thing any human can do to another is desecrate their earthly vessel." He uses quote marks when he says earthly vessel. "She told me it stops their soul finding peace. That they're stuck in a half existence for eternity." He grimaces. "Like I said, I don't believe in all that weird hippy shit. But that stuck with me. I don't know why."

"But you kill people for a living."

"Yep. But I don't mess with them once they're dead." He turns his body towards Isabella. "Even when I killed Kat. I carved three five nine into her face while she was still alive."

A pang, much like the blade of a knife hits Isabella in the gut. She slaps her hand over her belly and squeezes. "You what?" Her voice is raspy and she clears her throat.

"I added her to your count."

Isabella chews on her lip and holds Tom's gaze. "Have you noticed I haven't asked you about Kat?"

Tom nods and traces his fingers across the back of her hands.

"She needed to die."

Tom nods again, still holding Isabella's stare.

"But I thought of her as my sister. And despite what I said, I could never have killed her."

"I know."

Isabella bows her head. The sobs bubbling in her chest creep up the back of her throat. "But she's dead because of me, nonetheless." *Why does it still hurt so much?*

"Yes. Although..." Tom pauses and Isabella looks at him. "She also nearly killed Martha so..."

Isabella's eyes grow wide and she leans forward. "She nearly killed Martha?"

"It's James' big claim to fame. He came to the rescue, as he puts it." Tom rolls his eyes and lolls his head towards Isabella. "I mean, I guess he did. But I don't want him thinking he's a hero." He grins and Isabella nestles under his chin.

"Killing shouldn't be something we chat about like it doesn't matter."

Tom strokes her neck and rests his head on top of hers. "No, it shouldn't."

"Because it does matter." *It's always mattered.*

"Iz. There will be no killing on this trip. We go to your home. We bury your father. We get out of there." Isabella sits up. "No one will know who we are. We will just look like bumbling British tourists."

Isabella jerks the corner of her mouth up. "Wandering about with a box full of ashes?"

"Yes. It's our custom." He reclines his seat all the way and holds his arms out. "That and waving tiny Union Jack flags at the Queen."

Isabella reclines her own seat and lifts the arm rest. She shuffles across to nestle against him.

Tom wraps his arms around her, holding her against his body. "Don't be scared," he whispers in her ear.

"Okay." She closes her eyes and the images of her childhood bedroom and the bright airy kitchen in which her father would cook for her, flood her mind. She drifts off with the faint scent of borscht in her nostrils.

I'm coming home.

9

TOM

Tom throws the backpack into the boot of the car and glances back at the rural airstrip. *In and out in five days. Easy.*

A car door slamming shut brings Tom back to task. Isabella is in the passenger seat rifling through the glove box. Tom slides his hand along the roof of the black Mercedes. *Could be worse.*

Tom gets into the car and pulls a Wispa bar out of his pocket and tosses it in Isabella's lap. She grins at him and throws it in the glove box. "Provisions."

Tom nods and starts the car. "Provisions." He enters their destination in the satnav and reaches across, tucking Isabella's hair behind her ear. "Three hours, forty-five minutes to the border. You good?"

"Yes."

"Where's Alexei?"

Isabella looks over her shoulder to the backseat. "He loved a car ride." She grins.

Tom chuckles and pushes his foot down.

Isabella leans against the backrest and gazes out the passenger window. "What happens when we get to the border?"

"Hopefully, not much. Nathan Parker and Emily Maguire will be waved through with a quick passport check and visa presentation."

"Hopefully?"

Tom nods once, keeping his eyes on the road. "Hopefully."

"And what if it isn't so quick and easy?" Isabella bounces her knees up and down while clutching at her stomach.

"They could opt to search the car. And everything in it." Tom reaches across and rubs her thigh. Her legs still.

"Papa." The hand on her stomach pushes harder.

"Relax, Iz. He's a good excuse for our trip. I'm more concerned we'll miss the meet up in Minsk to get the weapons Martha arranged."

"She arranged weapons for us?"

Tom grins. "Have you met Martha?"

Isabella slides her hand off her stomach and laces her fingers through Tom's. "I guess weapons make sense. Just in case."

"Just in case." Tom notes her clammy hand and gives it a squeeze. *Nothing to worry about.*

TOM COUNTS THE NUMBER OF VEHICLES IN FRONT OF THEM IN THE queue. "Six."

"Six?"

"Six cars ahead of us." Tom turns to Iz and strokes her cheek. "Relax. Eat some chocolate." He nods at the glovebox. "We were waved through Terespol. No reason we won't be here as well." The waves of anxiety lapping at his gut, swell with each passing minute. He tries to ignore the unease as it continues to build, but his mother's voice echoes in his head. *Never ignore your intuition, Thomas. It's always right.*

"It's normal to be nervous at a checkpoint." Tom rolls the car forward as the one at the front continues through. "Completely normal."

"Are you convincing me or yourself?" Isabella breaks the Wispa bar in half and holds it out.

"Neither. I'm stating a fact." *Liar.* He takes the chocolate and shoves it in his mouth. "We'll be here for a while." He turns to Isabella and raises his eyebrows. "Wanna jump in the back and steam up the windows?"

Isabella laughs. "Stop it. Besides… not in front of my father."

"We can throw a jacket over him."

Isabella coughs and swallows her chocolate.

Tom laughs and rubs her back. "Sorry. Just trying to make you think about something else."

"Well, that subject doesn't calm me down."

"Fair. Me neither."

The next vehicle is waved through. Tom rolls the car forward again and looks up at the bus in the lane next to them. "Besides, the passengers in the bus would get a free show. Can't have that."

Isabella leans across and looks up at the windows. "And they all look old. They couldn't handle it." She smirks.

Ten minutes later a border control officer approaches the window. "Showtime," Tom whispers and grabs their passports and visa papers.

"Tsel' vashego vizita?"

Purpose of our visit? Avoid being killed. "I'm sorry I don't speak..." *Keep that ace up my sleeve.*

"Purpose of visit?"

"Ah, yes. Well, my wife has always wanted to visit. We hear the Nesvizh Palace is spectacular." Tom grins. *God, I sound like a twat.*

The border control officer looks at their passports. His left eye twitches. The officer looks up at him again. "You are British?"

"Last time I checked."

The officer bends forward and peers at Isabella. "And you?"

"Yes. British." Isabella nods.

The officer squints at her and looks down at the passports again. "Please move to adjacent lane and turn engine off."

Fuck.

Tom grins as Isabella gasps softly. "No problem." He moves the car where the officer points and watches as he disappears into a building in front of them, with their passports.

"Jesus, Tom." Isabella pulls at her shirt and squirms in the seat. "What's going on?"

"Okay Iz, listen to me." Tom leans across and drills his eyes into hers. "This is the only time I'll ever say this to you. But I need Irina, the assassin, sitting next to me right now. Do you understand?"

Isabella blinks once and draws in a breath.

"I need you to be calm, cool and unruffled. Okay?"

Isabella nods and closes her eyes. She breathes in and out a few times and drops her head.

Tom glances at the building the officer disappeared into. *Nothing.* He turns back to Isabella. Her face is down and her shoulders rise and fall with each breath she takes. She lifts her head and looks at Tom. Her eyes are hard and her jaw is clenched.

"You with me?" Tom cups her cheek.

Isabella nods. "Yes."

He strokes his thumb across her cheek. He looks up and sees the officer walking towards them with another officer alongside him.

"You are Nathan Parker and Emily Maguire?" The original officer glares into the car.

"Yes." Tom nods.

The second officer wanders around the car, he checks the licence plates before standing at Isabella's window. He taps on it. Tom turns the ignition so the window can come down. Isabella looks up at the officer and says nothing. Her right hand is gripped into a fist on the seat.

Relax Iz.

"Emily Maguire?"

"Yes."

The officer opens the door. "Please come with me."

Tom's stomach lurches and he grabs Isabella's arm. "Ah, why?" He slides his hand down and grips her wrist.

"Because we say so," the officer next to Tom snarls. "In meantime. Open boot."

Tom's heart races and his eyes dart between Isabella and the two officers.

"Is something wrong, Mr Parker?" The officer next to Isabella dips his head down and glares at Tom.

Tom composes himself and sucks a slow breath through his nose. He keeps hold of Isabella's wrist. "No. It's… we don't want to be late for our check-in."

"We will not take long."

"Where are you taking her?" Tom tightens his grip. Isabella's breathing is almost a pant and he softens his grip, rubbing her hand.

"We need to ask few questions."

"Can my husband come please?" Isabella's voice is strained and the tremble in her body is evident.

"Please get out of car, Ms Maguire." The officer grabs her other hand and pulls her from the seat, Tom keeps hold of her until her hand slips from his. The thump of his heart is so loud in his ears the other noises around him disappear. "I believe you were asked to openboot?" He glares at Tom before leading Isabella to the same building he came out of, shutting the door behind them.

Tom's throat is dry, and he struggles to swallow. He pops the boot and grips the steering wheel with both hands, his eyes fixed on where Isabella was taken.

He flicks his eyes to the rear-view mirror to see the officer bent over the boot. He pulls the backpack out and stands it in front of him. He opens it and rummages through, throwing clothes on the ground. He returns to the boot and Tom hears him opening the wheel cover.

Tom's eyes move back to the building in front of him. *No movement.* It takes all his inner fortitude to not run from the car and kick in the door that Isabella disappeared behind. The officer opens the back door and pulls the white box off the back seat. *Get your hands off him.*

"What is this?"

"Ashes."

"Ashes?"

"Yes. It's my father-in-law. He was Belarussian. We're bringing him home."

"You said you were British?"

"I am."

"And your wife?"

"She was born in London. Her father was not."

The officer shakes the box and Tom's stomach turns. *Put him down.* "Please stop." Tom bites his lip. The officer freezes and peers at Tom. *Shit.* "I mean. That's a human being. Please don't shake the box."

The officer appears to bow his head. "Of course. My apologies." He sets the box back down on the seat and shuts the car door. "You may repack belongings." The officer opens Tom's door and gestures to the pile of clothes and empty backpack lying on the ground.

Tom gets out of the car, his eyes glued to the building where Isabella is.

"Where is my wife?" Tom stands in front of the officer, keeping his arms at his side.

"Perhaps she needed bathroom?"

Tom stares into the officer's grey eyes for a few seconds before crouching down and shoving their clothes into the backpack. He tosses it into the boot and slams it shut with more force than it needs. His gut is coiled in a spring, threatening to explode at any moment.

The officer gestures for Tom to get back into the car.

"It's been a long drive. Wouldn't mind a leg stretch if you don't mind?"

"Get in."

"Right you are then." *Pulling out all the Britishisms.*

Tom gets in and the officer slams his door. Tom clenches his jaw and grips the steering wheel again. His eyes stay on the door.

Sweat trickles down the middle of Tom's back and each passing minute feels like a month.

"It seems to be a very long bathroom break." Tom looks up at the officer who is typing on his phone.

"You know what women are like." He jerks his head up and grins. "Ah, here we are."

Isabella walks from the building alone with their passports in her hand. Tom swallows and slaps his hand against his chest. He bunches his shirt up as Isabella opens the car door and slides into her seat.

She leans across and pecks Tom on the mouth. "I'm fine."

Tom lets out a breath and with it his jaw unclenches.

"Thank you for cooperation." The officer waves his hand, motioning for Tom to drive.

Tom waits until the checkpoint dips into the horizon behind him. He pulls Isabella into him and kisses her head, while watching the road ahead. "Are you okay?"

"Yes."

"What happened?"

"To be honest Tom. I have no idea."

Tom frowns. "What?"

"He sat me in a room with a table and chair. It almost looked like one of those interrogation rooms on TV. It had a mirror and everything."

"What did he ask you?"

"Nothing. He gave me a glass of water and sat across from me. He asked why I was coming into Belarus and I told him we were burying my father's ashes."

Thank God. "I said the same."

"And then we just sat. He said nothing, Tom. Nothing. It was kind of weird."

"Nothing?"

"Nope. He checked his watch a couple of times. A message

pinged on his phone, he read it and then stood up, walked me to the door and said I could go."

"That makes no sense Iz."

"No it doesn't."

"Which means it's weird."

"I agree."

Tom rubs his face and puts his hand on Isabella's thigh. "Well, let's stop in Minsk and stay the night. Then, tomorrow we take Alexei home."

"Home." Isabella nods and slides her hand over Tom's.

Wait a minute. "You said his phone pinged?"

"Yeah, he got a text."

Tom curls his lip. "They were buying time."

"To do what?"

Tom's mind ticks back to the officer leaning over the boot. He jerks the car to the side of the road and throws it in park.

"Tom? What are you—"

Tom gets out of the car and yanks the boot open. He throws the backpack on the ground and runs his fingers around the inside edge of the boot. *Nothing.*

Isabella appears next to him. "Tom?"

He pulls floor of the boot up and yanks out the spare tyre. He runs his fingers around the wheel rim. His left index finger hits a bump. He pinches it and rips it off the wheel.

"Fuck." He holds up a small black disc.

"What is it?"

"A track." He drops it on the ground and grounds it into the dirt with his foot.

Isabella grabs Tom's arm. "A what?"

"A tracking device. They were buying time to plant a track." Tom gut flips and he swallows the nausea creeping up his throat.

"They know who we are?" Isabella clutches at her throat.

"Maybe."

"Maybe?" Isabella wheezes and bends over her knees.

Tom pulls Isabella against him and cradles her head. "Without a track they don't find us. We'll get to Minsk, dump this car and disappear. It'll be fine."

Isabella nods against his chest.

"Iz?"

She lifts her face and blinks the tears out of her eyes. "I did this. We're here because of me. I'm sorry." She sniffles and Tom pulls her against him again. "We didn't even make it past the border before we were found." Her voice is muffled against his chest.

"And now they can't follow us. It'll be okay." He nuzzles his face to hers and finds her lips, kissing her. "I promise."

I promise.

10

ISABELLA

I sabella yawns and stretches, becoming aware of Tom's hand stroking her face and neck. She opens her eyes and blinks at the roof of the car.

"What time is it?" She pushes the seat control and sits up.

"A little before eight."

Isabella slumps against Tom and rubs her eyes. "Sorry. I couldn't stay awake."

"I know. Hungry?"

Isabella nods and looks around the early morning bustle of Minsk. The concrete buildings loom over them, blocking out the sun.

A tingle runs down Isabella's spine. She has only been to Minsk once before.

. . .

IRINA GLANCED DOWN AT THE PHOTOGRAPH AND BACK TO THE MAN *sitting at the bus stop. It was definitely the same man.*

"*Right where they said he would be,*" *she whispered to herself and skipped across the road. She sat beside him on the seat and he tipped his head in acknowledgement.*

"*I thought I was going to miss it. Last bus of the night.*" *She adjusted her top, making sure her cleavage was visible.*

"*I catch this bus every evening, it always runs a few minutes late. Always.*" *He smiled and ran his eyes up and down her body.*

Irina swallowed and gave him a smile that said more than 'it's nice to meet you.' He was exactly as they said he would be. He leered at her for a few more seconds while she crossed her legs and traced her fingers over her stocking clad calf.

The man shuffled across the seat to her. "*I haven't seen you on this bus before?*"

"*No. Today is a very special occasion,*" *Irina whispered in his ear, pushing her chest against him.*

"*Is that so?*" *His breath smelled of cigarettes and Irina wrinkled her nose.*

"*I was told I may meet a handsome stranger in this very spot this evening.*" *She locked her eyes on his, making sure he stared back at her as she slid her knife out of her jacket pocket.*

"*Handsome? I'm flattered.*"

Irina threw her head back and laughed while dragging her hand down the front of his business shirt, the knife against her palm.

"Surely you get told all the time?" She drifted the hand holding the knife down his body until it rested at the bottom of his ribcage. She made sure her other hand snaked inside his shirt and stroked his chest. The art of distraction was a specialty.

"Maybe, sometimes. Though none of them are as beautiful as you."

"Oh, you're too kind." Irina stared into his eyes and gripped the knife tight.

"Maybe we go somewhere and have a drink?"

"Maybe..." Irina pushed the knife up under his ribcage, piercing his heart. His eyes widened and his mouth gaped open. She pulled the knife out and he slumped forward making gurgling noises in his throat.

She waited until the sounds stopped and he became still. Grabbing his jaw she jerked his face towards her and carved the number 320 in his cheek before letting his head drop.

Irina shoved the knife inside her jacket pocket and pushed him back against the seat so he was sitting up again. She buttoned his jacket and patted his intact cheek.

"Maybe next time."

"Iz?"

Isabella shakes her head and turns to Tom. "What?"

"Do you want to go into that diner thing over there and order food? I'll get us another car. Yes?"

"Oh. Um. Yeah..." She unbuckles her seatbelt and Tom's hand comes over hers.

"Are you okay?"

"Yes. I just..." She shakes her shoulders out. "Nothing. It's nothing."

She gets out of the car as Tom is pulling the backpack out of the boot. He lifts it and hands it to her. "Are you alright with it?"

"Of course I am. I brought it with me all the way from Belgium, remember?" She smiles and heaves it onto her back.

"You did."

Isabella kisses him and nods towards the car rental across the road. "Are you actually going to rent one this time?"

Tom laughs. "No."

Isabella rolls her eyes and walks across the road. *I don't want to know.*

She finds a table at the back and sits down, she looks around the near empty diner and picks up the menu, printed on a sheet of paper.

"Kofe?" The waitress stands at the table with a pot of coffee.

"Oh. Da. Dva pozhaluysta." Isabella holds up two fingers and the waitress nods, pouring two mugs.

Her phone rings in her pocket and she pulls it out.

"Hey, Martha."

"Are you alright my dear?"

"Yes, why?"

"Well I called Tom and he didn't answer."

"No he's busy getting...acquiring another car."

"What's wrong with the Mercedes? Not fancy enough for him?"

Isabella laughs. "I can hear your eye roll from here. No. It was… compromised."

"Excuse me?"

"The border control put a tracking device in the boot."

"They what?"

"They planted a tracking device in the boot. So, someone tipped them off." Isabella lifts her eyes to the door as Tom walks in and spots her.

He plonks in the chair opposite and mouths *Martha*?

Isabella nods.

"But my dear. How?"

"I don't know. But Tom got us another car," she glances up at Tom as she says the words and he nods.

"Put him on."

"Um."

"Put him on."

Isabella holds the phone out to Tom, and he takes it.

"Martha."

The waitress comes back and Tom masks the microphone. "Just whatever their big fry up breakfast is."

Isabella laughs. *You're in for a shock.* "U menya budut syrnyye olad'i, i on zavtrakayet, pozhaluysta."

The waitress smiles and scurries away.

"… if I knew that we wouldn't be in this situation, would we?"

Tom grimaces and gulps his coffee. "Yes, thank you Martha. Now, just tell me where to meet this bloke for the guns."

Isabella leans across the table and holds a finger to her lips. "Lower your voice."

"They can't understand me, Iz."

"You don't know that."

Tom rolls his eyes. "Yep. Independence Square, small black Fiat. Right. Hey, tell me… do you think it could be any more obvious?" Tom purses his lips and looks at the phone screen.

"She hang up on you?"

"I'm going with... the phone dropped out."

"So, she hung up on you." Isabella laughs as the waitress puts two plates on the table.

Tom stares down at his plate. "What is this? Is that… cabbage?"

Isabella chews on a cheese fritter and nods. "Yep. With pork, potatoes and bread."

"But…" Tom lifts some of the cabbage with his fork. "Cabbage."

"Try it. It's delicious."

"Cabbage. For breakfast."

"We aren't in the land of baked beans and sausages now Tom."

Tom chews a forkful of cabbage and swallows. "By the way we're meeting our trusty weapons dealer in an hour. Then we can keep going to Polotsk."

As Tom mentions the name of her home, Isabella's stomach plunges. She puts her fork down and bows her head.

"Iz?" Tom slides his chair across and touches his head to hers. "Hey…"

"I haven't been back in so long."

Tom kisses her cheek.

Isabella reaches across and puts her hand on the top of the backpack, where her father's ashes sit inside. "Almost there, Papa."

AN HOUR LATER, TOM STOPS THE TINY GREY HATCHBACK HE STOLE in the last car space for miles.

"You couldn't have found a smaller car, huh?" Isabella grins as he unfolds himself from the car and gets out.

"Believe me, Iz. We're dumping this car as soon as we can." He stretches his arms above his head and peers across at a black Fiat, rolling to a stop on the other side of the street. The driver peers at the pair of them. "That'll be him."

"But we aren't in Independence Square yet." Isabella points down the street. "We need to walk the rest of the—"

"Wait here."

Tom jogs across the street and bends down to the car window before running around the other side and getting in.

Isabella watches them, biting her lip. *And he tells me to be careful.* Isabella purses her lips as Tom strolls back to her. She gets out of the car and holds her hand out.

"What? You want me to just casually hand you a pistol in the middle of the street?"

"No. Keys. I'm driving."

"Iz. It's fine. Get in."

"No. First of all it's the smallest car in history and you look ridiculous driving it. Second, you haven't slept. It's at least a three-and-a-half-hour drive."

Tom gazes at her a moment and blows out a breath. "Okay, fine."

He throws himself into the passenger seat and slides the seat all the way back.

Isabella adjusts her own seat and holds out her hand. "Now you can give me my gun."

"Oh, yeah." He pulls a pistol out of his waistband and shoves it in hers. "It's small but it'll do the job." He reclines the seat and crosses his arms over his chest.

Isabella bites her cheek and opens her mouth.

Tom reaches across and puts his hand over her mouth. "No. I've never had to say that before."

Isabella kisses his hand. "I believe you."

Tom smirks and closes his eyes.

ISABELLA ROLLS THE CAR TO A STOP AND TURNS THE ENGINE OFF. She stares at the ruin in front of her and covers her mouth and nose with her hands.

"My God."

She glances at Tom, sound asleep in the passenger seat and her chest expands a little. She pushes his hair off his forehead and he stirs but doesn't wake up. She reaches into the back seat where their backpack sits and scoops up the box of her father's ashes.

She walks through the crumbling front gate of what was her childhood home.

She presses her hand over her heart.

The house has fallen into disrepair, like many of the others along the street. Its front door hangs off the hinges and weeds and other growth has taken over. The roof has caved in and more tiles are missing from the parts still intact.

Isabella drops to her knees and gulps in air. Her nose blocks and tears stream down her face.

"Iz?" Tom's arm is around her shoulders. He drops onto the ground next to her and pulls her against him.

"I'm okay."

Tom strokes her hair, holding her tight.

"It's not quite the thatched roof cottage in the countryside, is it?" She sniffles and wipes her arm across her nose.

"You want to take me inside?"

Isabella looks up and smiles. "Yes."

Tom stands and holds a hand out for Isabella. She takes it and leads him to the front door. She looks to her left and sees a dead tree, branches have fallen to the ground and there are no leaves.

"I used to climb that tree and sit as high as I could." She swallows and presses her hand against the old front door. "Papa would always scold me, telling me I would hurt myself if I fell."

"I bet you kept doing it anyway."

"But of course." She pushes the old door and it swings inward on the one hinge still connected.

Inside, more weeds thrive throughout the tiny house. The lounge has a broken sofa and an old TV with a smashed screen. Water is puddled at the edges of the hall leading to the two bedrooms and bathroom. The air is thick and musty.

Isabella stops just before her bedroom and closes her eyes. She can almost hear the sounds of the old house, the way they used to be. More tears creep out under her eyelids and she smiles despite them. Tom rests his hand on her shoulder but doesn't say anything.

She walks into her bedroom. Her single bed is in the corner with a moth eaten and stained pink duvet. Animals have clearly made this place their winter shelter and Isabella wrinkles her nose up against the smell.

She cradles her father's ashes against her chest and looks out the tiny window to the small garden. The rotting stick right at the back that used to be a cross makes her heart twitch. She gazes at her mother's grave.

"Papa didn't have enough money for a cemetery plot. So he brought my mother home."

Isabella looks up at Tom and he strokes her cheek with the back of his knuckles. "Shall we reunite them?"

Isabella nods and they walk through the open-door frame at the back of the house where a door used to be.

Isabella kneels next to her mother's old cross and grabs a nearby stick. She pulls the hair tie out of her hair and winds it around the two sticks. She pushes it back into the ground.

"I wish it was fancier." She scratches at the earth at her knees, dusting away small rocks and pulling out a couple of weeds. Tom kneels next to her and digs his fingers into the dirt. She smiles and does the same. They both paw and dig at the earth until a hole big enough and deep enough for Alexei's ashes is made.

Isabella picks up the box and holds it against her. She bows her head.

"YA lyublyu tebya, papa." *I love you, Papa.*

She presses her lips to the top of the box, holding it against her heartbeat before dropping her forehead against it. Her shoulders shake and her tears fall freely. She lowers the box into the grave and sweeps the dirt over the top.

Tom and Isabella stand in front of the wonky cross. Isabella raises her eyes to the sky and pulls in a deep breath. Tom holds her hand, stroking his thumb along her fingers.

"I think I can go now."

Tom lifts her hand and kisses the back of it. They walk around the house to the crumbling gate and Isabella turns to look at the house one more time.

Memories flood her brain, as though trying to stop her from

leaving. She giggles as her eyes rest on what used to be a flower bed under one of the front windows.

"I had a pet goat." Isabella smiles, pointing at the old flower bed.

"A goat?" Tom quirks a brow and grins.

"Yes, Tom, a goat. My father found him abandoned as a kid and brought him home. I called him *Detka*."

"Baby."

Isabella nods. She wipes another tear from her cheek as it rolls down towards her chin. "I can't believe the house is still standing," she whispers. "Albeit, dilapidated."

Tom's hand slides across the back of her neck, coming to rest on her shoulder. Isabella feels his warmth against her back. She lolls her head back on his chest, staring at the house.

"Irina?" A deep voice invades the peaceful moment.

They both spin around and Isabella sees a man standing at the edge of the garden. She presses her hand against Tom's stomach to stay close to him.

The man is tall with insanely blue eyes. His close-cropped black hair and beard don't detract from the very generous gene pool he swam out of.

Isabella leans forward. *I know those eyes.*

The man takes a step forward and smiles, a deep dimple can be seen through the facial hair and Isabella's breath leaves her lungs.

"Nik?" She creeps forward, dropping her hand from where it

rested against Tom's stomach. Tom's hand catches hers and he holds on.

The man nods. "Da." His smile breaks into a grin and he walks towards her.

Isabella clasps a hand over her mouth, squeezing Tom's hand with the other. He squeezes back and it's as good as wrapping her in a security blanket.

"Nikolay Aristov?"

He nods.

Isabella claps the hand from her mouth to her chest and gasps in a breath. Her eyes are stuck on him as he stops around three feet from her. She wiggles her hand out of Tom's and lurches forward, hugging Nik around the neck. His strong arms wrap around her body hugging her tight. Tears seep through her closed eyes. *It's been so long.*

Isabella pulls back, holding both his forearms at arm's length, staring at him. "Eto deystvitel'no ty" *It's really you.*

Nik nods. "Da."

They stare at each other for a few seconds while Isabella squeezes his arms. She shakes her head slowly. Her mouth hangs open.

"So um, I'm Tom… in case anyone's interested."

Isabella jumps and drops her hands from Nik's arms. "Oh, yes. Tom." Heat rises in her cheeks and she closes her eyes a moment. "Ah, this is… Nikolay— Nik. Um, we used to be neighbours." Isabella's eyes move to the house across the road, also falling down and abandoned.

Nik's eyes flick to Tom and he holds a hand out. "English, I assume?" His voice still laced with a thick Russian accent.

Tom's arms remain folded over his chest and he raises his eyebrows. "You know what they say about assuming—"

"Ah yes!" Isabella jumps in between the pair of them. "English would be lovely. Tom can't speak the mother tongue." She looks back at Tom and narrows her eyes. "Can you Tom?"

Tom holds her stare for a moment and smiles. "No. Uneducated git I am."

Nik frowns. "Git?"

"Tom's…" Isabella shoots him another death stare and he gazes back at her, grinning.

She turns to Nik. "So, how are you? I mean… I… Um."

"I am well. As are you it appears." He runs his tongue along his top lip and fixes his eyes on Isabella's.

"Oh… um. Yes. How is your family? Your mother?" Isabella creeps backwards and stands against Tom's chest again. *I've forgotten how to speak.* She feels Tom's arms uncross behind her and come to rest on her waist.

Nik's eyes drop to Tom's hands before flicking back to Isabella's face. "Do you remember when we would bathe together?"

Isabella inhales sharply and coughs as spittle goes down the wrong way. She leans forward, slapping her hand against her chest. "Uh… "She swallows and straightens up. "Yes. I mean… when we were children." She twists her face around to look at Tom. He stares back, clearly hiding a smirk.

"Yes. When we were children." He pauses. "Of course."

"So what brings you here?" Isabella tries to steer the conversation away from her naked in a bathtub with her childhood neighbour. *Jesus.*

"I often come back through here." Nik looks around the street. "It was home for so long." He rests his eyes back on Isabella. "Before the violence." Her insides grow cold as his gaze appears to go through her. "Imagine my surprise to find you here."

"Imagine…" Isabella gives her shoulders a shake and clears her throat. "Well, we should… go."

"But it's been so long." Nik steps forward. "Will you not join me for dinner this evening?"

"Ohhhh, no. I mean… we don't ahhh…" Isabella bites her lip.

"Want to intrude," Tom finishes. "We don't want to intrude." He nudges Isabella in the back.

"Nonsense." Nik swats his hand as though shooing a fly. "It would be my pleasure to host you."

"I bet," Tom's voice whispers in Isabella's ear.

"Honestly, Nik. It's not necessary."

"You remember City Centre?" He raises his eyebrows.

Isabella nods.

"Wonderful. Katia's Kitchen? Seven?"

"Katia's is still there?"

Nik nods. "It is."

"Right," Isabella holds her breath trying to think of a way to decline and coming up empty. *Shit.* "Seven." She smiles and exhales through gritted teeth.

Nik walks forward and kisses both of Isabella's cheeks. "See you then." He nods at Tom before walking away.

Isabella watches as Nik's back retreats.

"Well. Wasn't that a hoot?"

Isabella spins and peers at Tom. She smiles and says nothing.

"Tell me. Did he show you his rubber duckie?"

Isabella pokes Tom's chest with her index finger. "You're jealous!"

Tom snorts. "I most certainly… am not."

Isabella nods and widens her eyes, watching Tom squirm. "Is that right?"

"Yes. That's right."

Isabella steps forward and slides her hands around Tom's waist. "Well, remember Tom… he saw me naked when we were four years old." She rests her mouth against his. "You see me naked all the time." She pecks his mouth. "And maybe you'll get to again later. So… you win." She winks and grabs his hand, dragging him towards the car.

Tom scoffs. "It's not a competition."

Isabella whirls around and presses herself against him. "Exactly." She nips him on the mouth one more time before opening her car door.

11

TOM

Tom pushes open the apartment door and throws the backpack on the rug.

"Fancy." Isabella walks past him, dragging her hand across his back as she passes. "For Polotsk anyway." She grins.

"The name of the place is *Lux* Apartments. I'd be demanding a refund if it was a shit heap." Tom collapses on the sofa and Isabella snuggles next to him.

Tom closes his eyes and tiredness washes over him. "We have time for a sleep right?"

"Of course we do. It's only lunchtime. And Belarussians love their food." Isabella yawns. "So you'll want to have room for dinner."

"Yeah, about that." Nik's smarmy face grins in Tom's mind's eye and he grimaces.

Isabella holds her hand up in a stop motion. "We're going."

Tom rolls his eyes. "We could order in and watch TV."

"Or we could go to dinner, relax and destress."

"Relax? Destress?" Tom jerks his lip at one corner and raises both eyebrows. "With Nik?"

"You're being ridiculous."

"No. I'm being cautious. I don't trust him."

"What?"

"He turns up in a deserted street in a deserted village and just *happens* to find us there?"

"He said he passes through all the time. His house was across the street." Isabella chews on her lips and traces the buttons on Tom's polo with her fingers. "Happy coincidence."

"Happy?"

"Stop it." Isabella kisses him and runs her hands up his neck into his hair. "You're jealous over nothing."

"I'm not jealous." Tom pushes his index finger against her mouth. "We were stopped at the border and a track was put on our car. Then this Nik character *happens* to appear in a deserted village?"

"Nik character?" Isabell laughs and gets off the sofa. She rummages through the backpack and grabs her toiletries bag.

"Yes. Character." Tom sits forward over his knees, lacing his fingers together. "A character is something you *pretend* to be."

Isabella huffs and looks at the ceiling a second before narrowing her eyes at Tom. "I'm having a shower. You can join me if you wish or you can sulk on the sofa. Choice is yours." She spins and stalks to the bathroom.

Tom squints at the bathroom door. "I'm not sulking."

"TOM! IT'S QUARTER TO. WE STILL HAVE TO WALK TO THE restaurant."

Tom sighs and pulls his shirt on, buttoning the front. "Iz, relax. I'm sure Nik will wait before he orders the garlic bread."

"Garlic bread?"

"Nevermind." Tom picks up his pistol and screws a silencer on the end.

"Tom, are you seriously taking your gun to dinner?"

"Yep."

"Why? Are you going to pistol whip the waitress if she takes too long?" Isabella plants her hands on her hips and tilts her head.

"Nope. I'm taking it for when Nik mentions you and he bathing together again." Tom shoves it into the back of his waist and shrugs his jacket on.

"Those green eyes of yours are looking greener by the second."

"Thank you. I eat my vegetables." He looks at Isabella a moment and gestures to the other pistol lying on the coffee table. "Well?"

"I'm not taking a gun to dinner, Tom." She picks it up and shoves it back into the backpack. "Forget it."

"Iz—"

"Enough." She holds her hand up and frowns. "We are going to eat dinner and talk about climbing trees and riding up and down the street on our bicycles. I don't need a pistol. And by the way neither do you."

"I'm taking it." Tom sweeps his arm towards the door and Isabella stomps to it. He grabs her elbow as she passes him. "I'm sorry."

Isabella stops and looks up at him.

"I'm on edge because something doesn't feel right." *Goddamn intuition voodoo magic bullshit.*

"Nik was like a brother to me, Tom. He isn't a threat, okay?"

Tom stares into her blue eyes and loosens his grip on her arm. "Okay."

A man on a phone is at the doors to the apartments and he brushes against Tom as they walk out. Tom glares at him a moment before following Isabella down the pavement.

"You don't have to take your bad mood out on everyone." She grabs his hand, lacing her fingers through his.

"I'm not. But who stands in a doorway on the phone?"

"You're not. Right." Isabella smiles and looks ahead. "Hey, there's a really old strip club along here somewhere. Maybe we should pop in for nostalgia's sake?"

Tom remembers her straddling his lap and her mouth against his neck. *Jesus.* "You want to make it to dinner, don't you?" He grins.

"Of course, but there's no reason we can have fun along the way."

"You were the one stressing about being late."

Isabella laughs and swings his hand as she skips along. "We've passed it now anyway. It's that red doorway behind us."

Tom looks back and sees a single red doorway tucked away amongst the buildings. A man stands next to the door reading a paper and smoking a pipe.

"Maybe on the way back." Tom squeezes her hand as she pushes open a glass door and pulls him inside.

She spins and puts her hand on his chest. "If you behave."

Tom rolls his eyes and sees Nik stand up from a booth across the room. *Of course, he's already here.*

Nik smiles and opens his arms out across the table in front of him. Isabella slides into the booth and Tom sits next to her. He taps his fingers on the table and Isabella covers his hand with hers.

"I am so glad you could make it." Nik smiles at Tom and his eyes are hollow. *Left your soul at home, did you?*

"Wow. I haven't been here since I was a little girl." Isabella kneels up on one knee and puts her arm on the back of the booth, surveying the room.

Tom can't help but admit it smells amazing. Thick scents of stews and hot bread fill his nose and his stomach grumbles. He slaps a hand over it even though there's no way anyone heard it over the bustle of the restaurant.

"I took liberty of ordering. I do hope that is okay?"

Smarmy git. "So generous." Tom gives him a tight smile.

Nik clicks his fingers at a passing waitress. "Vodka i tri stakana."

Fuck. Tom pulls his shirt collar away from his neck and swallows.

"Oh ah, thanks Nik. No, it's fine. Water is fine." Isabella sneaks a glance at Tom who stares back at her.

"But we must celebrate! It has been so long between drinks."

"Last time I saw you we were thirteen. I don't think we were having drinks." Isabella laughs and Tom hears the waver in it.

He clenches his fists under the table as the vodka bottle and three glasses are slapped in front of him. His jaw twitches and he clears his throat.

Nik pours and raises a brow. "Is something wrong Tom?"

"No."

"You seem tense."

"I'm tired. And hungry."

Nik slides a glass in front of him. "To friends. Both old and new. Eh?"

Tom bites the inside of his mouth and wraps his hand around the glass.

"Tom—"

"To new friends." He picks the glass up and downs the shot before tapping his empty glass on the table three times, as does Nik. The vodka slides down his throat and his bloodstream welcomes an old friend. Warmth spreads through his body and he squeezes his eyes shut.

Isabella's hand slides across Tom's thigh under the table. Tom grits his teeth and cracks his neck. Sweat lines his top lip and his shirt sticks to his back.

"Another!" Nik starts to pour.

Isabella holds her hand over her glass. "No. Thanks. We have an early start in the morning."

"Oh?"

Tom nods. "We're leaving." *First thing.*

"Is that so?"

Two waitresses bring plates of food to their table. Stew, vegetables and warm bread sits in front of Tom.

"Allow me." Nik picks up their plates before Tom can object and fills them with food. *Whatever.* Tom sweeps his eyes around the restaurant before resting them on his now overflowing plate.

Wait a second.

Tom looks up again and sees a man sitting across the room at a table. Reading the paper. Wearing a thick brown jacket and cap. The only thing missing is the pipe he was smoking. Tom's jaw tightens and he slides his hand across his back, under his jacket, before picking up his fork.

"Tom?" Nik pauses from laughing and talking to Isabella about childhood pets. "Are you okay?"

Shut up.

"I'm fine." He shovels stew into his mouth, and it irritates him that it's delicious.

"So, tell me. What is it you do for living, Tom?" Nik takes a bite of his bread and smiles as he chews.

"Well I'm—"

"An accountant. He's an accountant." Isabella nudges Tom. "Aren't you Tom?"

Could you have picked a more boring... Tom smiles and sips his water. "I love numbers."

"Of course. And how did you love birds come across each other?" Nik cups his chin in his hand on the table and eats more stew.

"Oh well…"

"She's my secretary." Tom grins at Isabella. *Two can play at this game.* "She types my… reports and makes me coffee. Don't you, Iz?" He nudges her.

Isabella smiles at Nik, ignoring Tom. "Well, who can say no to a polyester suit and cheap tie."

Oh, checkmate?

"You're only human, Iz."

The man reading his paper coughs and Tom's attention turns back across the room. *I need a closer look.* Tom drops his fork, and it clatters on the plate.

"Bathroom?" He widens his eyes at Nik.

A smile spreads along Nik's lips. "Of course. Down corridor past kitchen." He points across the room.

"Great. I'll be right back." He stands and throws his napkin on the table.

Isabella shoots him a look and twitches her left eye. Tom squeezes her shoulder and walks towards the kitchen.

As he approaches the table, he notices another man sitting at a table by the kitchen. This man stares at him and Tom flicks his eyes ahead and strides down the corridor.

There are framed photographs lining the corridor opposite the kitchen. Tom runs his eyes over the pictures and stops on one. Like all the others it is of people eating and drinking in Katia's Kitchen. But this one has a blonde woman. With a pixie cut and red lips. Tom's gut flips and swallows the bile threatening to rise. *Kat.* She is laughing and has her arm around the shoulders of a bearded man. Tom looks back at the booth and sees Nik laughing while Isabella grins and shakes her head. The photograph shows Nik smiling and clinking glasses with Kat. *Well, fuck me.*

A chair scrapes back in the dining room and Tom carries on to the bathroom. He opens the gent's door and pushes himself against the wall next to the door.

Three, two, one.

The bathroom door opens and newspaper man walks in. Before he can register that Tom is standing behind him, Tom grabs him around the neck and squeezes.

"Who the fuck are you?"

The man claws and scratches at Tom's arms and he loosens them so the man can speak.

"Yebat' tebya."

Fuck you? Really?

"Not the answer I was after." Tom throws him on the floor and stamps his foot in the middle of his chest. He pulls his gun out of his waistband and points it at the man's face. The man holds both hands up and glares at Tom. A pistol is visible under the man's shirt and Tom yanks it out. He holds it up and shakes his head.

"You see, this. Has no silencer. You can't bring a gun to a restaurant and think that the bang won't alert people that you've shot someone. Mine on the other hand..." He jiggles his pistol. The bathroom door swings open and the man that had stared at Tom from the other table stomps in.

"Piter," the man on the floor gasps.

"Ah, Peter. So nice of you to join us."

Peter pushes his hands down the front of his pants but before he can do anything else Tom swings his arm around and shoots him between the eyes. He flies back against the same wall Tom stood against and slides down to the floor. A perfect round hole in his forehead sends blood dripping down his face. Tiles explode on the wall behind him.

The man on the floor covers his ears with his hands. Tom leans down and pushes the silencer against his head. "Like I said. It's quieter. More time to do the job and disappear. Though, the tiles were a bit loud."

The man spits at Tom but it doesn't make it and lands on his own crumpled shirt, spittle dribbles down his chin. Tom grabs the man's tie and wipes his chin for him.

"Can't have you look like a dribbling mess when they find your dead body now, can we?" Tom twists the silencer against the man's head. "Last chance. Who are you?"

The man trembles. "Yebat' tebya."

Tom pulls the trigger and the man's head lolls to his shoulder.

"Fuck you indeed." Tom stands and takes both the men's guns and throws them in the bin. He unrolls a wad of paper towel and throws it in on top.

He shoves his pistol back into his waistband and strolls out of the bathroom.

Tom slides back into the booth as Nik is laughing and wiping his mouth with a napkin. Isabella gives Tom a look and raises a brow.

He pushes his mouth against her ear. "We need to leave. Now." He throws a smile laced with a smirk at Nik. "I'm so sorry Nik. I'm unwell. Isabella and I need to leave."

Nik's smile disappears and he puts both elbows on the table, resting his chin and mouth in his hands. "I am sorry to hear that."

"Yes, it's most unpleasant."

"Tom?" Isabella faces him in the booth.

"Well, before you rush away allow me to box some food up for your trip home." Nik stands up and fixes his eyes on Tom. "Such a shame you came down ill so very suddenly." He stares at Tom, his face blank.

Tom holds his gaze. "I'm bitterly disappointed."

Nik bows his head and leaves the table.

Tom grabs Isabella's hand and slides out of the booth pulling her with him.

"Tom. At least wait until—"

"I shot two men in the head in the gents. We're leaving." He hisses.

"Actually, take a seat." Nik voice slithers into Tom's ear as he bores holes through Isabella's confused eyes.

"*Actually* no. We're leaving. Thanks so much." Tom spins, still holding Isabella's hand and Nik's face is centimetres from his.

Something pokes Tom in the abdomen and he looks down to see a gun pressed against him.

"I said sit."

"Oh my God," Isabella whispers.

This is not ideal.

12

ISABELLA

Isabella sits and places both her hands palm down on the table. Her heart hammers so hard, the base of her throat pulsates. *This isn't happening.* Her nostrils flare as Nik slides into the seat across from both of them. He rests his gun on the table, his finger still on the trigger.

Tom pushes his leg against hers and slides his hand over her thigh. He squeezes her knee. The tremble in her body takes hold and her legs shake. Tom squeezes tighter.

"And here we are." Nik pours himself another vodka and throws it back. "Are you sure I cannot entice you Tom?" He holds the glass up. "From what I hear you do not mind a drink."

Isabella closes her eyes a moment. When she opens them, she looks at Tom who is staring at Nik, sweat glistens across his forehead.

"And how would you know a thing like that?"

"I have eyes everywhere."

What the hell is going on?

"Nik. What are you doing?" Isabella leans forward, glaring into Nik's smiling blue eyes. It's the first time his eyes have smiled along with the rest of his face. It sends a shiver through Isabella's body. *He's been lying the whole time.*

"My job. Irina."

"Your job?"

"Well, it is actually *not* my job. I usually get to frequent gentlemen's clubs and fancy bars. I drink and pay for women. But this job I wanted to handle *personally*."

"Head of the snake," Tom mumbles.

"What is that, Tom? You are thirsty?" Nik pours a vodka and places it in front of Tom.

The grip on Isabella's knee tightens for a second before he yanks his hand away and grabs the glass. He throws it to the floor; it smashes and vodka splashes over the tiles.

Isabella pushes her hand to her chest and gasps in a breath. Her lungs may as well have gone out to lunch.

"Now, now Tom. You only had to politely refuse."

Tom stares at Nik and doesn't speak.

Nik slides his eyes from Tom to Isabella. "Do you need some water, Irina?"

"Isabella."

"What?"

"My name is Isabella."

"I will humour you. For now."

"Can we hurry this up?" Tom slams his fist onto the table.

Nik observes his fist a moment. "My zakryty!"

Isabella jumps at Nik's bark and wraps her hand around Tom's arm.

The restaurant empties. People who had been halfway through their meals leave them and scurry out the door. Waitresses grab their bags and disappear. Within two minutes there are four men left sitting at tables around the room along with the three of them in the booth.

"What just happened?" Isabella already knows the answer.

"This is owned by our… Organisation."

Isabella nods. Visions of coming here with her father swim in front of her.

"STAY HERE, LITTLE DOLL. HAVE SOME BREAD WHILE I TALK TO Uncle Dimitri."

Alexei kissed the top of her head and walked to the other side of the restaurant. Irina watched as he sat and pulled a handkerchief out of his pocket. He mopped his brow and nodded while Uncle Dimitri spoke.

Irina broke some bread, enough for her and a nibble for her dolly. She sat and played tea parties, sneaking glances at her father. Uncle Dimitri was red in the face and her father held both hands out with his palms up.

Uncle Dimitri leaned across the table and said something in her father's ear before sliding a white envelope into Alexei's jacket pocket.

Alexei stood up and shuffled to Irina.

"Come Little Doll, we will not be having stew tonight."

ISABELLA LIFTS HER EYES TO NIK. "IT ALWAYS HAS BEEN."

Nik smiles and leans back against the booth. "Da."

The air leaves Isabella's lungs and she leans forward over the table.

"Iz?" Tom pulls her across and against him.

"My father…"

"Your father gave… information."

"But he… he was KGB. He…"

"He was. He was also a father who loved his daughter."

"They bribed him." Isabella tries to swallow but her throat is dry. She coughs and grabs her water.

"Da." Nik picks something out of his teeth and rubs it between his thumb and index finger before flicking it on the floor. "You were marked from birth."

"Fuck." Tom rubs his face.

"One default meant your death, Irina. And after the fall, your father planned to disappear. But…"

"They came for us. It was the middle of the night." Isabella's chest tightens and she closes her eyes. Tom wraps his arm around her.

. . .

"No! Please. Don't take her. Kill me instead. Take me."

Irina crept into the hall. Four men were in their lounge room. Two of them watched while the other two pushed Alexei to the ground and kicked him.

"Stop!" Irina fell to her knees. "Leave him alone."

"Run Irina! Get out of here."

The shorter and fatter of the two men watching stomped across the small lounge room and grabbed Irina by the neck of her nightgown. His teeth were brown, with a front one missing. He smelt of cigarettes and sweat. He hauled her off the floor.

"Take her." The other man, not involved in the beating barked.

"No!" Alexei screamed from the floor.

Irina reached towards her father, trying to get to him but the man holding her was too strong.

"Come little girl. Uncle Kostya will enjoy teaching you how to behave."

Isabella shudders and tears prick her eyes.

"What do you want, Nik?" Tom's voice is quiet and raw.

"Well, first. Let her go."

Tom pulls Isabella into his chest and cradles her head with his hand. "Next?"

Nik laughs. "You will go with my men."

"I will not."

"You will. Because if you do not. I kill Irina."

Isabella feels the muscles in Tom's chest tense, and she pushes herself up, putting her palms face down on the table again.

"What is this about, Nik?" She lifts her eyes to his, tears spill down her cheeks.

"You betrayed us."

"You?"

"This is now my family. Which means you betrayed *me*." Nik flicks his head and the four men sitting at tables stand and walk to the booth. "Tom. You go with them."

Tom stares into Nik's face and Isabella clings to him. "Make me."

Nik lifts his arm and points his gun at Isabella's temple.

Isabella buries her face in Tom's arm.

Tom's breathing shortens, his chest rising and falling in sharp bursts.

Isabella sits up. "Nik. Please."

Nik holds his palm up, still glaring at Tom. "Please do not assume I will not kill either of you. In fact Tom, you are someone I would very much like to shoot in head."

"You aren't the first."

Nik swings the gun to one of the four men waiting for Tom and shoots him in the chest.

Isabella gasps and pushes herself back into the seat.

"And he was one of mine." Nik leans towards Tom. "Now, I said go with my men." He holds the gun against Isabella's head again.

Tom stands up.

"No! Tom." Isabella grabs his hand and he squeezes it.

Tom drops Isabella's hand and leans forward, both hands on the table. "If you harm her or mark her…"

"I will do neither… as long as she is a good girl."

Good girl. Isabella holds her breath and wraps her arms around her middle.

Tom sits down and pulls Isabella's face to his. He kisses her and she runs her hands up his neck to his face.

He moves his mouth to her ear. "You run. Do you hear me? The second you can… you run."

Isabella trembles. "I'm frightened."

"I'll find you." He kisses her again. "I promise."

Tom is yanked out of the booth and he jerks his arm back. "I can walk. Thanks."

"So brave." Nik sips vodka and waves as Tom is pushed out the door.

Isabella pulls breath in and slumps against the booth. *I'm going to faint.*

"I see why you like him, so."

Love him. I love him.

Isabella pulls her knees to her chest and tries to make herself as small as she can in the corner of the booth.

"Irina. Do not be frightened. I will not hurt you. It is me. Nik."

Isabella drags her eyes to Nik's face and curls her lip. "Where are they taking him?"

"Somewhere safe."

"Are you going to kill him?"

"Not yet. I need him."

Isabella's heart squeezes. "Need him?"

"Much the same as you were used to bribe your father... I need him." Nik stands up from the booth and holds his hand out. "Shall we?"

Fuck you.

Isabella refuses Nik's hand. She stands in front of him, her eyes blaze. "I will cut your heart out, roast it over a fire and feed it to you if you hurt him."

Nik's eyes widen and a grin stretches across his face. "See, *now* you sound more like assassin." He winks and clicks his tongue. "Let us go."

13

TOM

Tom walks down the street, flanked by the three men. He recognises one of them from the doorway of the Lux Apartments. They round a corner, and he sees a white van with blacked out windows.

"A bit cliché wouldn't you agree?"

The man from the doorway squints at Tom. *No speaka the English.*

Tom's eyes dart around the backstreet as the tallest of the men grabs his hands, yanks them behind his back and cable ties them together. Tom's first instinct is to throw his head back and break the man's nose. *But Isabella.*

Doorway man stands in front of Tom and looks him up and down.

"Tak samodovol'no."

Smug? Me? I'm offended.

Doorway man pulls his fist back and slogs Tom in the gut. He bends forward and fights to pull a breath in. He slowly stands up and doorway man jabs him on the chin. Tom's head jerks to the left and he falls back against the van.

Tom grits his teeth and brings his face back to eye him. "Ouch."

Doorway man smirks and opens the backdoor of the van. He grabs Tom by the front of the shirt and pushes him inside.

Tom slides on the metal flooring, his hands catching sharp bumps on the floor. "Fuck."

He wiggles himself across and against the side of the van and rests there. He jiggles his jaw back and forth. *That smarts.* The third man climbs in after Tom and sits on the wheel arch. He stares at Tom and curls his lip. *You look about fifteen.*

Two van doors slam up front and the engine starts. A small window between the front cabin and the back of the van slides open.

"Khorosho?"

The man on the wheel arch nods. "Khorosho."

No. We are not good. I'm very uncomfortable.

"Is that your name?" Tom pretends to not understand what they are saying. The man stares at Tom but doesn't answer. He's a lot younger than the other two and is wearing a bearskin skullcap. "Where are we going?"

"Molchi."

Shut up. Fair enough.

Tom sucks on the blood in his mouth. He pushes against his teeth with his tongue and none of them move. *Must have bit my tongue.* He drops his head against the side of the van and closes his eyes.

They drive for around twenty minutes before the window slides open again.

"Sascha! Vpityvat' tryapku."

Tom opens one eye and watches the man—Sascha, grab an old tea towel and plunge it into a container of clear liquid. *Chloroform. You guys need some new material.*

Tom clears his throat. "Is your name Sascha?"

Sascha jerks his head up. "Molchi." *Shut up.*

"Where are we going?"

Sascha ignores him and continues to push the towel inside the container of chloroform.

Tom kicks the wall of the van. *You know what? Fuck it.* Irritation creeps up his neck and he kicks it again, harder this time.

Sascha puts the lid on the container with the towel still inside and drops it on the floor. He scrambles across to Tom and pulls his head up by the hair. "Stop."

Tom grins as laughter bubbles up his body. He hardens his eyes at Sascha and jerks his head out of his grasp. "Or what?"

Sascha's nostrils flare and he looks up at the closed window between them and the driver's cabin. He glances down to Tom and opens his mouth. He says nothing.

Tom raises his eyebrows. "Well?"

Sascha chews his lip a moment before grabbing a clump of Tom's hair again and twisting it in his fist. "Stop."

"Make me." Tom kicks the wall again, and again.

Sascha lunges at Tom and covers his mouth with his hand. "Ya ne khochu delat' tebe bol'no."

You don't want to hurt me?

Tom hides a grin so Sascha doesn't realise he understands him.

Tom eyes Sascha and kicks the wall again. The van swerves to the left and the brakes squeal.

Seconds later the back door of the van opens, and Doorway Man stands, scowling.

"Kontrolirovat' yego!" *Control me? Good fucking luck.*

"Da, Marat." Sascha dips his head.

The van door slams shut and Marat bangs on the outside of the van, above Tom's head. Tom grimaces and leans forward a fraction. *Testy.*

The van starts again and Tom watches as Sascha sits back on the wheel arch, avoiding his eyes.

"Are you afraid of them?"

Sacha jerks his head a little and ignores Tom. *Wait...*

"Can you understand me?" Tom leans forward, squinting at Sascha.

Sascha stares straight ahead and says nothing.

Tom pushes himself off the wall and shuffles towards Sascha. He snaps his head to Tom and drops to his knees. He pushes Tom in the chest so he falls back on the floor. "Stop."

"How old are you, Sascha?"

Sascha narrows his eyes at Tom and bites his lip. "Perestan' govorit' so mnoy."

Stop speaking to you?

Tom lets out an exaggerated sigh and flops against the wall again. "Hard to find good company." He slides his eyes to Sascha and sees him suck his lips in against a grin. *I see you.*

They travel in silence for the next half hour before the road becomes bumpy, and Tom sits up, trying to brace himself against the side of the van.

"Where are we?"

Sascha looks at Tom, almost as though considering him but doesn't answer.

Tom shrugs his shoulders and glares at Sascha. He is about to look away when Sascha opens his arms out like a plane and imitates flying.

"A plane? We're going on a plane?"

Sascha tilts his head and nods once, his eyes dart to the sliding window.

A plane...

"Moscow?

Sascha nods again.

Fuck.

"Isabella?"

Sascha curls his lip and folds his arms across his chest. "Dezertir."

"What did you just say?" Tom's blood warms and he grits his teeth. "Sascha?"

Sascha turns his face away from Tom and ignores him.

"Did you call her a deserter?"

Sascha continues to ignore Tom but his jaw jiggles back and forth. *Anxious much?*

"Is Isabella going to Moscow too?"

Sascha slowly turns his head and looks Tom in the eye.

Tom's pulse shoots up. *She'll be terrified.*

Moments later the van jerks to a stop and the back door opens. Marat and his friend stand, smirking at Tom. Marat flicks his head and Sascha scurries across to Tom, yanks him from the floor and drags him towards the door.

Once within reach the other two take hold and throw him on the ground.

Tom looks up and sees a ratty twin engine plane sitting on a deserted, dusty runway. *Looks like a Canadian Twin Otter.* He spits dirt out of his mouth.

"Khodit'" Marat barks at Tom.

Walk? No. I'm good. Tom pushes himself into a sitting position and glares at them both. Sascha stands behind him, saying nothing.

Marat looks at his tall mate and smirks. "Dolzhny li my Erik?"

Erik laughs before they both lunge forward. They grab Tom by each arm, hauling him off the ground. Another gut punch from Marat makes Tom lurch forward as the air leaves his lungs.

They drag Tom across to the plane, he stumbles as they pull him off balance, but doesn't fall. This appears to anger Erik and he throws a punch, landing on Tom's right cheekbone as they reach the door of the plane.

Pain prickles up into his eye socket and he closes his eyes, falling against the steps leading into the plane. His cheek throbs and he sees black spots in his vision.

"Tol'ko nachalo."

Just the beginning? Wonderful.

They drag Tom into the plane and discard him in the corner like a bag of trash. Erik sits in the cockpit with Marat next to him. Sascha scrunches down beside Tom, he holds the soaked towel in his hand.

Marat turns and glares at Sascha with his eyebrows raised. "Sdelay eto!" *Do it.*

Tom glances at the towel and up at Sascha.

Tom nods at Sascha as the plane starts to move. *I won't fight you. Let's just get where we're going.*

Sascha pushes the towel against Tom's nose and mouth. He breathes in deep breaths, the sweet scent envelopes his senses.

He closes his eyes and five minutes later, he falls into the dark.

14

ISABELLA

Isabella pushes herself against the seat in the jet and turns her face away from Nik. She claws her fingers into the plush leather of the arm rests and closes her eyes.

The plane climbs into the air and the tremble in her body matches the tremble in her chest. *I did this.*

"Irina."

Isabella ignores Nik and keeps her eyes closed. The sweat pushing out of every inch of skin does nothing to cool her down.

"Irina."

"My name is Isabella."

"No. It is not."

Isabella opens her eyes and glares at Nik. "Tell me Nik. How much money are you getting for finding me?"

Nik raises his eyebrows. "What?"

"There's a price on my head."

"Yes. Placed on it by me."

Isabella's insides disintegrate and she slumps lower in her seat. "You?"

"The original reward was wiped when you were… killed." Nik grins. "But upon hearing that you were still alive… I made new reward."

"Bummer for you then." Isabella turns her face away again and looks out into the night sky.

"Not so much. I have plans for you."

"I hope those plans don't involve me cooperating."

Nik chuckles and unclips his seatbelt. Isabella turns her head at the sound and watches as Nik slithers into the seat next to her. She grips the arm rests tighter and continues to look out the window.

Nik's hand cups her jaw and pulls her face towards him. "Tell me. I am curious. Why do you refuse to use the mother tongue?" His nose is within a centimetre of hers. She can feel his breath on her top lip. His blue eyes drill into her face.

"I no longer require the use of the mother tongue."

"I see. You speak like him."

"Who?"

"Your lover."

"He has a name."

"Whatever."

"Where are we going?"

"Home."

"My home is Polotsk."

"*My* home."

"Polotsk."

"Were you always this insolent?"

Isabella jerks her head away from Nik's grasp. "You tell me."

"You know. I always had crush on you Irina."

Isabella purses her mouth shut and refuses to look at Nik. *Best he doesn't know I had one on him too…*

"Do you remember just before you disappeared?"

Isabella cheeks warm and she folds her arms.

"In my bedroom?"

"We were thirteen Nik. It was nothing." *It was my first kiss.*

"It was something."

Isabella shifts in the seat. "Why are you doing this?"

"Whisking you away on luxury jet?"

"Kidnapping me, Nik. The word is kidnap."

"I need you."

"Well, you can't have me."

"Correction. I can have whatever I want."

Isabella leans forward, her nose brushes Nik's. "Good luck."

"Relax Irina." Nik runs a finger down Isabella's neck to her chest, stopping above her heart. "Your heart may beat for another, but I am sure with time you will come around."

"Fuck you, Nik." Isabella grits her teeth. "Your mother must be so proud of you."

Nik's grin falters and he drops his hand from her chin. Isabella moves to the far edge of her seat.

"You will not mention my mother again. Do you hear me?"

"Or what?"

"Or I order removal of Tom's left ear."

Nik glares at Isabella, his eyes flashing. "I swear on my parents grave Nik, you mark him, I *will* kill you."

"You are beautiful when you are angry." Nik whispers against her cheek.

Isabella grimaces and keeps staring out the window.

"My mother is dead by the way."

Isabella's gut plunges and she closes her eyes. "I'm sorry," she whispers.

TEN-YEAR-OLD IRINA SWIPED ANOTHER COOKIE FROM THE PLATE ON *Nikolay's dining table. They giggled as they clinked their glasses of milk.*

"Irina? Would you like to stay for dinner?" Oksanna smiled as she washed dishes.

"Can she stay over too?" Niklolay bounced up and down in his chair.

"She will have to check with her father."

"He won't mind. He was going to take me to Katia's Kitchen but I'm sure he would prefer to go alone."

Oksanna put the last dish in the dishrack and gave Irina a warm smile. "Of course." She bent down and pinched Irina's cheek. "Off you go you two. Play outside while the sun shines."

Irina ran outside after Nikolay and they climbed the tree outside his bedroom window.

"My tree is higher than yours." Irina taunted as she scrambled past Nikolay to the highest branch.

"Yeah, but mine is better for sitting." Nikolay sat next to her and they held hands.

"I like staying at your house."

Nikolay swung his legs. "Why?"

"Because you have a mother. And she's so nice to me."

"I'll share with you 'rina."

Irina dropped her head on Nikolay's shoulder. "Okay."

ISABELLA OPENS HER EYES AND WATCHES NIK. HE HAS MOVED TO his original seat and is reading paper from a manila folder.

"What happened to you?"

Nik looks up into Isabella's eyes. He closes the folder in his lap and wets his lips with his tongue. "I grew up?"

"And?"

Nik says nothing, fiddling with the corner of the folder. He slaps the folder on the seat next to him and places an elbow on each arm rest.

"And… I had to look after myself."

Isabella's eye twitches as she stares into Nik's sea of blue.

"Why did you need to do that?"

Nik observes Isabella a moment and tilts his head. He nods, more to himself than Isabella and takes a breath.

"You saw the state of our village?"

"Yes."

"The violence did not stop after you disappeared. Our whole town was pillaged. They killed my mother." Nik stops and bites his lip. "After they raped her."

Isabella's heart jolts and she sucks in a breath, willing her tears not to fall.

"My father took me away, but soon after he abandoned me."

"He…"

"He disappeared and never returned for me."

"Maybe he was killed."

"Maybe."

"And then?"

"And then… I was taken in by new...family."

"The Organisation?"

Nik nods. "I did jobs for them."

"How did you come to be in charge?"

Nik smiles, and the dimple deepens in his cheek. "I worked hard."

"Did you know what they did to me?"

"No."

"And if you had?"

"I do not know."

Isabella heart deflates. "You don't know?"

"What power would I have had? I was nobody then."

"But you're somebody now?"

"Da."

"Then why are you doing this to me?"

"You were the best at what you did. Everybody who knew, said so."

"So?"

"So… I need you."

Isabella clutches at her throat as the bile rises. "Fuck… you."

Nik smiles. "I am not who you remember. It is best if you do not expect me to be."

"I won't do anything for you."

"Then I kill Tom." Nik shrugs and inspects his fingernails.

The air leaves Isabella's lungs and she bends forward, clawing her fingers through her hair.

"We land in an hour. I do hope your attitude improves by then."

"It won't."

Tom's eyes peel open and he squints against the artificial light hanging above him from a single bulb. His head thumps and he reaches his hands up to massage his temples. Chains clink and he realises he is handcuffed and attached to a bolt in the wall.

He shuffles to sit upright from the concrete floor and looks around with his blurry eyes. He is in what appears to be an abandoned wine cellar. The room is no bigger than a walk-in wardrobe. One wall is exposed stone, the others concrete with a door at one end. His head spins and pounds and he feels as though he's going to vomit.

Not so lux.

He peers into the corner above the door and sees a camera with a red light blinking at him. *Say cheese.* He gives the camera the middle finger and slumps against the stone wall. He brings his knees up and realises his ankles are shackled. *Fuck's sake.*

Keys jangle on the other side of the door and it creaks open. Erik appears, swinging the keys on his index finger and grinning at Tom.

Tom nods towards his ankles. "Hands *and* feet. I don't know whether to be flattered or pissed."

Erik walks into the tiny room and Tom looks at the door, expecting Marat to be right behind him. There is no one.

"Your little friend not allowed out to play?"

Erik glares at Tom, clearly having no idea what he just said. He jabs Tom to the chin and his head bashes into the stone wall. Tom groans and sucks on his bottom lip, tasting the blood seeping out of it. Erik whips a pistol out and pushes the muzzle under Tom's chin, forcing his head up. Tom eyes Erik and doesn't blink.

"What are you waiting for?" Erik pushes the muzzle harder into his chin and Tom grins. "You aren't allowed to kill me. Are you?"

Erik pulls the pistol away and cracks it into the side of Tom's head. Pain rockets through his skull and his eyes slam shut. *Fuck.* Loud ringing reverberates through his head and he breathes out a pained moan. Warm liquid trickles down his neck from behind his left ear.

Erik stands and kicks Tom once to the ribs. Hard. He slumps forward against his chains and holds his breath. Erik bends down and holds his middle finger up in front of Tom's face.

"What if I'd blown you a kiss?"

Erik stomps out of the cellar, slamming the door behind him.

Tom stays where he fell on the floor, the crack he heard as Erik kicked him is enough to know he's broken a rib. *Been there. Done that.*

The door opens again and Sascha stands there holding a tray.

"Room service. How nice." Tom pushes himself against the wall and watches Sascha standing still. Tom raises his eyebrows and winces. "Well?"

Sascha walks in, closing the door behind him and puts the tray down at Tom's feet. He stays down on his haunches a moment, staring at Tom.

"Which body part do you want to attack?" Tom sucks his bloody lip. "I have a couple left to choose from."

Sascha looks up at the camera behind him before turning back to Tom. He bites his lip.

"You're kind of strange. Has anyone ever told you that?"

Sascha opens his mouth but before he can speak the door flies open and Marat stands, smoking a cigarette. He glares at Tom.

Sascha scrambles to his feet and slinks out of the room.

Tom blows a breath out and smiles at Marat. *Here we go.* "What can I do for you, Sunshine?"

Marat says nothing, smirking at Tom before closing the door.

Tom slides the tray towards him with his feet and peers at it. *What is it with you people and cabbage?*

He kicks the tray away and food litters the floor. *I'm watching my figure.*

He closes his eyes.

A HAND SQUEEZING HIS FACE WAKES TOM SOMETIME LATER.

"Rise and shine, Princess."

Tom blinks and focuses on Nik. He jerks out of Nik's grasp. "Where's Isabella."

"She is safe."

"That's not what I asked."

"It is not of your concern."

"Actually, it is."

"Hmm." Nik rocks onto his backside and observes Tom a moment. "You look little worse for wear."

"Where's Isabella?"

Nik sighs and raises his eyes to the ceiling. "Like broken record."

"You want another tune, answer my question." Tom pushes a hand against his ribs.

"You are hurt?"

"I'm peachy."

Nik grins and bites on his thumbnail. "Isabella sends her regards. She is sleeping after very eventful flight." Nik winks and spits his nail onto the floor.

Tom's stomach clenches at the thought of her in a plane, flying to Moscow. "Is she frightened?"

"Frightened? What is there to be frightened of?"

"Moscow. For one."

"It was her home for many years. She is not frightened."

She's petrified. "So what next?"

"I have some work for her to complete."

"Excuse me?"

"You know…" Nik leans forward and gestures a hand as though he and Tom are lifelong friends. "If you were better behaved, I could have used you, too."

"For?"

"I heard you are quite the killer."

Tom lets a smile spread across his face and his lip cracks. He sucks on the cut. "Kat."

"Kat. You will pay for that later."

"Is that right?"

"Yes. She was friend. You will pay."

"I look forward to it."

"Settle in." Nik looks around the tiny space. "I am sorry I do not have more luxurious room for you."

"It's fine. I won't be here long."

Nik's eyes widen and he smiles. "Oh?"

"I have a habit of getting out of tricky situations."

"This is *tricky* situation, is it?" Nik chuckles.

"Trickier than usual. But nonetheless…"

Nik stands and pulls an empty plastic water bottle from inside his jacket. He drops it on the floor.

"Your ensuite. Do not go crazy. Room service is lax."

Nik walks out, slamming the door behind him.

Tom glares at the empty bottle and then at the camera. He holds his middle finger up at it again and lays back on the floor.

He lifts his hands and inspects the cuffs. They are tight enough to hurt when he moves his wrist the wrong way, but loose enough not to cut off his circulation.

A TV would be nice.

16

ISABELLA

Isabella leans over the kitchen worktop and stabs a paring knife into the wood. It stands up on its own.

"Are you vandalising my home?" Nik stands at the door to the kitchen with amusement plastered across his face.

Isabella folds her arms and walks to the window, peering at the skyline of the city. "Your home? Or the home you took over, no doubt?"

Nik walks in and sits on a kitchen stool. "Took over?"

"You get to be in charge by getting rid of whoever is above you. Right?"

Nik gives a half shrug. "You helped. Unwittingly."

"Damir."

Nik nods. "Damir. And company." Nik reaches across and grabs Isabella's arm. He pulls her across until she topples into his lap. "You got all four." He rests his mouth against her neck. She presses her mouth shut, breathing deeply through her nose. "Impressive"

Isabella turns and slaps his face. Nik barely moves and laughs. He grabs Isabella's hands and pulls her into him again. This time their faces are practically touching. "I always get what I want."

"Only because you kill anyone who refuses you."

"I am offended."

"Where's Tom?"

Nik grins. "Would you like to see him?"

Isabella's heart wakes up and she gasps a breath in, before remembering who she is talking to. "What state is he in?"

"He is alive. If that is what you are asking."

"Where is he?"

Nik reaches for a tablet and swipes the screen. "I tell you what, Irina. I will give you glimpse. And then we talk business."

Isabella's eyes fill with tears and she grabs for the tablet.

Nik holds it away from her. "Uh uh… so grabby." He pokes the screen a few times and hands it to her.

She blinks and lets the tears fall down her cheeks to clear her vision. She sees a dimly lit cellar. Tom sits against the back wall. He's chained up. He looks up and glares straight at the camera. *It's me.* His face is bruised and dried blood is caked on his neck. Isabella holds the screen with both hands and sobs.

"You're hurting him."

There is blood on his shirt and jeans, he presses a hand against his ribs when he adjusts his position.

"He leaves me no choice." Nik grabs the tablet and lays it face down on the worktop. "He is quite the smart arse."

Isabella holds her hands out. "Please."

"You are going to do something for me now." He pushes his face into hers again. "Do you remember our first kiss?"

His lips brush against hers and she holds her breath, squeezing her eyes shut. She keeps her lips pressed together.

Nik pulls away and grimaces. He picks up the tablet and walks from the kitchen. "Maybe he needs few teeth knocked out?"

Isabella's body trembles. "No." She runs to Nik and pushes her mouth to his, keeping her tongue curled at the back of her throat. "Now let me see him again."

Nik stares down at her and slaps the tablet against her chest. "That does not count. But I will play your game, Irina. For now."

Isabella watches the screen. Tom is curled up and appears to be sleeping. "Oh God." She rests her forehead against the tablet and sniffles. "Nik. Please."

"You are adorable when you beg." He yanks the tablet out of her hands and she crumples to the floor.

"Where is he?"

"Somewhere secure."

"Where?" Isabella shouts, standing up.

Nik reaches across and strokes her face. "Sit down. Let us discuss your future." He gestures back to the dining table.

Isabella pushes him to the chest and stalks to the dining table. She throws herself in a chair and crosses her arms.

"Speak."

"Do you always address your superiors that way?" Nik sits across from her and folds his hands over the tablet.

"You aren't my superior."

"But I am."

"You're nothing."

"What about Kostya? Damir?"

The mention of their names sends prickles down Isabella's back and spine. "They were monsters." She glares at Nik. "As are you."

"Me?"

"Yes. Only you're worse."

"How so?"

"We were best friends. We grew up together. There was a time when the thought of hurting me would have made you sick."

"I am not hurting you."

"You're hurting Tom. And that hurts me."

Nik slides his hands across the table and holds it out. "Give me your hand."

"Fuck you."

Nik curls his hand into a fist. "You will come to realise that you have very little choices left."

"What do you want from me, Nik?"

"Well, since you ask." He stands and strides out of the room.

Isabella slides the tablet to her and it's dark. She taps the screen; it lights up and asks for a password. She drops her head on the table and sobs. *This is my fault.*

A hand slides beneath her chin and lifts her head from the table. "Irina."

Nik sits next to her and she turns her body away from him. He grabs her shoulder and twists her back around to face him. He stares into her eyes, narrowing his own.

"Get it over with Nik." She clenches her jaw and waits.

Nik pulls a photograph out of a large envelope and slaps it on the table in front of her. She pulls it towards her. A man in his mid-forties smiles at a child in a football uniform.

"He borrowed money from associate."

"And?"

"And he failed to abide the terms of contract."

"So?"

"So now he dies." Nik flicks his eyes to Isabella's. "And you will kill him."

Isabella swallows. "No."

"Then, Tom dies instead."

Isabella pushes a hand to her stomach and swallows again as saliva streams into her mouth. "Shit."

"Irina?"

Isabella jumps up from her seat and runs to the kitchen. She heaves into the sink, her neck tenses and her eyes water. She vomits the little she has in her gut. Her stomach clenches and acid burns her tongue. She grabs a dishcloth and wipes her mouth, and swallows the bitterness sitting in the back of her throat.

She turns and leans against the worktop, glaring at Nik. "Please don't do this to me." Her voice is husky and raw.

"You *will* kill him." Nik stands and walks to her. He puts both hands on her shoulders and bends down to her face. "It will be quick and clean. And you will brand him with your next number. The Orphan has returned and I want everyone to know."

"Why?"

"So they stay in line."

"And if I kill him?"

"Tom lives to see another day."

"I want to see him."

"I showed him to you."

"I want to touch him."

Nik stares into her eyes a moment and nods his head. "Okay. I am not unreasonable. But know this. This kill is only number one. Tom is not out of woods yet."

"How many do you have?"

"Three. But who knows what may pop up?"

Isabella looks at the tablet on the dining table.

Nik scoops it up and holds it against his chest. "Do not be greedy Irina."

"I'll need clothing. And knives." She slumps into a chair and stares out the window, pushing all emotion into the deepest part of her gut. *I don't want to feel.* She blinks the tears from her eyes and they roll off her chin.

"Consider it done, and Irina…"

Isabella looks at Nik.

"If you are that lonely… my room is on the top floor."

Isabella tracks Nik as he walks towards the hall, the tablet under his arm. He turns at the door as though remembering one more thing.

"Make yourself at home. But if you leave. Tom gets bullet to brain. Are we clear?"

"Crystal."

Nik smiles. "There is good girl."

17

ISABELLA

"Coffee?"

Isabella jumps out of her half-awake state to see Nik sitting at the end of the bed holding a mug. She slaps her hand against her chest as her heart pounds.

"Could you be any creepier, Nik?" She pulls herself up into a sitting position and ignores the mug being held out to her.

Nik shrugs and puts the mug on the blanket box at the end of the bed.

"What time is it?"

"Ten. I let you sleep."

"How kind."

Nik grins and stands up. "There is fruit and yoghurt in kitchen. Make sure you eat. You have big day."

"What?"

"Your target will be taking his child to football practice this afternoon. You will be dropped off and observed."

Isabella's throat closes up and she coughs. "Today?" *No.*

"Yes." He nods at the dresser. A pile of clothing is piled on top. "Your clothing and shoes. I took liberty of ordering some wigs."

Isabella's eyes drop to the selection of shoes on the floor.

"I would suggest soccer mum disguise." He winks. "You do not want to stand out."

Isabella glares at Nik's smug face. "I've done this before. But thanks for the tip."

"You are welcome." He turns to leave and flicks his head back. "You get job done. I take you to Tom. I am nothing if not man of my word." He shuts the door.

Isabella flops back onto the bed and lets tears drip down the side of her face. She rolls onto her side and screams into the pillow. *This can't be happening.*

Sometime later, Isabella wanders into the kitchen. A man stands at the worktop reading a piece of paper and he looks up at her.

God, you look about twelve. "Who are you?"

The man frowns.

Isabella rolls her eyes. "Kto ty?"

"Sascha." He holds a hand out to the fruit on the worktop.

"Vy khotite, chtoby ya yel." *You want me to eat.*

Sascha nods once. "Da."

Isabella grabs the plate of fruit and bowl of yoghurt and sits at the table. Sascha creeps around the worktop and sits at the other end. He watches as Isabella nibbles on a piece of apple.

"Are you taking me to the job?"

Sascha bites his lip and stares at Isabella.

She rolls her eyes. "Vy berete menya na rabotu?"

"Da."

Isabella's curiosity gets the better of her and she leans forward, peering at him. "Skol'ko tebe let?" *Seriously, how old are you?*

"Dvadtsat' chetyre."

"Twenty-four?" She pops a grape into her mouth. "You look about twelve."

Sascha smirks at the table and Isabella tilts her head.

"Do you understand me?"

Sascha's eyes flick up to hers. He observes her a moment, his eyes roam up and down her body. "Some."

"Some?"

Isabella looks around the kitchen and dining room and back to Sascha. "Do you work here?"

Sascha nods.

"For Nikolay?"

He nods again.

Isabella holds her breath a moment and fiddles with her spoon, stirring her yoghurt. *What have I got to lose?*

She looks at Sascha again. "Tom?"

Sascha sits up straighter and clamps his mouth shut.

You know.

Isabella moves to the chair right next to Sascha and peers into his face. "You know where he is?"

Sascha stares at her with no expression.

"I said, Ty znayesh' gde on?"

Sascha drops his eyes to the table and says nothing.

Isabella grabs his arm and he jumps as though shocked. "Where is he?"

"Well, this is so cosy." Nik's voice echoes through the room.

"You're here." Isabella slides away from Sascha and spoons yoghurt into her mouth.

"I was out. But now I am back. Sascha has been keeping you company?"

"Yes."

Nik nods and folds his arms. "He does what he is told. Unlike you."

Isabella swallows the yoghurt. "I'm eating. And I'll be killing later. Both of those things you requested. So I don't know what the problem is."

"Your attitude is problem."

"Get used to it." Isabella smirks and licks her spoon.

Nik leans on his fists on the table. "So smug."

Isabella holds his stare and says nothing. The silence lingers a few seconds more before Sascha shifts in his chair.

Nik blinks and checks his watch. "You best be getting ready. You do not want to be late."

Isabella drops her spoon into the bowl and stands up. "I need my weapons."

"In good time. I cannot have you wandering around house with knives at your disposal."

Isabella glances at the kitchen.

"Ah yes. After your stabby display yesterday I had knives removed."

Isabella steps into Nik and lingers her mouth within a breath of his. She stares into his eyes. "Are you afraid of me?" she whispers against his mouth.

Nik holds her gaze and grins. "No. But one cannot be too careful."

"You should be."

"Careful?"

"Afraid."

Isabella sweeps past Nik and throws a glance back at Sascha who is biting his lip, grinning at the tabletop.

SASCHA DRIVES, STARING AHEAD AT THE ROAD WHILE ISABELLA fiddles with her hands in the passenger seat. She swallows for what must be the fourth time in twenty seconds. Her gut churns and the small of her back is a pool of sweat.

Isabella flips the sun visor down and adjusts the ginger wig she chose. Perfect soccer mum hair do. Her bright red lips and large sunglasses disguise her face nicely. She wipes across her front teeth with her index finger, getting rid of a red smudge and flicks the visor back to the roof. The sudden thud makes Sascha flinch next to her.

"Are you scared?" Isabella leans on the centre console.

"Mne zhal'?"

Isabella sighs. "Ty boish'sya?"

Sascha takes a deep breath and shakes his head.

"Liar," Isabella whispers

Sascha grips the steering wheel tighter, his knuckles paling.

Isabella massages her stomach, willing its contents to stay down. Football fields crop up in the distance and her stomach rolls. She flops back against the seat and takes a few deep breaths. *Nope.*

"Stop!"

Sascha jumps. "Kakoy?"

"Stop the car!"

Sascha pulls the car to the side of the road and Isabella stumbles out the door. She grips the kerb with both hands and vomits into the gutter. Sour yoghurt and undigested bits of apple are carried by filthy water down the drain. Isabella heaves in air and spits the bitter acid out of her mouth.

She pulls herself back into the car and nods at Sascha. "Let's go."

Sascha's brow creases and he puts his hand on her arm.

Isabella looks down at his hand and up into his eyes. *Your eyes are kind.* "I said let's go, Sascha." She nods at the road again. *Let's get this nightmare over with.*

Isabella bows her head and closes her eyes. She takes a few deep breaths and visualises herself confident and cold. She remembers the feel of the knife in her hand and the sound it makes when it pierces someone in the heart. *People think it's silent. It isn't.* She lifts her face and opens her eyes. She pulls out the knife Nik slipped into her hand as she walked out the door. It has a wooden handle and a lovely sharp edge. She tilts it so the sunlight bounces off it. *Straight and true.*

"Pretty." She watches Sascha as he drives, ignoring her and her knife. *Give him a break.*

Isabella smiles to herself and slides the knife inside her fluffy jacket. *I look ridiculous.*

Sascha drives into the parking lot of the fields and finds a spot behind the amenities block.

Isabella swallows as the bile rises again and takes a breath. Her eyes scan the field in front of her.

"Wait here." She climbs out without waiting to see if Sascha understood.

She stands for a moment, steadying herself against the car. She shakes her head a couple of times against the emptiness.

"Quick and clean," Isabella whispers to herself. She closes her eyes and sees the image of the man with his son. *His son.*

She steps onto the grass and wanders through the people milling around the fields. Her eyes scan every face. She smiles and nods at those who acknowledge her but moves quickly through them so as not to start a meaningless conversation. The tremble in her legs becomes more insistent with every step she takes. She sits on a bench at the end of one field, taking in some slow breaths. *Calm down.*

The sounds of kids playing and laughing are at odds with her terror and unwillingness to be there. It's as though she is now glued to the bench seat. If she stands up she may find him. If she stays there, maybe she misses him and buys another day. *But Tom.* The picture of him bruised and bloodied. The pain on his face as he moved to sit up. As though stabbed herself, Isabella drops over her knees against the pain in her chest.

"Vy v poryadke, mem?" A voice above her asks.

Am I alright? No. No I am not.

She looks up and straight into the face of her target. *Jesus.* Her stomach drops and adrenaline pierces her body. *Now or never.*

She stands and wobbles, grabbing his arm to steady herself. She smiles and his eyes crinkle at the corners as he smiles back.

"Um, Tualety?" She asks where the toilets are, even though she is well aware.

He points and slides her arm through his own. "Prikhodi, ya tebya gulyayu."

You'll walk me? God. Why couldn't you be an arsehole?

They wander across to the very amenity block Sascha parked behind. Isabella stops and leans against the wall, behind the fields where no one else can see them. She slides her hand inside her jacket and with her other arm she pulls her target in to hug him.

"Spasibo." *Thank you.* She pulls the knife from against her body and pushes it through his shirt, up into his heart. His eyes widen and he stares into Isabella's face. He tries to sputter words, but gurgling and wet breaths are all he can manage.

Isabella's nose tingles and her eyes burn with tears.

"I'm sorry." She supports his weight as he crumples at her feet. She adjusts him so he leans against the wall. His breathing is shallow now and he is no longer trying to speak.

Isabella spins the knife in her hand and goes to carve 360 into his cheek and stops. Tom's words echo in her head. *It stops their soul finding peace.* She blinks and stares into the now lifeless eyes of her victim. She bows her head and puts the knife back in her jacket. *Never again.*

She runs to the car and throws herself into the passenger seat. "Go."

Sascha starts the car and drives. Isabella moves the rearview mirror and watches the dead man's body disappear from view.

Forgive me

18

TOM

Tom lies on his back and stares at the light bulb hanging above him. The filament flickers and he picks tiny fragments of stone off the floor to throw at the light. They ting softly when he makes contact, but none are big enough to smash the glass. He glares at the chains keeping him tethered like an animal.

Well, this is fun.

He pulls his knees up and the thick chain attached to his ankle cuffs slides against the concrete floor. He drops his head to the side and stares at the camera. He winks each eye, one after the other keeping time with the red light.

No one has been to see him in a number of hours. *Exactly how many? Who can say?* His stomach growls and he rubs a hand over it. *I'd even take the cabbage right now.* He eyes the bucket in the corner. *Although...*

He presses two fingers against his cheekbone. It's not as painful as it was a few days ago, which means it isn't fractured. *That's something.* He pulls in a deep breath, all the way from the bottom of his lungs to test his rib. Sharp pain cuts through to his back. *Definitely broken.* He pushes a palm against his ribcage and hauls himself into a sitting position. Leaning against the cold stone wall he counts the holes in the surrounding walls, where bolts used to be to hold wine shelves.

A sharp rap on the door and the jangle of keys draws his attention. The door opens. *Marat. Slimy bastard.*

"Sorry. Not fit for visitors right this minute."

Marat walks in and grabs the half-full ensuite replacing it with another. He stomps out without a word, slamming the door behind him.

"No mint for my pillow then?" Tom throws a handful of tiny stones at the door. *You could've taken the bucket too.* He wrinkles his nose up and glares at the bucket in the corner.

Tom scans the windowless room and tries to ignore the feeling of the walls closing in tighter around him. *I'm losing my fucking mind.*

He pulls his shirt up and inspects the bruising around his broken rib. He presses again and it hurts just the same.

The door swings open and bounces off the wall. Nik stands with a grin that spreads across his whole face.

Tom yanks his shirt down and sits up straighter against the wall. "Win the lottery?"

"In a way."

"I have a spare few minutes between engagements. Why don't you enlighten me?"

Nik scowls at the bucket in the corner. "Marat!"

Marat appears behind him in the doorway.

Nik juts his chin at the bucket. Marat grunts and takes it away.

"Maybe stop feeding me cabbage then?" Tom yells after him.

Nik squats down beside Tom and grins again.

"You gonna let me in on the secret?" Tom maintains his eye contact.

"Irina did a fine job today."

Tom's body gives an involuntary jerk. "What?"

"Irina certainly lives up to her... reputation."

"What reputation?" *Don't say it.*

"As the best of course."

"You made her kill for you?" Fury rises up his body and the pain in his ribs is forgotten. He scrambles onto his knees and swings his cuffed hands back. Before Nik can react, he slams them into the side of his head. Nick falls to the floor with a grunt. Within seconds Marat and Erik burst through the door and are on top of Tom. A knee connects with Tom's solar plexus and he gasps against the cold hard floor. A fist jabs him to the jaw, and he grunts, spitting blood down his shirt.

"Stop." Nik's voice cuts over the chaos.

Marat and Erik move back and Nik squats again, bruising already visible on his cheek and eye. "How did that feel, Tom?"

Tom fights for breath as he rolls onto his back to free his

lungs. The pain in his rib is back and mixes with his new injuries. *Fucking delightful.*

"I've had worse." He spits more blood from his mouth and stares at the ceiling.

Nik sniggers and stands up. "Well, do not get too comfortable. The worst is yet to come."

"Do check with my secretary on the way out and book a time."

The door slams and Tom rolls onto his side. His breathing slows but is laboured. He closes his eyes and thinks of Tesco, and nine loaves of bread on the floor...

A COLD COMPRESS IS PUSHED AGAINST TOM'S FACE AND HE OPENS his eyes. It's fuzzy and he blinks a couple of times.

"Sascha?"

"Yes."

"What are you doing? How long was I sleeping?"

"You need ice for face. Hold this." He grabs Tom's hand and pushes it against the ice pack.

Tom stares at him a moment and pushes his tongue against the new cut on his lip. "I knew you could understand me."

"Yes."

"What time is it?"

"Around eight p.m."

Tom glances up at the camera above the door and sees the red light isn't on. Sascha follows his gaze and shrugs. "They are all eating dinner and drinking. I disabled the camera and they have access to old feed for now."

"Where is Isabella?"

"Sleeping."

"Is she okay?"

"She is… distressed."

Tom drops his head back against the wall and closes his eyes. *Fuck.* Sascha starts to lift Tom's shirt and he snaps his eyes open. "Can I help you Sascha?"

"Your ribs."

"Oh."

"I will not bandage you. It will constrict your breathing."

Sascha drops Tom's shirt after inspecting the bruise. He grabs a bottle of clean water and holds it out for Tom. "Drink this."

Tom takes the bottle and inspects the seal.

"It is brand new." Sascha smiles. "No poison."

"It's not that I don't trust you. But… I don't trust you." Tom gulps the water. Thirst crashes over him and he sculls the entire bottle.

"That is fair."

"So, what gives?"

Sascha chews on his lip a moment and checks his watch. "I will not hurt you. I will not hurt Irina."

"Isabella."

"Isabella." Sascha nods and bows his head.

"Why not?"

"I need your help."

Tom squints at Sascha and looks around his cellar prison. "Don't know if you've noticed Sash but... I'm not quite in a position to be helping anyone."

"If I can get you out?"

Tom stops breathing and stares at Sascha. Sascha takes the ice pack and replaces it with a new one. "When you say get me out..."

"I will help you. And in exchange you help me?"

"And how do I know I can trust you, Sascha?"

"You do not. But... what do you have to lose?"

"Convince me I can trust you." Tom raises his eyebrows. "Then, we can talk."

Sascha watches Tom a moment before nodding. "I will prove it to you. But first, here." He holds out two white pills. "Painkillers."

Tom takes the pills and peers at them.

"They are not poison."

Tom tosses the pills to the back of his throat and swallows them. "Guess I'll soon find out."

"I will come back. At midnight. I have night watch. I will convince you." He stands and takes the ice packs and empty water bottle. "I was never here, yes?"

"I've been sleeping the whole time."

Sascha nods and scurries out the door.

19

ISABELLA

Isabella walks out of the bathroom connected to her bedroom and scrubs a towel over her hair. She slides knickers and a pair of tracks on as a knock sounds at her door.

"I'm not decent."

The door swings open. Nik stands in the frame. He runs his eyes up and down Isabella's body. Her wet hair shields her chest from view.

"Are you deaf?"

Nik walks into the room, kicking the door shut behind him. He stands in front of Isabella and twists her wet hair in his hand, revealing her left breast.

She squares her shoulders and glares at him. "What can I do for you Nik?" *By the way, you make me sick.*

"I see you are making good use of clothes I have provided for you."

"Well, I can't wander around naked. Can I?"

Nik shrugs. "It is not against rules."

Isabella stares at him and waits.

"I thought you may like to join us for dinner." He slides his hand around the back of her neck and pulls her closer to him.

"No thanks."

"But you must be…" He slides his eyes down to her chest and back to her face. "Hungry?"

Isabella smirks. "I'm fine." She grabs his hand, rips it away from her neck and slaps it in the middle of his chest.

"I visited Tom today."

Isabella's breath catches and she waits.

"He can be quite difficult. Can he not?"

"You said you'd take me to him."

Nik grins. "Well, this is true. But he misbehaved...so…"

Isabella stands on her tiptoes and inspects Nik's face. The bruise on his cheek is dark pink. "So I see."

Nik grabs the back of Isabella's head and pulls her face to his, kissing her mouth. She pushes against his chest and squirms. His breath veils her face and his scent makes her wretch.

"I see why he misses you so much. You taste delicious."

Isabella swings and slaps him hard across the bruised side of his face.

His head snaps to the side and he grimaces. He grabs her

arms, pushing her backwards onto the bed. He holds her down and straddles her hips.

She draws in long hard breaths through her nose and curls her lip. "Get...the fuck… off me."

Nik pushes his lips against her neck and slowly runs his mouth down to the middle of her chest. His close-cut beard drags down her skin and she pushes and fights against his arms. He stops and kisses the skin between her breasts before releasing her.

Isabella scurries to the top of the bed and hugs her knees to her chest.

"You know where we are if you change your mind."

The sounds of Marat and Erik drinking and laughing in the dining room don't entice Isabella to move.

"Get. Out."

"Sleep well. I know I will." Nik winks and shuts the door.

Isabella drops her face to her knees and sobs. The same visions of Tom languishing on the floor of the cellar flash in her mind and she sobs harder.

Wait.

She jerks her head up and sniffles. *He's in a cellar.*

She jumps off the bed and twists into her bra before throwing a jumper over the top. She slides trainers on and moves to her door. She opens it and peers into the hallway. *Empty.*

She slips out of the room and stays close to the wall. Reaching the opening to the dining room she peeks around the corner. The three men are huddled over shot glasses as Nik pours from a bottle. *I wonder where Sascha is.*

She leaps across the doorway and continues down the hall to the stairs at the other end. The stairs are dark and appear to lead to a basement. *Or cellar.* She checks over her shoulder but the hallway is empty. Off key singing and laughing floats down the hallway towards her but no one comes out.

Isabella continues down the stairs, feeling her way along the walls on either side. She gets to the bottom and feels for a light switch but thinks better of it and waits for her eyes to adjust to the dim surrounds. She is in a sort of anteroom. There are two doors either side of her. She is closer to the one on the right, she turns the door handle and it opens to a storeroom. She sees buckets and a mop and the overpowering smell of disinfectant. She closes that door and moves across to the other.

This has to be it.

She jiggles the doorknob and it doesn't turn. *Shit.*

"Tom?" she whispers loudly against the door. A quick glance over her shoulder tells her she is still alone. "Tom?" She taps on the door with her fingers. Silence.

She turns back to the storeroom and peers at the walls inside the door. There is nothing there. She runs her hands over the three shelves housing bottles of cleaning fluid and buckets. She knocks something to the floor and it tings against the concrete.

Her heart doubles it's pace and she picks up a key. Darting across to the locked door she takes one more look up the stairs and slides the key into the lock. It clicks and her heart hits her throat. She opens the door and sees...

Wine?

Rows of wine greet her. She runs her hands over the dusty bottles and shakes the tears from her eyes. *No. I was so sure.* She drops to her knees and wipes her face.

"If they find you here they will take it out on Tom."

Isabella heart pounds and she spins around. Sascha stands in the doorframe. He looks up the stairs and back to her. He holds a hand out. "Quickly. I will take you to him."

Isabella takes his hand and stands up. "He's here?"

"He is. But not in house. Come." He pulls her up the stairs, his eyes dart around the hall. He nods at the front door. "Go. It is open."

She runs on her tiptoes to the door and slides out. Seconds later Sascha joins her.

"We need to stay close to house. Camera will not see us under eaves." He grabs Isabella's hand and they run around the side of the house and down to the corner of the backyard and side alley.

Sascha nods to a concrete bunker style building at the very back of the yard.

"He's in there?"

"Downstairs. Yes. Underground."

"Under…?"

"Bunker has cellar. Come." Sascha sticks his head out and looks up at the house. He runs and pulls Isabella with him.

"What about the cameras in the yard?" Isabella's head swings around the deserted yard.

"There are none. Only at front of house." Sascha pushes down the door handle and throws his shoulder against the door. It opens and he ushers Isabella inside. He follows her in and closes the door. He turns on a torch and Isabella sees a tiny room with a couple of laptops set up on a rickety card table. "Wait. I need to fix camera." He sits at the table and taps on one of the laptops.

Isabella sees a narrow flight of stairs leading down to her left and creeps to the top of them. She peers down but it's pitch black. Her heart beats faster and she cups her hands over her mouth.

"Okay. Come." He shines his torch down the stairs and Isabella runs down.

She grabs the door handle at the bottom to open it. "It's locked."

Sascha smiles and the warmth in it catches Isabella off guard. *Who are you?* He pulls a small ring of keys from his pocket and slides one into the lock. He turns it and pulls down on the door handle, pushing the door open. He holds an arm out gesturing Isabella inside.

Tom is lying on the floor, beneath a flickering light bulb. His head jerks up from where it rests on his outstretched arms.

Isabella runs to him and drops to her knees. She pushes her mouth against his and kisses him, placing her hands either side of his face.

"Iz." He breathes against her face.

Isabella nods and kisses him again. The warmth of his mouth and his face against hers unknots her shoulders and she slumps against his body.

He sucks in a sharp breath and presses his hand to his ribs.

"You're hurt."

"A bit."

Isabella sniffles and lets tears wet her cheeks. "Oh, Tom." She drops her forehead against his. "I'm so sorry," she whispers. "This is all my fault."

"Stop."

"But—"

"Stop." He runs his fingers over her face before pulling her to him and kissing her again. "Are you okay?"

Isabella raises a brow. "Me? Look at you…" She looks around the tiny room.

Sascha is at the door, he clears his throat.

They both look at him.

"I have disabled camera but we cannot stay long. It is too risky. Da?"

Isabella nods. "Da."

Sascha closes the door and she turns back to Tom. "I need to do some jobs for Nik."

Tom tries to push himself into a sitting position against the wall and grimaces. He pushes harder against his ribs and heaves himself up. "No."

"No?"

"You don't kill anymore, Iz."

"But if I don't, they *will* kill you."

"I'll get out… listen to me." He grabs her face and pulls it against his. "You need to run. Do you understand?"

"Are you insane?"

"A little bit." He gives her a half smile.

"I'm not leaving you here."

"I'll get out. And I'll find you. I promise."

"Tom. No."

"Iz—"

"Tom! We're here because of me. You're hurt because of me. No. I'll do what I have to do and we get out together."

"You don't kill anymore."

"For you. I kill." She presses her lips against his and kisses him as though she will never get to again. *What if I don't?*

She sobs against his chest and he wraps his arms around her.

"Sascha wants to help us." Tom's voice rumbles in his chest.

"What?"

"He said he would do something to show me I could trust him."

"And?"

"He brought you to me."

Isabella looks at the closed door.

"Use him. And run."

Isabella closes her eyes against Tom's face. "I can't."

Sascha knocks once and opens the door. "We must go."

Tom kisses her again. "I'll find you."

"I love you."

Tom grabs her hand and kisses it as she stands up.

"I love you too, Iz."

20

TOM

Hours pass and Tom sleeps, albeit fitfully. He wakes often and hears nothing but silence. He can still feel Isabella's cheek against his and see tears glistening on her face.

Run Iz.

A key clicks in the lock and the door opens. Sascha appears.

Tom watches as he slinks into the cellar. A glance at the camera reveals the red blinking light active.

"Are you alone?"

"Yes." He kneels beside Tom shielding them from the camera view. He reaches into his pocket, pulling out two blue pills.

"What are you? Some kind of street level dealer?" Tom peers at the pills and back to Sascha. "What are these?"

"They are sedative."

Tom's eyes widen. "A sedative? Why do I need a sedative?"

Sascha looks back towards the door and pulls a water bottle from his jacket. He grabs Tom's hand and pushes the pills into it.

"Please. Take them. You will need to be relaxed and calm."

Tom's gut squeezes and he flicks his eyes to the camera and back to Sascha's face. "And why would I need to be relaxed and calm, Sash? Am I about to be probed?"

"Of course not. Though...that may be more pleasant."

"What the fuck?" Tom's chest shudders.

"Take the pills. We are running out of time."

Tom throws the pills down his throat and swigs water.

"They will not make it painless but maybe they will help." Sascha takes the water bottle from Tom and hides it inside his jacket.

Tom grabs the front of Sascha's shirt and pulls him off balance. He slumps against Tom before sitting up. "What.The.-Fuck is going on?" Tom snarls. "Time to win more trust, Sascha."

"They are going to teach Irin... Isabella a lesson. I could not stop it. I am sorry. Please know I had no part."

"You aren't filling me with confidence here, Sash." Tom swallows the dread creeping up the back of his throat. *Dread tastes a lot like bile.*

Noise from above travels through the open door. Voices and laughter accompany footsteps. Sweat dots Tom's top lip and drips down his temples. *This won't tickle.*

Sascha stands up. "I will help you after. I swear."

After? After what?

Nik appears in the doorway and flicks his head at Sascha. Sascha runs to the door and disappears. *Well, fuck.*

Nik folds his arms and gives Tom a smile laced with phony sympathy. "I am so very sorry for what is about to happen. But you see Tom… Irina did not carry out her job as instructed. And now, she will see consequences of such defiance."

"Well, aren't you just a ray of sunshine on a gloomy day." Tom pushes himself into a sitting position and rests his arms on his bent knees.

Nik stands and watches Tom without saying anything. His smug smile remains.

I'm going to love killing you.

Marat and Erik appear behind Nik and he steps to the side. Marat holds a large blow torch while Erik holds a branding iron in the flame. They both sneer at Tom. The iron glows red.

It's glowing fucking red.

Something akin to an electric shock shoots through Tom's gut. He instinctively scrambles backwards against the wall, knowing he can't get any further away but continues to try.

Nik smiles and squats next to him. He pulls on thick gloves "You should feel special, Tom. I had this custom made. Just for you."

Tom's breathing is a pant and sweat coats every inch of his skin. He pushes himself harder into the wall and his fingers claw into the concrete floor.

Marat and Erik walk to him and Tom kicks his legs out. The chain attached to his ankle cuffs is heavy but the adrenaline pulsing through his body takes over. He squirms and thrashes his body against the hard, cold floor and Erik and Marat try to grab hold of him. His shirt rips at the sleeve and Marat throws the useless rag on the floor.

"No!" He kicks again, landing on Erik's knee. Erik stumbles backwards before regaining his balance. He snarls and punches Tom under the chin, causing his head to jolt back against the wall. A heavy smack thunders through his ears and the scene in front of him slips away as darkness takes over.

TOM WAKES TO A HAND JIGGLING HIS JAW. HIS ARMS ARE outstretched above his head, held against the floor by Marat. He blinks a couple of times and remembers where he is. Erik sits on his legs at the knees and laughs as Tom's eyes widen and he thrusts his hips in an effort to throw Erik off. Exhaustion comes swiftly and he slumps against the floor, panting and spent. *Fucking sedatives.*

"Oh, Tom. You fought a gallant fight. But alas, knocking yourself out against wall was not helpful for you." Nik pulls his gloved hand away from Tom's face and pouts. "But I am so very glad you could join us again. You do not want to miss main show."

Nik pushes Tom so he rolls onto his side. His broken rib is now flush against the floor and pain throbs through his chest and back. He gasps air in against the sharp ache.

Nik pushes Tom's shirt up to expose the side of his ribs and hip. Tom thrashes as hard as he can but it's weak and pointless. He grits his teeth and squeezes his eyes shut.

"So, as I was saying… I had this made special for you. Open your eyes. Admire craftsmanship of blacksmith."

Tom ignores Nik and keeps his face against the floor.

Nik grabs his face and jerks it up. "I said, have a look."

Tom opens his eyes and sees the red-hot branding iron in Nik's hands. His eyes are blurry, and he can't make out what it is shaped as. *Is that a three?* A tremble begins in his gut before travelling through his blood stream to every other part of his body. His adrenaline goes into overdrive and he shakes.

Nik stands and stamps his foot against Tom's hip. "Here we go…" Tom finds every ounce of strength hiding within him and tries in vain to throw Erik and Marat off his limbs. They stay where they are and laugh. Tom pushes his face back into the floor and closes his eyes. He hyperventilates as a red-hot burn hits him in the ribs inches below his arm pit. It remains for several seconds, though it feels like a lifetime.

He howls into the floor, his body trembles as air rushes out of his lungs and he fights to fill them again. He draws in a ragged breath and moans against the concrete. His pained sounds echo off the walls of the small room.

"There." Nik taps the fresh burn with his gloved fingers and pain shoots through Tom's body. Tom swallows the howl in his throat. *I won't give you any more.*

All pressure is released from his limbs and he curls into the foetal position. His body quivers and he struggles for air. Tom opens his eyes and Nik stands over him. He squats down and grabs Tom by the hair, lifting his head from the floor. Tom clenches his jaw and breathes sharp breaths through his teeth.

"Maybe next time, when I give Irina clear instructions, they will be followed." Nik pushes Tom's head back to the floor. Tom slams his eyes shut and concentrates on slowing his breathing. *Fucking impossible.*

A door slams and quiet settles around him. All he can hear is his own breathing as it shudders from his mouth. Pain throbs and burns relentlessly on his raw skin. He opens his eyes and the room spins and morphs around him. Nausea sloshes in his gut and tingles erupt at the back of his throat.

Fuck.

He heaves and vomits on the floor, his face resting in the puddle. It makes him vomit again, the acid burns his throat and his eyes prick with tears. With everything he can muster, he shuffles backwards against the opposite wall. Moans escape his mouth involuntarily and he clenches his hands into fists.

The sedatives were a fucking waste of time.

21

ISABELLA

The forks and spoons jangle as Isabella slams the cutlery drawer shut. *He actually did confiscate the knives.* She pulls open a cupboard and eyes the drinking glasses. *I could smash one and take a shard.*

"What are you doing?"

Isabella throws a glance at the doorway. "Whatever I want?"

Nik smiles and strolls to the worktop and leans on it. He folds his hands together under his chin. "You are cute when you are being witty."

"Whatever." She slams the cupboard shut and glares at Nik. "I was searching for a knife."

"For?"

"So I could stab you in the jugular."

"I see."

Isabella drops her eyes to his shirt. "What's all over you?"

Nik smiles without looking down at his shirt. "Dirt."

"Dirt?"

"Yes.."

You've been with Tom. Isabella raises her eyebrows. "What made you dirty?"

"I have been tending to some... business." He smiles again and jiggles his eyebrows up and down.

Isabella scoffs and stomps out of the kitchen and down the hallway. She flings open her bedroom door and doesn't bother shutting it. *He'll follow me anyway.*

She walks to her window and stares down at the concrete bunker where Tom is being kept. Her stomach clenches and her throat aches.

"Maybe next time I instruct you to do something, you will do it."

Isabella turns as Nik walks in, puts one foot up on the blanket box and leans on his knee.

"What?"

"You did not carry your job out as instructed yesterday."

"I killed him for you. Didn't I?"

"You failed to mark him. As instructed."

Isabella purses her lips. "I don't do that anymore."

"You do if I tell you to." Nik whips his tablet out from under his shirt and taps the screen. He throws it on the bed and nods at it.

Isabella leans over and picks it up. A hole opens in her chest and she holds her breath. The ache sitting in her throat ignites.

She watches as Tom thrashes on the ground while Nik holds a red-hot branding iron. Heat creeps up her neck and sweat dribbles down her back. *Jesus Christ.* He stomps on Tom and jabs the iron on his skin. Isabella's knees buckle and she drops to the floor. Her eyes are glued to the screen. Nik pushes the iron down hard with both hands before releasing it. Tom jerks and she sees the pain ripple through his body.

She drops the tablet and lurches forward onto her hands and knees. She coughs and gasps as a wail builds and escapes her mouth. She wraps her arms around her middle and rests her forehead on the floor. She wails louder, squeezing every last ounce of pain and terror out. Her own scar aches in response.

"Irina." Nik's hand rests on her back.

She straightens and pushes him away. He falls onto his backside and she lunges at him, straddling his waist as he did to her the evening before. But instead of kissing his neck she punches his face and his head jerks back. He grunts and grabs her wrists. She wriggles until she has a knee on his stomach. She pushes down, moving her hips to pound into his stomach with her bent knee. Air whooshes out of his mouth and he growls at her as he thrusts his body upward.

Isabella topples off him and he scrambles on top of her, pinning her to the floor.

"You silly girl. You think acting this way will help Tom?"

She sobs, pushing against Nik and getting nowhere. The pain in her chest and throat is too much and she has no fight left. She goes limp, the only part of her body moving is her chest as she heaves in air and pushes out her pain.

"Right now he is in immense agony, Irina. Because of you."

Because of me.

"Do you remember when you were burned? The pain lasted days, yes?"

She closes her eyes as tears push their way out from under her eyelids. Hot breath hits her face as Nik leans over her, his mouth hovers over hers. She opens her eyes and presses her mouth closed. Her body trembles beneath Nik and she stares into his eyes, refusing to blink.

"I branded Tom with the number three sixty." Nik runs a hand down Isabella's face, stopping at her neck and pushing against her throat. She squeaks and concentrates on breathing. "It's a pity the vision has no sound. You could have heard him howl and scream like the weak piece of rubbish he is."

Isabella's nostrils flare and she pushes against Nik, getting nowhere. He loosens the grip around her neck and slides his hand down, resting it on her chest.

"So, Irina. Here is how it is going to work. Tomorrow you and I will be leaving for two days. I have another job for you. This time I will escort you personally."

She drops her head to the side and closes her eyes.

"We may even have time for sightseeing."

"Fuck you."

"Perhaps. If there is time. But know this… if you do not carry out my instructions to the letter. Tom's punishment is on your head." Nik kisses her closed lips and she squirms. "Is that clear?"

"Yes."

"If you thought the branding was horrific, you do not want to defy me again."

Nik releases her and stands up.

Isabella rolls onto her side and curls into a ball. She pushes her hand against her stomach, over her own scar. The pain of her branding flashes in her mind. *I can never forget.*

"You held the iron on him for too long," she mumbles.

"Pardon me?"

Isabella turns her face to him. "You held the iron on his skin longer than necessary."

"Correct." He grins and runs his tongue over his teeth. "It was particularly satisfying."

"Take me to him."

Nik chuckles and walks to the door. "Goodnight Irina."

Isabella lies on the floor, staring at the ruffles around the bottom of her bed. Tom's broken, jerking body replays over in her mind and the pain in her chest throbs. She wants to cry but has nothing left inside her. Emptiness is all she feels.

She pulls herself off the floor and wanders to the window, pressing her hand against it. She glares down at the bunker and bites on her lip, moments later she tastes blood.

A soft knock echoes through the room. Isabella turns and

frowns. She creeps over and rests her ear and mouth against the door. "Who is it?"

"Sascha." His voice is low and urgent.

Isabella opens the door and says nothing.

Sascha looks up and down the hallway before pulling Isabella through the door.

"Tom needs you." He holds a finger to his lips and Isabella nods.

Her heart quivers and she follows him as he hurries down the hall. The house is dark and silent. They get to the front door and Sascha turns to her.

"Same as yesterday. We stay against house at all times."

Isabella nods.

They scurry down the side of the house and across the lawn. Isabella glances up at the mansion as they reach the bunker. *Dark.*

Sascha opens the door and pushes her inside. "Wait. I must divert camera feed to old vision." He sits and drops a small bag beside him that Isabella hadn't noticed him carrying.

"What's that?"

Sascha looks at the bag and back to Isabella, his face rigid. "Dressings and medication."

Isabella swallows and nods.

"I will be with him for next forty-eight hours. I will help him as much as I can."

"Nik will be away. With me."

Sascha nods. "Yes. And others always party when he is away. They leave me to do all work."

"You'll look after him?"

"I will do my best."

Isabella hops from one foot to the other and looks down the dark stairs.

"Okay. Let us go." Sascha picks the small bag up and slings it over his shoulder.

Isabella follows him down the stairs, her heart pounds against her ribcage. Sascha opens the door and stands back to let her in.

She sees Tom, his face is hidden between his arms and his body is shaking. She skids to her knees next to him and slides her hands beneath his head. "Tom."

Tom jumps and opens his eyes. He blinks a couple of times.

"I'm here. I'm sorry." Isabella drops her face against his and cries.

Tom claws at the front of her shirt and holds her against him. "Iz…" He sucks in a breath and drops his head into her lap.

She runs her hands into his hair.

"I must dress your burn. It will hurt."

Tom makes a sound somewhere between a moan and a grunt as Sascha lifts his shirt.

Isabella cradles his head in her lap and strokes his face. She sees the burn on his skin, angry and blistered. Her gut pangs and bile rises in her throat. *I will rip Nik's fucking face off.* The area around the burn is red and swollen.

Sascha produces a soaked cloth and presses it against the burn. Tom jumps and moans against Isabella's stomach.

"What are you doing to him?"

"It is a cloth I soaked in ice water."

"He's in pain," Isabella glares at Sascha before softening her eyes. *It isn't his fault.*

"I know. I am trying. Please." Sascha drags the bag closer and rummages through it with his free hand. He pulls out a bottle of pills and hands it to Isabella. "Get two out and make him take them. They are strong painkillers. They will also help him to sleep."

Isabella takes the bottle and shakes two pills free. Sascha hands her some water.

"Give them to him while I dress burn." He pulls the cloth away and Tom pants against Isabella's body, the warmth of his breath comforts her.

"Tom?" He grabs her hand and squeezes. "Tom, I need to give you these."

Tom groans as Sascha dabs clear ointment on his blistered burn. His muscles tense and he trembles. "Fuck," he mumbles into her stomach.

"Look at me." She dips her face to his and he opens his eyes. His usually bright green eyes are dull and full of pain. She holds two tablets against his mouth. "Take these for me."

He opens his mouth and she pushes the tablets in. "Drink." She tips water into his mouth and he swallows. He drops his head back into her lap.

Sascha tapes a gauze bandage over the burn and gently slides Tom's shirt back down.

Isabella gazes at Sascha. "Where do you get this stuff?" She nods at the bag.

Sascha smiles and zips it up. "My wife is nurse. I tell her what has happened, and she gets me what I need."

Isabella smiles at Sascha. "Thank you."

Sascha nods. "I will leave you for little while. But you should get back soon. If Nik wakes and finds us here…"

"I know. Thank you."

"Make him drink more water."

Tom makes a noise, almost like a chuckle. "So bossy," he mumbles.

"Sascha?"

Sascha stops at the door but doesn't turn around.

"When I get back from wherever Nik is taking me. We will talk about what you need."

Sascha bows his head for a second before nodding. "Thank you."

Isabella looks at the closed door a moment before Tom grips her hands. She looks down at him.

"Hey." She smiles and swallows down the sobs threatening in her throat.

"I told you to run." He keeps his head in her lap.

"And I told you we leave together."

Tom grumbles something Isabella can't understand and she lets out an involuntary giggle. "Shut up, Tom."

Tom relaxes against her, becoming heavier in her lap. *The pills are working.*

"I thought you were… here to comfort… me." His words come out between sharp breaths.

"I am. Go to sleep. You need rest." She strokes her thumb along his cheek and he nestles against her body. Her sobs win the battle and she sniffles as tears wet her cheeks,

"Don't cry." He pulls her hands to his mouth and kisses them.

The door opens and Sascha gestures Isabella to the door. "Quickly. You need to get back. Erik is on his way."

"What? Why? Shouldn't he be sleeping?" Adrenaline spikes through her blood and her breathing hastens.

A loud crash from up the stairs starts Isabella's heart. She looks down at Tom who has fallen asleep in her lap. "Shit."

Sascha looks up the stairs and back to her. "There is a storeroom just here to left." He jerks his head. "Get in and stay there."

Isabella slides out from under Tom's head, placing him gently on the floor. She runs to the storeroom and squashes herself inside. It's unusually warm and Isabella realises the heat is coming from the discarded branding iron, lying on the cold concrete floor. She swallows the acid at the back of her tongue and holds her breath.

Sascha and Erik argue as they stomp down the stairs.

"On ne pisknul." Sascha's voice is insistent.

He hasn't made a peep…

"Mozhno li doveryat' Sasha?"

Can Sascha be trusted? Isabella smirks to herself despite the situation she finds herself in. *He can be trusted by Tom and me...*

A thud against the storeroom door makes Isabella step backward and her leg brushes the hot iron. She winces and sucks air through clenched teeth.

"Ty mne ne nravish'sya Ne day mne povoda prichinit' tebe bol'."

Isabella rests a hand against the door as Erik threatens to hurt Sascha.

Shit.

It feels like hours pass before Sascha opens the storeroom door a fraction. "He is gone."

Isabella slides out through the door. "Erik said he doesn't like you?"

"No. He does not. But I do not like him either so..." Sascha shrugs and gives Isabella a small smile.

She moves to go back to Tom and Sascha stops her.

"You should go. It is too dangerous. Erik is drunk and who knows if he may return." Sascha rests his hand on her arm. "Besides, Tom will be sleeping for some hours."

Isabella nods. "You'll take care of him?" Her voice wavers.

"You have my word."

22

TOM

A crash on the floor beside Tom's head snaps his eyes open. The cellar wobbles and slides into focus. A tray of food is beside him and alongside that, a pair of boots.

Tom peers up into the snarling face of Marat.

"Eat."

He turns and marches out and Tom stays still. The pain in his side is intense. A throbbing burn unlike anything he has ever felt before. It shortens his breathing but he reaches across and pulls the tray towards him. Leaning up on one elbow he tries to ignore the pain and heat radiating from his side. "God damn it."

Potatoes and some sort of poultry sits in the tray next to a lump of mashed peas. *At least it isn't cabbage.* He pushes the tray away as the nausea swells in his gut. He drops back to the floor and stares at the opposite wall.

The door opens again and Tom closes his eyes. "I'm sleeping."

"It is me."

Tom opens his eyes and watches as Sascha picks the tray up and replaces it with a bottle of water.

"That is last you will see of Marat and Erik for two days."

Tom leans back up on his elbow and takes deep breaths to try and quell the pain. "Why?"

"Nik has taken Isabella away with him, so others will leave everything to me."

Tom's pulse jumps. "Where to? Why?"

"A job."

"Fuck." Tom gulps water.

Sascha falls onto his backside next to Tom. "May I see your wound?"

Tom nods and Sascha lifts his shirt. Tom frowns at the white bandage. "When did that get there?"

"You do not remember last night?"

Tom stares at the wall and blinks. He feels Isabella's hands on his face and his head in her lap. "Iz."

"Yes. She was here with you. I dressed burn and gave you more painkillers."

"You're going to turn me into some kind of addict, Sash."

Sascha grins. "No. Only two a day from now on." He pauses. "Unless…"

Tom nods and gulps more water. "Unless."

"I will bring you better food."

"I'm not that hungry." Tom stops and takes in a few deep breaths.

"You must eat."

Tom rolls his eyes. "You and Iz make a good pair."

Sascha smiles. "I like her."

"She's quite likable."

"She said we will talk about helping me."

"Why wait?" Tom shifts to try and sit up but the pain is too much and he slumps back to the floor.

"Well. You need rest."

"I'm also bored shitless. Give me something to think about." He bites the side of his cheek to try and relieve the pain shooting through his body.

Sascha turns to face Tom. "I need to get out. Like Irina did. I want to defect."

Tom watches Sascha as he fiddles with his shoelace, his eyes on Tom's.

"Why?"

"Because I do not want this life."

"But how did you end up here?"

"My wife and I do not have much. I needed money for food and rent."

"Go on."

"Nikolay offered me delivery job when I was only twenty-one."

"Delivering what?"

"At first it was canned goods. Imported food."

"And then?"

"And then he decided he could trust me and gave me other jobs."

"Such as?"

"I became his chauffeur. His errand boy. His personal assistant." Sascha stops and blows a breath out. "I have seen him beat people. Maim people. Kill people. He trusts me. But he makes me sick."

"Have you tried to leave before?"

"Yes."

"What happened?"

"He took my wife. Held her for three days and threatened to kill her."

"I see."

"And now there is no one above him. He is in charge. He is worse."

"I bet."

"So I know Irina got out. It is possible."

"That was different."

"How?"

"They actually sent her out, Sascha. On a plane. She got out because she never returned as she was supposed to."

"But…" Sascha's face falls and he chews on his lip. "My wife. I am scared that one day they will kill her because of me."

"Nik trusts you now?"

"He said if I tried to leave again he would cut my wife's throat. So, I have given him no reason not to trust me." Sascha widens his eyes and leans closer to Tom. "I have helped you. I have tried to make it easier for you. I brought her to you."

Tom closes his eyes and nods. "You have."

"Please."

Tom stares at a spot on the floor. "I need a phone."

"A phone?"

"Yes, Sascha. That thing you use to talk to people who aren't with you."

"I know, but… It will not work in this room. You are underground."

"Well, Sascha. You want my help. I need to use a phone."

Sascha's eyes drift towards the open door. "Okay."

"Okay?" Tom moves to sit up and again the pain pushes him back to the floor. He winces and sucks on his bottom lip.

"I will take you upstairs and let you use phone."

"You're serious?"

"I told you. I need to get to safety. Take my wife away from danger. She is pregnant."

"How pregnant?"

"A few months. But I want to get her out before baby comes."

"Jesus, Sash. You don't want to make this easy do you?"

Sascha stands. "I must go and take care of other things. I will return with painkillers and food. You must eat."

"Yeah, yeah." Tom flops back to the floor and stares at the ceiling.

"Tom."

Tom's eyes flutter open and his head is heavy. "Fuck Sash. Whatever pills you keep giving me are making me feel half dead."

"You prefer pain?" Sascha smiles.

"No."

"Okay. Eat this. And take these." He hands Tom a sandwich and two more painkillers.

"A sandwich?"

"It is cheese."

"A cheese sandwich." Tom sits up and stops short as the burn intensifies and makes him dizzy. "Shit."

"You do not like cheese?"

"I'd prefer a steak." Tom steadies himself and takes a bite of the sandwich. "Not that I want to sound ungrateful."

Sascha produces a ring of keys and sticks one into Tom's ankle cuffs. They come apart and Tom kicks them off. He rotates his ankles and relishes the feeling of blood warming his joints.

"Give me your hands."

Tom takes the last two bites of his sandwich and holds his hands out. Sascha unlocks the cuffs and they swing open. Tom rotates his hands out of them and rubs at his raw wrists. He flexes them back and forth.

"You have no idea how good that feels."

"I got you phone. It is upstairs. Can you walk?"

"Excellent question."

Sascha holds his hand out and Tom grabs it, bracing himself

against the wall with his other. He tries to lift himself off the floor but the pain in his burn, coupled with his raw ankles halt his effort. "Well, fuck." He drops back to his backside and takes a breath.

"Are you okay?"

"I will be." *I have to be.* "C'mon. Let's go again." He grabs Sascha's hand and pushes his other hand against the wall. He bites his tongue and stands up. Every joint in his body creaks and crackles. His burn sends heat and razor-sharp pain cascading down to his stomach and legs. He bends forward and puts both hands on his knees.

"Tom?"

"Yep. Peachy." He stands up and nods at the door. "After you." He holds his breath and hobbles after Sascha. He looks up the stairs and counts them. "Thirteen steps." *It may as well be five hundred.*

"Can you make it?"

"Yep." Tom grabs the splintered handrail and takes the first step. The effort is excruciating and he leans against the wall. "Fuck!"

Sascha jumps and skips back down three steps to him. "Let me help you."

"Nope. I can do it. Just go up and keep watch. If we get sprung I can't exactly dash away."

Sascha scurries to the top and Tom follows, step by step and with a breather on each one.

Ten minutes later Tom reaches the top. Something stabs pain

through his burn and he doubles over and moans. Liquid dribbles down his side and he dabs at his shirt. "What the fuck?"

"Oh no." Sascha lifts his shirt. "Your blister has split."

"Fucking delightful." Tom sees a chair and lowers himself into it.

"I must dress this and clean it. It will not be pleasant."

"Just give me the phone." Tom holds a hand out.

Sascha picks up a mobile and hands it to him. "This is yours. When we get out, you keep it."

"When we get out, huh? You're optimistic."

"Should I not be?"

"No. You should." Tom punches Martha's number into the screen and waits.

"This is Judith."

"Martha."

"Tom! What the hell is going on? Where are you? I haven't been able to contact you or Isabella in days. Are you alright? What's happened?"

Tom scratches his cheek and looks at the ceiling. "Are you done?" Sascha peels the bandage off Tom's burn and he grimaces, sucking in a loud breath. "Fuck."

"What are you doing? You sound hurt."

"Perceptive. That's because I am."

"Jesus Christ, Tom. What the hell happened?"

"A few things."

"Starting with?"

"Well, we got a track put on us at the border. I ditched the car and got a new one. Isabella ran into a childhood friend called Nikolay, who turned out to be the new Damir, we were captured and I've been beaten and branded." Tom stops to wince as Sascha dribbles saline onto his split blister. *That fucking hurts.*

"This is no time for humour, Tom."

"I'm not laughing, Martha. Isabella's been forced to kill targets for Nikolay and I got branded with a red-hot iron." Sascha dabs it dry and Tom trembles as adrenaline spikes to deal with the pain.

Martha clears her throat. "Jesus."

"He hasn't been overly helpful."

"So how are you calling me?"

"I've made a friend." Tom's eyes slide to Sascha as he reaches for the burn ointment and a new bandage.

He smiles and holds the ointment up. "Ready?"

Tom nods. "Hit me."

"What?" Martha's irritation is palpable.

"Not you. My… new friend wants our help."

"To do what?"

"Get out of Russia."

"And in turn he helps you I'm assuming?"

"But of course." Sascha dabs ointment onto Tom's open blister and he nearly jumps out of the seat. "Fuck me!"

"Sorry."

"Tom, what the hell are you doing?"

"My friend is… helping me."

Martha huffs. "Give me the basics."

"I'm being held in a cellar somewhere."

"And?"

"And Isabella is being made to stay with Nikolay... and I swear he touches her I'll rip his arms off."

"Yes, very admirable Tom. But more to the point. What can I do for you right now?"

"I need paperwork and British passports for Sascha and his wife. He will get the details you need and send them to you. Yes?"

Martha sighs into the phone. "This is risky, Tom."

"I don't have many other choices right now, Martha."

"Are you going to get yourself killed?"

"No. And despite my valiant efforts at being beaten to death, I'm still alive. So, yay me."

Sascha pushes a clean bandage over Tom's burn and tapes it.

Tom bites his lip and scrunches his face up. "So look out for Sascha's details. I'll call again when I can."

"You expect me to just relax and soldier on?"

"Yes. You know what they say... keep calm and carry on." Tom pauses and inhales, holding it for a moment. "Relax okay? Iz and I are coming home. I promise."

"I know you believe that but—"

"But nothing. I'll call again when I can." He is about to end the call and remembers James. "Oh, and if you're chatting to James... tell him I said it's okay to let you in on the job I gave him."

"You gave him a job?"

"Yes."

"To do?"

"Ask him. But his answer may complicate things."

"Complicate things?"

"Yep. Chat soon." Tom drops the phone onto the card table and leans over it. The pain throughout his body is making him nauseous. "Sash?"

"Yes?"

"Do you have a bucket?"

"A bucket?"

"Cheese sandwich, incoming."

23

ISABELLA

Isabella sits in the passenger seat of Nik's luxury Aurus Senat. It's been two hours already and the early start makes her grumpy. She has one foot crossed over her knee and her toes tap the glove box.

"If you don't mind, Irina. That is premium leather."

Isabella turns her head and glares at Nik, before kicking the glove box harder. And again. "Sorry, Nik? What was that?"

Nik purses his lips and shakes his head. "I thought you loved Tom?"

"I do."

"Then, behave." Nik pulls the car to the side of the road and grabs Isabella around the throat.

She kicks the glovebox again. "What're you gonna do to him this time, Nik?" *How much worse could you possibly get?*

"Some precise cuts and further burns may teach you lesson.

No?" Nik stares into her eyes, his clenched teeth on show. "You do not want me to ruin that oh so handsome face. Do you?"

Isabella drops her foot to the floor of the car and turns her head away.

"Good girl. Now you are listening."

Isabella looks out the window and ignores him.

"And while we are on subject. If you try to run or disappear, for which you have shown talent in past." Nik pauses and his breath hits her ear. "Look at me, Irina." Isabella pushes herself into the seatback and glares at Nik. "As I said, you try anything smart. I will kill Tom. Personally." He strokes her cheek and neck. "Do you understand?"

Isabella controls her breathing and ignores the tremble building through her body.

"Yes?" Nik raises his eyebrows.

"I understand."

"Good girl." Nik moves back to his seat and begins to drive.

Isabella stares ahead of them but doesn't see anything. Her mind wanders to the English countryside, and a white cottage with a thatched roof. *He promised to take me back there.*

Half an hour passes with nothing spoken before Isabella's stomach grumbles. She slaps her hand over it.

"We shall stop soon."

"Why are you driving anyway?"

"Excuse me?"

"Shouldn't someone of your... status." Isabella rolls her eyes. "Be driven places?"

"Yes. I should. But… I felt this trip would be better just two of us."

"Is that right?"

"Yes. That is right."

"You're going to be bitterly disappointed."

"Perhaps." Nik shrugs.

"Where are we going?"

"Saint Petersburg."

"We're driving the whole way?"

"We are."

"It's like seven hours, Nik. What the hell?"

"You do not like flying. Do you?"

Isabella pauses. "Well. No."

"So I wanted to spare you stress."

"You wanted to…" Isabella leans across the console and squints at Nik. "You're taking me to kill someone."

"Correct."

"So, I'm gonna be stressed." She flops back into her seat. "Idiot."

"The less stress you are under the better. This job is complicated."

"What the fuck does that mean?"

Nik nods at a briefcase on the backseat. "Take envelope out and read papers."

Isabella yanks the large yellow envelope out and looks inside. She pulls out a photograph of a woman in a tailored suit and three pages of notes.

"Annika Durov."

"Yes."

Isabella reads the first few lines of accompanying notes. "A political figure? Are you crazy?"

"No. She is making things difficult for connections in other parties."

"Your friends."

"Associates. Either way. She needs to go."

"Do you understand what you're asking of me?"

"Yes."

Isabella's heart convulses and she massages her throat as acid singes the back of her tongue. "I can't," she whispers.

"You can. And you will."

"Nik, please don't do this to me."

"You want me to cancel contract because you do not want to do it?"

"I want you to stop being a monster."

"I am not monster."

"Bullshit." Isabella folds her arms and closes her eyes, resting her head against the headrest.

"Do you remember when we would draw pictures in dirt?"

Images of a dusty garden and sticks being poked and swirled in the dirt appear behind Isabella's closed eyes. She adjusts herself in the seat and shakes her head. "Stop it Nik."

"And we would laugh and draw pictures of other children in village?"

"I said stop."

"Why?"

Because it hurts.

"Because, that Nik is dead." Isabella opens her eyes and looks at Nik, who is chewing on his lip. "You killed him."

"I did not kill him. He was taken."

"He didn't have to leave."

"You do what you need to, to survive."

Isabella opens her mouth but slams it shut again. *Like me.* She curls into a ball on the seat.

"Now you understand."

Yes.

ISABELLA WAKES TO THE SEAT BELT RETRACTING ACROSS HER chest and a warm hand brushing her arm.

"Would you like some food?"

She sits up and looks out the window. They are parked outside a restaurant. "Where are we?"

"Veliky Novgorod." Nik looks at the restaurant in front of them. "I used to come here for vacation as child. My family would eat here often."

Isabella thinks of Oksanna and smiles. "Does it measure up to your mother's cooking?"

"No. But nothing does." He opens his car door and steps out.

I guess I have to eat.

Isabella follows him inside and they are seated near the back beside a window.

They order and Nik leans back in his chair. "That is all you are eating?"

"I'm not hungry." The grumble in her belly threatens to expose her lie. *I don't want to dine with you.*

"Why must you be difficult?"

Isabella narrows her eyes at Nik and leans forward. "Are you kidding me?"

"No."

"You kidnapped me and Tom. Locked him away somewhere. You are making me *kill* people for you and your... people. And if I refuse you maim Tom."

"Yes."

"And you're asking why I'm difficult?" Isabella taps the side of her head. "You've lost your mind."

"Do you realise, Irina, that if I was serving my... people... I would have had you killed. You are a wanted woman. You betrayed whole Organisation. You should be dead."

Isabella swallows and stares at Nik.

"You should be thanking me."

Isabella scoffs and drops her face into her hands.

"Would you prefer I torture and kill you? As was order placed upon your retrieval?"

She traces her finger along the embroidery in the tablecloth and refuses to answer. The waitress arrives with their food.

"Ah." Nik sweeps his hands out as the waitress puts their

plates in front of them. "Here we are. Eat up like good girl and we will be on way."

"Stop calling me that."

"What?"

"A good girl."

"You are not a good girl?"

"I'm stabbing people to death, Nik. No. I am not a good girl." Isabella shoves food in her mouth and chews so she doesn't have to keep talking to him.

Nik chuckles and sips his water. "So feisty." He leans forward and grabs her hand, stroking the back of it with his thumb. "I look forward to seeing how feisty you can get."

Isabella pulls her hand back and stands up, her chair hits the floor. She throws her napkin on the table.

"I'll be in the car."

NIK ROLLS THE CAR TO A STOP OUTSIDE THE FOUR SEASONS Hotel in Saint Petersburg. He jumps out of the car and speaks with the valet.

Isabella sits in her seat and folds her arms. She eyes the clock on the dashboard. *One forty-seven.*

Her door opens and Nik holds out his hand. "Come."

Isabella rolls her eyes and gets out of the car, refusing Nik's hand. She stomps into the lobby and leans against a large marble pillar. She watches as Nik speaks with the reception and is handed a card.

He walks to Isabella. "The valet will bring bags. Come with me."

She pushes herself off the pillar with one foot and walks behind Nik.

He stops and turns. "Now now, my wife should walk alongside me. Afterall, we are equals." He smiles and grabs her hand. He squeezes her fingers. Hard. And a glint flashes across his eyes.

Isabella inhales through her nose and walks with him. She follows him into the lift and stands against the back wall, crossing her arms. The doors slide shut and they are alone.

Nik turns and presses himself against her, his hands planted above her head. "Your job is tomorrow morning. So perhaps you can relax this evening. If you require my assistance with that…" He brushes her nose with his.

Isabella stares straight into his eyes and pushes her mouth against his. "You make me fucking sick."

He grins against her lips before running his hand from the nape of her neck up into her hair and kissing her.

Isabella pushes Nik to the chest with both hands but he doesn't budge. She holds her breath and keeps her mouth closed, but Nik continues as though there is no obstacle.

"You need to breathe sometime, Irina," he whispers against her mouth.

The lift dings and the doors open.

Isabella exhales as Nik pulls away from her. "Well, saved by bell, eh?"

Isabella's heartbeat is in overdrive and she pushes past Nik and sees that the floor they are on has a number of doors down the hallway. *This can't be right.*

"Are you sure this is our floor?" *Surely you booked yourself the penthouse.*

"Yes. Alas, they only had room with one queen bed left." Nik shrugs. "So inconvenient." He slides his hand into the small of her back and walks her forward. "I am sure we can... adapt."

"You're a lying piece of shit."

"So much anger."

24

TOM

Tom is hunched over his arms on the card table. The burn throbs and prickles through his skin and down his body. *Is it hot in here?*

He sits up and wants nothing more than to stretch out his arms and back, but the burn stops him short. He stands, hobbles to the filthy window and peers out. The dusk light is soft with mauve and pink lighting up the sky. His eyes drift to the looming, dark mansion at the other end of the yard. He bites down hard on his lip as a shadow moves into view from the side of the house. Tom's pulse reacts until he realises it's Sascha. He shuffles back to his seat and falls into it. Moments later the door opens.

"It is me." Sascha is carrying two cardboard takeaway containers.

"What have you got?"

"You wanted steak?" Sascha drops the boxes onto the card table and shuts the door.

"You cooked?"

Sascha laughs. "No. I cannot cook. This is UberEATS."

"You have UberEATS here?"

"Of course. We are not savages." Sascha grins.

Tom laughs and slides the box towards himself. He opens it and is enveloped with the scent of steak and potatoes. His mouth waters and he grabs the plastic cutlery.

"You really are my hero, Sash."

"Eat slowly. You have not eaten properly in days."

Tom pops the first bite into his mouth. "Okay, Mum."

Sascha chuckles and cuts his own meal. "I look forward to being parent." He chews and swallows. "Not yours though. No offence."

"None taken." Tom grabs the water Sascha brought and opens it. "Is this your first child?"

"Da." Sascha smiles. "It was not exactly planned but I am so happy."

Tom nods and swallows another bite. His gut twists and he puts his fork down.

"Are you okay?" Sascha raises a concerned eyebrow.

"Yep. Just... "Tom runs a finger around the neck of his shirt. "Is it hot in here?"

"No." Sascha looks down at his coat and back to Tom. "It is quite cold."

"Maybe it's the effort of eating." Tom shrugs and picks up his fork.

"I told you… slowly."

Tom rolls his eyes and smiles through a mouthful.

"So, you can stay out of cellar until they come back. Erik and Marat will not be around."

Tom nods.

"There is a bathroom through that door but please do not shower or they will know."

"It's okay. I'm getting used to my own unpleasantness." *I'm actually not.*

Sascha reaches into his bag and pulls out some papers. "I got what you asked for." He slides them across to Tom.

Tom looks at the papers.

"Tom?"

"Yeah?"

"Is Isabella love of your life?"

Tom's gut pangs and he looks at Sascha. "Why are you asking me that?"

"Because my wife is love of *my* life."

"I should hope so."

"I need you to understand lengths I will go, to keep her and my unborn child safe."

Tom looks at Sascha a moment and says nothing. *I understand.*

Sascha smiles. "You do not have to answer. I can see that she is."

"How?"

"Look at you. What you have endured for her."

"I haven't had much choice, Sash."

"No, but. I am right. No?"

"Yes," Tom mumbles through another mouthful.

"So… you will understand why I am doing what I am doing."

Tom watches Sascha for a moment. "Phone?"

Sascha pulls out the phone and gives it to Tom. He grabs the phone as a wave of nausea hits him. He slaps his hand to his stomach and sucks in a breath.

"Tom?"

"I'm fine." He ignores the sweat dripping down his back and dials Martha's number.

"This is Judith." Martha's voice brings him a moment of comfort and the image of her bringing him warm milk at bedtime flits past.

"It's me." Tom sucks in another breath as dizziness cocoons him.

"Tom?"

"Yep."

"Are you alright?"

"Yeah…" He shakes his head and sips his water.

"Tom?"

"Yes. Sorry. I'm going to send you Sascha's information... and his wife…" Tom reads the birth certificate. "Mischa's too."

"Right." Martha waits and Tom breathes a few more breaths. "Tom? What are you doing?"

"Nothing. Just…" The nausea eases and he sips more water. "I ate food."

"Is that a new activity?"

Tom grins. "No. It's just been a few days."

"Are you alright?"

"Amazing." He rests his head on the table top.

"Hmmm."

"Have you spoken to James?"

"Yes."

"And?"

"And… he said Malcolm hasn't done anything weird."

"Malcolm's always doing something weird."

"Agreed. Just not more than usual I think he means."

"But he told you about the money and the car?"

"Yes. I'm onto it."

"Lucky Malcolm."

"If he has done what you are implying… his number is up."

"He's done it. It's the only explanation."

"I would agree. Anyway, send me the information. I'll get it done."

"Okay. I'll do it now."

"And Isabella?"

"She's…"

"She's?"

"Away at the moment. With Nikolay."

"Another job?"

"I assume so."

"You need to get yourselves out of there."

"Thanks for the tip."

"Tom…"

"Talk soon." Tom hangs up as sweat trickles down his face. "What the fuck…" He takes his shirt off and throws it on the floor. His burn erupts in white hot pain and he grits his teeth. *Jesus.*

"Tom?"

"It's too hot in here."

"No it's—"

"Sascha! I'm on fucking fire."

Sascha leaps off his chair and puts his hand to Tom's forehead.

"Again with the Mum thing." Tom slumps onto the table.

"You are burning up."

"Newsflash." Tom grabs the bottle of water and pours it over his head.

"Mischa."

Tom looks up as Sascha speaks on the phone.

"U nego zhar."

I have a fever. Yes.

"Seychas?" Sascha's voice is shrill and his knuckles turn white as he grips the phone.

Now? Now what? Tom's heart speeds up.

"No my ne gotovy."

We aren't ready for what? Tom moans against the table. *God, I feel like death.* A shiver ripples through his body and he wraps his arms around himself. *Fucking freezing.*

Sascha mumbles something into the phone Tom can't hear. He sits up and nausea along with dizziness takes hold. Tom blinks and tries to focus on the table in front of him. It's blurry and appears to slide to the left. He shakes his head again before toppling off his chair.

"TOM?"

Tom blinks. Sascha is leaning over him. Something cold is on Tom's neck. He tries to sit up and fails, falling back onto the floor.

"Can you hear me, Tom?"

Tom nods.

"We have to go."

Go? Go where?

"Go…" Tom takes a breath and tries again. "Go where?"

"Somewhere safe. You need medicine."

Tom shakes his head and grips Sascha's arm, sitting himself up. The room spins and he closes his eyes and waits for it to pass.

"I'm not going anywhere without Iz."

"I will bring her to you."

"Sascha." Tom breathes in and out a few times and looks at Sascha. "Are you insane?"

"No, but… You are running high fever. If you don't get help it will be very very bad."

Tom grabs Sascha by the shirt front. "I am not leaving without Iz."

"Then you will develop sepsis and die."

"Sep… what?"

"You have infection. You need medicine I cannot give you."

"We can wait."

"No we cannot."

"Sascha—"

"No!" Sascha's voice is loud and firm.

Tom blinks and focuses on his face.

"Listen to me. If you refuse to leave you will die in cellar. And what help are you to Isabella then?"

Wait a minute. "And you. Right?"

"Yes. I make no apologies. I need you too. So we leave."

"But they'll kill her." His gut twists again and this time it's not nausea.

"No. I will figure something out."

"You aren't filling me with…" Tom stops and heaves a breath. *Fuck.* "Confidence here, Sash."

"Have I proved you can trust me?"

"Yes."

"Then you must trust me. I will get her out."

Tom leans forward, his head between his knees and concentrates on his breaths. "A soon as they see we're gone they're going to put a bullet in her head."

"I will fix live stream so it is old footage. It will buy enough time for me to get her out."

"Sasha…"

Sascha puts his hand on Tom's shoulder. "Please. You must trust me. Or you are dead with or without their input."

Tom looks up at Sascha. Sweat trickles down the side of his face and he falls back onto the floor.

He's right.

TOM LAYS IN THE BACKSEAT OF SASCHA'S CAR AND SHIVERS. "How… is it I'm wrapped in a… fuck...ing bear skin coat and I'm still freezing." His teeth chatter and he swallows, trying to stop the nausea.

"Fever." Sascha answers, while driving.

"You really are… Captain… Obvious." Tom manages before grabbing the bucket Sascha brought and vomiting into it.

"I tried to keep your wound as clean as possible. I am so sorry."

"Stop fretting. Just… drive, Sash." Tom rests his forearm over his face and closes his eyes.

"We are almost there."

"Please tell me you aren't taking me to the hospital."

"No."

"Or your own house?"

"No. My wife… her parents have a small home just outside city."

"Does Nikolay know about…" Tom stops and takes a breath.

"This house?"

"I do not believe so."

"You better hope so."

Sascha doesn't answer.

"Sash?"

"Da?"

"If Isabella is harmed or... killed because you... took me away. I *will* shoot you in the... head." Tom swallows the acid burning his throat. "Do you understand?"

"Da."

25

ISABELLA

Isabella steps out of the shower and grabs a towel. She presses her ear against the door and hears nothing. *He's still out running.* She pats herself, leaving her skin slightly wet. The fresh cool of the air against her wet skin helps her feel clean against the dirty job she's been tasked with. She drops her towel on the floor.

Opening the door, she scrubs a hand through her wet hair and looks up.

Her gut clenches and she gasps in a breath. Nik is in the armchair on the other side of the bed. He steeples his fingers beneath his nose and watches her. *I should have known.*

Isabella's instincts are to run back to the bathroom and lock herself in but instead she squares her shoulders and glares at him.

"What are you doing here?"

"It is my room too, Irina."

"You said you were going for a run."

Nik shrugs and leans forward over his knees, his eyes run up and down Isabella's body. "I changed my mind."

"You're creepy as fuck." Isabella rummages through her bag.

"You are one who walked out naked."

"Whatever. You can't have it anyway."

"Is that so?"

Isabella grabs a pair of knickers and slides them up her legs and over her hips. "Yep."

Nik stands and in two strides he is in front of Isabella. "You are forgetting I get what I want."

"And you're forgetting I can stab you dead."

"With what?"

"I'll improvise."

Nik traces both hands across her shoulders, meeting in the middle at the dip in her throat. Isabella's pulse thumps in her neck and she tightens her jaw. He pushes lightly and drills his eyes into Isabella's. She stands taller and swallows against his thumbs.

Nik walks into Isabella, forcing her to fall backwards onto the bed. He grabs her hands and pins them either side of her head. "You see how easy that was?"

"For every action there is a consequence, Nik."

Nik runs his lips across Isabella's taut jaw and down her neck. He stops where her pulse thumps. "Where did you learn such philosophy, Irina?"

"Kostya."

"Kostya? How interesting. Kostya was fool." Nik continues drifting his mouth down Isabella's chest.

She holds her breath as involuntary goosebumps pop up. "You're no better."

Nik lifts his face to hers. "How so?"

"I didn't want to give him what he wanted either. But he took it by force."

"Am I hurting you?"

"Not physically."

"But?"

"You make me sick… so…there's that."

Nik pushes his mouth onto hers and she can't close her lips in time. She squirms as his tongue invades her mouth. She waits for the right moment before clamping her teeth together.

Nik rips his mouth away. "Blyad'!" He slaps a hand to his mouth.

Isabella smiles. *Fuck indeed.* She twists out from underneath him and grabs her bag. She runs to the bathroom and locks the door. She slams her palm into the door. "And that is what you call a *consequence*, Nik. Make note."

"Perhaps Tom will also learn from your mistakes, Irina." Nik's voice is muffled against the door.

"If you touch him again, I'll rip your throat out while you sleep." *I am done.*

Silence.

Isabella grabs clothing and gets dressed before opening the door again.

Nik is sitting back in the armchair reading papers. He glances up as she walks in.

"Sit down. I must brief you about your job."

"What?"

"I said sit down. I have ordered room service for dinner."

Isabella frowns and stares at Nik. *What the actual fuck?*

"Please do not make me repeat myself, Irina." Nik doesn't look at her, keeping his eyes on the papers in his hands.

Isabella sits on the bed. "I want to see Tom."

"No."

"Show him to me. Then I'll listen to you."

Nik's eyes flick up from the papers. "And what else will you do for me, Irina?"

"I won't kill you."

Nik smirks. "You have sense of humour. Okay…" He pulls his tablet out of his briefcase and taps the screen. He stares at it a moment, frowning.

Isabella's heart jolts. "What's wrong?"

Nik peers at the screen closer.

"Nik?" *Shit.*

Nik continues to frown and blink at the screen for what feels like a year. Isabella ignores the butterflies in her gut and takes a deep breath. *Please be okay.*

"Ah." He smiles and hands her the tablet. "The wi-fi would not connect."

Isabella takes the tablet and watches Tom sleeping on the floor of the cellar. His body trembles as his arms rest above his head.

I'm so sorry. Tears gather at the corners of her eyes and she blinks to free them.

"That is enough." Nik yanks the tablet from her hands and throws it facedown on the bed. *No! Please.* "Take these." He thrusts papers at her and she takes them, wiping her eyes with her other hand.

"I have a bad feeling about this, Nik."

"She will be at this hotel tomorrow morning for media event." Nik points to the floor.

"Did you hear what I just said?"

"Yes. But I do not care how you *feel*, Irina. You will do your job." Nik juts his chin forward. "You will see on schedule that her event is in Grand Ballroom. She is holding breakfast reception."

"Two hundred guests? Are you insane?" Isabella looks at Nik, her eyes wide and her mouth agape. "What am I gonna do, Nik? Just march up and stab her in the heart in front of all these people?"

Nik shrugs. "She has to use bathroom sometime."

"Fuck you." Isabella leaps off the bed and throws the papers on the floor. " And fuck this. No."

Nik picks his phone up and holds it to his ear. He watches Isabella. "Ah, Marat. YA khochu, chtoby ty otrezal Toma ot ugolka rta do kazhdogo ukha."

Isabella digs her nails into her stomach. "No!"

Nik raises a brow and puts his hand over the phone. "No?"

"Don't cut his face."

"But you do not wish to follow instructions."

"I also don't want Tom cut from mouth to ear."

"And so?"

Isabella sits on the bed again and ignores the vomit threatening to rise. "And so, I'll do your job," she whispers. She swallows and stares out the window at the lights of Saint Petersburg before dropping over her knees and clawing her hands through her hair.

"Ne obrashchayte vnimaniya na Marata. YA soglasen."

You have compliance? Ha.

Isabella sniffles and glares at Nik as he ends his call. "You don't have compliance. I just don't have a choice."

"Same, same." Nik shrugs.

A knock turns Nik's attention from Isabella. He answers the door and pulls a cart loaded with silver cloches inside.

"Dinner is served." Nik sweeps a hand out and smiles at Isabella. "Come. You must eat."

"Not hungry."

"I said you must eat."

Isabella huffs. "Whatever." She can't ignore the mouth-watering scent of beef stew and fresh bread. *I'm starving.*

Isabella looks for a knife. "What am I supposed to butter my bread with?"

"Ah, allow me." Nik pulls a butter knife from under his napkin and butters Isabella's bread. She watches him and chews on the inside of her mouth.

"Are you going to hide all sharp objects from me forever?"

"I believe that is wise."

"And you think a butter knife is sharp?"

"No. But I know your skill. And so it is still dangerous."

Isabella squints at him as he drops the buttered bread on her plate.

He nods at the bread. "You are welcome."

"I didn't thank you."

Nik chuckles and spoons stew into his mouth. "Delicious."

Isabella shoves bread into her mouth and ignores Nik.

I hate you.

Nik lies in the bed reading a book as Isabella emerges from the bathroom. The fresh mint taste in her mouth is soured by the scene before her.

"Guess I'm on the floor." Isabella grabs a pillow.

"Get in the bed, Irina."

"Oh, did I misunderstand? *You're* sleeping on the floor?" Isabella raises her eyebrows and watches Nik.

He closes his book and puts it on the nightstand. "No. I am staying right here." He nods at the pillow next to him. "I said get in. You must sleep well. You have a busy morning."

Isabella clenches her fists and glares at Nik. Her nostrils flare as she breathes heavy breaths in and out.

Nik eyes her up and down and she stands strong, in her knickers and singlet top. He pats the bed next to him. "Well?"

Isabella rips the duvet back and gets in. She turns her back to

Nik and punches her pillow a couple of times. She closes her eyes, knowing full well sleep isn't coming.

A hand slides over her hip and across her stomach. Nik's hot breath hits her neck. "There. Now this is more comfortable than the floor, no?"

Isabella tenses her abdominal muscles as Nik's hand rests against them. She clenches her teeth and goes to rip Nik's hand away before halting and smiling to herself.

Fine. You asked for it.

She glides her hand over the top of Nicks and intertwines her fingers through his. She rolls onto her back and looks into his face. He is up on his elbow and peers down at her. He squeezes the hand laced with hers.

"What is this?"

Isabella slides his hand down her stomach stopping at the top of her knickers. "Isn't this what you want?"

"I did not think we shared this idea."

Isabella shrugs and smiles, lifting her chin so her lips are against his. "Well, I have time to kill. And I'm just so tense."

"Tense?"

"Very." She runs both her hands into his hair, leaving his hand at her knickers. She kisses his mouth and pulls him on top of her. His hand slides under her knickers and she tenses a moment before giggling against his lips. He slides his hand back up and traces her breast, before moving his knees either side of her hips. He pushes himself against her. *Wow. So generous.*

"Wait," Isabella whispers. She drifts her hand down his chest and stomach and into his boxers. She kisses him again and with her other hand, she reaches to her bedside and picks up her hairbrush.

"I knew it was only a matter of time." Nik nuzzles her neck.

"It's been difficult to resist, I must admit."

"Do not resist, Irina. You know where you belong."

Isabella grips the hairbrush tight and pushes the handle into the skin on Nik's neck, right against his pulse. He freezes and plants both hands on the bed, either side of Isabella's shoulders.

"What are you doing?"

Isabella puts her mouth against his ear. "You're a weak piece of shit, Nikolay. And if this was a knife you'd be dead."

She releases him, rolls from beneath his body and out of the bed. Nik heaves in air and grabs the bedsheets in his fists.

Isabella drops her hairbrush on the nightstand and folds her arms. Nik glares at her and she smiles, nodding towards his groin. "Bathroom's free if you need to take care of that."

Nik leaps from the bed and pushes Isabella against the wall. He snarls in her face and rests his hand at the base of her throat.

Isabella holds her breath and stares straight into his eyes. She raises an eyebrow and waits.

"That was mistake, Irina."

"Yes. It was. You should be more careful. Next time it won't be a hairbrush."

Nik pushes his hand harder against her throat and she resists the urge to squirm. He takes some deep breaths and releases her, slamming his hand against the wall.

"I'm not afraid of you. Take what you want. It means nothing to me."

Nik's eyes darken and he grabs Isabella's shoulders. "I will not."

"You will not?"

"That makes me no better than those who raped my mother. I refuse."

Isabella's throat constricts as she remembers Oksanna's warm smile and the love Nik had for his mother. *That poor gentle woman.*

Isabella looks down below his waist and back up. "Like I said, the bathroom's free." She ducks out from under his arm and crawls into bed. "Sweet dreams."

26

TOM

Something pinches the back of Tom's hand and he opens his eyes. He blinks a few times as a room comes into view with shelves and tinned food. He jumps as his heart convulses and he tries to sit up.

"No. Stay still. You are sick." A soft female voice to his right soothes.

He looks at the woman beside him and blinks again to try and focus. His heart is running away from him and his breathing tries to catch up.

"What..." He looks around the room again. *Is this a store-room?* "Where am I?" He lifts the hand that pinches and sees an IV tube connected to a drip. "What the..."

"You are safe. Please. Lie down."

"Iz. Where's Iz?" He flops back down and tries to catch his

breath. The pain in his burn cuts through him and he winces. *What day is it?*

"Sascha will bring her to you."

"No, but… how did I end up here? Where am I?"

"You are in my parents storeroom."

"Storeroom?"

"Yes. They had it built many years ago under house. It is for… unexpected trouble." The woman rolls her eyes and smiles. "It is secret room."

"A secret...room." Tom swallows against his dry throat. And peers up at the bag connected to his IV. "What's in that?"

"Antibiotics. You are very unwell."

"But I need to know where Iz is."

"No. You need to rest."

"I don't remember coming here."

"I would think not. You had such fever. You are lucky you got here when you did."

Panic crawls up his body and he grabs the woman's hand. "They're going to kill her."

"No. Sascha will get her out." The woman pats his hand and places it on the bed.

"But…" Tom grits his teeth and closes his eyes. *I need to go back.* "How long have I been here?"

"Thirteen hours."

Fear grips his body. "What?"

"You were given something to make you sleep. You were in very bad way."

"By who?" *Fuck.*

"Me. I am nurse."

Tom stares at this petite smiling woman who radiates warmth and he tries to stop panicking. He slows his breathing and bites his lip. "Mischa?"

She nods. "Yes. I am Mischa."

Tom tries to sit up again and she gently pushes his shoulder down. "Stay still."

"How long do I need to be on this drip?"

"Another day at least."

"Another day?" Tom slaps a hand over his eyes and groans. "Wait… thirteen hours." *She'll be back soon.* "I need to speak to Sascha."

Mischa observes him a moment and bows her head. "Okay, I will call him for you."

"What time is it?"

"Just after eight in morning."

Tom's gut flips and he hopes Isabella did what he told her to and ran. *She didn't.*

"Are you hungry?"

"No. Yes. I don't know."

Mischa pats his arm and stands up. "I will bring you something to eat."

Tom looks around the tiny room now that his eyes have focused. Rows of shelving line one wall with cans of food and bottled water. On the other side of the room there are stacks of toilet paper, soap and flour. He looks down at where he lies and sees it's a sofa bed. A door at the opposite end of the room to where Mischa left is ajar and Tom sees tiles and a basin. *Bathroom.*

Tom lifts his arm and peers at the bandage over his burn. It's clean and fresh. *Still hurts though.* He drops his head on the pillow and stares at the ceiling. The angst in his gut is still there and it crawls up his body until he grunts and bites his lip.

"Are you in pain?" Mischa's voice floats through the room from the door.

"No. I'm…" *I feel useless and uneasy.* "I'm just thinking."

Mischa smiles as she walks to him with a bowl and a rotary phone on an extra-long cord.

"This is kasha." She puts the bowl down on the small table by the sofa and slides an arm around Tom's shoulders. "Let me help you sit up."

Tom manages to get into a sitting position with Mischa's help and he takes the bowl she holds out for him.

"And what is kasha?" Tom looks into the bowl.

"It is grains. Cereal."

Tom pushes the grains around. "I'm just happy cabbage isn't involved." He spoons it into his mouth and is pleasantly surprised.

"Cabbage?" Mischa sits on the end of the sofabed.

Tom smiles and swallows. "Nevermind." He nods towards the tiled room. "Is that a bathroom?"

"Yes. Would you like to shower?"

"Yes. I would love to shower." *May I sit there for a week?*

"Once you are finished eating I will get clean clothes for you."

"Sascha and I don't quite look the same size."

Mischa laughs. "No. You are not. But…" Her cheeks warm. "I took liberty of checking tag on your trousers when you arrived. I sent Sascha out to get you something to wear."

"You looked in my trousers, Mischa?" Tom raises a brow.

She bows her head as her face glows red. "Yes."

"Okay, but just this once." He spoons the last of the kasha and puts the bowl down. "Thank you."

"You are welcome." Mischa stands and nods at the bathroom. "You will find towel and soap inside. Take your time. Your bandage is waterproof."

Tom shuffles to the edge of the sofa bed.

"But please…" Mischa holds a hand up. "You must take drip with you and do not overexert yourself."

Tom grins and slowly stands up, gripping the side of the sofa. Black spots dance in front of his vision and he closes his eyes a moment. "What do you think I'm going to get up to in there?"

Her cheeks deepen in colour again and Tom laughs.

"I promise to be good." He winks and moves towards the bathroom, sliding the pole with his drip along with him.

"I will have fresh clothes for you."

Tom turns at the door of the bathroom and nods once. "Thank you, Mischa."

Tom sits on the floor of the bath as the hot shower pelts down. The steam wraps around him and it's the most amazing feeling he's ever had. *Except for Tesco that time.* He pumps liquid soap out of the bottle and rubs it all over himself. The cellar grime feels as though it's embedded itself in his pores all the way to the bone. The clean scent of citrus swirls through the steam and it's heaven. He grabs the shampoo and scrubs it through his hair before sitting and letting the water wash the suds away.

He closes his eyes and imagines Isabella's nose against his and her hands on his chest. In the same moment ice cold shards stab his heart and the panic from earlier comes back. He can't escape the feeling something is wrong. *And I'm no fucking help whatsoever.* He digs his fingers through his hair and rests his head against the tiles. Water pummels his face and he breathes the steam in, cleansing his lungs of the dirt and filth of the cellar. He grabs the toothbrush and piles toothpaste on it. He cleans his teeth forever; the fresh mint is like a drug he can't give up.

After a time he turns the water off and gets out of the shower. He dries his hair with the towel before wrapping it around his waist. He peeks out the door and sees Mischa sitting on the sofa with her back to him. She is talking on the phone. Tom walks over and sits beside her. She smiles and nods towards the pile of clothing on the sofa bed. Tom notices the sheets are fresh and crisp. He smiles. *I hope you burned the old ones.*

Mischa hangs up the phone and stands. "Sascha will call back in a few minutes. I will let you get dressed in private."

Tom grins. "Thanks Mischa, but you really need to stop blushing."

"I will try."

"Okay."

Tom waits until she closes the door and struggles into the fresh clothes. The phone rings and Tom picks it up. *What century have I fallen into?*

"Sascha?"

"Hello. How are you feeling?"

"Average. But I'm alive and clean, so that's a bonus."

"It is."

"Where's Isabella?"

"They are not back yet."

"When are they coming back?"

"They are due back this evening. I believe her job was scheduled for this morning."

Tom's gut flips, thinking of her killing. *She'll be devastated.* "And what are you going to do when they get back?"

"I have doctored feed on camera so it is replaying time between your burn and letting you out."

"Are they that stupid, Sascha?"

"Not long term. They will notice it is not right at some point."

Tom's chest shudders. "You better hope you have Iz out of there before they do."

"Yes. That is my aim."

Tom rolls his eyes. "Sascha. Listen to me. I need more than an aim. I need you to protect her." Tom's pulse pushes against his neck and heat rises up his back. "You aren't filling me with confidence."

"Remember I told you I would do anything for my wife?"

"Yes."

"I intend to drug Marat and Erik before Nikolay returns."

"You… what?" Tom scratches a hand through his hair. "You need to kill them. Dead."

"I will not let them turn me into killer. You need to trust me. I may look naive but I am not so weak. I will get her out."

Guilt settles on Tom's shoulders and he sighs. "You're right. I'm sorry. It's hard for me to not be involved." *And it's twisting my gut into knots.*

"I understand."

Neither say anything for a moment. Mischa peeks in the room and Tom waves her in.

"Sascha?"

"Yes?"

"Your wife looked in my trousers."

Sascha laughs, uninhibited and loud. Mischa blushes again and puts her hand over her mouth.

"She did. Do clothes fit you?"

"Yes. I look like I'm going to a funeral but…"

"I thought black was best."

"You're probably right."

"Tom?"

"Sascha."

"I need you to trust me with Isabella. I will protect her. The same I would protect my own wife. I promise you this."

Tom's eyes slide to Mischa who is changing the bottle on Tom's drip.

"I trust you, Sascha."

"They are due back around seven pm. All going well she will be in your arms by midnight."

In my arms.

27

ISABELLA

I sabella sits at a fancy table and sips Earl Grey tea. The black wig she is wearing itches the base of her scalp and the long gloves make her hands sweaty. *Not ideal... considering.*

She turns to the door and sees Nik. He catches her eye and nods once before retreating. She rubs her stomach with one hand while sipping more tea. She grimaces and puts the cup down. *It's dishwater.*

A plate is put down in front of her and she stares down at the fancy corn fritters and bacon. *When in Saint Petersburg...* She picks up a fork and spears a piece of bacon.

She chews and scans the room. Annika Durov is at a table near the front. She is smiling and posing for photographs with reporters and other party members. Isabella's eyes flick to the clock on the wall. *Nine thirty-seven. You've been here for an hour. Can't you just pee already?* The butterflies in her stomach have turned into oversized bats and they slam into her ribs. She swallows the bacon and fights the urge to throw it back up on the crisp white tablecloth in front of her.

She slips a hand under the faux fur stole over her shoulders and finds her knife, hiding inside a pocket sewn on the inside. *Ultimate female assassin couture.* She runs her fingers along the handle of the knife and her spine stiffens. She breathes a slow breath through her nose. *Hello Irina.*

She lifts her eyes to the front of the room as Annika stands and makes her way to a lectern standing in front of a Russian flag. The room erupts in applause and Isabella claps along with them. *This is a fucking nightmare.*

Ten twenty-three. Longest speech about nothing I've ever heard. Isabella keeps her eyes on Annika as she moves from the lectern and whispers into another woman's ear before walking towards the bathrooms. *Go time.*

Isabella dabs at the side of her mouth with her napkin and stands. She nods politely to those seated around her and moves through the tables to the bathrooms. She takes one more scan of the room before pushing open the lady's door.

Two of five stalls are occupied. Isabella takes off her gloves, leans over a sink and turns the water on. She washes her hands and neither door opens. Isabella swallows and gets a lipstick out of her pocket. She peers into the mirror and smooths the pale pink stick over her lips. *Come on.* A toilet flushes and a woman Isabella doesn't recognise walks out. They exchange smiles and nods as the woman washes her hands and walks out. Isabella creeps to the door, hangs an out of order sign on the knob and locks it from the inside.

Seconds drag on and Isabella's gut twists and clenches. A toilet flushes and Annika emerges from the stalls. She glances at Isabella and smiles a photo-worthy smile with no feeling behind it. She leans over the sink and holds her hands under the water.

Isabella steps to the left and pushes her knife against Annika's back. She looks at her through the mirror, waiting for Annika to meet her gaze.

"Do you speak English?"

Annika nods and Isabella sees a tremor start in her hands as they stay under the running water. Isabella leans over and turns the taps off and pulls a paper towel out of the dispenser. She hands it to Annika while the knife stays firmly at her back.

"Excellent. Listen to me. You have a contract out on your life. Do you understand?"

Annika nods again as she wipes her now dry hands with the soggy towel. Her breathing is shaky and her teeth chatter.

"I want you to call your publicist and tell her you need assistance in the bathroom."

Annika stares at Isabella, the soggy towel now ripping as she continues to wipe her hands.

"Annika?"

"Da." She drops the towel in the sink and pulls her phone out of her handbag. She puts it to her ear while Isabella holds her stare in the mirror. "Tanya? Ty mne nuzhen v damakh."

Isabella nods as Annika drops the phone back into her handbag.

"I am going to unlock the door for Tanya. If you do anything stupid I will stab you and her. To death. Do you understand?"

"Da."

Isabella walks backwards to the door and clicks the lock. A moment later it opens and a woman peers in.

"Tanya?"

"Da."

Isabella flicks her head and Tanya slips into the room and hurries to Annika. Isabella clicks the door locked again and stands in front of both women. She spins her knife in her hand and holds it at her hip.

"I want you to understand that I could stab both of you through the heart within moments and leave you to bleed out on the floor. So please do not try anything heroic."

Annika's mouth drops open and Tanya peers at Isabella as though she is simple.

Ignoring Tanya, Isabella turns to Annika. "You are going to climb through that window and get as far away from here as you can."

Annika turns and looks at the window. "But…"

"You must. Please. If you stay. I have no choice but to kill you."

"Kill... me?"

"Da." Isabella turns to Tanya in her fancy suit and heels. "Tanya?"

"Da?"

"You are going to release a media statement saying that Annika was stabbed to death in the bathroom of the Four Seasons Grand Ballroom this morning."

"This is madness." Tanya glares at Isabella.

"That may be. But I have no problem driving this knife through your heart and killing you both."

"I will have you arrested." Tanya steps forward and stares into Isabella's face.

Oh, honey.

Isabella sweeps her leg behind Tanya and knocks her off her feet. She hits the floor and air huffs from her mouth. Within a second Isabella is straddling her hips and pushes the knife against her abdomen. "You think I am messing with you, Tanya?"

"No..." Tanya raises both hands in surrender and sucks on her bottom lip.

Isabella grabs Tanya by the jacket and pulls her up. "I need you to understand that you simply must do as I say."

"Okay. Da. I understand." Tanya nods as tears roll down her cheeks.

"If you fail to do so as instructed I will come after you. Do not try me." *I won't, but...*

Isabella's eyes flick back to Annika. She is gripping the basin, her chest heaving and fear etched all over her face.

Isabella closes her eyes a moment and sees Tom being branded.

"One more thing," Isabella moves to Annika and lifts her top. Annika whimpers and falls against the basin. "I need to cut you."

Annika pulls in a breath and clutches her chest. "Cut me?"

"Da."

The tremble that had taken over Annika's body intensifies and she crumples to the floor. She wheezes and gasps in air as panic encompasses her. Isabella's heart shrinks and squeezes as she kneels next to Annika.

"I am sorry. But I need you to bleed. And I need to mark you. It is either that or death."

Annika lifts her face to the ceiling and cries. She bites her lip and nods. Isabella nods with her and turns to Tanya.

"Tanya, come." Isabella grabs Annika's hand and holds it out to Tanya. "Hold her hand. Let her squeeze your fingers. This will hurt."

"O Bozhe." Tanya covers her mouth with one hand and grabs Annika's with the other.

Oh my God is right. Isabella grabs the pen sticking out of Tanya's jacket pocket and slides it between Annika's teeth. "Bite on this." She lays Annika back on the floor and pushes her top up to her bra. "I am going to cut into your stomach. I will be quick. Da?"

"D… da…" Annika shakes and twitches.

Isabella takes a deep breath and shakes out her shoulders. *Come on, Irina. Get it done.* She pushes the tip of the knife into Annika's skin and dark red blood trickles over the blade. Annika moans and squeals from her throat.

"Here we go." Isabella quickly drags the knife around and forms a three. Annika writhes and trembles. *I'm going to vomit.* Isabella swallows and moves to write a six. She flicks her eyes to Annika's face and sees her sweating and her pale skin is now a bright red. *God, I'm so sorry.* Isabella blinks back tears and swallows acid. She pushes the knife into Annika's skin one last time and drags it down to write a one. Annika tenses and cries escape her clenched teeth. Her body shakes and twitches.

Isabella drops her hand and clutches the handle of the knife. *I'm sorry.* Blood dribbles down Annika's stomach and soaks into the waistband of her trousers. Isabella wipes a hand across the blood and smears it on the floor. She waits a moment and smears more blood on the floor. Annika squirms and cries, the tremble in her body envelopes her. Tanya clasps her hand to her mouth as tears fall and her nose runs.

"Annika?"

Annika's eyes open and she looks at Isabella. "Take some long deep breaths. You are in shock." Isabella gently pulls the pen from Annika's mouth. "In and out. Da?"

Annika manages to nod.

Isabella draws in a breath and pulls out the digital camera Nik gave to her. *Didn't trust me with a phone. Fair.* She snaps a picture of the number, making sure to include some of the blood on the floor. She shoves the camera back into her pocket.

"Can you stand up, Annika?"

She shakes her head. "Niet."

"You must try."

A loud knock hammers through the room. *Fuck.* Isabella glares at Tanya. "Get rid of them."

Tanya scrambles from the floor and runs to the door. Isabella turns her attention back to Annika. She pulls her top down and helps her sit up.

"Now, you must run. Get outside and run. Do you understand?"

"I cannot. It hurts."

"I know. I'm sorry. Please understand I did not want to hurt you."

"Then, why?"

Isabella dips her face down and closes her eyes. "I had no choice."

"We always have choice."

"Not me." Isabella shakes her head and helps Annika stand up. She opens the window and looks out. *No one around.* "Are you ready Annika?"

"Da."

"You are first. I will follow."

Isabella turns to Tanya as Annika goes through the window. "You remember what you must do?"

"But… do I call Police?"

"The story will be enough. By the time it is exposed as a hoax, it will not matter." *God willing.*

"Okay."

Isabella slams the passenger door shut. "Drive."

Nik pulls away from the front of the hotel without saying a word. *Keep it that way.* He holds his hand out and clicks his fingers. Isabella grunts, slides the knife out of her stole and puts it in his hand.

The handle is covered in sticky blood and Nik huffs. "You could not have cleaned knife?"

Isabella jerks her top lip and glares at him. "Are you fucking for real?" She holds both hands up, covered in the same sticky blood and nods at the front of her blouse. "I just knifed a poor woman to death. Sorry if I'm not in pristine condition."

Nik shrugs and drops the knife in the side pocket of his door. "Just do not smear leather."

"Ever heard of a red rag to a bull, Nik?"

"Excuse me?"

Isabella slaps her hands on the glove box and rubs blood along the leather. She does the same thing along the seat, either side of her legs. "Ooopps."

Nik grins, swings the car into a side street and slams the gear stick into park. He shoots a hand out and grabs Isabella around the throat. She digs her nails into his arm and glares at him.

"Irina. When will you learn that you cannot win against me?"

Isabella breathes short sharp breaths through the tiny airway left open in her neck.

"You think Tom will fare well after this display? Combined with your behaviour last night?"

Isabella grapples Nik's arm with both hands and rips it away from her throat.

"Don't fucking touch me."

"I see." Nik turns back to the wheel and begins to drive. He presses a button on the steering wheel and dial tone fills the car. No one answers and Nik grunts. He presses the button again and waits.

Isabella stares out her window with her body twisted away from Nik. She presses a hand into her belly, willing it to stop tumbling and twisting. Acid climbs up her throat and she swallows in vain as saliva pools on her tongue.

"Stop the car," she mumbles.

"What?" Nik makes a fourth call, still no one answers. "Speak up girl."

"I said... stop the car." She swallows again and the urge to vomit intensifies.

"No."

Fine.

Isabella leans into the backseat and grabs Nik's designer briefcase. She yanks the zip open and sticks her face inside. Her stomach contracts and squeezes, pushing its contents up and out of her mouth. She retches as bitterness coats her tongue and tears stream down her face.

"Irina! No."

Isabella gasps in a breath before vomiting again, her empty stomach shrinks and her neck strains. She pants and keeps her face in the case a few more seconds until she is sure it's over. Clearing her throat, she sits up and dabs at her mouth. She zips the case closed and gently places it on the back seat.

"My apologies. That case looks expensive."

"How dare you." Nik's knuckles change colour as he grips the wheels and grimaces.

Isabella smiles to herself and leans back in the seat. "I asked you to stop the car."

"You want to play this game?" Nik mumbles and pushes the button on the steering wheel again. "I will even speak in English so as not to *offend* you."

Fuck you, Nik.

Loud dial tone fills the car and this time the call is answered.

"Da?"

"Sascha."

"Da."

Isabella's heart jumps and she turns to watch Nik.

"Where are Marat and Erik? I have been calling."

"They are in cellar. They must not have signal."

"Good. Exactly where I want them to be."

No.

"Please instruct Marat to cut Tom from mouth to ear on both sides."

Isabella's adrenaline spikes and she trembles. "No! Nik. Please." Isabella grabs his arm and claws at his shirt.

Nik shrugs Isabella off. "Do it now. I want to see his happy, smiling face upon my return."

"Da."

Nik ends the call and laughs. "And here I was thinking you loved him. Clearly not."

Isabella hunches over her knees and scratches her fingers through her hair. She sobs and sniffles and doesn't care that her nose is running down to her mouth. She wipes her arm along her top lip and sits up, glaring at Nik.

"That handsome face. Cut to shreds."

"You're an animal." Isabella's voice is husky as sobs linger in the back of her throat.

"Can you love a man with a disfigured face? I doubt it."

"You think it's because of his face that I love him?"

Nik doesn't answer. His eyes fixed on the road.

"You have no idea how to love anyone do you, Nik?"

"Whatever. I win."

"I pity you."

"Why?"

"Because the boy you were was kind and thoughtful. Now, you're nothing but a soulless void. When you die, no one's going to care."

Nik snaps his face to Isabella and curls his lip. "You think you are so smart. You do not know anything."

"I know that you have a one-way ticket to hell."

"Now now, Irina. I am not all bad. I intend to let you see Tom when we return. He will be grotesque. I very much will enjoy watching your reunion."

Isabella twists in her seat and stares out the window.

Please forgive me, Tom.

28

ISABELLA

Nik pushes open the door to his house and sweeps his hand aside, gesturing Isabella in. She pushes past him and turns with her arms folded over her chest. "Take me to him."

"You need to shower. You are covered in blood… remember?" He grins. "Although, I suppose you do not have to be in immaculate condition to visit Tom. But I prefer you clean and crisp."

Sascha appears in the hallway as Isabella glares at Nik.

Nik turns to Sascha and claps his hands together once, like a child opening a present on Christmas morning. "Sascha! Tell me… is Tom suitably… happy?"

Sascha nods once. "He is."

Isabella's stomach plummets and she grits her teeth, glaring at him. *We trusted you.*

"I shall wander down and visit my smiling friend." Nik throws

a glance at Isabella. "I will come and collect you once you are…
clean enough."

Fuck. You.

Isabella spins and continues to her room, slamming the door
shut behind her. She walks to the window and stares down at the
bunker. *God, what have I done?* She dashes into the ensuite and
turns the water on. It steams up the room while she peels her
clothing off. She steps under the hot water and lifts her face
upwards. *I'll never be clean enough again.*

A loud bang sounds through the tiny ensuite as the door is
thrust open. Isabella rolls her eyes. "Get lost, Nik."

A hand reaches in and fingers wrap around her upper arm.
What the hell? She pulls her arm back and Sascha stumbles
against the shower screen.

"What is it with everyone wanting to see me naked?"

"Please. You must come with me. Now."

Isabella swings a hand back and slaps Sascha across the face.
"You're a *fucking* traitor. We trusted you." She resists the urge to
spit on him. "I'm going to cut your liver out and feed it to you for
dinner." The quiver in her body is back and clenches her fists.

"Tom is not cut."

"Liar," Isabella hisses through gritted teeth.

"I swear on the life of my wife. He is not."

His wife.

Isabella glares at him for a few seconds. "Give me two
minutes. Not that I should even be talking to you." *Traitor.*

"No. You do not have two minutes." Sascha grabs her arm

again and yanks her out of the shower. He throws a towel at her. "Wrap yourself in this. We must go. I have clothes for you to get into in car." He holds up a black bag.

"I'm not going anywhere without Tom." Isabella wraps the towel around herself and drips water onto the plush carpet.

"He is not here."

Isabella's chest collapses. "What?" *Where the fuck is he?* Adrenaline races through her blood and the quiver in her body intensifies.

A door bangs downstairs and Sascha jumps. "Der'mo!"

"Shit? Why shit?" Isabella grabs Sascha around the throat and squeezes. "What the hell is going on Sascha?"

"Sascha?" Nik's voice hollers up the stairs. Loud footsteps ascend the stairs and Sascha claws at his chest.

"What's wrong with you?" Isabella peers at Sascha. "Are you having some sort of panic attack?"

Nik appears in the door and looks Isabella up and down. "Out of the shower so soon?"

"I forgot my shampoo." Isabella raises an eyebrow.

Nik turns to Sascha. "Sascha. What is going on?"

"Ah, what do you...mean?"

"The cellar."

Sascha's Adam's apple bobbles as he swallows and draws in a breath. "The cellar?"

Isabella looks between Nik and Sascha, unease bubbles in her belly as her adrenaline continues to run riot.

"Yes, Sascha. The cellar." Nik walks into the room and stands toe to toe with Sascha. "Can you explain to me…" He stops and glances at Isabella. "Why I am halfway across yard and you are not accompanying me?"

Sascha appears to slump and he chuckles. "Ah, sorry I was…"

"You were watching Irina in shower?"

"Da. Niet. I… No."

Tom isn't here. Sascha said Tom isn't here.

"I requested soap." Isabella tilts her head.

Nik and Sascha both look at Isabella.

"You… requested soap?"

"Yep. Yes."

Nik turns and stalks into the bathroom. Isabella frowns at Sascha. Nik returns with a bottle of liquid soap in his hand. "This soap? That was in your shower?"

"Yes. Well… *now* it is. Sascha… brought it in for me."

Sascha nods. "Yes. You are welcome."

Nik pushes the bottle of soap against Isabella's chest. "Well, you should finish washing."

Isabella slides her eyes to Sascha who is biting his lip and staring at the floor. "Yes, the sooner I'm clean, the sooner I see Tom."

"Maybe I will stay and make sure you can reach your back." Nik runs his eyes down Isabella's body and back to her face.

"Ah, I understand Marat was waiting for you to arrive." Sascha flicks his eyes between Isabella and Nik.

Isabella huffs and shakes her head. "Just let me know when you've both figured out what you want to do." She walks back to the still running shower and steps in, not caring that the door is wide open. *I may as well just wander about naked.*

Isabella washes herself, watching through the steam to see Nik and Sascha speaking to one another. She foams her hair full of shampoo and runs her fingers through it. Nik looks at Isabella one more time and she flips him her middle finger while rinsing her hair. He strides into the bathroom and opens the shower screen. Isabella drifts her hands down her neck and chest and smiles.

"Can I help you, Nik?"

Nik grins and strokes his hand across Isabella's cheek. "You will. You started something last night that I intend to finish this evening."

Isabella leans forward so her nose is brushing Nik's. "Good luck."

"I feel that luck will be on my side once you see what a mess we have made of Tom."

"I'll never give you what you want." As she says the words her knees buckle and she smells Kostya's sour breath and rotting teeth in her face.

"You will willingly lie in my bed. It will happen."

Isabella swallows. "You have big dreams, Nik."

Nik smirks and runs his hand down her neck, the middle of her chest and stops at her stomach. "Dreams can come true, Irina."

He steps back and walks out of the bathroom. He nods to Sascha and holds one finger up, to which Sascha nods in return.

Nik looks back at Isabella one last time as she turns the water off, before he disappears out the door.

Isabella grabs her towel and wraps it around herself. "You aren't going with him?"

"I convinced him that I should make sure you did not leave the house."

"How? He knows I would never leave Tom."

"I said now that Tom is disfigured you have no reason to stay."

Isabella gut clenches. "You said Tom isn't there?"

"No." Sascha pulls her by the arm out the door and down the hall.

Isabella scurries along leaving wet footprints on the floor-boards. "Where is he?"

"He is safe." Sascha opens the front door and pulls her down the driveway. Isabella's chest relaxes and her nose tingles.

"Safe?"

"He got very ill. I had to get him out or he could have died in that cellar."

Isabella's heart twitches. "Sick? He's sick? He could have died? What the fuck Sascha?" Her voice is a screech and she pushes her hand against her throat.

"He developed infection in burn. High fever."

Isabella stops walking. "What?"

Sascha grabs her hand and pulls her to his car. "Mischa is looking after him. He is okay. I promise."

"Where is he?"

"I take you to him now. Please… get in." Sascha opens the rear passenger door of his car and pushes Isabella in. She slides into the seat and Sascha hands her the bag.

"So what is Nik going to find in the cellar?"

"Marat and Erik. Sleeping."

"Sleeping?" Isabella dries herself as best she can in the back of the tiny hatchback.

"I drugged their food."

Isabella gasps and stares at Sascha through the rearview mirror as he frowns at the road ahead. "You what?" She pulls the clothing on that Sascha packed for her and climbs into the front seat. She scrubs at her hair with the towel. "Why didn't you kill them?"

"I am not a killer."

"You aren't a killer?" *Holy shit.*

"That is what I said."

"Oh my God."

Sascha flicks his eyes to the rearview mirror and back to the road as he hurtles his tiny hatchback along the street. His phone starts to ring and he pulls it from his jacket pocket and hands it to Isabella. "It will be Nik."

She looks at the phone. "Do you want me to answer it?"

"Da. And then we turn it off so he cannot trace us. We have an hour and a bit drive ahead of us."

Isabella presses answer. "Nik."

"You have death wish?" His voice is oddly smooth and calm.

"Should I?"

"When I find you and Sascha, I am going to slit his throat and hang him upside down to bleed out like pig he is."

"Graphic."

"And you."

"What about me?"

"I will torture and kill you like I should have when I found you."

Isabella gasps loudly and giggles. "Stop talking dirty to me Nik. It's such a turn on."

Isabella looks at Sascha, his hands are gripping the steering wheel so tight his knuckles are beyond white and heading to purple. She reaches across and puts her hand over his. He looks at her and she smiles. He gives her a tight smile and looks back to the road.

"You think you can stay hidden from me?"

"Well, I'll give it my best shot."

"I have eyes and ears everywhere. You think you can get across border without me finding out?"

There's something I haven't considered. Isabella's stomach drops to the road below but she swallows and shrugs. "We'll find a way, Nik. You can't be everywhere."

"That is where you are very much mistaken."

"Okay well, it's been lovely to chat. But I must go. People to see, places to go. You know how it is." She ends the call and turns the phone off.

"Throw it out window."

Isabella puts her window down and drops the phone out of the car. "Sascha?"

"Da?"

"Do you have a plan?"

Sascha chews on his lip, staring straight ahead.

"It's okay if you don't."

"My plan stops at your escape… so far."

"Well, you did good." She squeezes his hand again before settling back into the seat. She closes her eyes and breathes in, almost feeling Tom's mouth against hers.

29

TOM

Tom jiggles his jaw back and forth, his eyes glued to the clock on the wall.

"It's almost midnight."

"It is." Mischa nods as she fiddles with the bag on Tom's drip. "One more day of this and we can take you off it."

Tom doesn't shift his eyes from the second-hand ticking around the clock face. "Sascha said she'd be in my arms by midnight."

"Stress is not good for you, Tom."

"What if something's happened? What if he didn't get her out? Fuck." *God, I need a drink.* Tom swallows and swipes the water bottle off the table. He gulps to quell the relentless thirst in his throat.

Mischa sits on the sofa next to him and puts her hand on his arm. "Tom?"

He moves his eyes away from the clock and onto her soft face. "Yes?"

"It will be okay. You should sleep. You are still not better. You need rest."

"I'm fine. I feel fine."

"That does not mean you are better. You are very sick."

Tom huffs and flops back onto the pillow. "Fine. I'm lying down." He turns his head to Mischa. "Happy now?"

"Almost."

Tom raises both eyebrows. "Almost?"

"Once you close your eyes and go to sleep I will be happier."

"I need to know what's happening with Iz. Surely you understand?"

"I understand. But I also know my Sascha. And if he said he will bring her to you. Then, he will."

"That's not enough, Mischa."

"Do I need to give you something to make you sleep?" She widens her eyes and purses her lips.

Tom rolls his eyes and smiles. "You're going to be a good Mum." He nods at her tiny bump.

"How so?"

"You're already bossy and strict." *And I owe you my life.*

Mischa giggles. "I fear that I will be overwhelmed with love for my child and be too soft."

"Nothing wrong with that."

"Is your mother still too soft with you?"

"My Mum died when I was eleven."

Mischa's hand flies to her mouth. "I am so sorry."

"Don't be. It was a long time ago."

"But it was your mother. Time makes no difference."

You're right.

Tom shrugs. "I was looked after." He looks back at the clock. *Ten to twelve.* He clenches his teeth.

"What will help you relax?"

Tom smiles to himself. "I don't suppose you could warm up some milk?"

"Warm milk?"

"Yeah. Stupid but…" *If I can't have whisky...*

"It is not stupid." Mischa stands. "I will be right back."

Tom stares at the shelves of tins and long-life milk. He squints and leans forward, reading some of the labels. *Cabbage in a can?*

"It's bad enough in a stew," he mumbles, sitting back into the sofa cushion. He lifts the hand with the drip and inspects the cannula. He taps it a couple of times with his other hand and sighs. *Un-fucking-believable.*

Eyeing the clock, he grimaces. *Five minutes left til deadline, Sash.* He runs a hand over his gut in an effort to stop the squirming but it doesn't work. He drops his head back on the sofa and stares at the clock, watching as the second hand makes its way around the clock face another five times.

The door opens and Tom's heart jumps to his throat. He sits up as Mischa walks in. Alone. She has a mug in her hands.

Tom's shoulders slump but he gives Mischa a smile as she hands him the mug. "Thank you."

"You are welcome." She sits on the end of the sofa. "Is that a common drink in England?"

Tom sips and raises his eyebrow. "Warm milk? You've never tried it?"

Mischa shakes her head.

"Well, I don't know about common but... I used to have it when I was a kid and I couldn't sleep."

"A nice memory from your mother."

"She... she didn't drink milk. I lived in foster homes after she passed. And..." Tom stops and takes another sip. "My foster... Mum... gave it to me for the first time." *God it feels weird calling her that.* "Anyway, how did you meet Sascha?"

"Meet him?"

"Yeah... give me the story... I need to do something to pass the time or I'll go around the twist." He winks as Mischa giggles.

"We were childhood friends. I was very shy child."

"No... I don't believe it."

Mischa's cheeks turn pink. "Yes, I still am. I know it."

"So you were at school together?"

Mischa nods. "Yes. I had few friends because I was so timid. Sascha came and sat with me one day when we were only seven. He shared his sandwich."

Tom smiles, putting his mug on the table.

"Anyway, from that day he sat with me always and we became best friends."

"Love at first sight, huh?"

"Something like that. Only... at seven you don't know what

love is." She looks up into space a moment and shrugs. "Or maybe you do."

"How long have you been married?"

"We got married when we were twenty-one. So, three years." Mischa looks at Tom and tilts her head. "What about you?"

"Me?"

"Yes, and your love. Will you marry her?"

"Oh… um." Tom inhales. "I… haven't really thought about it?"

"Do not pretend. Of course you have."

"No, well." Tom shrugs and looks at the cans on the shelves. "I mean… I almost got married once."

"Almost?"

Tom stares at the cabbage in the can. "She…" He slides his gaze to Mischa. "She passed away."

Mischa covers her mouth with her hand. "Oh. I am so sorry. Forgive me."

"Don't apologise."

"That must have been horrific."

Tom looks down to his lap. "It was… difficult."

"I see now why you are so protective of Isabella."

"Protective?" He smiles. "Well, yes but… in truth she can handle herself."

"But you are frightened to lose her. Now that you know what that feels like."

"Maybe."

"Do you want children one day?"

Tom snaps his head up. *Kids?*

Mischa bites her lip and shakes her head. "I am sorry. It is none of my business. I got too comfortable."

"No. It's fine. I just…" Tom squints. "I guess I never really thought about it before."

"You don't like children?"

"No. I mean. Yes. Kids are great. I just don't know that I would be a very good parent."

"Why? You are kind and have much love in your heart."

Tom laughs. "How can you tell something like that?"

"Look at you. You love Isabella so much you endured torture for her."

"Endured yes. But I didn't have much choice."

"You know that Sascha could have got you out earlier. But you would not have left her. Would you?"

"No."

"He told me you would be difficult when it came to her."

"Did he now?" Tom smiles again and nods.

"Yes. But he meant because you would not leave her."

"He was right."

"So tell me again why you would be bad parent?"

"I never had a father. So… I wouldn't have a clue how to be one."

"It is within you, Tom. You do not learn it."

Prickles pierce the back of Tom's neck and he takes in a big breath. *Let's shift some focus here.* "Andis Sascha ready to be a father?"

"Oh yes. He was a little scared when we first found out but… now he is so happy. That is why he is doing all of this." She gestures towards Tom. "He wants a better life for us. A safe life."

Tom nods and yawns.

"Anyway." Mischa stands up. "Please try and sleep. I promise to bring her to you when they arrive."

Tom clenches his jaw and looks at the clock. *Twelve ten.* "Okay. I'll try."

"You are exhausted. You will sleep like that." Mischa clicks her fingers.

Tom chuckles and lies on the pillow. "Okay."

WARM HANDS SLIDE OVER TOM'S FACE AND SOFT LIPS PUSH against his mouth. He opens his eyes and blinks. *Isabella.* He wraps his arms around her and pulls her against his chest.

"Iz."

Isabella's shoulders shake and she sniffles against his skin. She brings her hands back to his face and strokes across his cheeks with her thumbs. "Your face."

"My face?"

"I thought they cut you and hurt you."

"Cut my face?"

"Yes." She leans up and kisses his cheeks and mouth. "I'm just going to keep doing this for a while." She smiles against his lips as she kisses him again.

Tom rakes his fingers through her hair. "Are you hurt?"

Isabella shakes her head. "No."

"What time is it?"

"A little after one thirty, why?"

"I'm going to have words with Sascha."

"Why?"

"He said you'd be in my arms by midnight."

Isabella giggles against his neck. "Don't be too hard on him. He did good."

"He did."

Isabella looks up at the drip. "God Tom, what happened while I was gone?"

"Oh, well… I got to eat a steak."

Isabella rolls her eyes. "And that put you on a drip, did it?"

"Well, no… the infection put me on the drip. I started burning up and collapsed. It was very dramatic."

"Sascha brought you here?"

"Yep. His wife's a nurse."

"Yes. I know. He told me after you were burnt and he was helping you."

"I have no recollection of that."

"You were pretty out of it." She lifts a hand and brushes his hair back from his face. "I almost took advantage of you." She winks and raises one eyebrow. "But you weren't looking up for it so…"

"What about now?" He nuzzles his face into hers.

"Now?"

"Do I look up for it now?" He slides his hands under her shirt and up her back.

"Honestly? No... "She grins and nestles her mouth against the dip in his throat.. "You don't appear to be overly energetic."

Tom holds Isabella against him and breathes her in. "I just need to hold you."

Isabella brings her face back to his and kisses him deeply. "That's enough for me."

Tom pulls in a breath and drops his forehead against hers. "I love you."

Soft tapping rouses Tom from sleep and he pulls Isabella against him, burying his face in the back of her neck.

"Have you got clothes on?" He smiles against Isabella's skin.

Isabella giggles. "Yes."

"Mischa blushes a lot."

"Bless."

Tom chuckles and pushes himself into a sitting position. "Mischa?" He calls towards the door.

The door opens and Mischa walks in with a tray. She keeps her eyes on the floor.

"It's okay Mischa, you won't turn to stone if you look at us."

Her cheeks deepen in colour and she looks up. "I do not wish to intrude."

"You aren't."

Isabella sits up. "Good morning, Mischa."

Mischa smiles and slides the tray with two bowls and two mugs onto the sofa bed.

"Oh, is that kasha?" Isabella pulls the tray towards her and picks up a bowl. She spoons some into her mouth and closes her eyes. "Amazing."

"It's cereal, Iz." Tom smiles and spoons his own kasha into his mouth.

"Yes, but... don't you ever eat something and it just reminds you of happiness and warmth and all those things that you took for granted as a child?"

Tom glances at the mug of milk on the table that he fell asleep before finishing. "Yeah, I get it."

"Well, my father would always make me this. It's my favourite."

Mischa stands up. "I will leave you to enjoy the kasha."

"Wait." Tom puts the bowl down. "Where's Sascha?"

"He will be down soon. I wanted to let him sleep. He has been quite stressed these last few days."

Tom nods. "Of course."

"I must go and get antibiotics in pill form so you can be taken off drip. I will see you at lunchtime." Mischa bows her head and leaves the room

Tom furrows his brow and stares at the closed door. *This is just the beginning.*

"Tom?"

Tom looks at Isabella and smiles. "I'm so glad you're here."

"I told you. I'm never going to make you think you've lost me again." She runs her hand into his hair and kisses his mouth.

He falls back onto the bed and she lies on his chest.

"We should...stop." Tom mumbles through their kiss. He pushes his hand under her waistband and squeezes her hip.

"We should."

"But we won't."

Isabella shakes her head. "No."

Tom rolls slightly onto his side and winces, taking in a sharp breath.

"Tom?"

"It's fine. I'm fine."

"Oh God, your burn." Isabella lifts his shirt and pulls the taped bandage from his skin. Her fingers trace around the outside of the angry red, blistered skin, her touch makes the pain bearable.

Tears drop from her eyes and trickle down her face. "You'll have a scar," she whispers.

Tom brushes the tears from her cheeks and pulls her face to his. "Maybe I'll just get a tattoo." He presses his lips against hers.

"I'm sorry." Isabella sobs against his face.

"Stop."

"It's my fault," she whispers.

"Stop."

30

ISABELLA

Isabella runs her fingers through Tom's hair as he sleeps across her lap. Her head is lolled back on the sofa and she is counting the spots on the ceiling. *Forty-seven.*

A soft tapping brings her back gaze to the door and it opens. Mischa and Sasha peer in and Isabella smiles, waving them over.

Mischa looks at Tom asleep in Isabella's lap and gives a soft shake of her head. "He will not admit he is still unwell."

"No. You're lucky if he admits he needs to pee half the time." Isabella giggles as Mischa and Sasha perch on the far end of the sofa bed.

"I'm awake you know," Tom mumbles against her stomach. He draws in a breath and pushes himself up. Isabella's hand trails down his neck to his lower back as he sits up. She dips her hand under his shirt and gently strokes his skin with her fingernails.

"Are you feeling okay?" Mischa jumps up and examines the now empty bag on the pole.

"Like I could move mountains, Mischa."

"Really?" She raises both eyebrows.

Tom chuckles and shakes his head. "No. I feel weak as shit. But… I'm fine."

Mischa takes hold of Tom's hand with the cannula. "I am going to remove this. Are you ready?"

"Absolutely."

Isabella looks at Sascha at the other end of the sofa. "How are you doing Sascha?"

He shrugs. "Okay."

"So, not well then?" Isabella raises her chin and smiles.

"He has not slept." Mischa smooths a square plaster on the back of Tom's hand. "He is stressed." Mischa gives him a pointed look.

Sascha gazes at Mischa a moment before bowing his head. "I admit I am concerned about our next move."

"You know what our next move is?" Isabella laces her fingers through Tom's and smiles at Sascha.

"Niet." Sascha shakes his head. "I have no idea." He gives a small grin.

Isabella looks at Tom. "He reminds me of someone…"

Tom purses his lips and raises an eyebrow. "No idea who you're referring to."

Isabella snorts. "Anyway… We can't stay in this basement forever Sascha. Your in-laws must be having kittens."

Sascha frowns. "Kittens?"

"Yeah… frightened? Freaking out?"

"They are… anxious. But they also know that you can help us."

Isabella nods. "We *will* help you."

"Speaking of." Tom leans towards Sascha. "Did you send those details to Martha after I collapsed in a heap?"

"The number you had been speaking on?"

Tom nods.

"Da." Sascha pulls the phone out and hands it to Tom. "Her reply was puzzling."

Isabella peers at the phone over Tom's shoulder as he opens the text messages.

I expect you over for a Sunday roast more often after this debacle.

Isabella snorts and Tom grunts. "So demanding," he mumbles, dropping the phone on the bed. "Do you have that other phone down here, Sash? I need to call *she who must be obeyed.*"

Sascha jumps up and grabs the old rotary phone sitting on one of the shelves next to the cans.

"Is that phone from the stone age?" Isabella widens her eyes and sticks a finger in the dial, making it move. "This is a dinosaur."

"There is no reception in this room. So, old school it must be." Sascha shrugs.

Tom is already dialling and holds the receiver to his ear. He wraps an arm around Isabella and pulls her into his body. She nestles against his chest. *Don't ever let me go.*

"Hey." Tom grimaces and looks up at the ceiling for a moment. "Yes, thank you, Martha. I've been doing my best to stay alive the last couple of days, sorry I haven't checked in." He rolls his eyes.

Isabella shakes her head. *He's back.*

Tom looks down at her. "Yes, Iz is here and she's fine… hang on…"

Tom hands the receiver to Isabella. She giggles and takes it, sitting up. "Hey Martha."

"My dear, are you alright?"

"Yes. I'm fine. Thank you."

"Is Tom being a royal pain in the arse?"

"I don't know about royal…" She sneaks a glance at Tom who raises a brow and sips from a bottle of water.

"That's a yes, then?"

"Don't stress. I'll make him follow orders."

"Good luck. I've been trying since he was thirteen."

Isabella laughs. "Well, *I'll* come over for a roast, even if he claims he's too busy." Isabella twitches her eyebrows at Tom who swipes for the receiver. Isabella jerks backwards and wiggles a finger at him. "Stop using all your strength," she whispers with her hand over the mouthpiece.

"You're as bad as her," Tom mumbles, folding his arms over his chest.

"My dear?" Martha's voice cuts back into her ear.

"Yes, sorry."

"No bother. Now I have a contact in Moscow who can get passports to you."

"Wonderful."

"I'll set it up for today. I'll call back on this number you dialled from."

"Okay."

"And my dear?"

"Yes?"

"If Tom thinks he is going to do anything other than what he's told. Swat him across the back of the head, won't you?"

Isabella fixes her eyes on Tom's and smiles. "Definitely."

"I'll be in touch." Martha ends the call and Isabella places the receiver back in the cradle.

"She's given me permission to swat you across the back of the head."

"I bet she did."

Sascha chews on his lip and looks at Tom. "We need to get out of Russia."

"Thanks for the newsflash, Sash." Tom grins. "It's a pity though. I'm getting quite accustomed to your basement."

"It will not be easy."

"No, it won't."

"We still have to consider the Nik factor." Isabella tilts her head and stares across the room. "He's going to be on the warpath."

Sascha nods. "Yes. He will want blood. Mine mostly." Sascha smiles and shrugs. "I drugged two of his men and took Isabella from right under his nose."

"I'm so proud of you Sash." Tom sits back against the sofa and brings his knees up, resting his wrists on them. "Growing up right before our eyes."

Mischa giggles softly from where she is standing next to the shelves. "Babyface," she smiles at her husband, her eyes full of warmth and love.

Isabella gazes at Mischa. *Oh, they are so cute.*

The phone rings and all four jump. Sascha scrambles to answer it. "Da?" He nods once and holds the receiver out to Isabella. She grins at Tom and takes it.

"Yes?"

"Four p.m. today. Outside Lenin's Tomb."

Isabella's chest constricts. "Red Square," she whispers.

"What?" Tom sits up and tries to grab the phone. Isabella moves back and holds a finger up at Tom.

"Yes. I couldn't convince him to meet anywhere less conspicuous. He wants to be out in the open. Will that be a problem?" Martha's voice brings Isabella's attention back to the phone.

"Ah. No. It won't."

"Can you manage this, Isabella? I'm assuming Tom is still out of action?"

"Yes... he thinks he isn't but he's not going anywhere." Isabella looks straight at Tom whose jaw twitches and he stares straight back. *Calm down.* She reaches across and puts her hand on his leg.

"My contact will find *you*. Wear a red scarf."

"Okay." Isabella's throat is dry and she swallows in vain.

"My dear?"

"Yes. It's fine. Thank you." *Fucking Red Square.*

"Please contact me afterwards and tell me you're okay."

Isabella smiles. "Of course."

Isabella clicks the receiver back into its cradle.

"Well?" Tom raises both brows and leans forward.

"I need to go to Red Square and get the passports."

Tom hisses in a breath. "Are you insane?"

"We need those passports. Or we can't go anywhere."

"Fine. I'm coming with you." Tom shuffles to the edge of the sofa, stopping at the edge to take in a breath.

Isabella rolls her eyes. "Tom, don't be ridiculous. You can't even get off the bed without needing a breather."

"I'm not negotiating this with you."

"May I make suggestion?" Sasha stands up and holds a hand up.

Tom grunts. "Go nuts. Suggest whatever you want. But I'm not changing my mind."

"I will go with her."

"Sash, no offence but you may as well put a beacon on your head and stand in the middle of Red Square."

"I understand. But... you cannot go. You are still weak—"

"I'm not—"

"By your *own* admission five minutes ago."

Tom scoffs. "I can point a gun and shoot."

"As can I."

Isabella kneels on the bed and leans into Tom's face. "Do I need to swat you in the back of the head?"

Tom presses his lips together and stares into Isabella's eyes. She pecks his mouth. "You seem to be forgetting my former profession? Not to mention I know Red Square like the back of my hand." *And the whole goddamn place creeps me out.*

"He'll have eyes all over Moscow looking for us. You." Tom nods at Sascha. "Him."

Sascha sighs. "This is true. But what choice do we have?"

Isabella nods. "We can't cross any borders like *normal* people without passports."

Tom slumps against the sofa. "Fuck."

"Did Tom really want us to send his regards to Lenin?" Sascha and Isabella walk across Red Square towards the tomb.

Isabella snorts. "No, Sascha. That's Tom being funny."

"Oh. I should have laughed?"

"No. Don't encourage him." Isabella pulls the red scarf she was given by Mischa tighter around her neck. The cold wind whipping around them is unsettling and eerie. Isabella pulls in a shaky breath and spies the poles and chains forming a barrier around the entrance of the tomb. "Let's wait here a bit."

Tourists wander about and although it isn't peak season yet, Isabella is comforted by the amount of people around them. *Less chance of a scene. Maybe.*

"I do not see anyone." Sascha is scanning the square, his hands tap against his belt as though itching to pull his gun out.

"You need to calm down, Sash. We're just a couple of tourists checking out the pretty St Basil's Cathedral."

"Pretty?"

"To tourists maybe." Isabella grimaces.

"Not to you?"

Isabella looks at Sascha as he peers at her, with an eyebrow jerked and sucking on his bottom lip.

"Well...I..." Isabella looks at the colourful building. "It doesn't symbolise anything for me, I guess." *I've seen too much.*

"Did it ever?"

Isabelle shrugs. "I don't know."

"I was conscripted when I turned eighteen." Sascha gazes at the building.

"How long did you serve?"

"Just mandatory year. My mother was ill. I was needed at home."

"How did it make you feel?"

Sascha shrugs. "It is difficult to understand how to feel when you are drafted into something without choice."

"I understand." Isabella smiles into her scarf. "Although, I knew exactly how I felt about it. I still didn't have choices, mind you."

"Da." Sascha nods. "But you understand why I want out of here?"

Isabella nods. "Da." She looks around the tomb, the queue of people waiting to walk inside to see the embalmed body inside.

She spots a man walking towards them. He stops every few steps and looks around the square. He gazes up at the Kremlin and over at the tomb before walking again. His eyes meet Isabella's.

"Here we go," Isabella whispers.

"What?"

"The man in the long black coat. He's our guy."

"How do you know?"

"Because he keeps looking at everything and trying to appear casual. And failing might I add. And he keeps looking at me." She rolls her eyes. "Not conspicuous at all."

"You are very pretty woman."

Isabella swallows down a giggle. "Thank you Sash but what I mean is—"

The man narrows his eyes at Isabella flicks his head, gesturing her towards him. She swallows and steps forward.

"Where are you…"

"Just wait here a sec."

The man's eyes continue to dart around the square as Isabella walks towards him. She is around ten feet from him when he slides his hand inside his jacket. Isabella shoves her hand into her pocket and grips the knife hiding inside. *Never trust anyone.*

He pulls his hand out and Isabella sees a manilla envelope. She exhales and quickens her steps. The man watches her and his head jerks violently forwards. Isabella stops walking. As though in slow motion he crumples face first into the ground, landing three feet from her. Air escapes her body, and she wheezes a breath in to refill her lungs. She pushes a hand into her chest.

Dark red blood seeps onto the ground, brain matter is splattered down the back of his neck and into his shirt collar. A gaping hole stares up at Isabella from the back of his head.

"Jesus Christ." Isabella's heart plunges, she clenches her teeth while her knees tremble.

Sascha's voice is behind her. "I will go help—"

Isabella grabs Sascha's arm. "No, you'll leave with me. Right now." She pulls him away as people gather around the man and inspect him. Her heart is in free fall and the shake in her legs intensifies.

"But what…"

"He's been shot." Isabella is running now, pulling Sascha along with her. "Which means they know."

"But what about passports?"

"Fuck the passports, Sascha."

"But—"

Isabella pulls Sascha behind the cathedral. "Do you understand there's a sniper somewhere?"

"Yes."

"And who do you think he is going to shoot next?" Isabella pulls the red scarf off and throws it on the ground.

Sascha stares into her eyes, fear races across his irises. "I know. I was reckless. But we need those passports. I did not use any of my training or judgement. I am sorry." He drops his face and rubs the back of his neck.

I understand desperation. "C'mon." Isabella grabs his hand and they run. "We need to get back before Tom has a conniption."

31

TOM

Tom throws a pill down his throat and chases it with water. He shakes the bottle and peers through the brown glass, counting the pills. *A week's worth.*

"How long did you say the drive to Moscow is again?" Tom frowns at the clock.

"It is around an hour and a little from here."

Tom moves his gaze to Mischa. "It's nearly six. They should be back by now."

"Tom, you must stop clock watching. They will be back soon."

"But—"

Mischa sticks a thermometer in Tom's mouth. "But nothing. Stop worrying and relax."

"I can't," Tom mumbles past the stick in his mouth.

Mischa smiles as she removes the thermometer and reads it. "Much better."

"I told you, I feel fine."

Mischa shakes her head, smiling. "How does Isabella put up with you?"

Tom stands up, stretching his arms above his head. "You'll have to ask her that."

The phone rings and both Tom and Mischa snap their heads to it. Tom's pulse jumps and he leaps across the room.

"Yes?"

"Tom?"

What the? "James?"

"Thank fuck."

"How did you get this number?"

"I'll explain later. Listen to me. Where's Isabella?"

"She's... wait. Why?"

"Tom will you just fucking trust me? Where is she?"

The urgency in James' voice makes Tom's scalp tingle. "She went to get our passports."

"Red Square?"

"Yes. How did you know that?" *Martha wouldn't say anything.*

"Shit. Have you heard from her?"

Tom's gut rolls over and he grips the phone tighter. "What the fuck are you on about? Where's Martha?"

"She's... taking care of..."

Tom's eyes widen and he's sure they're about to fall out of his head and roll across the floor. "Taking care of what, James? What the *fuck* is going on?"

"Okay, listen I don't have time to explain. But wherever you are, wherever this number is connected… you need to get out. Now."

Tom's throat closes up and he draws a hard breath through his nose. "What?"

"They know about Red Square and they know about this number. Which means they're going to find you."

"How do you…" Tom spins and looks at Mischa. She is clutching at her blouse, her chin quivering.

"I hacked Malcolm's computer."

"You what?"

"I backdoored his computer and found what he's been up to."

"You can do that?" *I hate it when you impress me.*

"Yes. But… now isn't the time to celebrate my talents… You need to get out and run. All of you. Malcolm hacked Martha's computer and phone and told them everything. *And* got paid a shit tonne for doing it."

One Porsche isn't enough? "Please tell me Martha is currently stringing him up by his nuts on a rusty chain?" Tom spits the words down the phone, gripping the receiver so hard his fingers ache.

"Well… she's locked him in an interrogation room."

"Close enough." *I'll fucking kill him myself.*

"Get out and call us when you're safe. Don't fuck around, Tom."

"But Iz isn't back yet… they *should* be back. Fuck."

James blows a breath down the phone. "Okay, listen to me. This number is connected to wherever you are. They know it. They're coming for you. I've read the text exchange. Some bloke… Nik… he wants you and some Sascha person dead. Like… *dead* dead."

"They'll kill her parents," Tom mumbles to himself, watching Mischa as she sits on the sofa, her hand over her heart.

"There's other people with you?"

"I'm in a basement at a house. Yes."

"Okay well, get the fuck out of the basement."

"As soon as Iz—"

"No, Tom! Are you fucking listening to me? Now!"

Tom hearts slams into his ribs and he spins to Mischa. "Get upstairs and get your parents in the car."

Mischa gasps. "Why? What is—"

A loud crash echoes above their heads followed by two gunshots. *Fuck.* Tom drops the phone and runs across to Mischa, he grabs both her shoulders and pushes her further into the basement.

"Stay away from the door. Remind me again… this is a secret room?"

Mischa nods. "Yes. It is room behind another storeroom. If you do not know it is here you would not find it." Her body shakes and she wraps her arms around herself. "Are they dead?" She looks into his face, her eyes flooded with tears. "Tom?"

Tom keeps both hands on her shoulders and drops his head. "It sounds that way."

Mischa slides down the wall and onto the floor. "Mama i Papa. Pozhaluysta net." Tears tumble down her cheeks. She closes her eyes and more water squeezes out and falls down her face. She curls into a ball against the wall and hides her face against her knees.

Tom crouches beside Mischa and rubs his arm. "Mischa?"

She looks up through her puffy eyes. "Da?"

"I'm sorry."

She claps both hands against her mouth and sobs. *God, I'm sorry.* Tom pulls her against him and lets her cry into his shirt. He raises his eyes to the ceiling and listens. Faint footsteps stomp around somewhere above his head. *Still here.*

He turns his body and looks at the closed door. The single, thin door separating them from whoever is upstairs looking for them.

"I promise. They will not find us here." Mischa sniffles.

"It's a whole room Mischa."

"Yes and it is hidden behind storeroom and wine cellar. My parents were worried after The Fall, they would be harmed. They built this as panic room." She smiles and presses both hands to her chest. "I do not think even *they* thought it would one day be used for actual purpose." She smiles a weak smile and rubs her nose.

Guilt wraps Tom up in chains and he rubs his face. "I don't know what to say to you."

A loud crash echoes through the room and Tom jerks his head to the door. *Still closed.*

"They must be in cellar or storeroom," Mischa whispers.

Tom nods and holds a finger to his lips. Blood whooshes through his ears as his pulse hammers against his neck. Sweat drips down the sides of his face and this time it's not a fever.

"Nichego!" A gruff voice booms, though it's muffled through the door.

"Nothing…" Tom swallows. *Marat.*

"Oni uzhe ushli." Another voice joins the first, claiming they have already left.

"Da. YA ne khochu govorit' Nikolayu."

Tom snorts softly. *I wouldn't want to be the one to tell Nikolay either.* He creeps to the door and pushes his ear against it.

"You understand them?" Mischa is behind him and puts her hand on his arm.

Tom sucks a breath through his teeth and smiles. "Yeah… Maybe I should have told you, huh?"

Mischa shrugs. "I had feeling…" Her face crumbles into sobs again and she stays silent as her shoulders shake and tears flood her cheeks.

Tom opens his mouth to comfort her as four gunshots ring out above, all in quick succession. *They're shooting someone else.*

Mischa drops to the floor and blocks her ears. Tom's heart jolts and he forgets he is meant to be hiding. He runs to the door and yanks it open. *Iz.*

He takes the stairs two at a time and ignores his laboured

breathing and the pain shooting through his burn and down his body. *Fuck this.* He pushes against his bandage and winces as the pain bites back.

He pauses at the top of the stairs and takes a rough breath. He holds his forehead against the door a moment to prepare himself for what's on the other side. *I promised to protect you.*

The door is thrust open from the other side and Tom holds his breath.

32

ISABELLA

Tom's eyes fix on Isabella's face and his mouth drops open. "Iz!" He lurches forward and pulls her against him, cradling her head. "I thought you were going to be dead on the floor."

Isabella squeezes her arms around him, careful to avoid his burn. Sascha's gun is hooked around her finger.

"Have some faith in me." She rests her cheek against his heartbeat as it thumps too fast. "I'm okay, Tom. Calm down."

Sascha pushes past both of them and runs down the stairs. Tom twists his body and watches as Sascha descends.

"Fuck," he whispers.

"Her parents are dead, Tom. Shot in the head." Isabella's voice is muffled against his chest.

"I heard." He turns back and looks over her shoulder. "You didn't miss, either."

Isabella turns and observes the body on the floor. "Not my weapon of choice, but still…" She turns the gun over in her hand and shrugs. "Erik ran. He's still alive, took off in a car."

Tom moves to Marat's body and crouches beside him. He scoops up the gun that lies on the floor.

"Cheers Marat." He shoves it into the back of his waistband. "We need to get out of here." He pilfers spare magazines from Marat's pockets.

"I know."

A loud wailing cry winds up the stairs and Isabella bites her lip.

"I'm so sorry," she whispers. Her chest aches and she bends forward at the hips, wrapping her arms around herself.

"It's not your fault." Tom's lips are at her ear and she nods, holding back her sobs. His arm slides around her waist and he pulls her back against him. "Take a breath. We need to have our heads screwed on. This is far from over."

"I know." She wipes the back of her hands across her eyes, and bites on her lip to stop it trembling.

Sascha and Mischa appear in the doorway and Isabella's heart jolts forward. *We are one.* She runs to Mischa and wraps her up. Mischa bows her head into Isabella's shoulder and cries.

"Pozhaluysta, prosti menya. ya sozhaleyu." *I'm so sorry. Please forgive me.* Speaking Russian feels alien to Isabella and yet strangely comforting in this moment. She holds Mischa tight and strokes her hair.

"Mne nuzhno ikh uvidet'." Mischa's voice is soft and shaky against Isabella's shoulder.

Isabella looks up at Tom. "She wants to see them."

Tom winces and looks towards the lounge room. "It'll be distressing."

Mischa head snaps up. "I must see them."

Tom's eyes soften and he nods. "We can wait."

Mischa moves towards the lounge, wiping her eyes. Sascha places his hand on her back and the two of them crumple to the floor next to the dead bodies of her parents.

"Let's wait outside." Tom grabs Isabella's hand and pulls her towards the front door.

Isabella trails behind Tom, listening to Mischa and Sascha say hushed prayers in Russian. *Oh God, this is heartbreaking. And it's because of me. All of it.* Isabella pushes against her heart as the ache spreads through her whole body.

Waves of pain and torment rise from her belly and she clenches her teeth. Tears flood her face and she doesn't bother wiping her nose. *What's the point?*

She turns to Tom and presses her palms against his chest. Her breathing is fast and it does nothing to dull the ache in her chest.

"Tom. I can't do this anymore." She drops her head against him. "It's too much. I want to go home." She coughs and pulls in a jagged breath. "I need to go home."

He slides his hands up her neck and into her hair. He doesn't say anything, but he doesn't have to. He presses her against his chest and holds her there. He scans the darkness in case Erik is still out there.

The door opens behind them.

Sascha and Mischa walk outside, hand in hand. Mischa holds Sascha's hand with both of her own. Her tear-stained face is blotchy and her eyes are swollen.

Isabella gasps in a breath as she makes eye contact with Mischa, and tries to curb her sobs.

"We must go." Sascha gestures towards the car on the street.

"Mischa?" Isabella embraces her. "Pozhaluysta, prosti menya."

Mischa holds her tight and rests her head on Isabella's shoulder. "I do forgive you."

I don't deserve your kindness. Tears sting Isabella's eyes as Tom drapes his arms around both their shoulders and leads them to the car.

Isabella slides into the backseat next to Tom and he holds her close to him. "Where to Sash?"

"I must think." Sascha pulls out from the curb and puts his hand on Mischa's leg. "Vse budet khorosho. Obeshchayu."

Isabella smiles, watching Sascha promise his wife it will be okay. She rests her head against the window and closes her eyes.

"We must take back roads." Sascha looks in the rear-view mirror at Tom and Isabella. "Nik will have blocks set up. He has police in pocket."

Isabella rolls her eyes. "Of course he does." *They always have.*

. . .

IRINA GRIPPED THE KNIFE IN HER POCKET AND CROSSED THE STREET. She was only a few blocks from where she was to find her target and the nausea in her gut swelled. I can't keep doing this. *A car beeped its horn as she scampered off the road.* Shit. Pay attention!

A police officer stood on the opposite corner, holding a radio while his partner spoke with a teenager sporting a pink and purple mohawk.

A volt shot through her chest to her throat and she scurried across the pavement towards him. Her body clenched as she processed what she was doing.

He's a policeman. He's here to help.

She stood in front of him and cleared her throat. "Excuse me?"

He looked up from his radio and slid his eyes up and down her body. His blank face broke into a grin and he stepped forward. "Are you okay, Miss?"

"No. I need help."

The policeman scratched a finger up under his police hat and nodded for her to continue.

"I am being held. I am being made to hurt people. I need safety. Please."

The policeman frowned a moment and bit his lip. "What are you talking about?"

"I am being held captive by The Organisation. They make me

hurt people for them." I can't admit to being a murderer. *"I know it sounds ridiculous but—"*

The policeman held a finger up and tilted his head. "And what is your name?"

"Irina. Petrov. I am eighteen."

"I see. And Ms Petrov how long have you been... captive?"

"For five years. Please help me." I can't go back there.

The policeman squinted his eyes a moment and pulled a phone out of his pocket. "One moment. Go sit on that bench." He jutted *his chin towards a park bench and held his phone to his ear.*

Irina's heart skipped and she stumbled to the bench and sat. She pressed a hand against her chest to calm her heartbeat. Oh my God. What am I doing?

She watched as the policeman spoke into his phone, his eyes never leaving her face. Maybe he's organising somewhere for me to go. Maybe he's telling his boss he needs assistance... maybe...

The policeman snapped his phone shut and sauntered across to Irina. "Ms Petrov?"

Irina nodded.

"Irina Petrov?"

She raised an eyebrow and sucked on her bottom lip. "Why are you asking me? I already told you."

"Please stand up."

Irina stood up. "Are you taking me to your police station?"

The policeman pulled a pair of handcuffs from his belt and pulled her hands towards him.

"What are you..." Irina's body shook and she widened her eyes, staring at the policeman.

"When I started my shift today I could never have imagined how profitable it would be."

"What?"

"Your Uncle Kostya will be here in twenty minutes. Sit down."

Irina's lungs collapsed and she grasped her throat. "What?" Her voice rasped as though being strangled.

"You do not run from The Organisation. They have eyes and ears everywhere." He shook his head and gave her a look of pity. "Silly girl."

TOM PRESSES HIS LIPS AGAINST ISABELLA'S FOREHEAD. "YOU'RE shaking."

"I'm cold," Isabella lies.

Tom chuckles against her head. "Okay."

Isabella sits up. "Sascha?"

"Da?"

"Where are we going?"

"A budget motel. Men take mistresses there when they do not want their wife to find out. They will not ask questions."

Tom snorts. "And how does someone like you know about a place like that?"

Isabella doesn't have to look at Tom to know he's grinning.

"Men like Marat frequent it. Not me." He looks at Mischa who slides a hand across and through his hair.

"He knows I would cut his testicles off."

Tom gasps. "Mischa. I never."

Mischa turns in her seat and offers a small smile.

Isabella smiles back and holds out her hand.

Mischa takes it and squeezes. "It will be okay. I trust Sascha with my life."

"Me too," Tom says.

"Me three." Isabella smiles at Mischa before noticing bright lights. Flashing. Bright. Lights. *Shit.* She claws at Tom's leg.

"Shhh. It's fine." He holds his lips against her temple as she digs her nails into his thigh. "Steady on, you know I'm still weak right?" She feels his mouth grin against her skin.

"You'll never be weak."

"Don't be so sure."

Isabella looks up into his face and he gazes back with his clear green eyes.

Isabella can't help herself and she lifts her chin, kissing Tom's mouth. "Weakness is strength, Tom."

He huffs out a half laugh. "If you say so." He wraps his arm tighter around her as the car slows.

The police wave Sascha behind some barricades and he manoeuvres the car into the lane. They wait as a police officer walks around the car. He bends down at the front and checks the number plate before looking back up and peering through the windscreen.

"Please tell me you didn't steal this car, Sash?" Tom leans forward resting his chin on the side of the driver's seat.

"I rented it."

"Rented it? Under what name?"

"My dead father."

Tom fingers tighten around Isabella's. "And tell me, Sash," Tom hisses in Sascha's ear. "Does Nik know your dead father's name?"

"Da."

"Excellent." Tom leans back in the seat. "What's a mad dash for our lives without a bit of drama?" He chews on his lip.

Isabella takes hold of his hand again and squeezes.

Sascha winds his window down and looks up at the policeman standing by the car. "Dobryy vecher ofitser."

"Ty segodnya vecherom pil?"

Isabella relaxes into the seat as she hears the officer ask if Sascha had been drinking this evening.

"We need to dump this car," Tom murmurs in Isabella's ear as Sascha blows into a small black box being held in front of his face. The box beeps a couple of times before the policeman checks it and waves them through.

Isabella's shoulder loosen and she lets out a steady breath. She peers out the back window as they drive away from the police checkpoint.

SASCHA PULLS UP IN FRONT OF THE SEEDIEST, MOST RUN-DOWN looking motel Isabella has ever seen. She leans forward and peers through the windscreen. "Oh wow."

"Jesus…" Tom follows her gaze.

"We stay one night. Work out our next move and go." Sasha gestures everyone out of the car. "I must get rid of this car." He twists in his seat and looks at Tom. "Please keep Mischa with you until I return?"

Mischa grabs Sasha's arm. "Sascha…"

"Shhhh… Ostavaysya s Tomom. On budet derzhat' vas v bezopasnosti. "

Mischa holds tighter to Sascha's arm and shakes her head. "Niet…"

"Like he said, I'll keep you safe." Tom reaches across and puts his hand on Mischa's arm. "I promise."

After a few more moments of Mischa gripping Sascha's arm and refusing to let go, Tom pulls her hand free and holds it.

Isabella sweeps Mischa's hair back from her forehead and smiles.

"Come on," Tom whispers and the three of them get out of the car.

Sascha takes off straight away and Mischa folds at the waist and sobs.

Isabella's heart aches and she wraps her arms around Mischa, resting her cheek against hers. "He will come back."

Mischa nods, leaning back against Isabella as her body trembles.

"Let's get inside." Tom grabs Isabella's hand and leads the girls into the tiny reception area.

The man sitting behind the desk looks like a cheap version of John Travolta in Saturday Night Fever, and he eyes both girls up and down as they sit on the rickety fold up chairs.

Isabella grimaces and looks at Tom as he glares at the slimeball.

"Dve komnaty." Tom raises his eyebrows until the man slides his eyes off Isabella and Mischa.

"Dva? Ty uveren?"

Isabella bites her tongue. *Yes he's sure he wants two rooms, you sleazy piece of...*

Tom tilts his head and hardens his glare. "Da."

"Two rooms?" Mischa squeezes Isabella's hand.

"Yes. But stay with us until Sascha comes back." Isabell gives her a smile and nods. "We won't leave you alone. I promise."

Mischa nods and dips her head.

"Well I'm not most customers," Tom barks. "Do you have two rooms available or not?"

"If you wanted English you only had to say…"

"Excellent, may I also request less sleaze?"

"I am just saying… one room would save money and... effort." He grins a yellow toothed grin.

"While I'm at it, may I request rooms *without* hidden cameras? Or is that standard in a piece of shit place like this?"

"We may not be Hilton, but I do not spy on my guests." He sniffs at the suggestion and pulls out two keys. "Are you sure you want whole evening? It is cheaper for just couple of hours…" His eyes slide to Isabella and she curls her lip.

Tom snatches the two keys off him and flicks his head towards the door. "Let's go."

The girls stand, and Isabella glares at the slimeball as he grins at her, running his tongue along his top teeth.

"I know you want to stab him, but let's go." Tom stands at the open door.

Isabella stops in front of Tom and lifts one corner of her mouth. "So bossy."

"I'm feeling better."

"Evidently."

33

TOM

Tom slams the door to the room shut and slides the chain along the lock. Isabella hugs Mischa against her as they sit on the bed.

Tom's chest pangs and he kneels in front of Mischa.

"I'm sorry. I don't know what to say."

"There is nothing to be said. But please do not feel responsible." She puts her hand on Tom's cheek and smiles. "You seem better."

Tom smiles. "Thanks to you."

The phone in Tom's pocket rings and he yanks it out. "Yes?" He stands and his eyes sweep over the room.

"I have set fire to car. I will be back soon."

"How are you getting here?"

"I will steal car."

Tom smiles. "I feel like a proud father, Sascha."

Sascha chuckles. "Desperate times…"

"Stay safe." Tom hangs up and sits next to Isabella on the sagging bed. "Well, isn't this… quaint." He looks at the stained comforter and feels invisible crawlies on the back of his neck. He rubs a hand through his hair and puffs out a breath. "Just so we're clear Iz… I'm picking the next holiday destination."

"And here I was thinking this topped Paris." Isabella laughs as a loud bang on the adjoining wall echoes through the room. She slaps her hand over her mouth and stares at Tom.

Tom reaches for his pistol and hears a muffled moan, followed by a squeal. More thumps against the wall confirm what Tom is already thinking.

He smirks and sticks his pistol back into his waistband. *No further banging required…*

The thudding against the wall gets faster and louder before fading.

Tom stares at the wall a moment before nodding once to himself. He turns to the girls and opens his mouth, about to suggest they try and sleep when an enormous thump hits the wall accompanied by a lingering moan, tinged with panting breaths.

He slams his mouth shut and bites the inside of his cheek, raising an eyebrow at Isabella.

Isabella drops her face and Tom chuckles watching her shoulders shake. The moans and squeals grow louder and more urgent until finally an unbridled scream erupts and a husky female voice curses loudly.

Tom tilts his head and waits as silence settles around them.

Mischa gasps while Isabella snorts and rubs her forehead.

Tom bites his lip. "Good for them."

Isabella raises an eyebrow and grins. "Jealous?"

"A little…" *But not in this dive.*

Mischa stands and walks to the window, rubbing her hands up and down her arms as though cold.

"He is on way back?" She peers out the dirty curtains into the empty car park.

"He is."

"I am so tired." Mischa drops her head and sniffles. "And I do not think I have any tears left."

Isabella stands and walks to her. She hugs Mischa. "Sleep now. We'll watch over you until Sascha returns."

Tom pulls the covers back on the bed. He breathes in a sharp intake of air at the grey patches on the sheets that used to be white.

"God, this is putrid."

Mischa pulls her shoes off and climbs into the bed. "But it is better than being dead." Her voice wavers and she dissolves into sobs.

Isabella climbs into the bed and pulls Mischa into a hug, cradling her head against her chest. "Shhh… sleep now."

"Yes. Both of you sleep." Tom sits on the floor and leans against the bed, facing the door.

"I'm fine," Isabella whispers.

"Sleep, Iz."

"So bossy…"

Tom grins and drops his head back against the bed.

TOM'S EYES SNAP OPEN AND HE SITS UP ON THE FLOOR. THE ROOM is dark with the only light a constant neon flash from outside shining through the thin curtains. He scrambles to his feet as the door to their room jiggles. His nerves stand on end and his burn prickles, reminding him it's still there. He sidles to the door and peeks through the peephole, but there's no one there. Tom frowns. *Did I imagine it?* He pulls his phone out and looks at the time. *4.28am.* His heart contorts and he looks over at the girls, sound asleep. *Where the fuck is Sascha?*

Tom pushes Sascha's number and slaps the phone to his ear. The phone doesn't ring, going straight to an automated voice claiming it's off. Tom's gut rolls over and he pushes Sascha's number again. Again, the phone is off. *Fuck.* He pulls in a couple of deep breaths and looks out the window at the deserted car park.

Frustration gets the better of him and he thumps the heel of his hand against the window. "Fuck!"

"What is it?" Isabella's voice is croaky and she sits up in the bed, rubbing her eyes.

"Sorry, it's just… Sascha isn't answering his phone and he

isn't back." Tom watches Mischa as he speaks, not wanting her to wake up.

Isabella climbs out of the bed and walks to Tom. "He doesn't have a phone."

"What?"

"After Nik called and threatened us, I threw it out the car window."

"What phone was he on earlier?"

Isabella shrugs. "Payphone?"

"Jesus Christ. He goes out to dump a car and steal another one with Russian mafia goons probably out looking for him and has no phone?"

"Correct." Isabella slides her arms around Tom's waist and rests her head against his chest. "What now?"

"We wait for Sascha. Though... he should be back by now. I'm concerned." Tom drops his chin onto Isabella's head and wraps his arms around her shoulders.

A gasp from the bed draws both their attention. Mischa is sitting up, clutching at her chest.

"He is not back?"

Shit.

Tom sits next to Mischa. "No. But he will be. It's okay." *You could try and sound convincing...*

"But... what time is it?" Mischa scrambles out of the bed and stumbles to the window. She peers out, still clutching at her chest.

"It's four thirty." Tom clenches his teeth and waits.

"He has been gone eight hours?" Mischa spins around and stalks to Tom. "Where is he?"

Tom stares back into her trusting, wide brown eyes and his heart squeezes. "I don't know."

Mischa crumples to the floor and Isabella runs to her.

Tom's anxiety reaches a peak and he strides to the door. "I need some fresh air." He slams the door and storms along the gangway. *This is not good.*

Movement out of the corner of his eye slows his steps and he pauses. The tell-tale prickles erupt down his neck and he tilts his head. He looks behind him and sees nothing but tattered brown doors with paint peeling off them. He leans over the railing and looks below. A couple of derelict garden beds littered with empty bottles and torn condom wrappers line the walkway. *Classy.*

Something lights up across the road and Tom's eyes snap up to a black car parked next to the kerb. The dull glow of a phone screen disappears from the driver's side window as Tom watches. The car remains parked with the engine off. Tom walks back a couple of steps and reaches into his waistband for his pistol.

A soft scuffle behind him makes Tom spin and point his pistol.

"Fuck me." He lowers his arm a touch and glares at Elvis. "Can I help you?" Tom holds his breath a moment, trying to ignore the burning pain in his side.

The car across the road starts, peels away from the kerb and speeds down the street. Tom watches it disappear and turns back to Elvis.

"One of your friends?"

Elvis gives Tom his yellow toothed grin and shrugs. "I was simply coming to check you had all you need."

"What's your name?"

"Tima."

"And tell me, Tima… do you *always* lurk behind your guests at four thirty in the morning?"

Tima opens his mouth and Tom holds a hand up.

"Stupid question. Of course you do. You're a filthy perve. My mistake."

Tima slams his mouth shut and glares at Tom. "Do you need anything?"

Tom blinks once and holds his gun up at Tima's face. He jerks his head towards the door of his room. "In you go."

"Excuse me?"

"I said… In. You. Go."

"Ah… there seems to be some misunderstanding. I do not… shall we say… participate in whatever it is you may be… doing in my rooms. I simply facilitate your… requirements." He smiles again and Tom grips the pistol tighter so he doesn't pull the trigger.

"Do I look like I need your help in that department, Tima?" Tom squints. "Honestly?" *I'll officially give up.*

"No…"

Tom jerks his head again. "In."

Tom follows Tima into the room, his gun firmly poking into Tima's back.

Isabella looks up and grimaces while Mischa wipes her eyes.

"What's he doing here?" Isabella stands and shields Mischa from Tima's leering face.

"Well, he thought I needed help." Tom pushes Tima onto a moth eaten armchair and stands in front of him, tapping the pistol against his thigh.

"Help doing what?"

"You and Mischa. Apparently."

"Ugh. Can I stab him now?"

"Let's hear what he has to say for himself…" Tom blows a breath out and stares at Tima.

Tima says nothing, watching Tom.

"So, who was your friend in the car?"

"I have no friend in car."

"Bullshit."

"I have no idea what you talk about."

Tom squats in front of Tima, resting his pistol on his knee. "Do you think I'm stupid?"

"Define… stupid." Tima leans into Tom's face and grins.

Tom smiles back and slams the pistol into the side of Tima's head. He shouts and grasps his ear as blood trickles down his neck.

"Try again?" Tom raises his eyebrows, staring into Tima's face.

Isabella walks Mischa into the bathroom and closes the door behind them.

For the best.

Tom narrows his eyes at Tima and wraps a hand around his throat. "Do you know who we are, Tima?" Tom squeezes his thumb against the gland in Tima's neck. Tima grips the arms of the chairs and eyeballs Tom. "Don't get me wrong. I've wanted to strangle you since I met you. But I feel like now I have more of an excuse other than you're a filthy piece of garbage."

Tima's eyes move to the clock on the wall and back to Tom.

Tom grins. "I see."

"You see nothing." Tima spits at Tom and it lands on his neck.

"Well, fuck me." Tom wipes the saliva away and pushes harder against Tima's throat, peering into his face. "Not bright are you?"

"And you are? You come here… not my usual clientele. Those women are beautiful and you are… well let's just say you do not need to be in place like this."

"I'm flattered, Tima."

"You think The Organisation does not send out alerts? You think I can maintain my… lifestyle running this filthy motel?"

Tom grits his teeth inside his mouth and grimaces. "Fuck's sake Sascha."

"Who?"

Tom stands up. "Fuck."

Tima's eyes move to the clock again and Tom's pulse ratchets.

"Iz!"

The bathroom door opens.

"We're leaving."

"But what about…"

"We'll find him." Tom crouches down in front of Tima again. "Where are your car keys, Tima?"

"Fuck you."

Tom slams him to the side of the head again with his pistol. Tima howls and leans forward over his knees, clutching at his ear.

"I asked you where your keys are."

"And I said fuck you."

Tom smiles and nods. "Okay Tima. Fair enough. Iz?" His eyes don't leave Tima. "Take Mischa downstairs. Find Tima's keys on that shit heap desk he sits behind and start his car please."

"Tom?"

"I'll be right behind you. I just need to finish this little… meeting."

Isabella leads Mischa out of the room, every sob and sniffle Tom hears from her stab him in the chest but he keeps glaring at Tima.

Once the door closes, Tom pushes the pistol against Tima's heart.

"One more chance before I shoot you dead. Who did you tell about us?" *Like I need confirmation.*

"You will not shoot me."

"No?"

"Look at you… do you even know how to use gun?"

Tom pushes his hand into his chest and gasps. "Well that's just offensive."

"I aim to please."

"Me too."

Tom pulls the trigger and Tima slumps sideways in the armchair.

Tom stands and cracks his neck side to side.

"I can't be the first person who's wanted to do that."

He spins and slams out of the room.

34

ISABELLA

Mischa cowers behind the desk after a single gunshot rings out above their heads. Isabella glances at the ceiling before continuing to pull apart the papers and drawers.

"Keys keys keys…" Isabella chews on her bottom lip and rips open a filing cabinet in the corner. Loose paper flies out while squashed folders and crinkled copy paper is smooshed inside. "Shit."

She turns and sweeps her eyes over the faux timber back wall and spies the keytel Tima pulled their room keys from earlier. Isabella bolts across and grabs key after key, reading the tag and dropping them on the floor.

"What normal person doesn't hang their keys on a key hook?"

"Tima wasn't normal." Tom's voice fills the room as he stalks through the door.

"Wasn't?"

"Dead."

Isabella nods.

Mischa starts to draw in deep breaths from the floor while she covers her mouth and nose with her hands.

Isabella crouches next to her and rubs her back. "Sorry. Tom and I forget we do that."

Mischa shakes her head. "It is okay. Let us find Sascha. Please." She clasps her hands together under her chin and looks at Isabella.

"We'll find him," Isabella whispers before standing up.

She spies a coat hanging on the ratty office chair and grabs it. She rifles through the pockets and finds a set of keys. Her heart dances and she holds them up. "Tom!"

Just as Tom turns towards her, loud screeching of car tyres screams through the early morning quiet.

Tom looks through the window. "Fuck." He turns and his eyes dart around the room before resting in the corner. Isabella follows his gaze and sees a set of stairs. The stairs are rickety and look almost like a ladder. He nods towards them. "Go."

Isabella jerks her lip and lets out a laugh. "Are you crazy? I'm not leaving you here." *You're in no shape to be a hero.*

Tom rolls his eyes. "I'm fairly sure we've had a conversation about getting into the roof before, Iz? And I was right that time too was I not?"

"But—"

"No buts. Get in the roof." Tom turns back towards the door. "Now!"

"Tom, I really think—"

"I really think we're about to have our first real argument if you don't get in the fucking roof, Isabella."

Isabella grunts and throws her hands in the air. "Fucking fine."

Isabella grabs Mischa and they run to the stairs and climb into the cramped ceiling cavity.

"Will they not look here?"

"Tom will shoot them before they get anywhere near us." Isabella crawls to the back of the space and gestures Mischa across. *I hope.* Butterflies of dread flutter in her gut as she sits against the wall. *Don't get yourself shot, Tom.*

Mischa's eyebrows reach the top of her head. "Shoot them?"

"Yes." Isabella puts her hand on Mischa's knee. "Did you have any idea what Sascha was caught up in?"

"Well… not a first. But then they took me and tied me up in basement. Sascha had to agree to keep working for them, doing everything his boss told him to do or they were going to kill me."

Isabella nods. "They would have."

"Isabella?"

Isabella looks at Mischa. "Yes?"

"Is my Sascha dead?" Her breath catches and she pushes a hand to her stomach. Isabella looks down at Mischa's hand and swallows the ache in her throat. *Your baby.*

"No Mischa. Of course not. We'll find him. I promise." *Don't make promises you can't keep. Stupid fool.* Isabella pulls Mischa against her and pats her back. "It'll be okay. Tom won't let anything happen to us." *Though I may tear his nuts off for being an arsehat.*

"He should not be putting stress on himself. He was so very ill."

Isabella smiles against Mischa's head. "No point telling Tom what he *can't* do. He will just keep right on doing it."

"You love him a lot."

God, I really do. "Yes. I'd be dead if it wasn't for him." Isabella closes her eyes and thinks of Paris and her father. "But he's more than that."

Mischa nods. "I understand."

"I know."

Loud clambering fills the tight space and Tom appears at the top of the stairs. "You okay?"

Seeing Tom in one piece calms the nerves dancing through Isabella's blood stream and she sits up. "Yes. What's happening?"

"They've gone up to the room. So no doubt they'll be back here in minutes."

"Is it Nik?"

"Yes and Erik." Tom hauls himself into the space and closes the hatch. Splices of early morning light filter through the cracks in the ceiling. "If we're lucky they won't look up here."

Isabella snorts.

Tom shrugs. "Stranger things have happened."

The door to the reception area opens, the little bell above the door rings and loud voices filter through to the roof space.

"On byl durakom. Konechno, Tom ubil yego." Nik's voice is brash and angry.

Isabella's heart speeds up and she pushes herself harder against the wall. *You're right, Nik. Tom did kill him.*

Mischa squeezes her hand.

Tom crouches, poised at the hatch, his pistol at the ready.

Banging, crashing and cursing float up from below and Isabella holds her breath as Nik and Erik tear the office apart.

"Tom…" Isabella whispers.

Tom holds a finger to his lips.

"Oni by ne torchali." The anger in Nik's voice is tangible and Isabella grits her teeth.

Tom raises his eyebrows at Isabella as Nik claims they would not have hung around.

Isabella shakes her head slowly. "Wow," she whispers.

"Oni ne mogli zayti slishkom daleko. Davay."

Mischa draws in a sharp breath. "They are leaving?"

"Sounds that way. They think we are not too far ahead and can catch us." Relief washes over Isabella's shoulders and she sits up.

Mischa shifts against the wall and a loose board on the floor creaks.

Tom whips his head around and shakes his head at the girls. The three of them freeze and wait.

The silence from below is the loudest thing Isabella has ever heard. *Jesus…*

They keep waiting and it feels like a hundred years before the tiny bell over the reception door tinkles.

Isabella lets out a low breath and clutches at her stomach. She rests her eyes on Tom as he stares at the hatch.

"Podozhdite." *Wait. Oh God.*

Isabella's stomach clenches again and she grips Mischa's hand tighter.

Tom raises up onto his knees and points the pistol at the hatch.

The deafening quiet does nothing to calm the beat of Isabella's heart. Seconds pass, but it feels like eons. Footsteps echo through the roof cavity as someone climbs the stairs to their hiding place.

Isabella swallows a moan of terror and bites down on her lip.

Mischa buries her face against Isabella's shoulder, the tremble in her body infiltrates Isabella's and they both huddle together.

The hatch shifts and Tom's shoulders rise as he holds his breath.

A gunshot rings outside through the dawn silence and Mischa startles, muffling a squeal against Isabella's arm.

Isabella slaps a hand against her heart and claws at her shirt.

Tom rocks forward, pushing both fists against the floor, heaving in deep breaths. He turns to the girls and Isabella stares at him.

The bell tinkles again as the door slams.

35

TOM

Tom crawls across to the girls and pulls Isabella against him. Feeling her warmth against his neck calms his breathing and he relaxes his shoulders. "I'm sorry."

"Me too."

"For what?"

"I called you an arsehat and threatened to tear your nuts off. Well… I thought it anyway…"

"I see."

Isabella shrugs. "I was pissed off. And thought you were gonna get shot."

Tom grins. "And your thoughts about me in my possibly final moments were that I'm an arsehat?"

"Yes."

Tom nods. "Fair."

Tom rests his chin on top of Isabella's head and the three of them sit in silence a while longer. Tom's eyes drift to the cracks in the roof, now streaming with soft early morning sun.

"Did you say you found keys, Iz?"

Isabella nods and pulls a ring with three keys hanging from it out of her pocket. "They were in his coat."

Tom looks at Mischa. "Let's go find Sascha."

"What if he is dead?"

"He isn't." *But he must be.*

Tom lets go of Isabella, drifting his hand down her arm and letting go of her hand as he crawls back to the hatch. He slides it across a fraction and peeks down. Satisfied he hears nothing; he moves it an inch further. *Nothing.*

Tom flicks his head at the girls. "Let's go."

TOM FOLDS HIMSELF UP IN THE DRIVER'S SEAT OF TIMA'S RED Dacia.

"Renault knockoff," Tom whispers to himself, pushing the key into the ignition. He flicks his eyes to the rearview mirror at Mischa. "Okay?"

Mischa nods, but says nothing more.

"This car is disgusting," Isabella mumbles, shuffling her feet through the empty takeaway containers and rubbish in the passenger footwell.

"Sorry, Iz. I ran out of time to rent us a beamer."

"Well, frankly it's not good enough."

Tom grins, they turn out of the car park and slams his foot down. *To where? Who fucking knows?*

"Okay, Iz. Where are we going?"

"No idea."

"Fantastic." Tom pulls his phone out of his pocket and gives it to Isabella. "He may call…"

Tom looks at Mischa again and she is staring out her window with tears running down her cheeks. He trains his eyes forward and grips the wheel. A quick look in his rearview mirror shows a grey SUV behind them at a distance. *Nothing to worry about.*

Tom turns left and drives on. Moments later, the SUV appears behind them. He opens his mouth to say something and closes it again. *It's probably nothing.*

He eases his foot off the accelerator and watches. The grey car stays the same distance back from them. *Interesting.*

"Okay so…" Isabella looks up from Tom's phone. "Around six miles from here there's another hotel - looks nicer than the last shit heap and it has a restaurant. And I'm starving. We can go there, regroup and work out a plan to find Sascha. Yes?"

Tom watches the grey car as it pops up behind him after every turn. *Aren't you a pest?*

"Tom?"

"Huh?"

Isabella huffs. "About six miles—"

"Well, fuck." Tom swerves the car to the side of the road and folds his arms across his chest, his eyes stuck on the rear-view mirror.

"What the hell, Tom?" Isabella leans across the console. "Are you even listening to me? Or are you being an arsehat again?"

Tom watches as the grey car stops in the middle of the deserted backroad around fifty metres from where they are.

Isabella twists in her seat and looks out the back window. "We're being followed?"

Mischa gasps and hunches down on the back seat. "By who?"

"Well… Yes. We are." Tom continues to watch the car as it sits, idling in the middle of the roadway. "But I don't think it's the baddies."

"Then who?" Isabella chews on her lip still looking out the back window.

Tom reaches across and lifts Isabella's shirt. A gun is tucked inside her trousers. "Excellent. Well…" Tom pulls his own gun out and plonks it on his knee. He starts the car again. "Let's find out."

"What?"

"Mischa? Stay down. Just in case."

Mischa lays across the backseat and covers her face. Tom sees her shoulder trembling and hates that it's because of him.

"Tom? Have you finally lost your last marble?" Isabella rips her gun out and racks the slide.

Right, well that was hotter than it should have been.

Tom bites his lip as he throws the car into reverse and pushes his foot down. "Hold on."

The car jerks backwards and Isabella drops her gun in her lap and slams her palms onto the glove box. "Jesus, Tom."

Tom spins the car around and rolls it to a stop next to the grey SUV that hasn't moved. His heartbeat thunders through his ears. *I hope I'm right.* He grips his pistol in his lap, keeping it below the window line.

The window of the SUV glides down and the driver's face comes into view.

Tom grins as Isabella gasps. Tom winds his own window down. *What is this 1965?*

"Hey, Sash."

"Moya dorogaya!" Mischa leaps from the car and Sascha gets out of the Rav. She wraps her arms around his neck and kisses all over his face. "U vas tak mnogo problem, mister."

Tom and Isabella follow Mischa out of the car and lean against it watching them reunite. He holds Isabella against him and listens to Mischa berate Sascha for disappearing.

"I'm sorry I called you an arsehat again."

Tom laughs. "It's fair though."

Isabella snakes her hand up under his shirt and gently traces around the bandage stuck over his burn. His skin tingles and prickles and although it's unpleasant, having her fingers on his skin is comforting.

"You've gone through all this…" she whispers against his chest.

"Don't." He kisses the top of her head and turns to Sascha. "We need to go, Sash."

Sascha nods, pulling himself out of Mischa's grasp. "We must.

Come. We will take this car. Yours looks as though it will give up."

"It's a dustbin on wheels." Tom ushers Isabella into the SUV.

She gets inside and leans into him past the open door. "I love you." She pushes her mouth to his and kisses him.

Tom runs his hand into her hair and holds her against his face. "And I love you. It's going to be okay. I promise." He holds his forehead against hers a moment before pulling away.

Isabella nods and sits back so Tom can close the door.

Tom slides into the front passenger seat and Sascha starts to drive. Tom pulls the spare magazines out of his pocket and notes how many rounds are in each. "Okay, Sash. What the hell happened?"

Sascha blows a long breath out and rubs his face with one hand. "I got rid of other car. I found service station and called you. But as I hang up, I saw black car I recognise pull in to fill up. I hid in restroom."

"Nik."

Sascha nods. "Da. It was only hour from motel. He had to be heading there."

"Then what?" Tom slides his hand over his bandage as the burn heats up. *Shit.* He holds his breath and watches Sascha.

"Then, after they left I took attendant's car and tried to get back to you before them."

"You know in hindsight it may have been wise to call and let us know… just… saying."

"Yes. I am sorry. I am still overwhelmed."

Tom reaches across and squeezes Sascha's shoulder. "You did good Sash." His burn stabs a pain through his side, and he sucks in a breath.

"Tom?" Isabella leans forward.

"I'm fine."

"Lie."

A rattle sounds from the backseat and Mischa holds a jar of pills over his seat. "I picked these up when you forgot to take them. You must take two."

Tom grunts and takes the bottle. "Thanks Mischa."

"Now. Take two now."

Tom turns and grins at her before popping two pills and swallowing them rough. He slaps his hand against his chest a couple of times and looks at Sascha. "Go on."

"So I arrive and see black car. It is just sitting on side of road. I turned off and parked before hiding in a garden. I watched and waited. The car sat for very long time. I could not risk returning to you all."

"He was waiting."

"Da. And then all of sudden car takes off."

"When I came outside and found Tima lurking around." Tom nods to himself.

"Once car left I waited a little while longer just in case. I saw Mischa and Isabella run into office. I heard gunshot and saw you also run into office. I was about to join you when black car returned."

"We were in the roof."

"I was so worried. I saw Nik and Erik run inside. When I did not hear gunfire I guessed you were hiding."

"Yes."

"So I wait. I see Nik come to door eventually. He pushed it open but then turned back. I panicked thinking he found you. I took gun and fired single shot into air to distract them."

"Sash, you have no idea how close they were to finding us before you did that."

Sascha nods. "They ran out and jumped in car and took off. I could not risk them seeing me and knowing you were still there so I wait. Then you ran out and left in red car so I follow."

"And you knew I'd probably shoot you if you came up on us."

"Da. I wait for you to come to me."

Tom smiles and claps Sascha on the back. "Look at you being all clever and stealthy."

"I am fast learner."

Isabella leans forward again. "Okay, but where are we going now? I was thinking somewhere where there's food might be good?"

Tom leans his head back so his face is next to Isabella's. She nuzzles her cheek against his and pecks him on the lips.

Tom smiles against her mouth. "You need a Snickers."

36

ISABELLA

I sabella shoves a forkful of pilaf in her mouth and chases it with ice cold kvass.

"Jesus, Iz. You keep eating like that, I'm going to need a cold shower."

Isabella rolls her eyes at Tom and swallows her food. "I feel like I haven't eaten in days."

"We kind of haven't." Tom swallows his own pilaf and nods towards Isabella's drink. "What is that anyway?"

"Try it." She holds the kvass out to him.

"No thanks. It looks like marmite with bubbles."

Isabella takes a gulp and slams the glass down. "Delicious."

Tom smiles and sips his water.

"Okay. So now we need plan." Sascha looks around the almost deserted roadside restaurant and back to Tom.

"Yep," Isabella covers her mouth with her hand as she chews. "We don't have passports. So we're buggered, basically."

"That's what I love about you, Iz. Your optimism."

"It's just going to be difficult is all." Isabella looks around. "Where's Mischa?"

"Bathroom. She is always needing bathroom these days."

Isabella giggles. "Pregnant problems, huh?"

"Something like that." Sascha smiles. "Thank you."

"For?" Isabella picks up her glass and watches Sascha over the rim of it.

"Helping us. I cannot bring child into a world where all this bloodshed and terror is normal." Isabella watches Sascha as he dips his head down and her chest swells. *You are the sweetest thing.*

"It's not like we had a choice, Sash." Tom rests an arm on the back of Isabella's chair.

"True. But…" He shrugs.

"It's fine. We'll get out of here. And you'll simply love the weather back home. It's delightful."

"Really?"

"No. It's bollocks."

Sascha snorts into his food. "I look forward to it."

Mischa scurries to the table and sits in her chair. "A woman looked at me strangely in bathroom. We should hurry." She scoops food into her mouth and chews.

"Relax, my little butterfly. You also thought waitress looked at us strange and old lady slurping soup in corner. You are paranoid." Sascha kisses Mischa's temple. "We are hours from where he last found us. Stop worrying. It is not good for baby."

"He's right." Isabella smiles and reaches across, taking Mischa's hand in hers. "We'll work this out." Isabella scans the restaurant, noting they are the only ones there apart from the old lady in the corner.

"I'll call Martha." Tom slaps his phone to his ear and a moment later he snorts. "Well, aren't you the ray of sunshine we need right now." Tom grins at Isabella and rolls his eyes. "Yeah, he landed face down on the passports and soaked them in blood so… no go." Tom rubs his eyes and leans onto the table. "Yes... well I'm fine and fully capable of…" He sighs loudly and holds the phone out to Isabella without saying a word.

Isabella takes it. "Martha."

"My dear. I'm so sorry about Red Square. I had no idea Malcolm had the information. James told me, but it was too late."

"It's not your fault." Isabella pokes her fork into her food.

"How's Tom? Truthfully?"

"He's fine." Isabella smiles at Tom as he peers up from his meal. "Impossible as usual."

"Standard."

"Yes."

Tom tilts his head and squints at Isabella. She shakes her head and gestures for him to keep eating. He stares at her and raises a forkful to his mouth. He chews slowly and raises a brow.

"He's so cute when he's irritated."

"Hmm… he's a pain in the backside is what he is."

"Agreed."

Tom flaps his hand about wanting the phone back, so Isabella stands up. She walks to the window and looks out at the highway. "So, we're kind of stranded."

"Yes. You are."

"We need to get smuggled out of here. It's the only way."

"Well, that doesn't sound dangerous at all."

"I know, I know." Isabella scratches her hand through her hair. "And then there's the added bonus of Nik looking for us. And no doubt finding us again."

"Do you have any friends left over there? Any contacts at all?"

"I doubt it. I'm a very profitable prize right now. I can't trust anyone."

A beep sounds in Isabella's ear and she holds the screen in front of her a moment. *Another call?*

"Martha, there's another call coming in.. gimme a sec."

"My dear—"

"Hello?"

"Are you missing me yet?"

Isabella's stomach drops to the floor as though full of concrete.

Shit.

"How the fuck did you get this number?"

"How the fuck do I get anything I want? I threaten and kill people to make them do things for me. Remember?" Nik chuckles. "Or pay handsome sum."

Malcolm.

Isabella runs back to the table. She stands in front of Tom and speaks into the phone. "So how long have you been tracing this number, Nik?"

Tom's eyes widen and he drops his glass. Water spills across the table and he stands up.

Mischa scrambles to mop up the water while Tom peers at Isabella as she listens.

"Some time. It has been enlightening watching where you end up. I'll leave you to your lunch now. I enjoy watching you run. I may not kill you quite yet. But keep your eyes open, my dear Irina. You never know where I may appear."

The phone goes dead and Isabella stares at the screen.

"How the fuck did he get that number?" Tom grabs the phone and rips the sim card out before dropping it and smashing it with his foot.

"Paid a handsome sum?" Isabella's eyes widen and she watches Tom's face change as he comprehends.

"Malcolm."

"But how…"

"I used the phone just before I passed out to call Martha. James hacked her phone and computer and found that Malcolm had done the same. I didn't know at the time."

"So he's been tracking us this whole time. Maybe Tima didn't…"

"Of course he did. You're worth a lot of money. Pity I killed him before he could cash in." He stalks towards the door.

"Tom! You can't just go waltzing out there." Isabella grabs his elbow.

"Iz."

"No! One, you're still not a hundred percent. Two, he will shoot you if he's out there. And three…"

Tom raises his eyebrows. "Three?"

"Well, I don't have a three."

"Hmm." Tom rips his pistol out from under his shirt and marches through the door.

"Am I speaking some language you don't understand?" Isabella follows him outside but there's no one in the deserted car park.

Tom looks around, holding the pistol down beside his thigh.

"Tom!" Tom spins and fixes Isabella with an intense stare and she pushes her hand to her chest. "Calm down."

"Do you understand what's going on here, Iz? We're stuck in a country that we can't get out of; Nik knows exactly where we are and has done for the past two days. He could have killed us at any time. I'm still weak as shit and it's *pissing* me off…" He sucks in his bottom lip and takes a breath. "He's playing with us. And I don't like being played with."

Isabella steps in to him and puts both hands on his chest. "I'm sorry. I'm sorry for all of it. We should never have come here. It was selfish of me."

Tom lets out the breath he had drawn in and wraps an arm around her shoulders. "No. It wasn't selfish."

Isabella rests her ear against his heartbeat for a moment and closes her eyes. "How are we going to get home?"

"I don't know." His heartbeat increases and Isabella runs her hands up his neck and through his hair.

She looks into his eyes and smiles. "We'll figure it out. We always do."

Tom drops his forehead against hers. "Yeah."

"Tom?" Sascha's voice interrupts their moment and they turn around. He holds a phone up.

"Where did you get that?"

"I offered old lady slurping soup two thousand rubles for her phone. Code is five oh one one." He drops the phone into Tom's hand. "We must go."

Isabella leaps at Sascha and wraps him up in a hug. "Thank you."

"It is nothing."

Isabella steps back and giggles as Sascha's face glows bright red.

"He has never been good with women throwing themselves at him." Mischa grins and walks towards their car.

An engine revs from behind them. Isabella turns and a black car shoots out from behind the restaurant and drives directly at Mischa.

Tom runs and jumps, grabbing Mischa around the waist and the two of them tumble down in front of their SUV. The car misses Mischa by a breath and she squeals as she hits the ground.

The black car continues on, making a sharp turn out of the carpark and onto the roadway.

Isabella runs to them and kneels beside Tom. "Nik," she pants. Her heart races and she runs her hands over his face. "He's taunting us."

Sascha pulls Mischa against him as she sobs.

"I'm fine, Iz." Tom sits up and pushes his hand into his side, against his burn. He heaves in air and Isabella hears the shake in his breath.

"No. You aren't." Her nose tingles and stings as tears gather in her eyes. *It's all because of me.*

"Mischa?" Tom leans across and squeezes her shoulder. "Are you okay?"

Sascha is covering her in a hug and whispering in her ear.

"I think so." She rolls onto her knees and stays on all fours, catching her breath.

Isabella shuffles to her. "Oh my god, are you in pain? Is your baby okay?"

"I am fine." Mischa squeezes her arm and stands up.

"I'm so sorry Mischa."

"You were not driving car, Isabella."

But I may as well have been.

Mischa runs a hand over her tiny baby bump. "I am okay. It is okay."

"C'mon." Tom stands, leaning against the car. He heaves in a few more breaths. "We have to go."

"Tom? Are—"

"I'm fine!"

Isabella slams her mouth shut and stares at Tom. He shakes his head and refuses to look at her. "Let's just get the fuck out of here." He pulls open the rear door and flicks his head. "C'mon, Iz. Get in."

Isabella gets in and sits, folding her arms across her chest. Tom slams the door and gets into the front.

"Let's go Sash."

"You think he is waiting for us?"

"No doubt." Tom huffs again as he leans forward and presses against his side.

Isabella's heart softens and she leans forward. "Tom?"

"I'm fine. It's just… tender."

"But—"

"Iz! Leave it. Please."

Isabella bites her lip and sits back. She swallows the lump in her throat and stares out the window.

37

TOM

Tom chews on the inside of his mouth and glares out of the windscreen. *Ugh. I was a bastard.* He sighs and rubs his eyes. The burn in his side throbs and prickles and every other uncomfortable sensation possible. He is tired and spent. *I should not feel this shitty.* The heat radiating from Isabella in the backseat slaps him in the back of the neck. *Yep. Bastard.*

He pulls the old lady's phone out and dials Martha's number.

"This is Judith."

"It's me."

"New phone?"

"Nik traced the old one. Malcolm must have given him that number as well."

"I see."

"Yep."

Tom watches the landscape zip past as they fly down the highway. He bites on the inside of his cheek and turns to see Isabella glaring out the side window, her arms folded.

"So where are we at?" Martha's voice brings him back to the task at hand and he turns to the front.

"We need to get the fuck out of here."

"Yes. As we discussed before you left. Airspace is impossible. The borders will be crawling with Nik's spies so a vehicle is also out… What?"

"What?"

"One moment Tom."

Tom huffs and drops his head back against the headrest and stares at the roof of the car. Martha's muffled voice drifts in and out. *What the fuck is she doing?*

"Tom."

"James." Tom bites down on his lip.

"I think I can help you."

"Well…" Tom blows air out of his mouth. "This fills me with trepidation and annoyance all in one go."

"Annoyance?"

"Let's just say I'm questioning my whole existence."

James laughs. "Oh yeah… this would be what... the third time I've saved your arse? You're welcome by the way."

Tom rolls his eyes. "You haven't saved anything yet. What's your plan?"

This oughta be good.

"The HMS Arrochar is currently in the Barents Sea doing exercises."

Tom lets the silence linger. *Not the Navy. Please.*

"What if we can get you on it?"

"I'm listening."

"Well… that's my plan so far."

"Ingenious."

"Can you get yourselves to Murmansk?"

Tom looks at Sascha. "Can you get us to Murmansk?"

Sascha turns to look at Tom, his eyes wide. "That is at least two day drive."

"It's a two day drive." Tom focuses back on the phone.

"That's good. Gives me time to work it out."

"You're not filling me with confidence, James."

"Get to Murmansk. I'll call you when I have more."

"But—"

The line goes dead and Tom glares at the screen a moment before redialling.

"Tom?"

"James."

"Did you need something else?"

"You hung up on me."

"I…did. Yes."

"*You* don't hang up on *me*."

"I don't? Sorry I—"

Tom grins to himself and shoves the phone in his pocket. *That feels better.* He turns and looks at Isabella again. She hasn't moved, still staring out the window with her mouth pressed in a thin line. *Okay, that doesn't feel quite as good.*

"Iz?"

She turns her face and peers at him with her eyebrows raised. Her mouth remains pursed.

Tom clears his throat. "Are you okay?"

"I'm fucking dandy, Tom." She gives him a pointed look and resumes looking out the window.

Tom watches her face and runs his tongue across his top teeth. "You don't *appear* to be dandy…" Tom braces himself as Mischa snorts softly and Sascha shakes his head.

Isabella drags her eyes away from the window and glares at Tom. "How observant of you."

"So I was a dick—"

"I really don't want to discuss any of it with you right now."
Ouch.

Tom sighs and turns back to the front of the car.

"You are brave man," Sascha whispers.

"Hmm."

IT'S A LITTLE AFTER MIDNIGHT WHEN TOM OPENS THE DOOR TO their hotel room and steps back to let Isabella in. She stomps past him and goes straight to the bathroom, slamming the door behind her. A few seconds later she opens it again and marches out.

"There's no fucking bathtub." She crosses her arms.

"We're in Pushnoy, Iz. Not Paris." *Remember Paris?* "I mean… the fact there's a clean toilet and shower is a bonus, really."

Isabella grunts and sits on the end of the bed. Her arms are still folded.

Tom sits next to her and they both stare at the wall in front of them.

"So… that was a twelve hour drive and you barely said three words."

"I had nothing to say."

"Are you gonna let me apologise now?"

Isabella tilts her head. "Go on."

"I was irritated and angry and I shouldn't have taken it out on you."

Isabella says nothing and keeps her head tilted.

"And… I'm sorry…"

"Okay."

"Okay? That's it?" Tom grits his teeth.

"What do you want me to say? I've made it pretty fucking clear that I blame everything that's happened on myself." Isabella jumps off the bed and turns to face Tom. "What happened to you was my fault. Mine. No one else's. *I* brought us here. *I* insisted we have dinner with Nik. *I* failed to carry out his instructions. All of it." She throws an arm out to illustrate her point. "*Me*. Tom." She slaps her hand against her chest. Tears fill her eyes and she blinks, sending them down her cheeks.

Tom's chest caves in and he stands up. "Iz, you need to stop blaming yourself."

"No... No I don't. But maybe… just maybe Tom, if I'm trying to ask you if you're okay, or helping you… or whatever… fucking deal with it! And don't get all defensive and angry. Because I've had it."

"Iz—"

"No. I need to yell at you so just shut up." She sniffles and wipes the back of her hand across her nose and mouth. "You turn into a six year old who has his favourite toy taken off him when you don't get your own way."

Tom clamps his mouth shut and raises an eyebrow at Isabella.

They both stand, eyeing each other and saying nothing.

"Are you done?"

Isabella stomps across to Tom and pushes him to the chest with both hands. He doesn't move and looks down at her.

"So… you aren't done?"

Isabella lets out a grunt, turns away and stares out the window. "I'm really fucking angry."

"Yes. You've made that apparent."

"Good. Take note."

"Iz?"

"What?"

Tom reaches across and puts his hand on her shoulder. He turns her around and runs his hand up her neck and tilts her chin up. "I'm sorry."

She looks into his eyes. "Stop it. That's not fair."

"What?" He slides his other hand up her neck and cups her jaw. "What's not fair?" He touches his lips to hers and kisses her.

She half-heartedly pushes against his chest but then digs her nails in and bunches his shirt in her hands.

"You play dirty," she whispers into his mouth, her breath brushes his top lip and it sends a tingle down his neck.

"Always have." He walks her backwards and they fall onto the bed. He rests his elbows either side of her head and tangles his fingers through her hair, kissing her harder.

Isabella wraps her legs around him and yanks his shirt up over his head. She runs her fingers down his sides, tracing around the outside of his bandage.

Tom sucks in a breath as the prickles erupt beneath the gauze. *Not now.*

"You should be sleeping," Isabella mumbles against his chest as she kisses her way across his skin.

"Can't. Busy."

Isabella's hands reach the top of his trousers and she pulls the buttons apart. Tom drops onto the bed next to her and yanks his trousers off, throwing them on the floor. Isabella rips her own clothes off and adds to the pile on the floor.

She drapes herself across Tom's body and brushes his nose with hers. His hands find her hips and he grips tight, holding her against him.

"Just so you understand… I'm still mad at you." She dips her lips to his and nibbles his lip.

Tom closes his eyes and nods. "I'm okay with that."

Isabella pushes her face harder against his and kisses him. Tom drifts his hand down and strokes the inside of her thigh, barely touching her skin. She exhales roughly and Tom smiles.

"Are you still mad?"

He drifts his fingers higher.

Isabella burrows her face into his chest. "Yes."

He rolls her onto her back and runs his mouth over her neck and down to the dip in her throat. He dances one hand across her breast, the other floats between her legs and her sharp intake of breath makes Tom grin against her neck.

"Now?"

"Somewhat."

Tom drifts his fingers back and forth and around in circles and Isabella arches her back, gripping the sheets in her fists.

"Well… you just let me know."

"Know what?" Isabella gasps between breaths.

"When I should give up apologising." He slides his hands up the sides of her body and along her outstretched arms until he laces his hands with both of hers. He pulls her arms above her head and kisses her deeply.

Isabella tangles her legs with his and pushes her hips into him.

"You've got a lot of making up to do."

Tom grins and pushes into her, catching her moan in his mouth. Her heat wraps around him and he exhales against her neck.

She squeezes her thighs against him and knots her fingers in his hair.

"Understood."

A PHONE RINGING DRAGS TOM OUT OF HIS DEEP SLEEP. HE SITS UP as Isabella grumbles and rolls over next to him. He scrambles for the phone in his trouser pocket and lies back on the pillow.

"Hello?"

"It's me." James' voice is too loud at this time of the morning.

"Fuck, James. It's like six a. m."

"Yes. Well it's four a m here so I feel I have the raw end of the deal."

"Do ya? I'm stuck in Russia with the mafia chasing us so... I'm trumping you on that one."

"Right well... I have a plan."

Tom scratches a hand through his hair and shuffles to a sitting position against the cheap pine headboard. "Hit me."

"I spoke to Uncle Pete and—"

"What?"

"He's the fucking Admiral of the Royal Navy, Tom. It's *his* ship we wanna use. Plus... you have something he wants so..."

"God I hate it when you make sense."

"May I continue?"

Tom sighs as Isabella slides across the bed and rests her head against his chest. He looks down at her and strokes her hair. "Go on."

"He will arrange a chopper to pick you up from Murmansk and get you onto the ship. Then you'll disembark in Norway and fly home."

"He's doing all this out of the goodness of his cold black heart is he?"

"No. He's doing it in exchange for you destroying all the records you have of his extracurricular activities."

"What about Iz?"

"Well…"

"Fuck."

"One thing at a time, yeah? Get to Murmansk and call me. I'll get him to arrange the chopper."

"A navy ship." Tom's gut clenches and he hisses a breath out through his teeth.

"Yes. Is that bad?"

Yes. It's very fucking bad. "It's… no. It's fine. I hate to say it but you impressed me, James."

"Third time saving your bacon… surely I'm kind of a hero now?"

Tom swallows and says nothing.

James chuckles down the phone. "Murmansk. Call me." James hangs up.

Tom looks at the phone screen. "He hung up on me again."

Isabella sits up and stretches and Tom watches as her hair falls down her back and shoulders and her chest erupts in goosebumps.

"Well, fuck." He grabs her face and kisses her.

She drops her hands to either side of his neck. "We don't have time for this."

"Like hell we don't."

38

ISABELLA

Isabella emerges from the bathroom, her wet hair twisted in a knot on top of her head. Tom is at the window with his back to her. She wanders over and slides her hands around his waist, resting her cheek on his back.

He covers her hands with his and squeezes.

"Good to go?"

"Yeah. Though, it feels gross showering and putting the same clothes back on."

Tom turns around and wraps his arms around her. "No corsets to buy around here, huh?"

"Nope. But I ditched the knickers completely."

"God, Iz. Don't."

She giggles. "They'll be waiting for us outside. Let's go."

"Yeah but… now I know you aren't wearing knickers." Tom follows her to the door.

She turns around and leans against the door. "We should argue more often." She stands up on her toes and pecks his mouth.

Tom pushes her against the door and kisses her.

"Stop," she mumbles against his mouth, continuing the kiss. "We need… to go…"

Tom kisses her harder. "Ahuh."

Isabella reaches behind and turns the door knob. She pulls the door open, walking into Tom. She stops kissing him and smiles.

"We have to go." She flicks her head towards the end of the hall.

"Spoil sport."

Isabella grins and squints down the hallway. Sascha and Mischa walk out of their room and Sascha drapes his coat over Mischa's shoulders.

Isabella pouts and lets out a breath. "They're adorable."

"You sound like their aunty or something."

Isabella slaps Tom in the arm. "I'm just grateful. And… they're cute."

They walk to the end of the hall and Mischa turns and smiles at Isabella. "Did you sleep well?"

Isabella's cheeks flush and she nods. "Yes."

Tom snorts and Isabella slaps him in the arm again.

Sascha turns from peering out the glass doors. "We have around seven hour drive ahead of us."

"Okay," Isabella nods.

"Let us go. We can stop and get some breakfast in a while."

"So efficient." Tom nods towards the glass doors. "Let's go then."

Sascha pushes his backside against the door and it swings open. "Maybe we can find you more cabbage dishes, Tom." Sasha grins and turns, taking a step outside.

"Please don't."

Isabella smiles. "You know Sash, I always wanted a little broth—"

Isabella's words jam in her throat as a perfect round hole appears in Sascha's forehead accompanied by a wet thud. He falls backwards. Blood pools from under the back of his head, staining the pebblecrete pathway he lays on.

Tom grabs Isabella around the waist and wrenches her back into the hall. Mischa screams and collapses to her knees. Her scream is a blood curdling, high pitched wail and it grips Isabella's heart, tearing it in half.

Isabella pushes her hand into her chest and wheezes. "Oh... God." She stares at Sascha's lifeless body, his eyes staring blankly into nothingness.

Tom pushes past the girls and yanks his pistol from his waist.

Mischa drops to all fours and digs her fingernails into the threadbare carpet. She tries to crawl towards the glass door but Isabella wraps her arms around her shoulders and pulls her back.

"We can't Mischa. You need to wait. I'm sorry."

Mischa wails, sitting against the wall. She tilts her face to the ceiling and claws at her hair. She heaves breaths in only to wail and sob them back out. Isabella's chest squeezes and she pulls Mischa against her.

"Shhhh… Mischa." She kisses her temple. "I'm sorry. Oh God… I'm so sorry." Isabella's heart beats too fast and black spots float in front of her eyes. *This isn't happening.*

Mischa cries and trembles against Isabella, who watches Tom as he stands at the door peering left and right. His pistol is poised.

Don't you dare go out there.

Tom pushes his hand down on the door handle.

"Tom! Don't you dare go outside. I'll kill you myself." Isabella's heart slams itself against her ribs and she grits her teeth.

"Yes. Tom. Why would you venture outside when it is so cosy in this hallway?"

Isabella freezes and her scalp prickles from the ice cold presence behind her. She breathes a long slow breath through her nose and blinks once, staring at Tom.

Tom aims his pistol at a point above her head.

Mischa whimpers against Isabella's arm and her tremble intensifies. Isabella rubs her back and cradles her head against her.

Nik stands over the girls, pointing his own pistol back at Tom. "Now, now Tom. Don't be so hasty. I clearly have another here with me." Nik juts his chin towards Sascha's dead body. "Such a shame. He was so very loyal. Or so I thought."

Tom moves from the door and pushes himself against the wall, keeping his pistol trained on Nik. "What are you waiting for, Nik? Take a shot. If you're good enough."

"Tom," Isabella hisses. "Jesus Christ." She swallows past her dry throat as Tom continues to eye Nik.

"Well, this is fun, but we cannot stay here all day."

Nik steps forward and holds his pistol against Mischa's head. She squeals and continues to hide her face in Isabella's arm.

Nik pulls another pistol from his back and points it at Tom. "Drop your gun, Tom."

Tom glares at Nik. "Two guns, Nik? You're so fucking impressive." Tom pushes himself off the wall and stands in the middle of the corridor, refusing to drop his gun.

"Stop. Nik. What do you want?" Isabella slides her arm out from Mischa grasp and holds both hands up. "I'm going to stand up."

"Iz! What the fuck are you doing?"

"He's not here for a tea party, Tom."

Tom narrows his eyes and curls his lip. "Thanks for the newsflash."

Isabella stands up and looks into Nik's face. "You came for me. Here I am. Now what?"

She hears the growl in Tom's throat. "Fuck's sake."

"Look after Mischa, Tom." Isabella keeps staring at Nik as he smirks at her. "Like he said… he brought Erik."

The glass door behind Tom explodes and he falls forward onto the floor. Mischa screams and pushes herself against the wall. Isabella's knees buckle. She collapses at Nik's feet; her nose tingles and tears prick in her eyes.

Nik's hand closes around Isabella's arm. Nik pushes the

muzzle of his pistol against her temple. "Get up." He shoves the second gun into his waistband.

He jerks Isabella off the ground and pushes the gun under her chin. He stands behind her, his breath hits her neck.

"Now, now Irina. Be good girl. You can't help Tom now."

Isabella's eyes are glued to Tom as he lays on the floor. Pain like she has never felt before climbs up from her gut and rips her insides apart. "No!"

"Erik is outside. Let's go before he comes in and keeps shooting."

"Tom…" Her voice struggles against the dryness in her throat.

Nik pulls her backwards and she stumbles into his body. His hand tightens around her throat, the gun at her temple.

Isabella slides her eyes to Mischa who is cowering against the wall, hugging her baby bump. Tears stream down her face and she shakes her head, watching as Isabella is pushed into a room.

Isabella falls to the floor in the dark room and gasps in air. Her chest is on fire and blood thunders through her veins, whooshing through her ears.

"Nik… please. Let me just see him."

"To what end? He is dead, Irina."

Isabella wheezes and splutters. Tingles threaten at the back of her throat and she swallows the acid pooling on her tongue. She heaves in more rough breaths as a light is switched on.

Nik lunges at her and flips her onto her back on the floor. He pins both her arms with his knees and sits down hard on her hips.

"I tell you what, Irina. If you can throw me off from this position I will concede."

Isabella knows she's pinned. She knows she can't win but she pulls in a breath and thrusts her hips and kicks her legs. She screams against his hold and fights until there is nothing left. Nik sits and grins at her, pushing harder with his knees until pins and needles trickle down her arms. She stills and sobs, turning her head away from him.

Isabella hears the slide being racked on a gun and looks back at Nik. The round pops out and he throws the gun across the room. He picks up his loaded gun again and pushes it back up under Isabella's chin. He grins and reaches to the bed, pulling a knife from his bag.

"I thought you might feel more comfortable with old fashioned knife through heart, Irina."

Isabella breathes laboured breaths and stares into Nik's freezing cold blue eyes.

The cool blade of the knife is pushed against her neck and she glares at Nik. He pushes his weight down on her again and puts his gun in his waistband. He runs his free hand down her body and lifts her shirt. His eyes drop to her tattoo.

"So sexy, Irina."

God, you make me sick.

"What are you waiting for, Nik?" Her pulse hammers against the knife blade.

"You failed to carry out the last job I gave you." He traces the roses with his index finger, and it makes Isabella nauseous.

"Correct."

"You let bitch go." He slides the knife from the side of her neck to her throat.

"She didn't deserve to die just because you didn't like her politics, Nik." Isabella swallows and feels the pressure of the knife against her skin.

"How very liberal of you." He continues to slide the knife down to her chest, cutting the material of her shirt down to the middle of her breasts. *That knife is fucking sharp.* Isabella holds her breath a second and bites her lip.

"Just get it over with." Isabella glares into his eyes. "Or are you afraid?"

Nik grins and pushes his mouth onto hers. He knots his other hand through her hair and pulls it. Pain stabs through her scalp as she wriggles and thrusts her body beneath him. He pulls away and leers at her. The knife against her skin doesn't frighten her and she manages to free one arm. She jerks her hand back and slaps Nik across the face.

He grunts and snaps his face back to hers, grimacing. "We were best friends, Irina. You ate dinner at my home. You loved my mother as though your own."

"Yes. And now look at you. Look at you!" Pain slices through her heart and it's not the knife. *Why does this hurt? I fucking hate you.* "How could you?" Tears sting her eyes, and she fights to keep them from falling down her face. *I won't let you make me cry.*

Nik frowns, running his eyes over her face, down her neck to her chest. He slams his mouth against hers again, forcing her lips open. She retches and pushes against his chest with her free hand.

Isabella squeals into his mouth and rips her face away from his. "Get. The. Fuck. Off. Me."

"Not until I get what I want. Then… I kill you."

"I thought you were better than that Nik? Isn't that what you said?" Isabella's body trembles and she hates herself for it. *I'm not afraid of you.*

"I did. But... desperate times…"

Gunfire erupts in the hallway and Nik startles. It's enough that Isabella can buck her hips and she wiggles out from under him. *Mischa!* She goes to crawl to the door and he yanks her back by the ankle.

Nik squeezes her throat and pushes his face in to hers. "I win, Irina. I always win."

Isabella closes her eyes and turns her face away. She forces her sobs to stay down; the ache in her throat is unbearable. *Nothing matters now.*

Nik grabs his gun, drags Isabella to the window and slides it open. All the fight has left Isabella's body. She lets Nik push her against the windowsill. *Where's the knife?*

"Not long now, Irina. Then it will all be over for you."

The room door slams open and the sound reverberates off the walls. Nik pulls Isabella against him again, his gun at her temple.

Isabella blinks. Tom stands in the doorframe. He holds his gun out at glares at Nik. "Leaving without me?"

39

TOM

Tom steadies his pistol, lining up the sights between Nik's eyes. Isabella slumps against Nik and presses her hand to her chest.

"Tom." She exhales and struggles against Nik's hold.

Nik yanks Isabella in front of him, his hand at her throat and pistol to her head. Tom grits his teeth. *Get your hand off her throat.*

"Tom. So nice of you to join us. What shall we talk about?"

"Let her go."

Nik laughs and holds Isabella closer to him. He runs his tongue down the side of her neck and she whimpers but there is disgust behind it. Tom's blood bubbles and beads of sweat roll down his temples. Nik peers at Tom from behind Isabella's shoulder and grins.

Tom blinks a couple of times and tries to push the image of

Claire being held by Natasha as a human shield out of his mind. *Not the same.* The ache in his chest betrays him and he rubs his free hand across his shirt. *It's not the same.* He straightens his pistol again and realigns the sights.

"This makes you uncomfortable, Tom?" He presses his lips to her neck and kisses her. Isabella jerks away but Nik pulls her back. "Delicious," he mumbles against her skin.

"Get the fuck off me, Nik." Isabella's voice is husky and Tom hears the fear in it.

Tom steps forward and Nik pushes his pistol into Isabella's cheek, resting his mouth against her neck again.

"Shhh… be good girl and all will be okay."

"You're such a damn liar." Isabella squirms.

"It's okay, Iz. Nik won't hurt you."

"Is that so? And what makes you so sure? She is traitor."

"Because, if you shoot her, I'll unload a full magazine into your chest, Nik. And we both know you're a cowardly piece of shit, so…" Tom shrugs and jiggles his jaw back and forth, eyeing Nik.

"Tell me. Why are you not dead on floor where we left you?"

Tom smiles and leans forward. "Missed me," he whispers.

"And then?"

"I'll enlighten you after you let Isabella go."

Nik laughs. "Ah Tom, so naive. Irina is not going anywhere." He winces. "Wait, that is not true. She is coming with me." He trails his hand down her throat and slides it inside the ripped t-shirt. Tom's pulse lifts and he bites on the side of his mouth.

"So soft and feminine." Nik nuzzles her neck.

Isabella stares at Tom, her left eye twitches and she raises her chin a fraction. Tom watches her eyes as they drop to the floor at the foot of the bed.

Tom lowers his gaze and steps back. He sees the gleam of a knife blade half under the bed. *I see.*

"Excellent, Tom. Now you understand. If you could just keep walking backwards and out door, that would be ideal."

Tom grins and lifts his face to Nik and Isabella. "You're a glass half full kinda guy aren't you, Nik? I applaud you. Such positivity in dire circumstances."

"Dire for you, maybe."

"Indeed." Tom flicks his eyes to Isabella.

Isabella nods once and bends forward at the hips. She heaves her elbow backwards into Nik's crotch. Tom grimaces as he hears the crunch. *Bullseye.* Nik crumples forward. Isabella clasps both hands together and slams the same elbow down on the back of his neck.

"Jesus, Iz." Tom keeps his gun trained on Nik as he retrieves the knife from the floor. "That's some serious Karate Kid shit." He pushes the knife into Isabella's hands.

Nik pants on the floor, both his hands at his crotch and the gun next to him. "Blyad'!" He huffs air in and groans it back out as he writhes on the floor.

Tom winces and crouches next to Nik. "Ouch. That looked painful. Do you need anything? An ice pack? A bucket perhaps? That one sounded vomit inducing…" Tom shakes his head slowly and tsks. "Poor bastard." Tom shoves his pistol under his arm and grabs the gun Nik abandoned. He drops the magazine out and racks the slide. He tosses the gun onto the bed.

Nik ignores Tom and continues to groan.

Tom grips his own pistol and taps Nik in the side of the head with it. "Hey… I asked you a question."

"Fuck… you…" Nik pushes his forehead into the floor and lets out a frustrated scream.

Isabella kneels next to Tom. "Oh, Nik. Your poor nuts. And I was so looking forward to what you had in store for me. I mean… that preview you gave me in St Petersburg was just so hot."

Tom's head snaps to Isabella. "Wait, what?" Heat rises up his neck as he thinks about Nik touching her.

"Oh yeah, Tom… I forgot to tell you. Nik's such a generous lover… I tricked him into thinking I actually wanted to sleep with him… his foreplay was *phenomenal.*"

Tom grins at the sarcasm in Isabella's voice. *Of course.*

"Really left me wanting more, hey Nik?"

Well, I can't let that go unpunished. Tom swings his arm back and slams Nik to the side of the head with his pistol. Nik grunts and cups his ear with one hand, leaving the other grasping his crotch. Blood trickles through his fingers and Tom nods to himself. *Nice one.*

Tom grabs Nik's shirt by the collar and heaves him into a sitting position, slamming him against the wall. He glares at Tom, his sweaty face nearing a purple hue.

Tom smiles and jabs Nik to the chin. His head jerks back and hits the wall.

"Okay, wait. That was fun." Tom jabs him again, his head hitting the same spot. *Just so satisfying.*

Nik kicks a feeble leg out, connecting with Tom's thigh.

"Um… ouch?" Tom lurches forward and grabs Nik's jaw and squeezes. "Not good at this are you?" Tom glares into his face. "Probably because you get all your lemmings to do your dirty work."

Nik bats at Tom with his hands, slapping at his chest. It's almost comical and Tom squeezes his jaw harder. "Best give up Nik. It's over. For you."

Tom rocks down onto his backside and rests his wrists on his knees. The hand holding the pistol stays ready to pull the trigger.

Nik takes a few deep breaths and stares up at the ceiling.

"Seriously, Nik. Do you need some ice? I don't want your last moments on earth to be… painful."

Nik curls his lip and says nothing.

"That's a no?"

"Get it over with."

Tom raises his eyebrows. "Hmm? What's that?"

"I said… get it over with."

"That's what I thought you said. But see, the thing is… you kinda tortured me. And you touched Iz… where you shouldn't have." Tom stops and sucks a breath through his teeth. "I mean… you haven't really covered yourself in glory." His burn awakens and it's like a million tiny thorns poking through his skin. Tom grimaces and takes a breath. *Fucks sake.* He swings his pistol again and hits Nik in the same spot over his left ear.

Nik yelps and dips his head forward. Tom shoots his leg out and kicks Nik to the ribs. He falls sideways, sliding down the wall.

Tom presses a hand against his bandage and leans over to Nik. "Broken?"

"Fuck you."

Tom grins, braces his hand against the wall and slams his knee into the same ribs. The crunch of bones breaking is particularly gratifying. Tom grabs Nik by the hair and yanks him back to a sitting position.

A wail from the hallway floats into the room and Tom's breath hitches. *Mischa. Sascha. Their baby.*

"I'll go see her." Isabella stands and runs from the room. Tom watches Isabella disappear into the hall before looking back at Nik, his hand still pulling his head up by the hair.

"He was about to be a father, Nik. Did you know?" Tom pushes his face directly in front of Nik's. Their noses millimetres apart.

"Well, he made choices. They were wrong ones."

Tom slams Nik's head against the wall. "That baby isn't going to have a father. Because of you."

"Why do you care? It is not your baby." He grins and Tom makes note that his teeth are still intact. *That won't do.* "Or maybe it is?" He raises an eyebrow.

Yeah, those teeth have got to go.

Tom's pulse spikes and he punches Nik square on the mouth. His head smashes into the wall and teeth fall from his face. He spits blood down the front of his shirt.

"You know what your problem is, Tom? You are too emotional. You care." Nik laughs. "That is big mistake."

"I actually agree with you on that, Nik. But then... here I am beating the shit out of you. So maybe I can be both?"

Isabella appears next to Tom and puts her hand on his back. "She's with Sascha."

Tom nods, still glaring at Nik.

Nik flares his nostrils and holds Tom's glare. "You are nothing. You think killing me will make difference? Someone else will take my place. There is always someone else."

"No doubt. Though... we plan to be back home in by then..." Tom shrugs and gives Nik a laddish grin. "And as much as I've enjoyed my time here in tropical Russia, I won't be hurrying back." Tom looks at Isabella. "Iz?"

"I'm never coming back."

"Well, there we have it. Russia's ticked off the bucket list." Tom tilts Nik's chin up with the muzzle of the gun. "Tell me Nik. Do you have a bucket list?"

Nik says nothing as blood trickles down his chin.

"Well, that *is* a shame. You've kind of run out of time to write one."

Isabella pushes past Tom and squeezes Nik's throat. He wheezes and sucks air through his nose, glaring in Isabella's face. "I know how annoyed you get when I disobey you Nik. So I promise to follow instructions this time." She releases his throat and with both hands she rips his shirt open.

Nik's eyes flick to Tom who shoots him a grin. "Isn't this fun?"

Nik's eyes slide back to Isabella and she shuffles forwards on her knees, until she is leaning right over him. "Try not to move. I don't want to muck up any of the numbers."

Nik's breathing hastens and he pushes himself back against the wall but gets nowhere.

"I feel you. Those walls really inhibit a quick getaway, huh?" Tom stares at Nik's face while Isabella starts to carve into his chest. *Feel every fucking knife stroke.*

Nik hisses air in through his teeth, watching her face and refusing to shy away from her knife blade. He trembles and his fingers claw into the carpet.

"Three..." Isabella whispers. "Six..." She sits up and spins the knife in her hand. "One more number. Are you doing okay? Need some water?"

Nik spits at Isabella but it dribbles down his chin.

Tom snorts. "Saps your energy doesn't it?"

Nik kicks out with his feet, not aiming anywhere and Tom pushes the muzzle of his pistol against Nik's knee. "I should have mentioned, I'm very apt at shooting out kneecaps. It's one of my talents. So... maybe stay still, yeah?"

Nik's glare intensifies at Tom and he kicks his leg out again.

"I fucking warned you." Tom pushes the pistol into Nik's knee and pulls the trigger.

Howling fills the tiny room they are cramped inside and Nik rolls forward, grabbing at his knee.

"Surely now we can interest you in that ice pack?" Tom raises his voice above Nik's howls and wipes blood from his cheek and neck with the corner of the duvet.

Nik continues to scream into the carpet, his face buried in the dirty threadbare pile. Blood pools beneath his shot out knee and his breathing ratchets. *Going into shock. Bless him.*

"C'mon Nik. Sit up and let Iz finish her fancy numbers." He grabs Nik by the hair again and sits him against the wall.

Isabella smiles at Nik and leans forward, her knife at the ready. She pushes the tip of the blade into Nik's chest as he slumps there, shaking and panting, with no fight left.

"Two." She finishes with a flourish and sits back. "Pretty."

Nik starts to laugh, softly at first before becoming louder - almost delirious. Tom tilts his head and raises an eyebrow. "Is something funny?"

Nik abruptly stops laughing and spits on the floor. He glares at Isabella. "Maybe not today after all, Irina. But one day… you will pay for your betrayal."

"Maybe, Nik. But… feel special. I don't usually work on a live canvas."

"I feel so very important."

Isabella smiles, drops the knife and steps away. "You aren't."

Tom raises his pistol and points it at Nik's face.

He pulls the trigger.

40

ISABELLA

I sabella peers at Nik, while Tom rummages around the bed and floor, collecting guns and magazines.

Isabella's eyes travel over Nik's twisted body, with a freshly carved 3 6 2 dripping blood down his torso. He no longer has a face and though it's disturbing and macabre, Isabella can't help but stare at the pulpy mess where it used to be.

"IRINA! ARE YOU COMING?" NIK CYCLED DOWN THE STREET, calling back over his shoulder.

"Slow down Nik! You're going to fall off."

The front wheels wobbled as he tried to turn a sharp corner and the bicycle slid out from under him.

Irinia's heart sped up along with her legs to get to Nik as he lay sprawled in the gutter. She skidded her bicycle to a stop and jumped off.

"Nik?" She knelt beside him and slid her hands under his head. "Are you okay?"

Nik groaned and rolled onto his side to sit up. "Yeah. I'm okay. I was going too fast."

"Told ya."

"Yeah well I like going fast."

"But what if you hurt yourself really bad next time?"

"I won't. But if I fall off, you'll be there to help me." He wrapped his arms around Irina and hugged her. "Just like I will for you." He jumped up and picked his bicycle up. "C'mon. Let's go."

"HEY. YOU OKAY?"

Isabella blinks as Tom slides his arm over her shoulders and pulls her against him. She nods, still staring at Nik's body.

"We should go be with Mischa," Tom whispers. "And... get out of here."

Isabella nods. "I'm right behind you."

"Iz—"

"I'll be one minute." Her eyes flash as she looks into Tom's face.

Tom kisses the top of her head and lets her go. "Okay. One minute." He walks out.

Isabella kneels beside Nik and his voice echoes through her mind.

I am not who you remember. It is best if you do not expect me to be.

She bows her head and bites her lip. "Go to your mother, Nik. Maybe she can forgive you." A tear falls from her chin and lands on the back of his hand. She takes his hand and swipes her thumb over the wet teardrop. "Because I never will."

She stands and walks out of the room, pulling the door shut behind her. Peering down the hall she sees Mischa lying on the ground outside the shattered door, nestled against Sascha's body. Tom is crouched beside them with his head down.

Tingles prickle in Isabella's nose as she walks past Erik's body in the hallway and ducks through the obliterated glass doors. Tom looks up at her, but Mischa doesn't move. Her eyes are closed, and she is whispering in Sascha's ear.

Isabella's chest aches and a hole opens up where her heart beats. Tom stands and pulls her into him. "Are you okay?"

"No."

"Fair."

Isabella slides down Tom's body and kneels on the ground. She puts her hand on Mischa's shoulder.

"Mischa?"

Mischa whimpers and squeezes her eyes shut tighter. She nestles her face into Sascha's neck, the tremble in her body giving away the silent sobs.

Isabella's throat aches and she tries to hold back her own tears but they flood her eyes and topple down her cheeks. She gasps a breath in and shuffles herself behind Mischa. She lays down and wraps her arms over her and they both lie with Sascha.

"Iz, we need to—"

Isabella narrows her eyes at Tom and shakes her head. *Give her time.*

Mischa sits up and she looks between Isabella and Tom, who is now sitting on the step of the building. Isabella reaches across and pushes Mischa's hair off her face.

"You want to leave?" Mischa whispers.

"No." Isabella shakes her head. "I don't want to leave, but… we need to, Mischa. We need to get you to safety. *Us* to safety."

Mischa's eyes are vacant and dull as she runs them over Isabella's face.

"Sascha trusted you," she whispers and bites her lip.

"He did. And we trusted *him*. With our lives."

A faint siren wails in the distance and Isabella's head snaps up as Tom jumps to his feet.

Mischa looks back to Sascha. She drops her face against his and kisses his cheek.

"YA tebya lyublyu." Her voice wavers and cracks as she tells Sascha she loves him.

Tom crouches beside Mischa and holds a hand out and she takes it. He pulls her from the ground and she collapses against him and cries into his chest. Instead of pulling her to the car, he holds her and waits. Isabella's heart warms as she watches Tom let her cry against him.

Isabella crouches next to Sascha and slides her hand into his trouser pocket. Her fingers curl around the car keys and she pulls them out. She is about to stand up when her eyes rest on his wedding band. She looks over to Mischa, her face still against Tom's chest. Isabella lifts Sascha's hand and wriggles his ring off. She slips the ring into her pocket and stands up.

"We really need to go. Can you walk with me?" Tom's voice is soft, all his attention is on Mischa, and Isabella falls in love with him all over again.

Mischa nods, she looks at Sascha and her face breaks into raw pain and torture. She slides both of her hands over her belly and cradles her bump. She presses her mouth closed and sniffles a great breath through her nose.

"Let us go." She walks towards the car without looking back at Sascha.

ISABELLA OPENS HER EYES AND LOOKS AROUND THE LANDSCAPE AS they drive. Mischa is asleep against her shoulder.

"Hey." Tom's green eyes crinkle as he smiles at her through the rear-view mirror.

She extricates herself from Mischa, climbs through the seats and sits next to Tom.

"Hey. Sorry. I only rested my eyes for a minute."

"Don't apologise. You didn't sleep much last night." He gives her a sidelong glance and squashes the smile playing at the sides of his mouth. "And you know… it was an eventful morning."

Isabella nods. "Eventful."

"Are you sure you're okay?"

"Yes. The Nik that died in that crumby motel room wasn't the Nik I grew up with."

"No."

"God, what must have happened to him?" Isabella shakes her head and watches the road ahead of them. They drive on in a welcome silence for a short while before Isabella shifts her body to face Tom.

"By the way…"

Tom raises his eyebrows but keeps his eyes on the road.

"How is it you're not dead?"

Tom grins. "Oh yeah. Well… like I said. The bumbling idiot missed me."

"But you fell?"

"Yes. And I played dead until I heard the door shut behind you and Nik. Then I got up and waited. I don't know what took him so long, but he burst in and I shot him. It's really not that fancy of a story." Tom shrugs. "Maybe he should have actually looked through the doors and aimed at me. Idiot."

Isabella giggles. "You sound like you're disgusted they *didn't* kill you."

"Well, if you're gonna do a job…" Tom grins. "But yes. I'm glad I didn't die. That would have been unpleasant."

"Yes well, it would have been inconvenient."

"And I'm sorry I didn't follow you into the room straight away. But… Mischa. Erik would have killed her if I left her."

"I know. And it's fine. I could handle Nik." She pushes against the pang in her stomach as Tom reaches across and squeezes her hand.

"Well, I'm sorry anyway."

Isabella nods and swallows the ache taking over her throat. "How long to go?"

"Around four hours, I guess. I'm not sure how much I trust this GPS on the old lady's phone."

The phone rings at that moment and Isabella picks it up. She glances in the back seat to see Mischa still sleeping.

"Da?"

"Isabella?"

"Hey, James."

"Hey. Is Tom about?"

"Driving."

"Are you okay? You sound weird."

Isabella smiles. "I always sound weird James. But yes I'm fine. We're fine."

Tom snorts and shoots Isabella a smirk. She raises the corner of her mouth in return.

"Okay I'm going to send you guys coordinates for the location the chopper will land to pick you up. What's your ETA?"

"Around four hours."

Tom nods.

"Okay. Be at the location I send you in five hours. Yeah?"

"Yes. No problem."

"It's nearly over Isabella."

"It is. Thanks to you."

"Yeah. Tell Tom I said hey." James chuckles.

Isabella drops the phone beneath her chin. "James says hey."

Tom grunts and Isabella slaps him in the arm.

"Fine. Hey." Tom squints at the road ahead.

Isabella laughs. "Thanks, James."

"Be safe." He hangs up.

Isabella drops the phone into a cup holder.

"Did James just hang up on you?"

Isabella rolls her eyes and giggles. "Shut up Tom."

ISABELLA WANDERS INTO THE OPEN FIELD AND LOOKS AT THE SKY. *Thank God we didn't come here in the dead of winter.*

Tom's arms slide around her waist. He rests his chin on her shoulder and kisses her neck.

Isabella leans against him and closes her eyes for a moment as his warm breath hits her skin.

"Where's Mischa?" Isabella turns and interlocks her fingers around the back of his neck.

"In the car." He turns and looks back at the car. "She's practically catatonic, Iz."

"Can't blame her. In the space of a few days she's lost everyone." Isabella pulls a breath in as her chest constricts. "Because of us." *Because of me.*

"I know."

"We're her family now." Isabella stares at the car. "You know that right?"

Tom nods.

"She's having a baby, Tom." Isabella's eyes fill with tears and she blinks them back. "God it's so unfair."

Tom cradles her head against him. "Stop. Ripping yourself apart doesn't help her. Or us."

"But I can't help it." She pulls away and wipes the tears from under her eyes with the back of her index fingers.

"I know." He smiles as the tell-tale sound of a chopper floats over them from somewhere in the distance. Tom raises his chin and listens. "It's a Merlin." He slides his hand down her arm and grabs her hand. "Showtime."

Isabella lets herself be pulled away from the middle of the field, her brain still a mess of guilt and frustration. *I'm such a cold blooded assassin.* They reach the car and Tom helps Mischa get out. She stands, staring into space.

"It's going to be loud and windy. Yes?" Both girls nod.

Isabella slides her arm through Mischa's. "I'm staying right here with you."

Mischa nods again but the blank expression on her face doesn't change.

The sound of the chopper gets louder until it appears over the edge of the tree line.

Isabella inhales a breath and stares. "Wow."

It lands in the middle of the field and Tom walks forward a couple of steps as a crewman runs from the chopper towards them.

He stands in front of them and looks at his clipboard. He glances up and down a few times and his eyebrows knit.

"Tom Grant and Isabella Wirth?" he shouts over the noise of the chopper. Isabella barely hears it.

Tom nods. "And Mischa Ustinova."

The crewman shakes his head. "No Sir. We only have authorisation for yourself and Ms Wirth. We had permission to fly over as part of an exercise. We shouldn't have even landed. If they find out we lied..."

Isabella's stomach clenches and she looks at Tom.

"Not possible," Tom shouts. "It's all of us." He swirls his finger around, indicating the three of them.

"No Sir. I'm sorry but—"

Tom steps forward and grabs the crewman by the shirtfront. "I've had a shitty morning. Actually... a shitty week or so. I'm tired. I'm angry and I'm fucking *done.*"

The crewman wrenches Tom's hand off him and rips his headset off. "Her name isn't on my manifest. She stays."

"You're gonna leave a pregnant woman in the middle of nowhere Russia?"

"Not my problem."

Tom grabs the crewman again and twists his collar. "Get Admiral Moore on the comms."

"What?"

"You heard me."

"Ah, well no I don't think…"

"Right. Then fly us the fuck out of here."

Both stand and glare at each other.

Tom caves first and sweeps his arms out either side of him. "Well?"

The crewman looks from Tom to Isabella and then rests his eyes on Mischa. Isabella feels Mischa trembling against her and wraps an arm around her shoulder.

The crewman flicks his head towards the helicopter and marches off, shoving his headset over his ears.

"Well, they could work on their hospitality. But… shall we?" Tom hollers above the whipping of the helicopter blades.

Isabella hugs Mischa.

Almost there.

41

TOM

The fucking Arrochar. Of all the ships.

It's windy and bitterly cold. Tom begrudgingly accepts the jackets the crewman hands to them as they climb out of the chopper. They walk across the ship's landing pad and come to a stop beside the hangar. The chopper blades power down and the noise dies away with them.

It's fucking freezing. Tom draws in a breath and instinctively stands closer to Isabella. She runs her hand over his and interlaces her fingers. Mischa stands next to both of them, staring out at the sea. Her face has not cracked since leaving Murmansk.

"Relax, Tom."

"I am relaxed."

"Is that why you're squeezing my fingers numb?"

Tom looks down at their hands and loosens his grip. "Sorry."

"Petty Officer Perkins will take you inside." The crewman nods towards a female sailor walking towards them.

Perkins? Oh please, no.

Tom's eyes land on her as she comes to a stop in front of them. Blonde hair tied in a neat bun at the nape of her neck and her uniform hugging every curve perfectly. *Still fit as hell.*

"Well I never." She grins at Tom. "Hey, Grant."

Fuck.

"Abbie. What a… pleasant surprise."

He squeezes Isabella's hand again.

"Tom!"

"Sorry."

Abbie looks over the three of them. "Well, why don't we get you checked out in the medical office? You look a little worse for wear and… forgive me but are you pregnant, Ma'am?"

Mischa slowly drags her eyes to Abbie and peers at her. She purses her mouth and her eyes water.

"Yes, she is. The medical office would be great. Thanks." Tom tries to smile but he's pretty sure it looks more like a grimace. *Ugh. The medical office.*

"Follow me. Although, you could lead the way, no doubt." She winks at Tom and walks.

"Wait a minute." Isabella steps in front of him. "Was this your ship?"

He looks at her and takes a breath. "Yep."

"Are you sure you're okay?"

No, I'm fucking not. "Yes. Great. Let's go."

Mischa slides her hand through Tom's elbow and he smiles at her. "Stay close. You're fine." *Me, on the other hand...* Tom imitates a blowfish, blowing a long slow breath out.

Isabella is a pace in front of them and she spins around and walks backwards, grinning at Tom.

"You know Abbie?"

Intimately. "Yeah, a bit." He shrugs as they walk.

"A bit?" Isabella throws him a grin. "Which bits?"

Tom winces and checks that Abbie is out of earshot. "All of them."

She laughs. "Oh, this is going to be fun."

"A God damn hoot."

They follow Abbie inside and she leads them down a labyrinth of gangways before she pokes her head through an open door. She gestures them inside.

"Take a seat. I don't know where the medic is but I'll find him." She runs her eyes over the three of them. "And I'll get you some clean clothes."

"It's fine, Abs."

"Don't stress Tom. I promise not to make it too *uniformy* for you." She winks and ducks out of the room.

"Uniformy?" Isabella sits down and hugs Mischa close to her.

"She's just being a smart arse."

"You didn't like your uniform?"

"Not really. It was like a straight-jacket."

"Visitors!"

Tom snaps his head around as the medic appears in the doorway. "Lieutenant." Tom nods once and stands up.

"Lieutenant Campbell. But you lovely people can call me Mike."

"Did you take over from Lieutenant Bradley?" *Did Bradley even have a first name?*

"That cranky old coot… yes. He retired eighteen months ago." Mike frowns at Tom. "How do you…"

Tom smiles a half smile and gestures to Mischa. "This is Mischa. She's…" He turns to Mischa. "How many months are you?" *Let's get the focus off me.*

Mischa raises her face, still clinging to Isabella. "Almost six."

Tom looks back to Mike. "Almost six months pregnant."

"Ah, how wonderful." Mike steps forward and holds a hand out to Mischa. She hesitates before taking it.

Tom slides his hand up Isabella's back. "We'll wait outside." He walks Isabella out and closes the door behind him.

Isabella leans against the wall and looks at Tom. Tom rests his hand on the wall above her head and holds her gaze. "What?"

"Nothing. You just seem… jumpy."

"I am jumpy."

"Why?"

"This is literally the most uncomfortable I have ever been. Ever."

Isabella slides her hand around the back of his neck. "I won't say I get it. But… If you want to talk about it…"

"There's nothing to talk about."

"Well, that isn't true."

Tom lets out a forced chuckle as Abbie appears holding a pile of tracksuits and shoes.

"I had to guess your sizes. Well… the girls anyway." She grins at Tom and Isabella snorts. Tom closes his eyes and pinches the bridge of his nose. *If the floor could swallow me up, that'd be great.*

Abbie shoves the tracksuits into Tom's arms. "You have beds in one of the staterooms." She pauses and clicks her tongue at Tom. "Bet you never thought you'd end up in one of those."

"No, no I didn't." Tom forces a smile.

The door to the medical office opens and Mischa steps out with Mike behind her.

"She's good to go. Everything is perfect. Now… do you two need anything?"

"No." Tom shakes his head.

"Yes." Isabella gives him a pointed look and flicks her head towards the open door. "In you go."

"Iz—"

"He has a severe burn over his ribs under his left arm." Isabella looks at Mike. "He also got an infection because of it and nearly died. So yeah…" She glares at Tom. "He needs a check-up."

Tom bites the inside of his mouth and rubs his face. "Fine." He stalks into the room and sits on the exam table.

Mike closes the door and wanders to Tom. "Okay, let's have a look."

Mischa looks down at her hands, clasped in her lap. "I do not know what to say."

Isabella wraps an arm around Mischa's shoulders. "You don't have to." She kisses Mischa's temple. "Well... you could ask Tom how you're meant to cook with two saucepans and five spoons..."

Tom scoffs. "I'm going out to get firewood. All I get is attacked around you two." He stands and walks out to the garden as the girls snort.

He walks into the crisp air and takes a breath. Staring out at the fields beyond the back gate he smiles to himself. He picks up the axe and sits a piece of wood upright to split.

"Aren't you meant to do that shirtless?"

He turns and Isabella is leaning against the house.

"Well, it's an option but it's also freezing." He grins and drops the axe. "Where's Mischa?"

"She's having a lie down."

Tom nods as Isabella walks to him and slides her arms around his waist. He cups her face in his hands and kisses her. "Want to walk?"

Isabella nods. He laces his fingers through hers and they walk out the back gate towards a couple of giant stones.

"She's going to be fine, Tom."

"I know."

"It's kind of you to let her stay here."

"Where else is she going to live? Also... that whole life saving stuff." He shrugs and stops walking.

"Well, yes. There's that." Isabella runs her hand up under his shirt and brushes over his burn.

Prickles erupt but he ignores the discomfort.

"I'm sorry, Tom."

Tom drops to the grass and pulls Isabella down into his lap. She faces him and wraps her legs around his waist. "I don't want to hear that again." He touches his forehead to hers.

"But—"

He pushes his mouth to hers and kisses her. "Stop," he mumbles against her lips. "No more. We're home and it's done."

"We should never have gone."

"But we did. What is it they say? Onwards and upwards? Or… something?"

"You know we've never really talked about… onwards."

A ball of anxiety starts to wiggle in Tom's gut. "What do you mean?"

"Well, I just turned up again. And hauled you off to Russia. We've not spoken about what's next."

"We're going back to our flat."

"*Our* flat?"

"Yes." He kisses her again. "Our flat. You know… if you… want." *Please say yes.*

"You do realise that we've never actually been out on a real date?"

"We haven't?"

Isabella giggles. "No, Tom. We haven't."

Tom yanks his shirt off and raises his arm. He chews on his bottom lip as Mike peels the bandage away.

"Oh my."

"Yeah. Cheaper than a tattoo."

"How on earth…"

"Do you really want to know?" Tom raises a brow.

"I really don't. But this needs cleaning and you need antibiotics."

"Oh yeah… I had some of those somewhere…"

Mike purses his lips. "Are you always this cavalier about your health?"

Tom sighs and drops his arm as Mike turns away, gathering saline and gauze. "No. Well… maybe."

"I see."

"I don't think you do."

Mike turns back around and gestures for Tom to raise his arm again. "So, former Petty Officer Thomas Grant. How does it feel to be back on board?"

Tom peers at Mike. "How did you…"

Mike nods towards a computer screen. "Your file is still there. How's the drinking?"

"Jesus."

"Relax, I'm not here to bust your balls." Mike watches Tom a moment before continuing. "Did you ever seek any sort of counselling after—"

Tom squeezes his eyes shut and huffs. "I really need you to shut the fuck up."

"I'll take that as a no."

"Why do you even care? I'm not a sailor on your ship. I'm not under your medical responsibility."

"No. That's true. But maybe I'm trying to right the wrongs of one Lieutenant Bradley. I can see in your file you came to him and—"

"You know what? No one listened back then... so excuse me if I don't feel overly chatty."

"I can see that the drinking and fighting started after—"

"Can we just clean me up and give me the magic pills?"

Mike clears his throat and squirts some sort of bright orange liquid on Tom's burn and it stings. Tom hisses a breath through his teeth.

"Yes. Antiseptic." Mike smooths a clean bandage over the burn. "Okay, that's waterproof but come see me tomorrow and I'll change it again."

Tom jumps down from the exam table. "Sure."

"And if you need a chat." Mike shrugs.

Tom frowns and takes the bottle of pills Mike holds out to him. "I'm good but... thanks."

Mike nods once. "Three times a day with meals until all gone."

TOM SCRUBS A TOWEL OVER HIS HAIR AS HE WALKS INTO THE stateroom assigned to them. Isabella is sitting at the desk. Her feet up on the seat, knees against her chest. He notes the two bunks and the extra cot that has been supplied for them. *First class treatment.*

"Feeling better?" Isabella stands up.

"Shower helps. What about you two?"

"I don't know what to do. Mischa hasn't said a word."

Tom looks to Mischa, who has claimed the cot and appears to be sleeping. *Bet she isn't.*

"So we get the bunks, huh?" Tom looks at the narrow beds and remembers how uncomfortable they are.

"I bags being on top." Isabella winks.

"I'm not complaining."

A knock at the door jolts Tom's already anxious nerves. "Fuck." He stalks over and opens it. Abbie stands with a tray of food. "Oh, hey." Tom steps back to let her in.

"Thought you guys might be more comfy eating in here for today. It's a zoo in the mess." She slides the tray onto the desk and spots Mischa. She covers her mouth. "Sorry. I didn't realise she was sleeping."

"It's fine, Abs." Tom sits on the seat Isabella had been on moments before. "Are you our assigned personal assistant or something?"

"I kind of am. Yes." She grins. "Hey, it could be worse. This is my last deployment so…"

"Last?"

"Yep. I'm out."

"Out?" *And what does your Dad think about that?*

"It's time to do other things." She smiles. "Anyway, you're one to talk."

"I am?"

"You disappeared! One minute you're engineering assault weapons. The next you're gone."

"Yeah…"

Abbie leans on the desk. "Did they kick your drunk arse out?"

"No. I was… headhunted for something else." *That'll do.*

Abbie shrugs. "Fair enough. Well… if you need some privacy there's the amenities closet about halfway down the gangway." Abbie winks at Isabella and saunters out.

"Amenities closet?" Isabella grins at Tom.

"Yeah… we used to… meet up in there…" He scratches a hand through his hair. "Anyway… this little frolick down memory lane is really taxing. Shall we eat?" Tom grabs a fork and shovels mashed potato into his mouth so he doesn't have to keep talking. *Bland.*

Isabella stands over him and runs her hand through his hair and kisses his cheek. "I'm sorry. I was being insensitive."

Tom swallows and drops the fork. He pulls Isabella onto his lap and wraps his arms around her, resting his head against her chest. Her steady heart beat helps Tom's own to slow and he closes his eyes.

"Only forty two hours, Iz."

"Until?"

"We can get off this fucking ship."

Isabella places her hands on his cheeks and tilts his face up. "Okay."

Tom gazes into her eyes and forgets the anxiety throwing a party in his gut. He pushes his mouth to hers.

A knock at the door shatters the moment and Tom grumbles. Isabella stands and answers the door.

"Petty Officer Grant." A voice booms.

Tom leaps to his feet and is about to stand ramrod straight when he remembers he doesn't have to. He half way goes to sit back down, hesitates and stands up again. *What the fuck is wrong with me?*

The owner of the voice chuckles and strolls into the room. "Old habits die hard, eh?"

Commodore Matthew Lawrence walks in and stands in front of Tom. Tom looks him in the eye a moment before dropping his gaze to his too shiny shoes. His heartbeat runs so fast it's humming.

"Relax Grant. You're allowed to eyeball me if you wish. Hell you could drop your trousers and moon me. You're a civilian. Remember?"

Tom looks up and stares at the Commodore. "Tempting." *Bastard.*

Commodore Lawrence holds Tom's stare a moment before breaking it and looking at Isabella. "Welcome aboard, young lady. Commodore Lawrence." He holds his hand out and Isabella shakes it. "I see our other guest is sleeping."

"Tell me, *Commodore.*" *Of course you've been promoted.*

Tom grits his teeth. "How pissed were you when Admiral Moore ordered you to pick us up?

"Ordered? Now Grant. I was happy to help. Citizens of the United Kingdom in distress? Why… it's our duty." He smiles but his eyes remain empty. "What luck I was overseeing these exercises."

"At what point did you find out it was me?"

"I knew the whole time. Like I said… it's our duty."

"Right." Tom swallows the distaste creeping up the back of his throat. "Well, thanks. You're a real hero." He sits down and folds his arms.

"Maybe I should have come with a flask and a couple of glasses, Grant? Toast to old times?"

Tom curls his lip and says nothing.

"Right well, sleep tight." Commander Lawrence holds Tom's glare a second before nodding once and striding out of the room.

Tom turns to the food and shoves another mouthful into his mouth.

No more talking.

TOM REACHES BOTH HANDS UP AND PICKS AT THE MATTRESS ABOVE him. The narrow bunk, thin mattress and the fact Isabella isn't in bed next to him doesn't make it any easier to sleep. *And I'm on the fucking Arrochar.*

Soft whimpering from Mischa's cot draws his attention. He

rolls onto his side and focuses his eyes on her in the dim light. Her shoulders shake and she hugs herself.

Flicking his eyes to the clock on the wall, the digital numbers read 04:48. Tom's burn prickles and his chest aches as he watches Mischa sobbing into her pillow. He rolls off the bunk and shuffles across to her. He sits on the edge of her cot and rubs her shoulder.

Mischa rolls over and wipes her eyes. "I am sorry. Did I wake you?"

"No. I've been awake for hours."

"You are not tired?"

"I'm exhausted. But… It's hard for me to sleep on a ship these days." Tom shrugs.

Mischa sits up and sniffles. "You are having hard time."

"In comparison to you? No. I'm being ridiculous." He smiles and holds an arm out. Mischa slides across and burrows against him.

"I am sorry."

"Don't be."

"The pain is constant. It does not go away."

Tom nods. "It's like a hole has opened up inside you. And it's on fire around the edges and it keeps growing and getting hotter and more painful." *Until you're completely consumed by it and drink yourself into oblivion.*

"Da. You have felt this pain?"

Tom bites his lip. "Yes."

Mischa looks up at Isabella, sound asleep in the top bunk, her arm hanging over the edge and her face smooshed into the pillow.

Tom follows her gaze and smiles. "That's what I love about her. She's just so glamorous." Isabella snorts and rolls over. "See? Glamorous."

Mischa affords Tom a tiny smile. "It is not Isabella that caused you this pain?"

"No." Tom shakes his head and rubs a hand over his gut. "Remember I almost got married?"

Mischa nods. "She passed away."

Tom drops his face and rubs his eyes. "Murdered. In front of me."

Mischa's hand slaps her mouth. "Oh, Tom."

Tom shakes his shoulders out. "So yes. I understand your pain. And if there's one thing I'll say to you, don't hide it away and pretend it doesn't hurt. That just makes it hurt more." *Believe me.*

"It is not your burden to bear."

"And you can't carry it alone. Trust me. You can't." He pulls her against him again. "Try and go to sleep. I'll stay with you."

"Tom?"

"Yep?"

"What is going to happen to me?"

Tom holds his breath a moment before letting it out slowly. "You're going to have a healthy baby and live somewhere quiet with your family close by."

"I have no family left."

"You have us."

A fresh wave of tears tumble down Mischa's face and she coughs out a sob. "I cannot burden—"

"You're not." Tom looks down at her and waits for her to meet his eyes. "You're not a burden."

"But—"

Tom holds his index finger up and shakes his head. "If not for you and Sascha, I would be dead and God knows what Nik would have done to Isabella." His gut clenches at the thought of Nik's hands on her. Tom clears his throat and looks up at Isabella, her back to both of them, still sound asleep. "It's our turn to look after you."

"I am so frightened."

"I know. But it'll be okay." He squeezes her shoulder.

Mischa drops her head against Tom again and closes her eyes. "Thank you."

"You're welcome." He rests his chin on top of her head. "Now, try and sleep."

Tom lolls his head back against the wall and for the first time all night, he feels calm enough to sleep.

TOM OPENS HIS EYES AND ISABELLA SMILES AT HIM FROM HER bunk. Mischa is nestled against him; her head has dropped to the middle of his chest and she is breathing steady breaths.

"Morning," Isabella whispers.

"Hey." He slides himself out from Mischa and lays her on her pillow. He walks to Isabella and rests his chin on her bunk, his nose brushes hers. "How'd you sleep?"

She pouts her lips and kisses his mouth. "Like a log. The whole boat thing must agree with me."

Tom snorts. "At least it agrees with one of us."

Isabella nods towards Mischa. "Is she okay?"

"Not really. I heard her crying and sat with her. She looked alone and scared."

"You're going soft, Tom Grant." She runs a hand through his hair.

Going? "It's becoming inconvenient."

"What is?"

"Having feelings and shit."

Isabella giggles and sits up, resting on her elbow. "What time is it?"

"A little after six. I need a walk."

"Okay." She smiles and kisses him again. "I'll stay here with Mischa."

Tom keeps his face against hers and kisses her again. He takes a step backwards to stop himself climbing into her bunk and relieving her of her frumpy tracksuit. *Focus, Grant.*

He walks out to the corridor and looks left and right. Two sailors wander past and tip their heads. Tom pushes the anxiety down and nods back. *Poor bastards.* He turns towards the gym, once his only place of solitude on this ship and it's where his feet automatically take him. He's in no physical condition to work out, but the familiarity of the room is what he craves. He trains his eyes on the floor and ignores all the familiar sounds of the ship that fill him with angst.

"Up early?"

Tom looks up and sees Abbie walking towards him. She's in her navy tracks and a towel is draped around her shoulders.

"You know me." He smiles. "Going to work out?"

"Just finished."

"Still bench pressing a hundred pounds?"

"Of course. A hundred and ten if you want to get technical." She winks and leans against the wall. "You okay?"

"Nah. I'm fucked." He grins and raises his arms up to tap against the bulkhead. *Seriously, I'm fucked.*

"Well, I was about to go have a coffee before the rec is overrun with loud smart arses. Join me?"

Tom chuckles and nods.

They walk to the rec room and Abbie sticks her head in. "Well, look at that. Free. I'll grab some instant. Be right back." She jogs away down the corridor and Tom walks inside.

He sits and rests his elbows on his knees. He looks to his left and though there's nobody there he sees a sailor sitting, smiling at him and challenging him to some offshore prank or another. Over at the table he sees another group playing cards and throwing chips at each other.

Tom shakes his head. *Fuck.*

"Black with no sugar. Yes?"

Tom's head snaps up. *That was quick.* He takes the coffee. "You remembered."

"Of course I do. The amount of coffee I made for you to get you through a hangover? It's ingrained in my memory forever."

She sips her own and sits, crossing her legs. "And all the covering for you I did with…" She rolls her eyes to the ceiling.

Tom gulps the coffee so he doesn't have to acknowledge the reminders of his behaviour on the ship. "He paid me a visit last night."

"Of course he did. Were you a prat?" She grins as Tom gives her an indignant look.

"I was perfectly respectful." He shrugs. "More or less."

"…a prat."

"So tell me. Is this really your last deployment?"

"Yep. Time to move on."

"I never thought you'd get out."

Abbie shakes her head. "You're right. I didn't either. But… Dad died three years ago and I just started realising that I wasn't here for me."

"You never were, Abs."

Abbie sits upright and shakes out her shoulders. "Anyway. What happened to you? One minute you're turning up late for duty in a crumpled uniform with bloodshot eyes… the next you literally disappear."

"I was… headhunted. Remember?" *Did we not have this conversation last night?*

Abbie narrows her eyes.

Tom sighs. "Commander Ford thought my skills would be of use… elsewhere. I actually think I was about to be charged with something and Claire told him to get me out. Though, neither of them ever admitted that to me."

"I won't lie. At first I was annoyed you ended our secret closet trysts after she came along.... but she made you happy. That was obvious."

Tom stares at the wall across from him and nods. "So what's next for you?"

"I have a few prospective jobs lined up. I haven't decided yet. Might take a few months to just chill out."

"I get the feeling you won't end up sitting in an office somewhere."

"Ha! No. I won't. I'd die of boredom."

"You would."

"So, how did you end up stuck in Russia and getting rescued by the navy?"

Tom runs a thumb over his bottom lip. *No point lying.* "Isabella's father died and she wanted to bring his ashes home to be at rest with her mother."

"Isabella is Russian?"

"She is."

"But she sounds like us. Like... born and bred."

"She had to learn. She defected and had to go into hiding."

"Hiding? What did she do?" Abbie leans forward and raises an eyebrow.

Tom shakes his head. "You don't want to know, Abs."

"That bad?"

Steady on. "No." *Yes.* Tom slams his mouth shut and cracks his neck, wondering why anger is bubbling through his blood.

"Then?"

Tom lets out a slow breath. "She defected. From Russia. That's bad enough isn't it?"

"Sorry. I didn't mean to…"

He runs a hand through his hair and stands up. "No, I'm sorry. I'm just on edge on this ship."

She hugs him. "I'm glad you're okay. I didn't mean to upset you."

"You didn't."

She picks up their empty cups and walks past him to the door. "Only another twenty something hours and you'll be in Norway. And off the ship."

"Yeah."

"Oh, by the way. Lieutenant Campbell asked me to remind you to go see him again today." She pauses and watches Tom for a moment. "You're unwell?"

Fucking Campbell. "No. I have a dressing he wants to change."

"A dressing?"

"Yes." *What the hell.* "I was branded with a red hot iron."

Abbie's mouth drops open. "What?"

"Yeah, I considered a tattoo but where's the fun in that?" He grins and holds a hand up to quell Abbie's clear discomfort. "I just have a burn that needs dressing. No biggie."

"Seriously Tom, what the fuck kind of job do you do these days?"

He slinks past her into the corridor.

"I'm an accountant, Abs."

42

TOM

Tom pushes open his door and he, Isabella and Mischa practically fall into his flat.

"Fifty two hours," Tom grumbles. He wanders to the cupboard next to his bedroom and pulls out a pillow and spare comforter. "You girls take the bed. I'll sleep on the sofa."

"No. Please. I will sleep—"

"You're six months pregnant. You'll sleep in the bed."

Isabella wraps her arms around Tom's waist and leans against him. "We're home."

Tom kisses the top of her head. "I was going to shower… you know… if you need one… too…"

Isabella giggles. "I may."

A loud knock comes from the front door. "Tom? Isabella? Are you there?"

Tom screws his face up and sighs. He stalks to the door and

pulls it open. Martha stands on the other side. Her hands are clasped in front of her, and her hair is unkempt.

You look a fright.

"Hey." Tom stands back a step and she scurries into the room; her eyes don't leave Tom's face.

She stands in front of him and clears her throat. "You're back."

"Yes. Like I said… on the phone to you no more than an hour ago."

"Well, yes. You did. I…" She stops talking and purses her lips.

Tom stares at her and frowns slightly. "Is there something we can do for you, Martha?"

"No. I just wanted to… check…"

Tom raises a brow and holds both hands out either side of him. "And?"

"Oh God, you two are frustrating," Isabella pipes up. "She wants to hug you, Tom. She's glad to see you."

Tom turns his head to Isabella. "We don't hu—"

Martha launches herself into Tom and wraps her arms around his waist. Tom's arms are still outstretched either side of him and he peers down at the top of Martha's head.

"Umm…"

"Hug her back, Tom." Isabella rolls her eyes. "Jesus."

Mischa giggles from the sofa.

He closes his arms around Martha and pats her on the back. *Am I in the Twilight Zone?*

Martha pulls away and pats down her blouse and tucks her hair behind her ear. "Yes, well. I'm glad you aren't dead."

"I'm touched." Tom smirks. "But thanks. I'm fine."

"Oh my God," Isabella whispers, shaking her head.

Martha nods once and turns to look at Mischa, sitting on the sofa with her hands clasped in her lap. "And you must be Mischa."

She nods. "Da."

"She's the one you should be hugging." Tom sits in the armchair and pulls Isabella onto his lap.

Martha gives Mischa one of her rare warm smiles and pats her knee. "We'll help you."

Mischa dips her face.

Tom watches Mischa and sees the exhaustion in her face. "Go to bed Mischa." He flicks his head back towards his bedroom.

I need to discuss tearing Malcolm limb from limb, anyway.

Mischa stands and Isabella jumps off Tom's lap and leads her out. Tom watches them disappear into the bedroom before looking back to Martha.

"Did you really nearly die?"

"Yes."

"And you're burned?"

Tom lifts his shirt and rips the bandage off. He sucks a sharp breath in as his burn reacts to the disturbance.

Martha leans forward and peers at his disfigured skin. She purses her mouth and her nostrils flare. "I see."

Tom drops his shirt.

Martha meets Tom's eyes and sits upright. "So I assume you have questions about Malcolm?

"If by questions you mean, what's his location so I can beat the shit out of him? Then, yes. I have questions."

Martha twitches her left eye while she stares at Tom. "You need sleep. You're still unwell."

"I'm fine."

"Tom—"

"I said I'm fine. Where is he?"

Martha sighs and rubs her eyes. "He's at the warehouse. In the holding cell."

"You've held him there all week?"

"Yes."

"But you're only supposed to—"

"Special circumstances." Martha eyes Tom and raises a brow.

"I wasn't complaining…"

Martha nods once. "You sleep tonight. And come in tomorrow. He's all yours."

Isabella walks out of the bedroom and sits on the sofa. "Are we talking about Malcolm?"

Tom dips his head and scrubs both hands through his hair. "Yep."

"Can I stab him?"

"Yep."

Martha grunts and stands up. "I'm leaving before I hear anything else I shouldn't." She stops at the door and turns around. "I'm glad you're both okay. I was worried."

Isabella leaps from the lounge and bounds over to Martha. She envelopes the tiny woman in a bear hug. "It's wonderful to see you, Martha."

Martha pats Isabella's back, much the same way Tom did to her earlier. "And you, my dear."

Tom grins, watching Martha stiffen at being hugged. Isabella lets Martha go and winks at Tom. "You're both just so affectionate."

Martha grunts and walks out the door, closing it behind her.

Isabella plops back into Tom's lap and he nuzzles her neck. "Are you saying I'm not affectionate?"

"You have your moments." Isabella slides her hand up and under the back of his shirt, the other presses against his chest. She pushes her mouth on his and kisses him. "I don't think Martha's the kissing type," Isabella whispers.

Tom grimaces against Isabella's face and she laughs, standing and pulling him out of the armchair.

"What were you saying about a shower?"

TOM SLAMS OPEN THE DOOR TO THE HOLDING CELL AND IT bounces off the wall. He stands in the doorframe and glares at Malcolm.

Malcolm startles and scurries on his backside against the back wall.

"Tom. You're back. No one told me... umm..."

Tom remains in the doorway and folds his arms over his chest. "Didn't they?" He pouts his lips like a duck and raises his eyebrows. "Strange. I mean… I'm *sure* you were waiting eagerly for my return. Yes?"

"Y... yes. Of course."

Tom steps into the cell and lets the door shut behind him. A loud, secure click echoes around the room. Malcolm stands up, presses himself against the wall and starts pulling at the front of his shirt. Sweat glistens across his forehead.

"Are you anxious?"

"Umm… should I be?"

"Absolutely." Tom grins and looks up at the camera mounted in the corner of the room above the door. "Well, best be getting rid of that." He jumps and grabs the camera, yanking it out of the wall. The burn in his side stretches at the action and stabs a pain through his body. Tom grits his teeth and glares at Malcolm. *Your fucking fault.*

Tom slams the camera into the floor and it breaks apart.

Malcolm jumps and slaps his hand against his chest. He sidles along the wall, his eyes glued to Tom.

Tom watches him, not moving, and a smile creeps along his lips. "Honestly Malcolm. You need to relax."

"I do?"

"No. This is going to hurt. Make no mistake."

"You can't."

"Can't I?"

"It's… against the law…"

"Yes. I agree. But then again… so is accessing government systems to gain benefit… like, you know… money to buy Porsches and such."

"Ahhh…" The shake in Malcolm's voice increases and he wipes his hands down the front of his shirt. *Bit sweaty, Mal?*

Tom's fingers itch, wanting to strangle Malcolm around his fat neck. Tom stalks to Malcolm and yanks him off the wall by the shirt front. He glares into Malcolm's face, twists his shirt and it constricts around his throat.

"Tom…" Malcolm's slaps at Tom's hand as he wheezes and slides down the wall.

Tom crouches over Malcolm and tilts his head. "Sorry about that." He lets go of Malcolm's shirt and smooths it down for him. "Crumpled your shirt."

"That's okay I—"

Tom jabs Malcolm to the chin, his mouth slams shut and he yelps. Blood dribbles from his mouth.

"Bite your tongue? Ouch." Tom jabs again and Malcolm groans, falling sideways to the floor.

"Fight *back* for fucks sake. I hate it when it's easy."

Malcolm wraps his arms around his head and lies on the floor. "They were going to kill me, Tom. If I didn't…"

"Bullshit. They waved money in your face and you took it."

"No, but I…"

"You?" Tom slides his hand around his waistband and pulls his pistol out.

Malcolm squirms on the floor and manages to pull himself back up against the wall. "Fuck, Tom. You're gonna shoot me?"

"Hmmm?" Tom looks at the pistol and back to Malcolm. "Oh. This? No... well... not right now." Tom winks and clicks his tongue. "It just makes such a satisfying crunch when you whip someone in the head with it. You know?" *You deserve the Nik treatment.*

"I... d...don't..."

"No? Let me show you." Tom slams the pistol into Malcolm's head and splits his left ear. Blood runs down his neck, staining his already sweat stained shirt. Rage bubbles under Tom's skin and he restrains himself from reducing the fat slob to a bloody pulp on the floor. *No, we can be more creative than that.*

"Hey so, you know what else, Mal? After they chained me up in a filthy cell, made me eat fucking cabbage and beat the shit out of me... you know what they did next?"

Malcolm trembles and tears roll down his face.

Tom grabs Malcolm's jaw and yanks his face towards him. "I asked you a fucking question."

"Wha... what?"

"I said... do you know what they did next?"

Malcolm's shakes his head, sweat flies off his face and hair. "No. No I don't. Please Tom—"

"They branded me like a fucking head of cattle, Malcolm."

"What?"

"They pulled out a red hot iron and they pushed it into my skin. You want to know where?"

Malcolm shuts his eyes and pushes his hands over his ears, yelping as he pushes against the bloody mess in the side of his head.

"Well, that's just fucking rude. I'm trying to share my holiday memories with you." Tom flicks Malcolm in the forehead and he flinches but squeezes his eyes shut tighter. "Should I cancel the projector and slide show?"

Malcolm pulls in a loud sniffle and continues to ignore Tom.

"Are you fucking seven years old? Open your eyes and face the consequences of what you did, you fat, useless heap of shit." Tom braces both hands against the wall above Malcolm's head and drives his knee into the side of his ribs.

Malcolm's huffs and groans, scrunching his body into the foetal position.

"Right there, Malcolm. That's where they slammed a red hot iron onto my skin and held it down." Tom leans down to Malcolm's face. "Have you ever smelt flesh burning? Your *own* flesh burning?"

Malcolm's sobs against the floor and refuses to look at Tom.

"I mean, I wouldn't recommend it in Lonely Planet…" Tom shrugs and squints at Malcolm. "You know what? We should go for a drive."

Malcolm spits blood on the floor and covers his face with his hands. "No. No just leave me alone. I'll take the jail time. Whatever. Just, no more Tom…"

"Bless your cotton socks, Mal. You think you can call the shots. That's cute."

"No… I just…" He pushes a hand into the ribs Tom crunched and winces.

"Get up."

"I can't."

"Get. The. Fuck. Up."

Malcolm's cries, openly and loudly. He leans against the wall and buries his face into his hands.

You're pathetic.

Tom leans down to Malcolm and whispers in his ear. "If you want to play with the big boys, you can't opt out halfway through the game. Now… I said *get up.*" Tom grabs Malcolm by the shirt with both hands and yanks him off the floor. He languishes against the wall, sobbing and refusing to look at Tom.

"Lovely. Now, the weather is simply delightful. I thought a nice drive in the countryside might just clear our heads." Tom sweeps his arm towards the cell door. "After you."

Malcolm's turns his body against the wall and sniffles.

Tom grabs him and throws him towards the door. "But you know what the worst part was, Malcolm?" Tom walks behind him, jabbing him in the back with the pistol.

Malcolm shakes his head as he stumbles down the empty corridor.

"They made me eat cabbage."

"So?"

"I fucking hate cabbage."

43

ISABELLA

om opens the door of the Porsche and throws Malcolm into the front seat.

"Hey." Isabella leans over from the back compartment and pinches Malcom's cheek. "Glad you made it. I was beginning to worry. Thought Tom may have killed you and I missed it."

Tom leans in, pulls Malcolm's hands together and slides a cable tie tight over his wrists.

Malcolm trembles and shakes his head. "I won't run, can't you just—"

Tom slams the door in Malcolm's face and gets into the driver's seat.

Isabella looks at Malcolm's cable tied hands as the car starts and winces. "Ouch. Yeah. I've been there. Hurts doesn't it?"

"Cable... tied?"

"Yeah… Tom tied me to a steering wheel once. God, it was hot." She fans at her face, leans between the two front seats to face Malcolm. She taps a knife on her palm.

Malcolm eyes the knife and turns his back to her. He leans his head on the window.

"Turning your back on me? That's very brave, Malcolm."

Tom looks at Malcolm. "Are you being rude again?"

"I'm sorry." Malcolm whispers against the window and his breath fogs up the glass.

"What was that?" Isabella cups her hand to her ear.

Malcolm turns to slide his eyes to her, side on. "I said I'm sorry."

"You think that's gonna cut it, Malcom?" She tuts and holds the knife up. "Sorry, bad pun."

Malcolm makes a noise from his throat that gradually rises until he is screaming and shouting nonsense as the car flies down the motorway.

Tom swerves the car to the shoulder of the road and slams the brakes on, lurching them all forward. He turns in his seat and grabs Malcolm around the throat. "We're trying to have a nice relaxing drive in a classic sports car. If you could shut the fuck up so we can enjoy the sound of the engine, I'd appreciate it."

Malcolm shrinks away from Tom as he lets go of him.

"Sorry about him," Isabella whispers. "He gets a bit hot headed."

Malcolm keeps his head buried in his arms and ignores

Isabella. Isabella flares her nostrils and her pulse speeds up as she gets no response from him. *You want me to hurt you?*

"And you know what I hate? I hate it when I'm trying to be nice and all I get is ignored." She grips the knife tighter and bites her bottom lip. "So… last chance. Turn around and chat with me."

Malcolm doesn't move.

Isabella grits her teeth and jabs the knife into the side of Malcolm's leg and yanks it out again. He jerks in his seat and yelps, clutching at the wound left behind. He slumps forward over his knees and presses his hand against the bloody stab wound in his leg.

"Now. Malcolm. Do I have your attention?"

He sobs into his knees and mumbles to himself.

"Malcolm? Yes? No? Maybe?" Isabella pulls her arm back again and gets ready to give him a matching puncture. "I'm rather skilled with a knife. In case you didn't know."

"Yes! Yes! You have my attention." He sits up and rests his head against the headrest, tilting his face to the roof and panting.

Isabella smiles. "Wonderful. So, I believe Tom told you all about his adventures?"

Malcolm squeezes his eyes shut. "Yes."

"Okay so my experience was a little different. Do you know what I did?"

Malcolm keeps his eyes shut and shakes his head.

"Well, where to begin? As you may or may not know… I used

to kill people. Lots of people. With knives." Isabella watches Malcolm a moment before continuing. "Did you know?"

"No."

Isabella's eyes pop wide open. "You didn't? That's interesting. So you didn't stop to wonder why the Russians were hell bent on finding us? Or... you didn't care as long as you got paid?" At this, Isabella plunges the knife into Malcolm's leg again, this time on top of his thigh. She yanks it out and grimaces at him. *God, you're disgusting.*

He shrieks and falls forward over his knees again and pushes a hand against his thigh.

"How very manly of you, Malcolm," Tom muses. "Though as I said, if you could keep it down?"

"Let me out... please? I just..." Malcolm's voice squeaks out, and it sounds bizarre coming from such a large man.

"Bless." Isabella leans forward. "Tom... Malcolm would like to get out of the car now."

"He would? Oh well..." Tom swerves the car to the shoulder of the road again. "If you wanted out Mal, you should have just said."

Malcolm opens his eyes and looks out the window. "I can... leave?"

"You can try." Tom smiles as though he's just asked him how his day has been.

Malcolm fumbles with the door handle but the car is central locked.

"Just kidding, Mal. You aren't going anywhere." Tom turns back to the wheel and slams his foot down.

The car lurches forward and Malcolm is slammed back into the seat. He lets out a noise somewhere between anguish and terror and claws at his shirt.

Isabella puts her index finger against her lips. "Shhh… just relax."

"Yes Mal. Relax. We've got a good forty minutes before we get there. Have a snooze maybe?"

"Yeah… a snooze." Isabella winks. "But maybe keep one eye open though." She grabs a corner of his untucked shirt and wipes her knife blade clean. "So shiny."

TOM STOPS THE CAR AT EPPING FOREST AND GAZES AT THE TREES in front of them. "Isn't that peaceful?" He swivels to face Malcolm. "Shall we go for a stroll?"

"My… my leg…"

Isabella winces. "Yeah. Sorry about that. You were giving me the dirts." She leans across and slides the knife under the cable ties and cuts Malcolm's hands free.

Tom appears at the door and opens it. He reaches in and lugs the quivering lump of a man out of the car and drops him. He hits the ground with a grunt and curls into a ball.

Isabella crouches down to whisper in his ear. "Malcolm? You are going to need to get up and walk."

"But you stabbed me in the leg."

"I did. Yes. Well spotted. And if you don't get up and walk, I'll stab you again. Yes?"

Malcolm makes a sound halfway between a grunt and a sob and stands up, using the side of the car for leverage.

He hobbles forwards and Tom stands behind him. "Just walk, Mal. I'll let you know when to stop. We might even get a spot of bird watching in. Won't that be delightful?"

"I do love birds." Isabella nods.

They walk for around fifteen minutes until Tom grabs Malcolm by the shirt and throws him against a tree. Hard.

Malcolm crumbles to the ground and leans against the trunk, one hand is pushing into his ribs and the other holds his stabbed thigh.

Isabella sits down next to him and turns the knife over in her hand. "You okay?"

Malcolm shakes his head. "No… no I'm not okay." His voice rises and a tone of indignation comes out with it. "You two can't do this."

Tom tilts his head. "No?"

"No!" Malcolm wipes his hand across his forehead and shakes the sweat off. Isabella swallows and grimaces. *How are you so gross?*

Tom crouches down in front of Malcolm. "Please enlighten me, Malcolm. Because from where I am… there's no one telling us to stop."

"Well if Martha knew—"

Tom and Isabella both laugh and Isabella pats Malcolm on the shoulder. "You're so funny Malcolm."

"Wha… what?"

Tom leans in and glares at Malcolm. "She *does* know, you git. You think you were kept in that holding cell for no reason? You think she doesn't know I wanted to beat the shit out of you?"

"But she wouldn't allow…" Malcolm frowns and looks between Isabella and Tom.

"You're stupider than I gave you credit for. Computer whiz. Yes. King of espionage and intelligence? No. No I'm afraid not." Tom shakes his head and stands up again. "Plus, it would be an effort to find a suit to fit you."

Isabella shuffles closer to Malcolm and pushes the knife blade flat against his cheek. "I'm going to let you pick, Malcolm."

"Pick what?"

"Where I'll slice you first."

Malcolm jerks and pushes himself harder against the tree. "Slice!?"

"Yeah… bastards choice."

Malcolm's legs pump as though he's on a bicycle as he tries to scuttle away from Isabella. She reaches across, grabs his arm and heaves him back next to her. "C'mon. Make it quick. Or I'll choose for you."

Malcolm looks up at Tom, who stares back at him with his arms folded. He shrugs and looks up at the trees around them.

"But I don't want to be sliced."

Tom drops and crouches in front of Malcolm again. "Well, isn't that a fucking shame? You don't *want* to be sliced? Well, newsflash. I didn't want to be beaten, burnt and locked in a cellar either. Iz?"

"I didn't want to be forced to kill another human being. I didn't want Nik slobbering all over my mouth and running his hands all over me. But well… here we are."

Tom quirks a brow and peers at Isabella. "He slobbered on your mouth?"

"Ugh. Yes."

"Well." Tom punches Malcolm in the gut and he doubles over, moaning and wraps his arms around himself. "Now I'm a damn sight angrier than I was before. How inconvenient for you, Mal."

As Malcolm is doubled over with his arms around his waist, Tom flicks his leg out and kicks him in the side of the head. He slams against the tree and falls to the ground, out cold.

Isabella stands up next to Tom and they both peer at Malcolm.

"A moment's peace," Isabella says. "It's quite nice."

"Have you got that rope?"

Isabella pulls a length of rope from the back of her waist and holds it up.

"Right then. Shall we?"

"We shall."

Isabella and Tom heave Malcolm into a sitting position against the tree and Tom loops the rope around him and ties it in some weird knot at the back of the tree.

"What kind of knot is that?"

"It's a constrictor knot. Practically impossible to untie once

"But I *did* take you to Paris."

"You did. That's true."

"And we've already braved Tesco together." *And I had to buy nine loaves of bread.*

"And if we can survive that…"

"Exactly."

"Okay. I guess it can be *our* flat. But… can I buy cushions?"

Tom wrinkles his forehead. "Cushions?"

"You have no colour in that place, Tom. It's like a morgue."

Tom purses his mouth. "Okay, fine. Cushions."

"And a plant."

"And a plant." He slides his hands under her shirt and up her back.

"And cookware."

He falls back onto the grass and pulls Isabella with him. "Cookware?"

"I'm not eating takeaway and protein bars all the time." She leans down to his mouth.

"Fine. Cookware." He slides his hands down to her waistband and dips them inside to her backside.

She lets a breath out against his mouth and drops her elbows either side of his head. She runs her fingers through his hair, keeping her nose touched to his. "And a new comforter."

"What's wrong with the one I have?"

"It's grey, Tom."

"So?"

"I'm not sleeping in a morgue." She kisses his mouth before he can get an argument out. *Cheeky.*

He squeezes her backside and rolls her onto the grass next to him. "Fine. A new comforter. You drive a really hard bargain."

"Am I worth it?"

A million times over. Tom shrugs. "You'll do."

it's tightened." Tom stands up and dusts his hands. "The navy taught me *some* useful stuff. Mind you, this idiot would probably struggle with a shoelace."

They both stand in front of Malcolm as he starts to moan and mumble to himself. He opens his eyes and looks around before realising he is incapacitated. His breathing increases and he tries to wriggle out from the rope around him.

Isabella crouches beside him and pulls out her knife. "You know what else I'm really good at?"

Malcolm watches her but doesn't answer.

"Carving numbers into flesh. I've come to get quite good at it over the years. Wanna see?"

Malcolm resumes his pointless wriggling and grunting. He becomes more frantic as the rope doesn't give. He stills for a moment and his skin flames. He looks down at his crotch as a wet patch slowly expands.

"Oh, sweetheart. You needed the bathroom?" Isabella pouts. "You could have simply asked for a moment to yourself."

Tom grimaces and shakes his head. "God, you're pathetic."

"I'm sorry," Malcolm pants. "Please don't kill me. Please. I'll do... I'll do whatever you want."

Tom bends down to Malcolm's eye level. "We aren't going to kill you. Killing you would be easy. Killing you would be a cop out. Now, don't get me wrong. I really want to shoot you in the head. But you're going to be faced with far worse in prison. So..."

"Don't flatter yourself. I wouldn't waste my time carving into your useless flesh," Isabella whispers.

"Right. Well we'll be off then." Tom holds a hand out and Isabella takes it. "Enjoy the peace and quiet Mal."

"You're gonna leave me here?"

"Yeah. But don't worry. Someone will walk past with their dog. Eventually."

"But… you can't." Malcolm squirms against his restraints. "I'm hurt. And bleeding and…"

Tom scrunches his face up. "You keep saying that. But… I can."

"And don't stress. We'll take good care of your Porsche." Isabella smiles and blows Malcolm a kiss.

"You will?"

Tom laughs as he and Isabella walk away. "If by taking care you mean… torch it. Then… yes."

Isabella stops. "Oh. Wait." She walks back to Malcolm. "Almost forgot." She stabs her knife into his uninjured leg and he howls. "Here's a knife for your rescuers to cut you free."

You're welcome.

44

TOM

Tom twiddles a knob, and the gas ignites on the newly installed cooktop. "Ah. There we go." He rummages around in a cupboard. "I'm pretty sure there's a whole pot and pan set somewhere here…" His head disappears inside the cupboard before he pulls out two small saucepans and a skillet. "Thought so."

His triumphant smiles fades as Isabella and Mischa giggle to each other.

Tom frowns. "What?"

"Where's the rest?"

"What do you mean, Iz?"

"You said you had a whole set."

"This isn't a set?"

"No, Tom." Isabella leans on the timber polished worktop. "Please tell me you have cooking utensils in the flat?"

"Yeah… when you say utensils…" He flicks the gas off now that he knows it's working.

Isabella massages her temples. "I guess it's lucky we're staying here for a month or two then." She sits next to Mischa and holds her hand. "We can get this kitchen into some working order first."

"It works." Tom squints at the old fire oven. "I think."

"I'm taking you to the doctor tomorrow, and then after that we can walk around town." Isabella smiles. "It's really lovely here. You'll make friends and fit in just fine."

"And once we have to go back to London, at least one of us will come visit every weekend," Tom says.

"I cannot expect so much of you." Mischa shakes her head gently.

"After what you lost because of us?" Tom folds his arms and leans against the worktop.

A single tear rolls down Mischa's cheek.

Tom walks over and sits next to her. "Are you okay?"

She nods. "You do not need to do this for me."

"Do what?"

"Let me stay in house."

"Are you kidding? Where are you going to live, Mischa? No offence but the flat is a tad small for all three of us. And… you aren't simply staying here. This is your home. For as long as you want it to be." Tom bites his lip. "And we can turn my old bedroom into a nursery." *Right. That sounds weird.*

EPILOGUE
6 MONTHS LATER

Tom drums his fingers on Martha's desk and glares at her empty chair. He chews on the inside of his cheek as the door opens and Martha walks in with Isabella, who is carrying two mugs.

Isabella walks over and sits next to Tom at the desk, plonking one of the two coffee mugs, down in front of him. "Stop scowling."

"I'm not scowling."

"You're scowling, Tom." Martha stands behind her desk and sips her tea.

Tom huffs and picks up his mug. "So, why are we here?"

"I thought we should talk about Isabella's future. Now that you've had a few months to recover from the Russian ordeal."

Tom's pulse spikes and he gives Isabella a sidelong glance while she smiles at Martha. "What about her... future? Iz?"

"Martha and I have been chatting…"

Tom raises a brow. "Evidently."

"And I want to fast track Isabella to be part of my team." Martha folds her hands and fixes her eyes on Tom.

Tom coughs as his coffee goes down the wrong way, and leans forward slapping the coffee mug onto the desk. "Fast track?"

Isabella pats his back. "Don't get all 'Tom Grant' about it."

"All what?"

"It's a term around here. Didn't you know? Like, all huffy and difficult. " Isabella grins.

Martha chuckles and paces behind her desk. "Now Tom, Isabella has proven herself to be a very resilient and capable woman. She is already trained in weaponry… probably better than half the people here. And she shows little fear when confronted with life or death situations." Martha stops pacing and looks between the pair of them. "Wouldn't you agree?"

"I… would," Tom grunts through gritted teeth.

"So, Martha reckons I can get through theory and basic training in nine months."

"Amazing."

"Yeah…" Isabella, watches him with her head tilted to the side. "Problem?"

"Iz, you don't need my permission."

"I know that. I'm not asking you. I'm… telling you this is happening."

"Fine. Great."

Isabella sighs and stares at the ceiling.

Martha looks at Tom and waits for him to meet her gaze. "I might leave you two to have a discussion." She sweeps her arm to the sofa. "Make yourselves comfortable. I'll be back in ten minutes. I'm expecting a call from Admiral Moore in around half an hour, so chat quickly." She strides to the door and leaves without another word.

"Tom?"

Tom flicks his eyes to Isabella who is perched on the edge of the sofa. He walks over and throws himself down next to her.

"It's a bit lumpy." Isabella wiggles her bum and tries to puff the cushion behind her.

"Try sleeping on it."

They both sit in silence a moment before Tom shifts and faces her. "It's dangerous."

"I know."

"What if you get hurt?"

"I expect to get hurt. It's part of the deal, right?" She gives him a small smile.

"You're a big girl. You don't need my or anyone else's permission. It's just..." He lifts the corner of his mouth. "Why couldn't you have been a Russian cupcake maker or something?"

Isabella laughs. "I'm terrible at making buttercream."

He nods and sits back into the sofa cushion. "Right."

Isabella puts her hand on Tom's arm. "I want to do this."

"I know."

"So... will it be a problem?"

He sits forward and scrubs his hands through his hair. "Do you really think it's a good idea? Given Moore still wants your head on a pike?"

"I've been thinking about that. And honestly Tom, what can he do? He has no evidence to back up his claims."

"Because there isn't any."

"Exactly."

The phone on Martha's desk rings and Tom looks at it. "It's probably Martha checking up." He walks to the desk and picks up the phone. "You said ten minutes."

"Grant?"

Fuck. "Pete. You're half an hour early. We were just chatting about you."

"Is that a fact?"

"Yes. What do you want?"

"Is that any way to speak to the First Sea—"

"What do you want?"

"I see. I called to speak to former Admiral Cole. You know… your superior?"

"She's busy."

"You know, for someone who owes me his life, you're being rather insolent."

Tom snorts. "Have you met me?"

"I must say it was rather serendipitous that Commodore Lawrence was overseeing the ship sent to retrieve you."

Tom grips the phone tighter. "Indeed."

"How was it to be back in familiar surroundings? You must have felt right at home on your old ship."

Tom's pulse hastens and he squeezes his eyes shut as sounds and smells from the ship invade his thoughts. "Home is a stretch."

Moore chuckles. "I bet."

Tom's patience evaporates and he grits his teeth. "Mark my words. I'll never set foot on another ship in your fleet. Ever again. You can hold me to that."

"That's fine with me Grant, my ships are better for it. But there was one other thing about your extraction that made me smile…"

"And what might that be?" Tom knows he's being baited, but that tiny part of his brain telling him to hang up isn't shouting loud enough.

"Lawrence is looking at nomination for promotion within the next twelve months. And your risky and dangerous extraction paints him in a very favourable light. A successful mission under adverse conditions. You must feel wonderful about helping an old friend?"

The smirk at the end of Moore's words leaves a sour taste in Tom's mouth and he swallows. "Was there anything else I can pass on to *my superior* for you?"

"No, I have actual matters of national security to attend to. Tell Admiral Cole I will be in touch. Oh, and do say hello to the Russian killer for me."

"Isabella."

"What?"

"She has a name." He turns and looks at Isabella who has inched to the edge of the sofa with her hands under her chin.

"You listen to me, Grant. I *will* send her back to Russia. I *will* win."

"You *won't* send her back. I'll kill you first."

Isabella stalks across the room and yanks the phone out of Tom's hand. "Admiral."

Tom presses the speakerphone button and purses his lips at Isabella.

"Assassin."

"Tell me… why did you rescue me from Russia in the first place?" Isabella waits and Moore doesn't respond. "Admiral?"

"Tom blackmailed me. I would have left you there to rot otherwise. But now he has nothing left to use against me…"

"I see."

"You're going back."

Tom leans over the speaker. "Well… thanks for the call. Always a pleasure." Tom presses a button on the phone and takes a breath "Fuck…"

"Can he really send me back?"

"He's blowing hot air." *I think.*

"Are you sure?"

"Honestly. It's fine. Nothing to worry about."

I hope.

www.ingramcontent.com/pod-product-compliance
Lightning Source LLC
Chambersburg PA
CBHW020540120726
47903CB00001B/64